Tangled in Texas

RULES

OF

PROTECTION

D1519691

Tangled in Texas

RULES

OF

PROTECTION

ALISON
BLISS

Entangled Publishing, LLC
2614 South Timberline Road
Suite 109
Fort Collins, CO 80525
Visit our website at www.entangledpublishing.com.

Select is an imprint of Entangled Publishing, LLC.

Edited by Theresa Cole and Gwen Hayes
Cover design by Fiona Jayde

Manufactured in the United States of America

First Edition August 2014

For Denny, Matthew, and Andrew, the three loves of my life.

Chapter One

I caught him eyeing me from across the room.

He was tall, dark, and…well, interested. I couldn't get a good enough look to see if he was handsome. Although dim lighting obscured his face, it highlighted the thick, gold chain around his neck and ridiculously huge diamond stud in his ear.

Nestled in downtown Chicago, The Jungle Room buzzed with flashy, well-lubricated businessmen with oversized wallets and scantily clad women with oversized racks. They circled each other like vultures, waiting to see who'd fall onto their backs first. It appeared the men were winning—a form of upscale prostitution.

Gina sat beside me at the bar, encouraging me to do the flirty eye thing with Shadow Man. "It's your twenty-eighth birthday. Everyone should get laid on their birthday. What better present to give yourself?"

"I can give myself an orgasm."

Gina laughed. "Not the same."

I shrugged. "Depends on the guy. Besides, I don't need birthday sex. I can hardly see him. He's probably ugly."

"It's a one-night stand. Only thing that matters is the size of his—"

"Then pretend it's *your* birthday!" I downed my cosmopolitan and spun the stool around. "Bathroom break. Keep an eye out for Dale."

I followed the hallway to the restrooms. A line formed outside, but moved fast. Two women stepped in behind me, giggling like teenagers. I half-assed listened to them when someone grasped my elbow.

I immediately recognized the jewelry.

The man was 100 percent Italian Stallion, sporting a tight zipper shirt and black hair slicked back over his ears. He was around my age with a decent face—definitely not ugly like I'd thought—and he was tall and nicely built. Actually, he wasn't bad looking at all. Maybe Gina was on to something with this birthday sex idea.

"Hey, sweetness. Saw you eyeing me back there." He looked me up and down, licking his lips. "Now that I'm here, what are your other two wishes?"

Oh, jeez. Did he have to open his mouth? I hate men who start a conversation using cocky, sexist remarks. They come off as piggish jerks.

"I wasn't eyeing you. I was…uh, looking for someone."

"Well, you found me."

"No, I mean someone else…the guy I'm with."

Okay, so I lied. Dale hadn't arrived yet, and even if he had, no one would believe he was my boyfriend. Ever. I didn't have the right equipment Dale's sexual preference gravitated toward. But this guy didn't need to know that.

"The name's Sergio. How about I buy you a drink, honey?" He rubbed a finger down my arm as I stared at his weird girly hands.

"No thanks," I said, moving away.

"Aw, come on. I'll wait for you, then we can go get that drink."

"Thanks for the offer, but I can't."

He grinned as if I had somehow encouraged him and leaned against the wall. "No problem. I don't mind waiting."

What the fuck? Is he deaf?

"No, really, I can't. My stomach's upset and I… I'm going to be in here for *quite* a while."

The two girls next to me made faces at each other, stepped out of line, and walked away. Oh, great. Did I just make them think I had diarrhea? Sadly enough, it didn't deter Sergio.

"Whatcha drinking tonight?" he asked, still not giving up.

I sighed, rolling my eyes. "Pepto Bismol."

A woman stepped out of the bathroom, and I ran in before the door could shut. I didn't know what was worse— me pretending to have diarrhea or Sergio not caring that I did. Gross.

Momentarily cornered, I tousled my hair, washed my hands twice while singing "Happy Birthday" to myself, and then reapplied my makeup. Hard to believe it was my birthday, and I was spending it hiding in a public bathroom eating a Tootsie Roll I found in the bottom of my purse.

I even realized something while in there. There isn't much to do in a bathroom to occupy your time—unless, of course, you actually have the shits.

I'd just finished chewing the chocolate candy when I poked my head out the door. Yes! He was gone. I hurried down the hall and rounded the corner, but Sergio stood at the nearby bar. I ducked back into the corridor, hoping he hadn't seen me.

I rubbed my hand over my eyes and breathed out. "Christ."

Then a smooth, deep voice asked, "You okay?"

It startled me at first, thinking Sergio had found me. I pulled my hand away from my face reluctantly and gazed up at a man with wavy dark brown hair. He was tall—probably a few inches over six feet—and wore black slacks and a white dress shirt. His steel gray eyes pierced mine, making it hard to form a coherent thought, much less breathe.

When I didn't answer, he asked again. "Are you okay, ma'am?"

"Um, I… I'm fine."

"Let me guess, avoiding someone?"

My sluggish brain finally caught up, and I recalled hiding from Sergio. "You could say that."

"I just did," he responded, a hint of southern twang fortifying his voice. "Pull the boyfriend card. It usually works on us clowns."

"I tried, but this guy is more persistent than most. My friends are somewhere on the other side of the bar, and I'm tired of hiding in the bathroom."

The man glanced at his watch. "Tell you what, if you're still here when I come out, I'll escort you across the room."

"Best offer I've had all night."

His eyes scanned my black miniskirt, stopping on my bare legs. "Somehow I doubt that." He turned and walked toward the men's bathroom.

I blew out the large breath I'd been holding and resisted the urge to loosen a button on my blouse. Sergio or no Sergio, I planned to stay put until he came back.

Okay, so I'm a hypocrite.

Sergio's remarks and lingering looks came off way more threatening than the new guy's did. Tall, Dark, and Delicious was virtually harmless and particularly flattering. It helped that he hadn't approached me with a line; he was more interested in helping… Ah, damn. Men are such weasels.

The guy played me. Of course.

He knew if he showed concern for my well-being, I'd drop my guard. That's why he did it. Sadly enough, it almost worked. After all, he was no threat; just a gentleman trying to help out a lady. Well, screw him! He could pull the hero crap on some other unsuspecting girl. I waited for him to come out to tell him to his face. But Sergio rounded the corner first.

"There you are, sugar. I wondered if you'd fallen in." Sergio handed me a shot glass filled with a pink liquid. "I got your Pepto, but I had to talk to three bartenders before I could get your order filled."

Seriously? Bartenders make a shot called Pepto Bismol?

I hadn't known it at the time, but what a lucky stroke of genius that was. Sergio must've thought it was a drink all along and hadn't realized I was a smartass.

The men's bathroom door opened behind me, and heavy footsteps approached. I was still irritated the douchebag had used a diversion tactic to hit on me, but the last thing I wanted was him to stroll up and ask me what I was drinking. It was one thing to let Sergio think I had an upset stomach, but it was a whole other thing to share that false information with the hunky weasel.

I threw my head back, downed the shot in one large gulp, and handed the empty glass back to Sergio. "Wait a minute," I said. "That wasn't—"

Two large hands captured my waist, spinning me sideways with dizzying speed, and a sharp, assertive mouth sheared the rest of the words from my lips. The stupid weasel was kissing me. I hadn't expected it, and it only furthered my irritation. I'd have to play along to make it look good. Either that or I'd be stuck with Sergio the rest of the night.

Damn. I hate weasels.

Begrudgingly, I kissed him back, but only to make it believable. At least that's what I told myself. If he wanted a show, then that's exactly what he was going to get. I leaned into him, curled my arms around the back of his neck, and moaned softly.

Immediately, his lips stopped moving against mine, and his body became rigid. I thought it was the end of the match, and we would each return to our respective corners. With me being the winner and all.

Boy, was I wrong!

The moment I began to back away, he firmed his grip on my waist and parted my lips with his tongue, deepening the kiss. No, actually, it wasn't a kiss, more like a molestation of my mouth. Who was I to complain, though? It was good. Really good.

My fingers slid through his hair. His tongue touched mine, and a fiery sensation rocketed through my entire body. Involuntarily, I shivered, and it set him off. His thumbs dug into my hips as he pulled me tighter against his growing erection. I gasped at his hardness and, remembering where we were, fought the urge to touch it.

A bathroom hallway in a packed nightclub wasn't where I wanted to partake in a public display of heavy petting. I must've surprised him when I responded to his kiss, but it all happened so fast I didn't have time to contemplate his motivation. Nor did I care to. Sergio had to be standing there with wide eyes and an open mouth, but I didn't want to stop long enough to check.

When I finally pushed the weasel away, he grunted in protest, but didn't stop me. Panting softly, I glanced around and noted the empty hallway. Sergio had disappeared.

I wasn't sure what to say. My brain shifted gears but had trouble getting up to full speed. So I said the first thing that popped into my head. "Did you wash your hands?"

A patronizing grin contorted his face, but he ignored my question and asked one of his own. "Why do you taste like Pepto Bismol…and chocolate?"

My cheeks flushed with heat. "Long story, but it doesn't matter. Why'd you do that?"

"Do what?"

"You kissed me. Why?"

"Long story, but it doesn't matter." He winked and then walked away.

His abrupt departure surprised me, but I was outraged he didn't ask for my name or phone number. Hell, he didn't even ask me to go home with him. As if he actually intended to save me from Sergio after all. And I never thanked him.

Back in the bathroom, I composed myself, fanning my face with a paper towel. I was hot, but it wasn't the kind of heat staved off by air conditioning. Only time—or possibly an orgasm—would cure the fever under my skin.

After a few minutes, I strolled back into the main room more in control of the brain fog that had overwhelmed me. I spotted Gina and Dale walking in the opposite direction from me on the other side of the dance floor. I yelled to get their attention, but the music was too loud.

Weaving through the crowd, I waved frantically and yelled again. "Gina! Dale! Hey, over here!"

By the time I noticed the step up in the floor, it was already too late. I tripped and reached for the closest thing to me, which happened to be a man. Trying to catch myself, I had an intimate moment with the bulge in his pants on the way down.

The floor punched me in the face, but the pain was slight compared to the mortifying beating my pride had just taken. Two seconds after I hit the floor, I decided to stay there. I wasn't sure if it was because I physically couldn't get up, or mentally didn't want to.

The man I'd felt up lifted me with ease, stood me upright, and held me until I steadied myself. Mortified, I refused to look up until I heard him ask, "Are you okay?"

No! It can't be.

My eyes shot up, looked directly into his, and I stopped breathing. It was the hunky weasel with the steely gray eyes. If I had to embarrass myself in front of someone, why did it have to be him? Where in the hell is Sergio when you need him?

The hunk smiled as if he read my mind. "I always wanted a girl to fall head over heels for me."

I stood motionless and tried to think of something to say that didn't sound stupid. "Well, next time I'm near your crotch, I'll be sure to bring my knee pads." Nope. That wasn't it. At least six guys turned their heads toward us and sucked in a breath.

A young Hispanic guy leaned over, flexing his eyebrows. "Damn, girl, where have you been all my life?"

"Out of it," I sneered. "Now, leave me alone. I'm talking to the weasel." Disappointed with our exchange, the guy turned away and shrugged to his buddies.

I turned my attention back to the man who lifted me from the floor and noticed he glared with one offended eyebrow raised. "The weasel?"

My cheeks flushed. "It's what I dubbed you, since I didn't know your name."

"Why a weasel?" He paused. "Wait… You thought I was hitting on you back there?"

"Well, yeah."

The confusion on his face changed to humor as he shook his head. "Nope."

I guess I should've been relieved, but I wasn't. Actually, I was insulted and…well, pissed off. "Why not?"

"Is that a trick question, where no matter what I say I'm going to be wrong?"

"Just answer the question."

"Damn," he said, grabbing my arm and jerking me away from the crowd. "Why are you yelling?"

"Because I'm mad at you."

"You don't even know me. Do you have a split personality disorder or something?"

I gritted my teeth and narrowed my eyes. "You're a weasel *and* a jerk!"

My outburst made him laugh. A lot. When he finally got himself under control, he grinned. "Look, I get that you have this head-turning ability and like to stand out in a crowd, but I don't."

"You think I turn heads?"

"Sweetheart, a man would have to be blind or stupid not to look." He smiled again. Damn, I wished he'd stop doing that. "Definitely a looker, but that makes you trouble. I don't need the unwanted attention you crave."

"I'd swear there's an insult somewhere in there."

"Darlin', if I insult you, you'll be the first to know. Now point out your friends. I'll see to it you get to them safely."

I scanned the room and found Gina and Dale sitting at a small, round table near the bar. No one could miss either of them in a crowd.

Gina had flaming red hair, bright blue eyes, and a spectacular chest barely covered by a low-cut top. Her boobs were a statement piece; I'm talking breasts for days. She was highly skilled in the sex department and didn't care who knew it.

Dale was Gina's roommate. He had blond hair with spiky tips, honey-colored eyes, and dressed ridiculously well for a man—designer jeans, expensive silk shirts, and Italian leather shoes. One look and you knew his sexual preference without a doubt. But he didn't care, either.

It's what I loved about them. Neither pretended to be something they weren't. They were sexually profound individuals who enjoyed sharing stories of their lively bedroom adventures with me. Even if I didn't have much to offer on the matter.

I wasn't a prude, but compared to the two of them, I may as well have been a nun.

I pointed out Gina and Dale and, without hesitating, the

weasel grasped my elbow and led me across the room, not stopping until we stood before them. They stopped talking the moment we walked up.

The weasel plopped me into the empty chair. He leaned down, brushing his lips across my ear, and whispered, "The name's Jake." Then he smiled and walked away.

Gina barely waited for him to get away from the table before fanning herself. "Who the hell was that?"

"That's Jake," I said nonchalantly.

Gina and Dale traded questioning glances and then Dale added, "Hellooo, Mr. Tall, Dark, and Yummy!"

"Was he the guy who gave you the eyes earlier?" Gina asked.

I shook my head. "No, that was Sergio. Jake helped me get rid of him."

"What's wrong with Sergio? Ugly?"

"No, but it's too bad about his personality. Not really the kind of guy a girl could fall in love with. He's already in a relationship…with himself."

Gina and Dale both laughed.

"Oh, and he has tiny girl hands," I said, figuring they would draw the same conclusion I had. Weird, girly hands probably said a lot about the size of his package.

Gina wore a wicked grin. "If you were a virgin and slept with Sergio, then you'd probably have to sleep with someone else after him just to make it count."

Dale and I laughed, but he still looked confused. "So how did Boy Wonder come into the mix?"

"You mean…uh, Jake?" Damn. I still wanted to call him the weasel. "He pretended to be my boyfriend to deflect Sergio." I wasn't going to go into specifics about the flirty encounter in the hallway. I needed something to tell them about later. It was all I had.

"He can be my boyfriend any time," Gina said, fanning herself again.

"He doesn't look like the type who'd use the 'take-a-number' dispenser next to your bed, Gina." Dale grinned playfully and then motioned to me. "He's probably available on a first-come, first-served basis, which means our little vixen here has already hired him. I hope it's for a permanent position."

"And what position would that be?" I asked.

Gina offered a mischievous grin. "Boyfriend, lover, missionary, sixty-nine…"

"Doggy-style," Dale added, giggling as he gave Gina a high five.

"Oh, stop it. He didn't ask me to go home with him. Besides, even if he had, I wouldn't have gone."

The two of them gave me a "yeah, right" look.

"Okay, I'd like to think I wouldn't have," I amended. "I'm not that kind of girl."

Dale smiled. "Honey, when it comes to a man like that, we're *all* that kind of girl." Then he shrugged. "Besides, every girl needs to get laid on her birthday."

"Is that some rule I don't know about?"

By the time the waitress came over, all three of us were fanning ourselves thinking about Jake. She focused on me, since Gina and Dale both had drinks. "Can I get you anything?"

"Vodka, straight up."

The waitress nodded and squeezed past us toward the bar.

"Getting worked up?" Gina asked.

"Of course not. Don't be silly. I'm just thirsty because it's hot in here." I undid a button on my blouse, opened it up, and shook it loosely around my cleavage.

When I looked up, Jake stood about ten feet away, his gaze lacerating across my chest. If he would've stared any harder, he could've seared it open and performed open-heart surgery on me. That would've been helpful since my heart had stopped beating the moment I spotted him again.

I shifted nervously in my chair and crossed my legs to keep from fidgeting, unintentionally exposing quite a bit of upper thigh. But it worked to my advantage. The waitress returned with my drink, but before I could pull out my cash, a large hand slid a twenty-dollar bill across the table at her.

"Keep the change," Jake said. He leaned over me, his eyes raking across my thighs with intensity. "Dance with me."

"I…uh…" His proximity removed all of the air from my lungs.

"It's not a request," Jake said, pulling me from my chair by force.

I looked to my friends for help, but Gina laughed. "He's better than a caveman."

Dale smiled flirtatiously at Jake from across the table. "Jake, honey, how's your gaydar?"

Jake gave a wolfish grin and winked at both of them. "*Everything* of mine is perfectly intact."

Gina and Dale drooled on each other as Jake dragged me toward the dance floor. Some support group they were. They threw me to the big, bad wolf, hoping he'd eat me, just so they could hear about it later.

Jake pulled me out on the floor and spun me into his arms as a slow song played. Dale and Gina watched us from across the room.

"You were flirting with my friends."

A smile played at the corner of his mouth. "Just giving them some food for thought."

"And getting them to take your side?"

"That, too."

"I thought you said I was trouble."

He scanned the room, looking everywhere but at me. "Yep, and I was right."

"I was minding my own business. You came over to me, remember? Why bother, if I'm so much trouble?"

"Because I need a favor."

That piqued my interest. "Favor?"

"Same thing I did for you. Put on a show to detour some unwanted attention."

"Y-you want me to kiss you?"

He glanced down toward his groin. "With extreme caution this time."

My mind instantly recalled the rock solid bulge in his pants from before, causing a surge of lust to run through me. I breathed out hard. "No."

"*No?* What do you mean 'no'?"

"You heard me. No. You do understand what the word means, right? Or maybe you've never had a girl tell you that before."

"Wait, I helped you. You owe me."

"I didn't ask you to kiss me."

"You didn't exactly decline, either."

"I was surprised, that's all. It won't happen again."

His stare was unnerving as he tightened his grip on my hand. "Like I said, you owe me."

Defensively, I yanked my hand from his and narrowed my eyes as the slow song ended. "You can't force me to do something I don't want to do."

"Oh, you *want* to. You're just being difficult."

People cheered as a faster song boomed from the large speakers; apparently, it was popular. I turned to leave the dance floor, but he grabbed me from behind, snaking his arms around my waist. His warm breath caressed my neck. My ass practically cradled his groin as he grinded into me to the beat of the music.

He stroked his large hands along the outside of my thighs, lifting my miniskirt slightly. Then he swiveled his pelvic area back and forth across my ass until my hips were as loose as his. Maybe he was just feeling frisky, but I had to admit the man had moves.

Gina, Dale, and I had a theory about how a man dances representing their sexual ability. In other words, a guy who can't catch a beat on the dance floor probably has no rhythm in the bedroom, either. So far, the theory had proven true. At least that's what Gina and Dale told me. If Jake's presence on the dance floor was any indication of what he was like in bed, then I'd let him dry fuck me any day of the week.

Jake spun me around to face him. He pulled me closer, though I didn't think it was possible without crawling under his skin. His dreamy eyes focused on mine intently, penetrating deep, as if he were probing my most intimate parts. He may as well have had his hand up my skirt. The thought alone made me whimper.

I should've kept walking instead of allowing him to stop

me. I don't know what I was thinking. Well, I know…but I shouldn't have been thinking it.

"I won't ask twice," he demanded.

Our faces were almost touching. My gaze traveled between his lips and his eyes, contemplating my decision. From our previous encounter, I knew what a tasty morsel he was, and I was starving for more of his…Oh God! *I'm going to hell.* Drawing a breath, I did what any self-respecting girl would do. I plastered my face to his and held on tight.

A low, guttural sound came from deep within his throat as his tongue glided over mine. My fingers locked behind his neck. His hand slid down to my ass, grabbing a handful, and a hot wave of sensation melted me against him.

My heart hammered against the walls of my chest. I knew nothing involving my heart could be good for either of us—especially since it's the one organ in my body I didn't intend to let him near. I tore away from him, stumbling back.

He looked surprised at first, but then averted his eyes to scope the room. "It worked. I don't see them anymore."

"*Them*?" I asked angrily. "Jesus, how many women are you trying to detour?"

"It's not like that."

"Sure it isn't."

He glanced over at me. "You're mad again?"

"I don't like being used."

"I didn't use you, at least not how you're making it sound. You knew what this was."

"What's your point?"

"You walked into this with your eyes wide open, and now you're mad because you didn't like what you saw."

My eyes narrowed. "God, why are men such assholes?"

"Because women are…you know what, never mind. I don't have time for this. I've got better things to do."

He walked away before I could protest and left me standing on the dance floor alone. Frustrated, I made my way back to the table where Gina and Dale waited impatiently.

"Where's the dreamboat?" Dale asked.

I gave him a sour look.

Dale laughed. "What, no love connection?"

Gina smiled as I picked up my vodka and chugged it. "Damn, girl. He got to you."

"Shut up."

She laughed, too. "You know if a man buys you a drink and you take it without going home with him, then you're a tease."

"Yeah, but if you go home with him, then you're a slut."

Dale grinned. "She's got you there, Gina."

"I'd rather be a slut than a tease any day. It's more fun."

"Well, I'm not you," I told Gina. "I'm not going to springboard myself into some guy's bed because he has a heartbeat and a blood supply that pools below his belt."

"Hell, I'm not sure Gina considers the heartbeat mandatory," Dale said.

She shook her head. "You two are wrong. I'm very selective when it comes to men."

"Are you kidding?" I asked, lifting my brows. "You choose men the same way a child picks out a new puppy; first one who crawls in your lap is yours."

Dale broke into hysterics.

"You guys are jerks," Gina said to him.

"It's a joke," Dale said, still laughing.

Gina crossed her arms, fuming mad.

"Well, I didn't get a chance to tell you earlier," I said to her. "But tonight, before you picked me up, I shaved my bikini area."

Dale and Gina both looked puzzled. "So what?" she asked.

"I thought I'd try something new and be…um…creative."

Dale looked confused. "What did you do?"

"Is it as bad as the last time?" Gina asked me, grinning.

"Worse."

Gina giggled. "Nothing could be worse than last time."

"Wanna bet?"

Gina completely lost it but pulled herself together long enough to explain the situation to Dale, who was irritated he was out of the loop. "The last time this one tried to get *creative*…"—she used two fingers on each hand to gesture air quotes—"…she ended up looking like she had mange."

They both laughed, but I didn't care. The three of us always made fun of each other. Dale and Gina were already roommates when I met them, and although they'd been friends longer, I never felt like a third wheel. A few months ago, they'd even asked me to give up my apartment and move into a three-bedroom with them. But I politely declined. Dale had a tendency to walk around naked, and Gina was a complete slob. No way I'd be able to clean up after her with my hands covering my eyes.

"Don't look now, but I think your boyfriend is staring again," Gina said, motioning to the back of the room.

I turned my head in time to catch a glimpse of Jake sweeping the crowd with his eyes before slipping through the doors leading to the private lounges. "He wasn't looking at me."

"Oh, he was," Dale said, confirming Gina's assessment. "Right before you turned to look. Maybe it was an invitation. I bet he wants you to follow him."

I shook my head and laughed. "He didn't even know I saw him."

"So what," Gina said. "It would be fascinating to see what happens between you two when there aren't a hundred pairs of eyes keeping those clothes of yours intact."

My stomach knotted up just thinking about it. "I'm not going to have sex with a random guy in some storage closet."

"Honey, I say the same thing every time I'm drinking in a hotel bar," Dale said with a chuckle. "But I always end up in a room, and I'm *never* alone."

Gina grinned knowingly. "This guy has you scared to death."

"What are you talking about?"

"Any time something scares you, you unleash the sarcasm," she responded. "It's what you do."

I rolled my eyes. "Whatever."

"See what I mean? Come on, follow him and find out what he's doing," Gina said. "He looked like he was hiding from someone."

Probably one of the women he tried to shake loose. I hated to admit it, but I was curious. His behavior intrigued me. He had looked around as if someone watched him, though I never saw anybody paying attention…unless you count us, of course.

"Okay, fine," I said, getting out of my chair. "I'll take a quick peek, but I'm not sleeping with him."

Dale laughed as I walked away. "Girl, you better watch out for those magicians. Like magic, he could easily make your panties disappear."

I pretended not to hear him and kept walking. When I got to the back of the room, I paused and leaned against the wall. What the hell was I doing? If I had any brains left, I'd go back to the table and forget the whole thing, but there was a problem. I couldn't get Jake out of my head.

From the first time I saw him, my mind clouded over, as if he shut it down and forced me to do things I wouldn't normally do. He caused my brain to fog, but I didn't know how or why. It was as if he put a dunce cap on my head, and I took it literally.

Now I had a decision: follow him or go back to the table. The smart thing to do was rejoin my friends, but nobody had ever accused me of doing the smart thing.

I let out a breath and swung through the door. It led to a narrow hallway undergoing some renovations. A ladder, some painting supplies, and a few boxes of new lighting fixtures lined the walls. The corridor was long and quiet with no sign of Jake.

Most of the fluorescent bulbs in the ceiling were broken or not working. One blinked constantly as if it were getting ready to go out. That alone made the passageway eerily dark, but I followed the length of it anyway.

When I got to the end, I wasn't sure what to do. I could go left or right, but had no way of knowing which way Jake had gone. So I used logic. The bulge in his pants had hugged one side more than the other, suggesting he was a righty. Therefore, I ended up going to the right, and moments later, came to a door labeled Lounge 3. I opened it and peered inside. Nothing. Entire room was empty, except a few pieces of furniture covered with thick, clear plastic.

I continued on and stopped at the next room labeled
LOUNGE 4. The last door in the hallway. If he wasn't here, I'd
have to try the other hall in the opposite direction. I turned
the knob and started to pull it toward me, but stopped when
I heard voices. Curious, I cracked the door open without
making a sound. I peered in through the two-inch slit and
caught a glimpse of more furniture covered with the same
thick plastic.

A familiar voice rose as a man walked into view. Even
by his profile, I recognized Sergio as he stood in front of the
plastic-covered couch against the wall. He spoke to someone
out of my eyesight.

"You know it wasn't me!" Sergio said in a tense voice.

"Take a seat," the other man said.

Sergio sat, but stayed nervously on the edge of the
cushion. "Come on, Boss. You know I wouldn't lie to you."

The mystery man finally strolled into view in his navy
blue tailored suit. He was a short, heavy-set man with a round,
pudgy face, a large, crooked nose, and a mole under his left
eye. "It's a shame, Sergio. I told you to lay low and I'd give you
a pass, but instead…"

Two men in sleek suits with short dark hair joined his
side. They resembled bodyguards, and both silently stared
at Sergio.

Sergio stood, waving his arms frantically. "Wait, Mr.
Felts. I'm telling you…"

The other man—the one referred to as Mr. Felts—shook his
head and clicked his tongue sarcastically. "We have a problem
that needs some attention. My associate on the inside says
someone's been feeding data about my operation to the feds.
That's no good. I can't afford to lose the respect of my family

and friends. I need a scapegoat to correct this problem."

"Please, Boss, I'm telling you…it wasn't me."

"Sit down, Sergio," Mr. Felts ordered. "And stop carrying on. You're something all right, but you're not a damn goat."

The two big men behind Mr. Felts chuckled. Sergio blew out a huge breath. Relieved, the tension melted from his posture as he sat back, kicking an ankle up over the knee of his other leg.

Sergio looked at Mr. Felts and grinned. "Then what am I, Boss?"

"The sacrificial lamb," Mr. Felts said, as he reached inside his jacket pocket and pulled out a long silver gun.

I barely recognized what it was until I heard a small noise and looked back at Sergio, who rested his head on the back of the couch as he stared blankly up at the ceiling. Blood and chunks of brain matter dripped down the white wall behind him.

It didn't register for at least a full three seconds. Something was wrong, but I didn't know how wrong until it hit me.

Then I gasped. Loudly.

Chapter Two

All three men looked my way.

The sound that came out of my mouth was loud enough for them to hear, but I hoped they wouldn't notice me through the crack in the door.

"Someone's out there," Mr. Felts said. "Take care of it."

I wasn't sure how I managed it while wearing stilettos, but I ran the entire length of the hallway. The men burst out the door as I rounded the corner to the next corridor. One shouted from behind me, "It's a woman, Boss!"

Mr. Felts's voice rang out, "Bring her to me!"

The second hallway was longer, but I didn't slow down. The two men chasing me would round the corner before I could get through the door to the main room, and I didn't doubt they were armed. At any moment, I expected to feel a sharp pain in my back as a hot bullet ripped through me. But it didn't happen. Surprisingly, I made it into the lobby without any new holes in my body. I don't know why, but I guessed their guns didn't have silencers and would draw far more attention than they wanted.

I burst through the lobby doors and dashed through the crowd, weaving and dodging, while watching behind me. Two big men flew out the doors seconds after me, but I ducked, concealing myself behind a wall of people. They spoke to each other briefly, both of them scanning the crowd, and then separated.

It wasn't much farther to our table — about twenty feet. Gina and Dale were still sitting there. I started to make a mad dash for them, but I had barely taken a step when someone grabbed me from behind, clamping a hard hand over my mouth.

"Don't scream," a man whispered into my ear, his voice barely audible over the music. "I want you to walk quietly with me out the exit on your left. If you alert your friends in any way, you'll only be putting them in danger. Do you understand?"

Frozen with fear, I managed a small nod.

"Good. Now, start moving." He uncovered my mouth and pushed firmly into my back, prodding me to walk.

He kept one hand on my neck, steering me in the direction of the exit, practically shoving me out the door. It opened to a dark alleyway, but as soon as we were outside, I spun on him. I hit him with everything I had, which unfortunately, wasn't much.

He lunged at me, knocking both of us to the ground, and gained control of my flailing arms. Gravel bit into my back as he straddled me, using his weight to pin my legs as he held my wrists tightly. I used the only weapon I had left. I bit his arm as hard as I could and held on tight.

"Sonofabitch," he ground out between his teeth.

He pressed his other arm into my throat, which cut off my oxygen supply and forced me to open my mouth with a gasp. After a quick check of his bite wound, he jumped off me and snatched me up from the pavement.

He pushed me against the brick wall and leaned in close. "Don't ever do that again," he growled.

The moonlight was dim, but bright enough to catch a glimpse of his face. "Jake…?"

His eyes met mine and he grinned. "Surprised?"

A rush of heat pulsed through my body, like a volcano building up pressure. I quivered, awaiting the furious eruption raging beneath the surface. Anger and fear are the worst combination of emotions to feel at the same time. It makes a victim irrationally combative.

"Not as surprised as you're going to be," I sneered, lifting my knee into his groin.

He crumpled to the ground, and although I briefly considered kicking him in the face, I chose to run instead. I jumped into a taxi parked in front of the nightclub and yelled for the driver to take me to the police station.

Jake stumbled out of the alley as we pulled away from the curb. The look on his face was murderous.

The adrenaline swimming through my veins kept my heart rate up and my breathing rapid. I figured it would slow on the way to the police station, but the cab driver kept watching me in his rearview mirror. It made me paranoid.

"You okay, ma'am?" he finally asked.

His concern came across genuine, but I wasn't taking any chances. "My car was impounded."

I'm not sure if he believed me or not, but he didn't ask

any more questions. When we got to the station, I glanced around and realized I didn't have my purse; it was still at the table with Gina and Dale. No purse. No pockets. No cash.

"I, um…"

The cab driver realized the situation as well. "It's okay. This ride's on me."

I thanked him, exited the cab, and walked numbly through the police station's sliding glass doors. A heavy-set dispatcher with short brown hair sat behind a bulletproof partition.

She glanced up at me. "Can I help you?"

Though I heard her, I couldn't bring myself to answer. Thinking of what I needed to tell her made my breath tighten, as if Jake's arm still pressed against my throat. My heart pounded in my chest, and my blood pulsed rapidly through my body, registering in my ears.

The dispatcher eyed me strangely. "Ma'am…? Is there something I can do for you?"

Shaking from head to toe, I finally managed to say, "He's d-d-dead."

At once, the entire scene rushed back to me. The room got darker as my eyes rolled up into the back of my head, and the last thing I heard was the sound of me hitting the floor.

When I woke up, I was sprawled on a gurney, and my head hurt. The paramedic at my side pulled a blood pressure cuff off my arm and pointed a penlight at my pupils to check their dilation. I did as he asked, following his finger with my eyes. Four uniformed deputies in the room watched silently while the he assessed my condition.

The medic glanced back at the officers. "She's okay, just

fainted and bumped her head. She'll have a bit of a headache, but it's nothing a little aspirin won't cure."

"Miss, we need to ask you a few questions," one policeman said. "Could you come with us, please?"

I stood slowly, my head hurting from the movement. The cop led me through the double doors and down a hallway until he angled into a small room marked "INTERROGATION UNIT." A small table, three uncomfortable-looking chairs, and a large mirror that consumed most of the far wall adorned the room. After I sat, I spied the small black camera mounted above the door. The red, blinking light flashed to a steady green. It wasn't hard to figure out they were taping me.

The man who sat across from me was probably close to retirement age. He had a full head of gray hair and a neatly trimmed mustache to match. "I'm Officer Stevens," he said, flipping open a small notepad. "And this is my partner, Officer Danforth."

Danforth was in his late thirties with dark hair cropped short. He offered to get me some coffee, but I declined. My hands trembled enough without the extra jolt of caffeine.

"Miss, our dispatcher said you told her a man is dead," Stevens said bluntly.

"Y-yes. He's…dead. I saw it. I watched him die."

"Did you kill him?"

"What? No, I watched him…oh God!" I covered my face with my hands.

"It's okay, Miss. We're here to help you," Danforth said. "Can you start from the beginning and tell us what happened?"

Stevens jotted down notes as I spoke. I told them everything I could remember until I had passed out in the lobby. They both looked at me as if I were loony.

Stevens shifted his gaze to the younger officer and, as if given a silent command, Danforth excused himself, disappearing from the room. I hoped they were sending a unit over to The Jungle Room to check out my story. I imagined it was difficult to believe anyone would be dumb enough to murder someone in a packed nightclub.

Officer Stevens asked me to repeat the entire story and forced me to go slower through the details this time around. When I got to the part about Sergio looking nervous, I completely broke down. Tears rolled steadily down my cheeks. My voice was barely a whisper. I knew how he had felt because I felt the same way when Jake had grabbed me. It's the fear of the unknown, as much as it's the fear that you know exactly what might happen.

Sergio was a creep, but he didn't deserve to die. Hell, what do I know? Maybe he did. He obviously had associations with some very bad men. No matter what, though, I didn't deserve to have his death forever stamped into my memory.

My face heated as I swayed a little in my chair. I wanted to pass out again, but having another meltdown would only prolong the inevitable. I gained some composure before continuing and tried to keep my voice from cracking while I calmly described the rest of the events that led me to the police station.

Afterward, Stevens led me to another room to search their database. Two long and tedious hours went by before I fingered the three men from the club. The officers were ecstatic, though I had no idea why. Only person I couldn't find in the system was Jake.

They let me take a break and issued another offer of

coffee. I accepted, knowing it might be a while before they asked again. A female officer escorted me to the bathroom, then deposited me back into the interrogation room, along with a cup of strongly brewed glop. I couldn't bring myself to try it, but the potent smell kept me awake.

Stevens excused himself, saying he needed to check on something, and left me alone. No clock on the wall. No way of telling how long he'd been gone. I knew it had been a lengthy stay when my ass fell asleep. My initial assumption about the chairs was right—they were uncomfortable.

I paced the floor for a while, then stopped to look at myself in the mirror. Holy hell. My curly blond hair resembled a raggedy bird's nest, my makeup was streaked, and my clothes were dirty and disheveled. Even my boobs looked crooked.

Casually, I glanced behind me and saw the green light shining on the camera in the corner. They were still filming me, but being alone in an interrogation room for hours does something to your mind. Apparently, it made me lose mine. I kept my back to the camera and my body close to the mirror as I reached into my blouse and adjusted my boob.

It was a familiar problem, since one of my breasts was a large B, while the other was a small C. It wasn't a noticeable difference, and most women have one breast that's larger than the other. At least, that's what I've heard. No explaining that to men, though. Every time I've tried, I always got the same response. *"Un-uh! Prove it! I want to see for myself."* Even Dale, who had more interest in a man's hacky sack than a pair of tits, said the same thing.

Men are idiots.

Tired of standing, I sat in the chair and laid my head on

the table. I could barely keep my eyes open, but every time I closed them, Sergio's face stared back at me with a blank look. I thunked my head on the smooth surface, trying to get the image out of my mind. Then the door opened and closed.

"Thank God," I said, lifting my head. "I want to get this over with — " I stopped breathing, and the room grew eerily still.

Jake stood there looking at me, measuring me up. The butt of a gun peeked out from under the edge of his jacket. The panic that had settled in my bones from earlier resurfaced, as if Jake himself had pushed the big red button.

His lips curled into a disgustingly sarcastic smile. "Rough night?"

Instinctively, I jumped out of my chair and screamed. He hurried to round the table as I ran to the other side near the door. He stopped coming forward when I picked up a chair and held it in a throwing position.

"Don't you dare," he said, his face knotting with anger.

Yeah, like I was going to listen. I threw the chair, but he turned at the last second, and it caught him in the shoulder. I tried to run out the door, but didn't make it before Jake grabbed me.

With warp speed, he shoved me against the wall, pinning me there with his body, making it hard for me to breathe. The intensity in his eyes told me he positively seethed with rage. That's when the door flung open as Officer Stevens burst into the room. Jake let go of me and backed away slowly with his hands in the air.

"We have the whole thing on camera," Stevens said. "Do you want to press charges?"

I looked at Stevens stupidly. "Of course I do! Arrest that

sonofabitch!"

Jake and Officer Stevens traded puzzled looks before both men burst into hysterics. I'm talking the kind of laughter that can easily make you wet your pants and not care because it's that damn funny.

"I was talking to *him*," Stevens said, still chuckling.

"What?"

The officer wiped his watery eyes. "Ma'am, you just assaulted a federal agent. This man here is Special Agent Jacob Ward. He works for the Federal Bureau of Investigation."

I glanced over at Jake. "FBI?" He grinned and cocked his eyebrow at me. "Fine. Officer Stevens, I want this *agent* arrested for kidnapping and assault."

The smile slid from Jake's face. "I didn't kidnap or assault anybody."

"Yes, you did. *Me!* You forced me to leave the club with you, then you assaulted me."

"Are you insane? That was self-defense. You spun around and attacked me. I was nice enough to hold back and keep myself from hurting you. And I didn't kidnap you. There was no gun to your head when I asked you to leave with me."

"Ask? You didn't ask! You threatened to kill my friends!" I pointed at Stevens. "Add that to the list, as well."

The officer looked confused. "I'm going to step out for a moment and let you two work this out."

Jake nodded. "While you're at it, get the camera turned off and clear the boys out of the viewing room. I need to talk to the witness privately."

Viewing room? Oh God, don't tell me I...

The officer hurried out the door as Jake picked up the

chair I had thrown. He set it back in place, then motioned for me to sit. Before I did, I watched the green light on the camera change to a red, blinking one. Holy shit! He really was a federal agent.

"Viewing room?" I whispered, biting my lip.

"Yep, we were making arrangements for you when you started fondling yourself. Then most of the men in that room had to make their own arrangements...if you know what I mean."

"I wasn't fondling myself."

"Hey, I can't help it if that's what it looked like."

"Oh God." I rubbed at my temple, trying to alleviate the headache that came back. "Someone should've told me a viewing room sat on the other side of the mirror."

"Do you live in a goddamn cave? Don't tell me you've never seen a cop show with a double-sided mirror before."

"Of course I have. I wasn't thinking. I was more worried about the camera. Excuse me for being stressed out."

"It's understandable." Jake eyed me for a moment. "You're in a shitload of trouble, you know."

I jumped up, making my chair fall backward, and my hands gripped the edge of the table until my knuckles turned white. "If you press charges on me, I'm going to...to..."

He glared back at me. "You're going to do what, exactly?"

I cocked my head and smirked. "I'm going to press charges on you for sexual assault."

"Okay, I've had enough of your antics. Now sit down."

"I don't have to listen to—"

"If you don't sit down and shut up, I'm going to arrest you for obstructing a federal investigation. A few hours in a cell might make you more cooperative. Besides, I already know you didn't tell Stevens about the kiss."

I picked up my chair, returned it to its rightful position, and sat in it. "It wasn't for your benefit, you creep. I didn't want them to think I was easy."

"You don't have to worry about that, sweetheart. Nothing's easy about you."

Jake opened the door and asked Stevens to hand him a file. He closed the door again and spread some pictures out before me. It was the three men from the lounge.

"This here's Frankie Felts. He's a low-level mobster with ties to drugs and money laundering. The other is Frankie's cousin, Arnold. Mostly a parasite, but Frankie keeps him around for amusement. The big guy is Curtis Manning, Frankie's hit man. As far as we can tell, he's never missed a mark…until now."

"What do you mean?"

"We've been trying to nail Frankie Felts for a long time, but every time we get close, the witness turns up dead or missing."

"Oh, that's comforting."

Jake grinned. "He covers his tracks well."

"So why are you telling me this?"

"Because you're a witness, and Felts isn't going to roll over and play dead. He's going to try to make sure *you* are, though."

Dear God. "Can't I be an anonymous tip or something?"

"Won't work. Not since they got a look at you."

"Then I'll recant my statement."

"Won't matter. To Felts, you're a loose end, and he doesn't leave loose ends. He'll kill you, just like the others. He murdered one of his own men tonight on suspicion alone, but Sergio wasn't an informant. All the intel we received was from bugs we'd placed throughout Frankie's organization."

"So he died for nothing?"

"Sergio wasn't innocent by any means," Jake said, shaking his head. "He squirreled away dollars from Frankie's bank account every chance he got. The drugs he sold helped line his pockets as well. Frankie just hasn't found out about any of it yet. Sergio had more brains than Felts gave him credit for."

No kidding. And most of them were on the wall behind his dead body. My stomach rolled at the thought, and I shook my head, wanting the images to dissipate. "What do I need to do?"

"That's where we come in."

I was confused, not connecting the dots. "Who's we?"

"The FBI and U.S. Marshals. We can give you a new identity and put you in a safe house."

"You mean the Witness Protection Program?"

"That's the one."

"Nuh-uh! No freaking way!"

His steely gaze fixed on me, and his jaw tightened. Jake didn't like being refused. "Three other witnesses have died in the past year. You want to be number four?"

"Should've put them in the program."

"We did."

"You mean they trusted the government to keep them safe, and they died anyway. Now, I'm supposed to take your word you'll keep me safe. You're crazy!"

"You don't have a choice."

"Sure I do," I said, standing to leave. "I'm going home and erasing what happened from my memory."

"You're not going anywhere. Sit down, Miss Stubborn-ass."

"Oh, puhleeeze!" I rolled my eyes as I stepped out the door.

Four uniformed officers stood outside the interrogation room, including Stevens, who looked up and smiled. "Can I get you something, ma'am?"

"A ride home would be great."

"Don't bother," Jake snarled, as he marched up behind me. "She's not leaving."

"You can't keep me here against my will. I want to go home."

"Tough. Like it or not, you're a witness in a murder investigation." He looked over to Stevens. "In fact, if she tries to leave again, shoot her."

Generating steam, I started yelling and stomping my foot. "You're violating my rights! I've been here for hours and answered all your stupid questions. I want to go home. Now!"

Jake smiled, as if he enjoyed my temper tantrum. "Patience is a virtue."

"Yeah, well, so is virginity, but I don't have *that* anymore, either."

A few of the men snickered under their breaths. Jake gave them all a stern look. The hallway went silent, filled with stagnant air nobody wanted to breathe. Jake grasped my elbow and tried to lead me back into the interrogation room. "I'm not done with you yet. You'll leave when I damn well say you can."

I dug my heels into the floor. "I want to see your badge."

"What?" He wheeled around, anger flashing in his eyes.

"You heard me. How do I know you are who you say you are?"

Jake never shifted his piercing eyes off mine as he reached into his shirt and pulled out a badge dangling from a chain around his neck. He held it up for me to get a closer look.

"Could be a fake," I told him with a shrug.

The other officers in the room grinned with amusement, but a vein popped out of Jake's temple. He was pissed. He pulled me into the interrogation room and pushed me roughly into the chair. Then he slammed the door on the laughter outside.

I crossed my arms and shook my head. "Has anyone ever hauled off and hit you?"

"You did...with a chair."

"Well, you deserved it. Maybe you should've identified yourself as an agent."

"It's not like you gave me much of a chance."

"Maybe you should've done that instead of shoving your tongue down my throat. Both times."

Jake's hard mouth turned up in a shameless grin. "So that's why you're being a pain in the ass? You're pissed about me using you as my cover."

"You're a bastard, you know that?"

His smile broadened. "I goofed and needed to do some damage control. If I would've known Sergio was the guy you were talking to, I wouldn't have interfered. I wasn't supposed to make contact with anyone in Felts's organization. But he saw me come out of the bathroom, and you probably would've stopped me if I walked past. So I kissed you to avoid talking to him."

"Oh, gee thanks." What an insulting thing to say to a woman. *I was forced to kiss you.* He might as well have thrown scalding water on me. "Jerk."

He was genuinely confused. "Hold on, I'm lost…"

"I could tell you where to go."

"What's your problem? I thought you'd want an explanation."

"I'm not a puppet, and I don't appreciate someone showing such disregard for my feelings."

"Feelings?" he asked. "There were no feelings involved. I was doing my job."

"Yeah, I could feel how hard your *job* was when it rubbed against my ass on the dance floor."

"Jesus," he said, exasperated. "When we leave here, I'm stopping to buy you a self-help book."

"Won't it defeat the purpose?" I asked, narrowing my eyes. "Besides, I already told you. I'm not going into your stupid program."

"That's still to be determined," he argued. "You don't seem to understand the full scope of the problem."

Oh, I understand all right. I'm about to be murdered, and it's freaking me the hell out. I just want to go home. I breathed out hard, crossed my arms, and tried a more promising tactic. "I'm done answering questions. If you're going to keep me here, then I want a lawyer."

"You're pushing my buttons. Why do you have to be impossible?"

"I'm not talking anymore until I get a lawyer."

"Don't be stupid. There's a fine line between dumb and ignorant, and you're about to cross it. Do you even know how to protect yourself?"

"I know enough," I said. "I can't complain."

"But you still do." He shook his head in disbelief, then tried to scare me into compliance. "Worst case scenario is they'll use you for target practice."

I refused to show him any weakness, though. "Better than being used by the King of Deception."

"Well, honey, I guess that makes you the Queen of Denial. But don't let me monopolize any more of your time, Your Majesty. By all means, go home and have a terrific life…what's left of it, anyway."

His words left me antsy, but it was too late to change my mind. The whole absurdity of the situation boggled me. When he wouldn't let me leave, the imagined dangers were surreal. Now that one of my get-out-the-door strategies actually worked, I wasn't sure I wanted to go. Not that I'd tell him that.

"You still here?" Jake asked in a snarky tone. "Thought you wanted to go home?"

"On a roll, aren't you?"

"Just making a point," he answered.

"No need. I got your point. You don't like me, and I don't like you. We'll never be Facebook friends. Good. But here's something for you… I don't care. You can go to hell." I threw open the door and marched out with Jake on my heels. "Officer Stevens, can I get that ride home now?"

Stevens tossed Jake a wide grin. "Do I have to shoot her?"

"No. Get her out of my sight."

The officer got up from his chair. "I'll pull a squad car around front for you, ma'am." Then he strode out a side exit.

"I'll wait outside." I walked out the lobby doors.

Two seconds later, Jake stepped out beside me. "You really should stay inside. It's not safe for you to be out here alone."

"I'm not alone," I replied curtly. "Officer Stevens is out here somewhere pulling a car around."

His hand curled into a fist, and he closed his eyes as if he were counting to ten. "Why don't you just admit you're wrong and cooperate?"

"Because I'm not wrong. And I'm sick of your bullying," I said as Stevens pulled around the building and parked next to us.

"You know what your problem is? Your mouth operates faster than your brain does."

"Is that all?"

"And you have a problem with authority," he added.

"Then why don't you stop profiling me and find another girl to use in your undercover operation?"

He laughed loudly and smugly. "I guess I struck a chord with your ego, since you keep bringing up that kiss. You must've really enjoyed it."

"Oh, the fuck," I said with a disgruntled roll of my eyes. "You're the one with the ego, jackass. I'd rather have a gerbil up my ass than to have you touch me again."

Jake put his fingers to my lips as he focused on something in the shadows across the lot. His grim, unblinking eyes startled me, but I tried to tamp down the fear welling up inside. A black sedan with dark tinted windows rolled to a stop in the parking lot with its headlights off. I couldn't tell if anyone was inside.

"I'm going back inside," I said nervously, scuttling toward the doors of the police station.

"No! Get down!"

Instead of dropping to the ground, I instinctually turned to see what had happened while still in the threshold of the sliding glass doors. The black sedan had flicked on its headlights, and the back window motored down. Jake's hand was on his gun, but instead of pulling it out, he propelled himself at me with breakneck speed.

Oomph.

The impact threw me off-kilter, and I landed on my stomach as the first shots rang out. Jake had thrown himself on top of me and shielded my head, but managed to grab his gun and fire back. I couldn't breathe. My first guess was I held the air in my lungs out of sheer terror. More shots rang out, and glass shattered all around us. Small shards nicked my hands and face as they ricocheted off me.

Three police officers from inside the building emerged, rolling onto the ground with their guns drawn. They each returned fire as the black car sped toward the highway. Two officers ran for their vehicles. Another called in backup over the radio on his shoulder.

Jake peeled himself off me, but the pressure of him lying on top of me wasn't what kept me from being able to breathe. My ears were ringing, and a burning sensation in my chest felt like a bullet had pierced my lung.

Then Jake shouted, "We need a paramedic!"

Chapter Three

I felt someone toe me.

"I'm not dead yet," I said weakly.

"I know," Jake said. "So why are you still on the ground?"

"Because I've been shot."

Jake paused for a beat. "No, you haven't."

I rolled over onto my back, which exhausted more effort than it should have. "Then why do I feel like I have a punctured lung?" I asked in a raspy, whispering voice. "I can barely catch my breath."

"Sorry," Jake said, hoisting me to my feet. "I must've knocked the wind out of you."

He hadn't lied when he said he held back during our earlier fight. A macho, all-American male. Probably even played football at some point. I wouldn't have been any match for him unless he had tried to keep me from getting hurt in that alley. This time I got hurt, but that's because he was trying to keep me from getting…well, dead.

"You're bad luck," I told him.

"I saved your ass twice tonight. How am *I* bad luck?"

"It's the third time I've scuffed the floor with my face since you've been around. If you're the undercover agent, how come I always end up being the one on the ground?"

"I like being on top," he said smugly. "Besides, none of those incidents were my fault."

"Two of them were," I argued, shaking glass fragments from my hair and dusting off my clothes as an ambulance came up the driveway.

"Look at the bright side. At least you're not the one who got shot."

"What, someone was shot?"

"Officer Stevens."

I covered my mouth. "Is he…?"

"No, he'll be fine. Stevens caught a stray bullet in the shoulder, but it doesn't look bad. He's lucky they were aiming for you."

A wave of nausea welled up from my stomach, making me woozy. "I…I need to sit down."

Jake spoke to the officer with Stevens. "I'm getting her out of here before she ends up on the ground again. Let me know if you find that car." He grabbed my arm and speed-walked me over to a black Yukon in the side lot, stuffing me into the back seat.

I drew in slow, deep breaths as he slid behind the wheel and cranked the engine.

"You look a little pale, like you're going to be sick. Need some Pepto?" His incredibly smug face peered back at me in the rearview mirror.

"You're such a prick."

Jake turned to face me, draping his right arm over the seat. He didn't dare laugh, but the smirk remained on his face. "So where to?"

Damn. He wanted me to say it.

I had refused the FBI's protection and demanded to go home, but had since changed my mind. Someone flinging bullets at you tends to have that effect. He already knew, but he wanted to make me eat crow. I seriously doubted it tasted anything like chicken.

I sighed. "Are you going to tell me how the stupid program works or not?"

"I knew you couldn't do it," he said, shaking his head. He turned around and drove us out of the lot. "Okay, in exchange for your testimony, you'll be entered into Witness Protection. You'll receive a new identity, be relocated to a safe house, and given twenty-four hour protection since it's a high-threat situation. FBI and U.S. Marshals are assisting each other on this case."

"Then what happens?"

"We put the bad guy behind bars."

"Sounds easy."

"It is…for you. We have the hard part," Jake said. "We have to keep you alive until then."

"That going to be a problem?"

"Nope. Everything's under control."

His reassurance should have put my mind at ease, but it didn't. I may have been new to the program, but I wasn't new to men. Jake was confident to a fault, which led me to believe he wasn't telling me everything. In fact, I was sure of it. Nothing about this would be as easy as he said.

We drove for half an hour when Jake pulled into the

parking lot of a run-down motel off I-74. The vacancy sign was half lit, and the landscaping consisted of weeds and spent cigarette butts.

"We're here," Jake announced.

"Does the FBI have a suggestion box?"

"What's wrong?"

"Are you fucking kidding me? Thirty minutes outside of town and a crappy motel is the FBI's idea of relocating me to a safe house?"

The corners of Jake's mouth threatened to erupt into a full-on smile. "Of course not. Don't be ridiculous. This is more of a transition station. Have a little more faith in us than that." Jake got out and opened the back door, keeping his eyes alert as he shuffled me toward a nearby room.

A female agent awaited our arrival. She had on black slacks, a cream silk top, and a pair of chic horn-rimmed glasses. Nerdy, but she had great hair. She smiled at me warmly, then nodded to Jake.

"Agent Ward, I presume? I'm Agent Vickie Rawlings from the FBI's Indianapolis Division. Two more agents, Agent Franklin and Agent Schafer, are with me. They're posted outside for the time being."

"I spotted them when we pulled in," Jake told her.

Agent Rawlings motioned to me. "Well, are you ready to do this? I have everything we need."

"Huh?"

"A new identity requires a new look. Lucky for you, my mother owned a hair salon, and I spent every weekend there until I graduated high school. I used to practice on my dolls when I was a child. Actually, you look like one of my old Barbie dolls with all that curly, blond hair."

I glared at Jake. "You didn't tell me I had to change my appearance."

"You have to change your appearance," he said, mocking me with monotone.

Rawlings grabbed my arm and pulled me toward the back of the motel room. "It'll be fine. You'll love it when I'm finished." She pushed me past the vanity and into the bathroom, closing the door with an echoing clang. It may as well have been the cell door closing on my freedom, leaving me with no control and completely at her mercy.

The tiny bathroom didn't have a mirror, so I couldn't see what she was doing. My scalp tingled, and the dye smelled caustic, but the color stayed a mystery. Leftover purple gunk in the bowl fueled images of me as a punk rocker sporting a Mohawk.

When it was time to rinse, Rawlings stepped out and came back in with a cellophane-wrapped plastic cup. I wanted to peek in the mirror outside the bathroom door, but didn't want Jake to see me with a towel draped over my shoulders and hair glued to my head. I was sure I looked as stupid as I felt.

Rawlings rinsed my hair over the tub, toweled it, and combed it before making the first cut. Every snip made me cringe as pieces of my now-brown hair fell to the floor, some segments at least ten inches long. I bit my lip to keep from crying.

Normally, I used a curling iron every day, since my hair is naturally pin straight. When she stopped cutting and blow-dried my hair, Rawlings suggested I keep it that way as part of my new look. My head felt strangely light, as if she'd shaved me bald.

Rawlings stepped back, admiring her work. "Done. You

can look now."

Reluctantly, I opened the door, letting her lead the way, and was glad when I realized Jake wasn't still in the room. I stepped over to the vanity mirror and peered at my reflection. My hair was a mousy brown color, and the layered cut sat barely past my shoulders. She had given me some face-framing pieces, blended them into the front layers, and added side swept bangs.

"I look like you," I told her, admiring my cut.

"That's the point," she replied, handing me a bag. "Here, now put these on."

We stepped back into the bathroom, and I opened the bag, half-expecting an ugly turtleneck or a pair of hideous polyester pants. Surprisingly enough, I found the exact outfit Rawlings wore, including a pair of horn-rimmed glasses.

Rawlings changed into my clothes, stuffed her own outfit into the bag, and put on a long, curly blond wig she adjusted on her head. When she put on a Kevlar vest, that's when it dawned on me. She was my decoy.

"Don't I need to wear one, too?"

"Won't be necessary," she said. "If someone is out there watching, then I'll be the one in danger. They won't recognize you."

She tried to comfort me, but I wasn't feeling warm and fuzzy. I had a knack for attracting unwanted attention. Sergio was proof of that. A vest would've made me feel safer but, then again, it wouldn't keep them from shooting me in the head.

By the time we came out again, Jake was back and joined by three men. Jake stopped talking and looked me over. He didn't smile or comment, just stared with piercing, impolite eyes. I imagined he liked the new look as well.

"Agent Franklin and Agent Schafer from Indianapolis," Jake said gesturing to the two men standing behind him. Then he motioned to the third man on his right. "My boss, Harvey Brockway. He's the Director of the FBI's Chicago Division."

The man wore a wrinkled navy blazer, light blue dress shirt, and a loose, slightly askew tie. His thinning gray hair was unkempt, and his bloodshot eyes drooped with bags underneath. He didn't look like anyone's boss. He looked like someone who'd rolled out of bed after a rough night.

"Pleasure to meet you, ma'am. I only wish it was under better circumstances," Brockway said, offering me his hand. "Let me assure you we'll do everything in our power to keep you out of harm's way." I nodded, and he gestured to the table. "I brought some documentation for you, Miss Foster."

I looked at him with confusion. "That isn't my name."

"It is now. From this point on, your name is Emily Foster. In the envelope is your new identity, complete with background information. You'll need to memorize it all. Agent Ward will oversee your transfer to the safe house we set up. From there, three U.S. Marshals will rotate shifts. Someone will be with you at all times. I took the liberty of having some of your personal items from your apartment sent ahead, but if you need anything else, please don't hesitate to ask."

"Thank you," I said, thinking Jake could learn a lesson from this man. The consideration Brockway showed in the last five minutes was more than I got from Jake all night long.

After Brockway left, Jake gave the agents their instructions and told them to get moving. Agent Franklin opened the door, looked around, and then walked out. Rawlings followed him closely, keeping her head down timidly as if she were a scared witness. Schafer fell in line behind her.

Jake watched through the peephole, making sure they were gone. "Okay, it's our turn, Emily."

Whoa! Emily? That would take some getting used to.

"I'm not going to walk beside you this time," he explained. "Don't act nervous or jittery. You're supposed to be another agent. Stay calm and get in the front seat. Got it, Emily?"

Jeez. I haven't had the name fifteen minutes, and I'm already sick of hearing it. "Yeah, I guess."

"Let's go."

I walked out casually, sauntering over to the Yukon, and slid into the front passenger seat. I tried to convey confidence and coolness, but I was sweating like a preacher in a whorehouse. As soon as Jake drove us out of the parking area, I blasted the air conditioner and turned the vents toward myself. It wasn't a good idea. I love silk shirts, but you can't hide hard nipples under thin material. I thought maybe Jake wouldn't notice, but of course, he did. After all, he's a man.

His lingering gaze gave me a slight rush. "What?"

"Nothing," he replied, grinning. "I'm waiting."

"For what?" It wasn't like my nipples were going to sprout tassels and dance for him.

"The nervous breakdown you haven't had yet."

"Why would I do that?"

"You've had some rather calm responses to what most people would deem disturbing situations. I thought you'd be crying by now."

I put on a brave face, not wanting him to know how

scared I really was. "I'm more of a screamer. But if you want to cry, by all means, don't let me stop you."

"Jesus. Always a smartass," he said, focusing his attention back to the road. "Get some rest. We'll be on the road for another couple of hours before we get to the airport."

"Airport?"

"A private jet is waiting to take us to a safe, undisclosed location."

"Which is where?"

"You do know what undisclosed means, right?"

"You're not going to tell even *me*?"

"Not yet," he said, shaking his head. "You still have phone calls you need to make to your family. I have a secure line you can—"

"No."

His eyes widened. "You can't call them later. It's now or never."

"Fine," I said with a shrug. "Never."

He stared at me strangely, not understanding my refusal. "You might want to reconsider and call them. You won't be able to attend family reunions or even their funerals if someone dies. You need to say good-bye—"

"I don't...have anybody to call."

He was taken aback by my response, his brows lifting in questioning slants.

"I buried both of my parents when I was fourteen and don't have any siblings. I'm alone."

"Who did you live with when your parents died?"

"Foster homes. Lots of them. Nobody wants a smart-mouth teenager. I figured that out quick."

"Any other relatives?" he asked.

"No. Probably some distant cousins somewhere who I don't know, but no one who would know I'm missing, except Gina and Dale. They're the closest thing I have to family."

"Your friends from the club? Why don't you call them?"

I kept my eyes on the window, watching the trees blur past. "I can't."

"Why not?"

"Because I can't—no, I won't—say good-bye to anyone else I care about. I've already done it too many times."

"Look, it's your last chance to contact someone from your former life. It doesn't matter who—family, friends, an old boss, or even an old boyfriend. You won't be allowed to do it later."

I shook my head and, for a moment, there was nothing but silence. He kept looking at me as if I were going to change my mind. "Okay, fine," he said. "Then you're officially in federal custody."

"Now will you tell me where we're going?"

Jake smirked. "Omaha, Nebraska."

"What happens when we get there?"

"There are some rules you'll have to follow."

"Wait. You didn't say anything about any rules. I hate rules. Too damn restrictive."

Jake rolled his eyes at me. "Heaven forbid the feds have rules that could save your life."

"Too many rules in life already," I argued. "Wear sunscreen, buckle your seatbelt, practice safe sex. Nothing good ever came from following rules. Okay, well, except for maybe the 'practice safe sex' one."

Jake smiled. "It's simple. You'll lay low at the safe house under a new identity until we need you to testify. No outside contact of any kind."

"And what if my cover is blown?"

"*You're* the only one who'll blow your cover. Don't ever tell anyone your real name. It would be like voluntarily ejecting yourself from the program and would most likely get you killed. You are Emily Foster. Remember that, because one slipup can change everything."

"Anything else?"

"Refrain from doing things you've done in the past. Change your routine…in fact, don't even build one. It'll keep you alive longer."

"You say that like you don't expect me to live."

"Some haven't," he said, matter-of-factly.

"What happened to the other three witnesses?"

"Not sure. It's possible they did something to endanger themselves, like using their real identities."

"No, I mean…how'd they die?"

He shook his head, and his jaw tightened. "You don't want to know."

"Yeah, I do."

"Okay, then you don't need to know."

"Come on, Jake! It's my life we're talking about. I have a right to know what happened to them."

Jake stared at me for a full minute before he spoke. "One woman was beaten to death with a hammer, one was shot in the head seven times, and the man's body was decapitated and dismembered…all *five* of his limbs."

"Five? But there's…oh, never mind." *Jesus. What have I gotten myself into?*

"Their bodies were all dumped in cornfields a few days after they disappeared."

"Eww," I said, cringing. "I'm never eating corn again."

. . .

We were landing just after sunrise when I remembered why I'd always hated flying. The plane was sure to crash on landing. I gripped the armrest tightly, turning my knuckles white, and closed my eyes. A warm hand touched mine and squeezed my fingertips. I cracked an eyelid.

Jake gave me a half-smile. "You'll be fine," he said.

Then I felt the jarring bump of the landing and said a silent thank you to the pilot, God, and my digestive system. The plane slowed and taxied down the runway. More relaxed, I opened both eyes. By the time the jet stopped on the tarmac, I was breathing normally. I followed Jake through the exit door of the plane, stopping to blink and adjust my eyes to the bright morning sun.

A black Suburban waited for us, along with two male agents, both wearing dark blue suits and aviator sunglasses. Like that wasn't a dead giveaway. Jake stepped out before me, shielding my body with his, while visually searching the immediate area with caution.

"Everything okay?" I asked.

"Just staying alert," Jake answered. "Quit worrying."

Easy for him to say. Hard to remain calm when he scrutinized my every move, as if I'd be executed any minute.

The driver opened the back passenger door for us. "I'm Special Agent Riggs and this is my partner, Agent Murphy."

"I'm Agent Ward and this is Emily." *There's that name again.* Jake gave the agent a quick handshake while steadily shoving me into the backseat. He didn't bother walking around to get in on the other side. Instead, he pushed me toward the middle and slid in next to me, sitting close enough that our legs touched.

Twenty minutes later, we pulled into a driveway with a two-car garage attached to a large house, and entered through the front door. I expected old and dilapidated. What I got was far from it. Well hidden on the back side of a lake, the three-bedroom, two-bath home had a stone fireplace, jetted tubs, hardwood floors, granite countertops, and stainless steel appliances. It was like my own private spa.

Jake was more impressed with the split entryway and walk out basement, explaining how it gave me a choice of exits if anything went wrong. Probably the reason they chose it. The pool table in the basement must've been a bonus for the unfortunate souls stuck guarding me for any length of time.

"We've already swept the house for bugs," one of the agents told Jake.

"Good," I said. "I hate bugs."

Both agents glanced at Jake, not knowing if they were supposed to take me seriously.

"She has a wisecrack for everything," Jake told them. "You'll get used to it."

Agent Riggs shook his head. "We're the security detail for the transfer, not babysitters. They won't arrive until tomorrow."

"What?" Jake yelled. "Three U.S. Marshals were supposed to be guarding her upon arrival. Who authorized the twenty-four hour delay?"

"Director Harvey Brockway from Chicago. He asked us to inform you of the change once you arrived, since four marshals from the Nebraska district were caught in an explosion during the night. They're down some manpower and adjustments had to be made. Director Brockway said to tell you he cleared your schedule for the next few days."

"Brockway, huh? I'm surprised he didn't call me himself."

Riggs shrugged. "You two are on your own, at least for tonight."

Damn. They were leaving us alone overnight. Probably not a good thing. Maybe I could avoid Jake and keep from talking to him. Yeah, right. Like I could go twenty-four hours without talking. Hell, no woman could do that.

Riggs smiled, reading the sheer panic on my face, before he continued. "The fridge is stocked, and there are clothes for each of you in your rooms. Brockway sent them. Explorer in the garage has a full tank of gas and is equipped with a tracking device in the GPS. Keys are on the counter, along with the code for the security system to the house."

As soon as the agents left, Jake locked the door behind them and activated the alarm. I went upstairs to the master bedroom to look for my clothes and the nearest bathroom. Jake followed me, then stood leaning against the bedroom wall. He watched as I dug through the dresser drawers and found a pair of bikini underwear, a white tank top, and a pair of green striped pajama bottoms.

I headed for the bathroom.

"Don't lock the door in case I need to get to you fast," Jake said.

"But I'll be naked."

He paused. "So let me get this straight. If the bad guys storm the castle, you'd rather be dead than for me to see you naked?" He glared at me with a controlled intensity that forced me to look away.

"Fine. I'll leave the door unlocked. But you better hope no one storms the castle while I'm in there."

I had planned to soak in the tub for a while, but after what Jake said, I opted to take a quick bath instead. He stood in the same position when I came back out, except some clothes had materialized under his arm.

As soon as I stepped clear of the bathroom, he walked in and turned the water on. I sat on the king-size bed across from the bathroom, thinking he'd shut the door. But I was wrong.

He removed his shirt, baring his nicely chiseled abs and well-defined pectoral muscles. A sexy treasure trail of hair led into his pants, and I salivated as I thought about following it. He was all hard muscles and tanned, firm skin. I had the sudden urge to run my fingers up his back and my tongue down his front.

He removed his pants, then pulled off his boxer briefs as I watched in anticipation. *Please, no ass hair. Please. Aha! There is a God.* I started to smile, but glanced up from his rear to see him looking back at me in the mirror. *Oops.*

"Might want to shut the door," I told him. "Especially if you're going to use my bathroom."

"Sorry, but without someone else here to keep an eye on you, we'll have to make do. If you don't want to look, then turn your head."

If I don't want to look? Was he fucking crazy? Of course, I wanted to look. That was the problem.

To spare my sanity, I averted my eyes. But it chewed my insides raw with frustration. As soon as Jake stepped into the tub, I thunked the back of my head against the headboard several times.

"What's that noise?" Jake yelled over the sound of the water.

Jesus. I couldn't even bang my head on something without having to answer to him. "It was me. Sorry."

Moments later, Jake turned the water off. I could hear him in the bathroom shuffling around, but didn't look. His glorious, naked body was a twist of the neck away, and I refused myself the view. It was cruel and unusual punishment.

Just so I wasn't tempted, I stepped over to the bedroom window and peered out at the backyard, watching a small bird flitter from tree to tree in the late morning sun. I didn't hear Jake approach me from behind, when he grasped my arm, startling me.

"Stay away from the windows," he said, moving me toward the bed. "It's the last place you want to be standing if someone shoots at the house."

Gee, thanks a lot. Like I needed that neurosis for the rest of my life.

I sat on the bed, but he stayed standing. His hair was damp, which made it look a darker shade of brown than it actually was. He was more relaxed and comfortable now that he put on a pair of Levi's and a T-shirt. It was strange, though. I didn't picture him as a jeans and T-shirt kind of guy. It looked good on him.

"I'm surprised you aren't wearing pajamas," I told him. "Aren't you tired?"

"I don't sleep in pajamas."

"You sleep in jeans? That's weird."

Jake gave me one of his incredible smiles, showing his gleaming white teeth. "I don't usually have anything on me in bed…unless it's a woman."

I struggled to maintain my composure, but practically melted into the mattress. I smiled back, though I think mine came off more like an Elvis impersonation. *What the hell is wrong with me?*

Seconds later, I answered my own question.

My mind did a mental rewind of the evening and paused on the memory of Jake kissing me in the club—not once, but twice—and my nipples tightened. Okay, I was obviously attracted to him. But he was a jerk, right? Before I knew he was an agent, I'd toggled between wanting to kiss him or slap him. So far, kissing had won out.

"We should probably talk about what happened between us last night," Jake proposed, sitting next to me on the bed.

I swallowed hard. I didn't want him to apologize for anything or tell me it was a mistake. It was his job…I knew that. But hearing him say his memories of our kiss weren't as fond as mine would be damaging to my mental well-being. I didn't want to rehash the evening with him because then I'd have to wallow in self-pity, something I refused to do with an audience.

Jake sat quietly, waiting for me to speak. His eyes met mine, and the swell of inner emotions restricted the blood flow to my brain. The intense way he focused on me made my mind and body feel out of alignment. I liked him. A lot. There's just something hot about a guy who's willing to take a bullet for you.

I tried to conquer the voice in my head, but it was no use. God, I was falling for him. Again.

After a dizzying deliberation, my brain went on hiatus, and I made a ballsy move. I grabbed Jake and kissed him. It was eager, aggressive, impulsive…and not returned.

Jake grabbed my arms firmly and pushed me away. His eyes trained on me as he gave me a pensive look and tightened his jaw. Jake's lips pursed as he breathed out through his nose, his eyebrows gathering over the bridge. Yep, definitely mad.

I couldn't breathe. Couldn't speak. I felt rejected, not to mention embarrassed. Was I so self-deluded that I hadn't realized the little effect I actually had on him? Okay, he could've faked the kiss in the club. But there was no mistaking the giant beanstalk in his pants.

"I-I'm sorry," I said, though I didn't feel particularly guilty. "I just thought…"

Without warning, Jake stood and crossed the room, putting distance between us. I didn't dare look at him with my heated cheeks. They were probably as red as I was stupid. Instead, I plopped back, pulled a blanket over my head, and tried to smother myself.

Naturally, I wanted to smooth things over, but I doubted he'd give me the chance. He made it unmistakably clear he wanted nothing to do with me. Maybe he was cranky and sleep deprived. Or maybe he didn't have to pretend anymore. Whatever it was, it left me scratching my head, but I refused to be interested in a guy who wasn't interested in me. Well, it sounded good, anyway.

I don't know if the long, traumatic night finally caught up with me, or if the oxygen deprivation had something to do with it, but I must've passed out. When I opened my eyes again, the sun had already gone down. If the clock next to the bed was correct, then I had spent the entire day unconscious.

Jake sat across the room in a chair with his laptop, notebook, and a pen. He didn't look up. I closed my eyes and pretended to be asleep, hoping he wouldn't talk to me.

"I know you're awake."

Crap.

Jake clicked his pen, and I heard him set it down. "We need to talk."

I opened my eyes to see him moving toward the bed with a masculine saunter. "Talk about what?"

"You know what."

I avoided making eye contact, but knew he watched me. His laser-sharp stare sliced into me with surgical precision. It was nerve-racking, though I craved his attention. The problem with Jake was that he was addictive. I don't know why I felt so strongly for a guy I barely knew, but I desperately wanted to quit him cold turkey. I needed a distraction until he left. Then, problem solved.

I shook my head and played stupid. "You have to be more specific."

"We need to talk about you kissing me this morning."

"No, we don't," I said, though I meant I'd rather gouge out my eyes with a dull pencil.

He sighed and rubbed at the back of his neck. "You're impulsive…and stubborn…and you don't think things through…and I—"

"I don't need you to point out anything. I'm not oblivious to my flaws."

"You're actually admitting you have some?"

"Jerk."

He grinned. "If I'm such a jerk, then why throw yourself at me?"

We both went silent. My eyes fastened to his, and I realized we were sizing each other up. I began to sweat. "Don't worry,"

I said, my voice growing more hostile. "I've regretted that decision ever since. It won't happen again."

He shook his head and sat next to me. "You know what your problem is? You're mad because you kissed me, and I didn't fall over with my dick hard."

My nostrils flared, and I saw red. "Funny, I don't recall your dick having any problems getting hard the other times."

"You know what? I was wrong. You don't need sex. You need a fucking Valium."

"Who said anything about sex? You're quite presumptuous. It was just a kiss, nothing more. No offer of anything else."

Jake grinned. "Oh, you made an offer all right, whether you admit it or not. Now you're mad because I didn't take you up on it."

My head spun, and my heart pounded. What he said was true, but I wasn't going to tell him that. "Better hope no one comes for me and accidentally shoots you between the eyes. It might puncture your ego and let all of the swelling out of your head."

"Excuse me for being a gentleman. I'm not a guy who takes advantage of someone in an emotionally vulnerable state."

"Laaaame."

"What's lame?"

"You are. And stupid. That's your idiotic attempt at shifting the responsibility onto me. Gentleman, my ass. You weren't such a gentleman in the club, either. So don't think for one second I'm buying it." Jake sat there stewing in his own juices. I had pushed his buttons, rendering him speechless. "Do you know what bothered you about that kiss?" I asked, not waiting for him to answer. "You obviously wanted it to lead to something more."

"Jesus Christ, woman! We don't have to have sex. There's enough damn friction between us to last a lifetime."

"What's wrong? Afraid you might enjoy it?"

"It's sex. Of course, I'd enjoy it. That's why it can't happen." Jake held my gaze. I recognized a battle of wills when I saw one. Not only that, but he was losing. That's why his feathers were ruffled. "Sex is intimate and has a psychological element to it," he added.

"Take the intimacy out of the equation."

"I can't," he said, giving me a contemplative look. "You know I'm leaving tomorrow. That leaves a moral and ethical dilemma to consider."

"You said it yourself, Jake…I *know* what this is. It's been clearly stated. There aren't going to be any issues to air out later. No strings attached. Just keep it casual."

Jeez. Either I was twisted, or my brain had taken a leave of absence. Everything coming out of my mouth was bullshit. I knew it, but I couldn't stop the flow. I'd relish in the moment and suffer the consequences later. And, as bad as I had it for him, there would be some definite consequences.

I didn't want him to leave. When my parents died, I refused to say good-bye to anyone else. Jake would be my first good-bye after all these years. He'd leave, and I'd be alone. It was a vicious circle.

With no warning, Jake grabbed me by the back of my neck and covered my mouth with his. I didn't hesitate to kiss him back as he dipped his tongue inside and swirled it in time with mine. His warm hand found its way under my shirt, cupping my breast, rubbing my nipple between his fingers.

I pulled at Jake's shirt until he released me long enough

to help jerk it over his head. He tossed it to the floor and yanked mine off as well. Then, he pushed me back onto the bed, sliding his hands over me. He slipped a nipple in between his teeth and gently tugged on it. Pleasure raced through my body in surges, making me arc farther into his awaiting mouth.

My nether region was on fire. The sensations were well worth surrendering to, but I'd pay dearly when it came time for him to leave. This was all we would have. One night together.

"Do you have a condom?"

"The FBI taught me to always be prepared," he said, grinning.

I smiled back. "Even when it's meaningless sex?"

His face turned serious. "I don't do meaningless sex."

I wasn't sure what he meant, but I didn't have time to respond before his hand found its way inside my pants and pushed them down. I kicked them off my feet as Jake hovered over me, staring down the length of my body. He wasn't moving anymore. One minute, he was unbuttoning his pants, and the next, he was frozen in time.

"Okay, what the fuck is that?" he asked.

Chapter Four

I glanced down to see what I had missed. "Oh, shit! Well, it's…uh…"

Jake's eyes met mine. "Did aliens invade your pants and leave crop circles in their wake?"

Heat filled my face. "It's a botched trim job. I forgot about it. If it's a problem, then we can stop…" I tried to roll out from under him, but he clamped his hand on my shoulder and held me there.

"I work for the Federal Bureau of Investigation," he reminded me. "It's my duty to investigate this, er…sighting… to the best of my ability." He grinned.

Wiseass.

"Stay here," Jake said. "I'll be back."

"Oh, come on! It's not *that* bad."

Once again, his eyes flitted down and back up. "No, but it isn't that good, either."

"Then don't bother." I tried to nudge him off me, but he

didn't budge.

He lowered his mouth to mine, kissed me hungrily, and then traced his tongue to my ear. "I'm just getting a condom," he whispered, his voice aching with desire. "Rules of Protection, right?"

"Oh," was all I said as he pushed himself off me.

He stood at the end of the bed and looked me over again, shaking his head with a smirk. His pants were undone, hanging loosely onto his waist, and the black boxer briefs outlined his raging hard-on.

Hmmm. Impressive.

Jake watched me lick my lips. "Hold that thought," he said, then stepped out of the room. Several minutes went by before he returned—with his pants buttoned. He snatched my clothes from the floor and threw them at me. "Get dressed," he ordered.

"What's wrong?"

Jake pulled his T-shirt on. "We've got company."

My first thoughts were that our escorts had returned to check on us, or maybe my babysitters had arrived early. Then Jake grabbed his gun off the table and stuffed an extra clip into his back pocket. I threw my clothes on faster than he had pulled them off me.

"Who is it?" I asked.

"I don't know, but they aren't FBI or U.S. Marshals."

"How do you know?"

"Because they're walking the perimeter of the house, looking through windows," Jake said in a low voice. "Any agent would know doing something stupid like that would get them shot."

"Are you going to call in backup?"

He shook his head. "Too far away. I need to concentrate on getting you out of here alive first."

"Are we safe as long as we stay inside?"

"We're sitting ducks. If we can get to the Explorer in the garage, then we'll make a run for it. If nothing else, I'll pick them off one by one."

"What if they pick you off first?"

He stared at me point-blank for a moment. Though he didn't say the words, I read his thoughts. *Then we'll both be dead.*

"Jesus," I said with exasperation. "Your crime prevention program sucks!"

Jake clamped his hand around my wrist, pulled me to the bedroom door, and peeked down the dark hallway. He gestured for me to stay quiet as he yanked me into the hall, keeping me behind him. As we got near the stairs, Jake lowered into a crouch, so I did the same. He looked around constantly. I leaned into his back, crowding him, and tried to look over his shoulder.

"Any sign of trouble, I want you to run to the garage and take the vehicle," he whispered. "Don't wait for me. You understand?"

I nodded, though I knew I wouldn't leave him behind. I didn't want to be left completely defenseless. And I didn't want Jake to die.

We flattened ourselves against the wall and tiptoed down the stairs. Jake peeked around the corner, then motioned for me to follow. We went through the dining room and into the kitchen, where the door to the garage was located.

As we rounded the corner, a gun became visible. A man in the kitchen pulled his weapon up to shoot us. Jake reacted with speed, grabbing the gun and pointing it away from us as the gunshot rang out. The bullet went wild, ricocheting off the stainless steel refrigerator and embedding into the tile over the kitchen sink. They each fought for control of the gun, bumping into me and knocking me backward onto my butt as the man aimlessly fired again.

I'd hit my lower back on the counter and tweaked my ankle as I went down but ignored the pain. I crawled around the island to the other side, ducking my head. I could no longer see what was happening.

Both men breathed heavily, grunting and fighting, until another round fired and someone landed with a thud on the kitchen floor. I was afraid to look, afraid of what I might find if I did look. What if Jake was the one who…? No, I couldn't finish the thought. It wasn't Jake. It couldn't be.

I scrambled to my feet. Jake stood over an unknown man slumped on the floor near the island. A dark red stain on his chest grew larger by the second, like a rose blooming in the midday sun. Still alive, his eyes were open. He gurgled frothy-looking blood from his mouth.

Jake barely glanced at me when he lifted his gun and pointed it at my head. Surprised by the quick movement, I didn't have time to flinch. He pulled the trigger, and a shot zinged past my ear. A loud crash came from behind me. I spun around with wide eyes to see a man lying on the floor with a knife in his hand and a bullet hole in his head.

Gunfire erupted through the kitchen windows, and Jake lunged for me, knocking me back to the floor. In a split second, our safe house had turned into a house of horrors, a dire situation filled with incalculable risks. He covered my head with my face turned toward the dead man. I got an up-close view of the bullet hole, which made me gag.

Once the shooting stopped, Jake ran for the nearest window, keeping himself to the side and peering out. I rolled away from the corpse.

"There must've been only three of them," Jake said. "Someone jumped into a car and is driving away." Jake walked over and checked on the man with the chest wound. "He's dead, damn it!"

"That's a bad thing?" I asked weakly, having a hard time finding my voice.

"It is when you need to question someone. Dead people have a tendency not to answer."

I kept my eyes on the window. "Is he coming back?"

"Doesn't matter. We aren't staying to find out. Your location's been compromised, so my main concern is getting you out of here. I'll go upstairs with you and stand guard while you throw some things in a bag. You've got two minutes."

"Two minutes? That's not enough—"

"That's all you're getting. Take it or leave it," he said, walking up the stairs ahead of me with his gun still in hand. I marched after him, making a mental list of everything I should grab.

Jake checked out the room before he relaxed a bit, but I ran back and forth trying to fit everything into a suitcase. It was hard to do with shaky hands. He grabbed his laptop from the desk and threw it into the bag as well. Next, we visited his room and did the same with his limited amount of clothing.

Then, cautiously, Jake led me down the stairs and into the kitchen. I don't know why I was surprised to see the two dead men still lying on the floor. I mean, where were they going to go? I guess it's because, in the horror movies, the bodies are never in the same spot as before. And this situation was as creepy as any thriller.

Jake surveyed the garage first, allowing me to enter after he deemed it safe. I tried to open the passenger door on the blue Ford Explorer, but he grabbed my hand to stop me. I watched as he slipped under the vehicle for a few seconds. Then he slid back out and popped open the hood.

"We don't have time for an oil change," I said with sarcastic frustration.

He closed the hood. "I was looking for a bomb," he said, his tone cavalier, as if it was an everyday thing.

"A what?"

"Don't worry. There isn't one." He grabbed the suitcase and chucked it into the backseat. Then he walked around to the driver's side. "Get in."

"No."

He lowered his gaze to look through the car windows at me. "Emily, get in."

"No fucking way! I'm not getting into a car that might blow up."

"That's why I checked. It's not going to blow up. Now get in."

I stood there, still not moving. Jake sighed and marched back around the front of the vehicle. "This is the last time I ask you nicely," he threatened.

"You're insane if you think—"

He snatched me up by my arm, opened the car door, and then manhandled me into the front passenger seat, slamming the door closed. Jake muttered expletives and shook his head as he walked back around to the driver's door. He got in and ripped the GPS off the dash, tossing it out the window.

I shook my head with disgust. "Feel better now, you big baby?"

"Tracking device," he explained.

When he cranked the Explorer, I nearly jumped out of my seat, waiting for an explosion that didn't happen. Then he pulled out of the garage, and I slid down in my seat, waiting for the stray bullet that didn't come. By the time we got to the highway, I was pretty sure I wasn't going to die. At least not tonight.

"Why haven't you called this in?"

"Because."

"Generous with words, aren't you? Care to elaborate?"

Jake glanced over at me. "Nope."

"Well, then at least tell me where we're going."

"I need to hide you somewhere safe."

"And where's that?"

"I don't know yet." He shook his head, as if contemplating something, then blew out a breath. "Shit."

"Something wrong?"

"I know somewhere I can take you. No one will find you there."

"Yeah, you said the same thing about the other place," I reminded him.

"It was safe, but things changed. I promise you, Emily, I don't make the same mistake twice. Once we get a few hours down the road, I'll need to stop."

"Wait, aren't you going to rename me?"

"The only identification you have is for Emily Foster. So, no, I'm not going to rename you. You aren't a pet turtle."

• • •

"Are you sure we're safe here?"

"We won't stay long. I need to check a few things on my laptop and make some phone calls. You can get some rest, if you want."

I peered around the room, wrinkling my nose. "If you wanted me to actually use the bed, then you should've chosen a more suitable motel."

Jake shrugged. "Nothing wrong with this one. It's functional."

"Sure, if you don't mind bedbugs and pubic lice," I said, glancing at the yellowed walls, dingy carpet, and stained comforter.

Jake didn't say anything as he opened his laptop.

"I guess I'll go rinse off, though I'll probably end up with fungus on my feet afterward," I said.

"Don't lock the door."

I could've taken his comment to mean he'd be joining me, but since he didn't look up, I figured I was on my own. Probably a good thing, since I couldn't imagine the bathroom being any more hygienic than the rest of the room. I didn't want an infected vagina any more than he probably wanted a sore on his dick.

I hurried into the shower…then hurried right back out. It was as disgusting as I'd imagined. Hardened soap scum coated the walls, rust stains encompassed the drain, and there were black, curly hairs in the bottom of the tub, none of which belonged to me. Instead of bathing, I used one of the washcloths—though it smelled funny—and sponged myself off at the sink. It took longer, but was more sanitary.

Barely.

He sat at the small table, still looking intently at his computer. I plopped into the chair across from him and admired the new brown do Agent Rawlings had given me in the mirror on the wall. The cut was perfect and, although I never thought I'd look good as a brunette, I loved it.

When I got bored with that, I flipped on the television. Sounds of a girl moaning blared from the television well before the black screen turned to a live color shot of a couple having sex. I tried to change the channel, but the button on the remote crushed inward and no longer worked. Frantically, I hit more buttons, including the one that turned the volume up. The man had a ginormous penis and pounded it into the poor girl while he slapped her rear end, making her scream like a…well, a porn star.

Jake looked at me with a raised eyebrow.

I smiled and shrugged my shoulders, but my face had to be as red as the girl's ass. I banged the remote on the table, smashing my finger in the process. Jake shook his head with irritation, crossed the room, and hit the power button on the television. *Why didn't I think of that?*

"We need to get on the road," Jake said, packing up his computer.

Outside, a man stood near the room next to ours, smoking a cigarette. He made a lewd gesture with his tongue, then winked at me. I got into the Explorer and locked my door.

"Did you see that?"

Jake nodded. "Want me to shoot him?"

"No, but you could show him your gun."

"Those walls are paper-thin. I'm sure that's what he thought I was doing to *you*. Why do you think he needed a cigarette?"

I gave him a dirty look, but it was dark enough in the Explorer that Jake missed it. Good thing, since it meant he couldn't see me blushing again.

"How did those men get inside the safe house?" I asked as we pulled out of the motel parking lot.

"Since the alarm didn't go off, I assume they had the code."

"How?"

"Someone must've given it to them, along with your location. Makes sense, otherwise, they wouldn't have known where to find you."

"Who, the agents who escorted us from the plane?"

"I'm not sure. I checked out their explosion story. They told the truth as far as I can tell."

I twisted in my seat, trying to get comfortable, though my sore, achy back wouldn't allow it. I made a small grunting sound as I shifted.

"Problem?" Jake asked.

"I can't get comfortable. When I fell in the kitchen earlier, I hit my back on the counter and twisted my ankle. I feel like someone threw me down three flights of stairs."

"So much for witness *protection*," Jake said with a laugh. "You keep getting hurt. You even smashed your finger in the motel room. Any other injuries I need to know about?"

I didn't tell him I almost shit my pants when he pointed the gun at me in the kitchen. That would've hurt, but only my pride. "I think that covers most of them."

"Maybe I should ransom you off to Frankie Felts. You might stand a better chance of escaping injury with him than you have so far with me."

He was kidding, but his words made my heart stop and my stomach churn with queasiness. The psychological implication of being abandoned weighed on me, making me wonder what would happen if Felts found me. Then I made the mistake of wondering how I'd die. Maybe I should've listened to Jake when he said I didn't want to know how the other witnesses had died. I had pressed him to tell me, but now I regretted it.

My mind tapped into the residual memories of the past twenty-four hours, and the sharp crack of reality split me in two as vivid pictures flashed through my head. Sergio's death replayed automatically, the images standing tall and casting a shadow over the more pleasant thoughts I conjured. Like him, I'd be dead. No gray area, just the black and white of it all. I'd been marked. Frankie Felts would do everything in his power to make sure I didn't live much longer.

Then I made the mistake of imagining my cold, lifeless body lying in a cornfield. The image overwhelmed me, making me numb, as my eye twitched uncontrollably. I couldn't take it anymore. My pulse raced, and my breathing deepened until my lungs stopped functioning properly. I hyperventilated in rapid succession until everything around me distorted.

I don't remember Jake pulling the car over, but he must've. I stood on the side of the road, doubled over, as my chest convulsed with spasms. I wanted to scream, but I couldn't in between all of the sobs bubbling in my throat. Wracked with fear, I became practically inconsolable.

"Don't panic," Jake whispered, trying to soothe me as he rubbed his hand on my back. "Take deep breaths."

It felt dreamlike, as if all of this had happened to someone else. I'd watched Oprah enough times to know the ugly cry wasn't attractive on anybody. Yet, I was on the side of the road doing just that.

Jake stood close with his arm around my shoulders, wrapping me in comfort and security, as well as compensating for my unbalanced posture. I was a crumbling mess under his hands. He tried to smooth over my rough edges, a further distance than the wheels of responsibility should've taken him. It was bad enough he saddled himself with the impossible, foolhardy task of keeping me alive—something he'd barely been able to do.

"I…I'm fine," I choked out, not wanting him to see me this way. "Leave me alone."

Jake grimaced. "Bullshit. Emily, I can plainly see you're not fine. Tell me what I can do."

He may be responsible for my physical well-being, but my mental state wasn't something he should have to deal with. It angered me that he looked at me with his eyes full of pity. "For one thing, stop calling me Emily."

"It's your name."

"No, it's not!" I shrieked. "My name is—"

"Not anymore, it isn't. Your name is Emily, even if I have to beat it into your head before I'm through with you. Now get in the car."

Never one for following orders, I resented Jake for issuing one. Annoyed by his demand and in the middle of a nervous breakdown, I underwent a mental time-out and said the first stupid thing that came to mind. "I hope the FBI has an extra-large dildo because all of you can go fuck yourselves."

I angled past him, walking away from the car, but Jake snatched me up before I could get far. "Don't be stupid. Are you trying to get yourself killed?"

I didn't answer him. In fact, I was careful not to look at his face until he stuffed me in the passenger seat of the Explorer. He stood there glaring, still waiting for an answer.

"Who cares, Jake? I'm dead, no matter what."

His hard expression softened around the edges. "So that's what this is about? You think you're going to die?"

"Looks that way, doesn't it?"

"Emily, I know your world just became more stressful with having to be relocated for a second time, but I'm not going to let anything happen to you. You have my word."

"I don't want to die." I straightened my face and tried to get ahold of my emotions, but a few stray tears rolled down my cheek. "I didn't even get my birthday sex."

Jake looked at me strangely, swiped the drops away with his thumbs, and then snagged a strand of my hair, pushing it behind my ear. His hands rested on both sides of my neck as he leaned toward me. "I don't know what the hell that means, but I can assure you that you'll have plenty more birthdays ahead of you. Trust me, okay?"

I nodded quietly.

Jake flashed a grin. "I love the sound you make when you're silent."

He was only trying to make me feel better, but I couldn't force myself to smile back. A flicker of light in his dark eyes called to me. How he had responded to my emotional needs stimulated me, and I desperately needed more. I inhaled his scent—a mix of soap and something unmistakably male— with every breath as I leaned slowly toward him. But before my lips touched his, he shifted away.

"Emily, it can't happen again." Jake wore a self-deprecating look. "It shouldn't have happened the first time. It was an unguarded moment, one where I should've considered the consequences first. I could've gotten you killed."

"But you didn't."

"Not this time, but I need to keep a clear head. And having sex with you is the exact opposite of that. We can't become intimately involved."

"You've already seen my vagina," I reminded him, sarcastically. "You can't get much more intimate than that."

His gray eyes liquefied to molten steel. "Wanna bet?"

My inner muscles contracted enthusiastically, and a hot wave of lust ran up to my breasts. I bit my lip to keep from asking him to do a show-rather-than-tell format of his theory. "I don't understand."

"You know what I mean."

"Not *that*. I mean, I don't understand why we can't—"

"Because there are rules about these things. I'd lose my job."

"But as long as it's off the record, then…"

"No."

"Jake, I'm a big girl, and we're both consenting adults. It's not like you're corrupting my soul or something." God, I sounded desperate.

"No, but fraternizing with a material witness could get the entire case thrown out of court. My choices are a reflection on the bureau, as well as on me. I have to do this right. It's important."

"I get it. More important than some piece of ass you're stuck babysitting, right? I'm glad you've made that clear." Nope, I was wrong—way past desperate at this point.

"Damn it. Why do women always have to analyze or

overthink everything?" He shook his head at me. "I didn't say you were some piece of ass." He blew out a breath. "I'm attracted, okay. I'll admit it. Attracted enough that I can't deny it, but some things are better left unspoken. I'm not saying it won't happen...but later, after the trial. Until then, let's keep things platonic."

"I guess that's your 'let's be friends' speech? And I'm supposed to wait for you to lift this sexual embargo?"

"That's all you can do. I won't change my mind. I need to put Felts behind bars."

"Wow! You're a fucking marvel. The backbone of our *relationship*," —I used my fingers to signal air quotes— "is dependent on whether I live or die?"

"That's not what I meant."

"It's ridiculous. You're prolonging this because you're afraid of being *that* guy."

"Which guy?"

"You know, the one who falls for the witness who gets killed."

"Damn it, Emily. I'm responsible for your safety."

"Then wear a condom!"

"Jesus," he said, breathing out hard. "I was right before. You definitely have multiple personalities."

My eyes narrowed. "Yeah, well maybe I do, and none of them like you!" I folded my arms across my chest and resisted the urge to gaze back at him.

Jake slammed the car door and stomped around the front of the vehicle, stopping long enough to bang his fist on the hood before getting in. His hand tightened into a death grip on the steering wheel, but he didn't try to strike up another conversation. I quietly stared out the passenger window as we got back on the road. I didn't have to look at him. I could feel him next to me. His anger vibrated the air and danced on my skin.

An hour later, we still hadn't spoken. Isolation fueled the depression I desperately tried to push away. The blahs tend to multiply when you are silent for long durations. I counted the bug splatters on the windshield to pass the time until we crossed into Oklahoma on I-35, and then, before I knew it, my eyelids drifted closed.

When I woke up, we were in a rest area parking lot. Jake leaned against a payphone outside my door with his back to me. Guess he didn't want to risk being tracked by using his cell phone. So much for his supposedly *secure* line.

He had left the car running and the air conditioning on high, which explained my icy-cold skin, goose bumps, and hard nipples. I turned the air conditioner down a few notches to keep from getting hypothermia and cracked open the window. That's when I heard Jake talking.

"It's a solo mission, but she doesn't have a bullet hole in her head. At least not yet."

What did he mean *yet*?

"We aren't exactly on speaking terms at the moment," Jake commented. "She trusts me, though. I'm good at this. Her decision to cooperate sealed her fate. Now it's up to me to make sure things go as planned." He paused for a second, listening to the person on the other end. "No, nobody knows her whereabouts or where she's going, including her."

Who the hell was he talking to?

"Yeah, I'm bringing her in. In fact, it won't take us much longer to get there. Probably another couple of hours. Get your guns ready," Jake said. "She's a live one. We may have to draw straws to see who gets to shoot her first." Then he chuckled.

The deep timbre of his laughter jolted through me like a high-voltage shock wave. Jesus Christ. I thought I was safe with an FBI agent and, all along, he planned to kill me. I thought Jake kidded when he said he should turn me over to Frankie Felts, but I was wrong. He was going to let me die. That shrewd, double-crossing bastard! I knew he was a weasel. No wonder he didn't want to have sex with me. I was practically dead already.

And he knew it the whole time.

Chapter Five

My brain felt clogged.

I had to get away from Jake, but I didn't know how. He manhandled me every time I didn't do something he asked, which, now that I thought about it, should've been a red flag. FBI agents went through psychological testing, right? If so, I don't know how Jake passed. He had anger issues.

Jake hung up the phone and slid into the driver's seat. "I'm glad you're awake. Do you need to use the restroom while we're here? We have a few hours to go before we get there."

This was my last chance to escape. "Yes, I need to go," I told him, trying to keep my voice even.

"Come on," he said, turning off the car and taking the keys out of the ignition. "I'll walk you over there."

Shit. I hoped he'd leave the keys behind. "No, that's okay. I can walk myself."

"You're not going alone. I can't protect you if I'm out

here."

"Protect me from whom…the elderly couple, the parents with their children, or the two teenagers skateboarding on the sidewalk? I don't think any of them are going to take me out."

"With you, you never know." He stepped out of the car and waited at the front for me to join him.

Pressing the issue would only make him suspicious. I couldn't risk him wondering what I was up to. If I managed to get away from Jake, it would be a small miracle. He had the keys and, chances were, he'd come after me in the car once he figured out I was gone. I wouldn't have much of a head start unless I could slow him down. Hmmm. Jake was too busy scoping out the area to see what I was doing inside the car.

As soon as I opened the car door, the heat slapped me in the face. It was like stepping into a hot oven, and sweat instantly formed on my lip. "Where are we…Hell?"

"Close. Texas."

The midday sun, bright and hot, seared into my skin. I shaded my eyes and surveyed my surroundings, mindfully planning my escape route. The busy four-lane highway wasn't a good option, but the mounds of dirt surrounding the rest area kept me from seeing what was on the other side and didn't look like easy climbing. "I thought Texas was supposed to be flat."

"We're in the hill country. Only things here that are flat are the armadillos in the road."

We walked inside the brick community building together and stopped outside the entrance to the ladies' room. "The men's room is on the opposite side," Jake said, grimacing.

"Men piss faster than women do. I'll be back before you come out."

"It'll take me a few extra minutes. I want to splash my face with some water while I'm in there."

"Two minutes. Don't make me come in there to get you."

His threat irritated me, but I smiled agreeably. "Okay, Jake."

I walked into the bathroom, but stood by the door listening to Jake's shoes clomp away. When I could no longer hear him, I peeked out to be sure he left. Since Jake was nowhere in sight, I scuttled out the door.

The moment I got outside, I sprinted for the highway. Traffic zoomed steadily by, and I had to wait for an opening to cross. I looked back and saw Jake come out of the building. He looked my direction, spotting me.

Gulp. It was now or never.

I had an overwhelming sense of imminent danger. I wasn't sure if it was the cars roaring past me at seventy miles per hour or the sinister face on the man running to catch up. I took my chances with the cars.

I shot across the highway and climbed over the concrete divider, but had to stop and wait for more vehicles to pass. Jake made it out to the highway quicker than I did, but still had to wait for his chance to pass. Once he had an opening coming, I couldn't wait any longer for the traffic on my side to clear.

I darted across too soon as Jake yelled out. A tan car headed straight for me. Standing frozen on the hot asphalt, I braced myself for impact. The car barely slowed, zigzagged around me, and sounded its horn relentlessly. I rushed to the shoulder of the road and observed Jake jumping the concrete divider.

Without wasting any more time, I ran away from the highway and into an open field. Long blades of grass went up to my knees, but didn't hinder my movement. Or Jake's.

He caught up quickly, tackled me to the ground, and straddled my waist. I immediately became combative, swinging my arms and trying to scratch out his eyeballs, but he captured and pinned my wrists above my head. His red face lit with fury, his eyes filled with hostility. "What the hell is wrong with you?"

I pulled my head up and tried to bite his arm.

Jake flicked me on the nose. Hard. "Damn you, Emily, if you don't stop trying to bite me, I'm going to cut off your head and send it to a lab for a rabies check."

Now, this is how hearing and listening are two very different things. I listened to what he said, but all I heard was he wanted to cut off my head.

"Help! He's going to kill me! Help me! Help—"

Jake muzzled me with his hand over my mouth, but he seemed confused. "Simmer down. What the hell's your problem?"

I started to cry, which shocked him into removing his hand from my mouth. "Please…don't kill me!" I begged.

"What?"

"I thought you wanted to help me," I sobbed. "You said…"

"Emily, I don't understand why you think I'd want to kill you. Well, besides the obvious reasons."

I sniffled. "You said you were going to shoot me."

"What? When?"

Jake relaxed his grip on my wrists and allowed me to pull

them free as he eased off me. We both dripped with sweat.

"On the phone."

"Oh hell, I was kidding around," he said with a laugh. "That's why you ran? Why didn't you just say something?"

"Oh, yeah right. I'm supposed to ask a murderer if he's going to kill me *before* I run. Give me a break. How was I supposed to know you were joking? And what the hell is funny about that, anyway?"

"I was talking to my uncle. We're staying at his house until I can figure out what's going on. Frankie Felts went underground after shooting Sergio. Someone on the inside must've leaked information to him about our location. I'm not taking any chances by putting you in another safe house. Apparently, they aren't very safe."

"So you aren't going to kill me?"

"No, but I might line you with bumper pads to keep you from killing yourself," he said, his voice as coarse as steel wool. He rubbed at his temples, then ran his hand through his unruly hair. "Come on. We need to get on the road."

"Uh…Jake?" I waited for him to turn around. "One problem. I still have to pee."

He half-smiled. "Yeah, me, too."

"I thought you went already."

He shook his head. "Never made it. I knew you were up to something."

"How?"

"When I said I was giving you two minutes, you were too agreeable. You didn't argue. And you *always* argue."

Jake led me across the highway and toward the building that housed the restrooms. He kept a firm hold on my upper arm as we passed a small crowd that had formed. Two teenagers stood there, skateboards in hand, eyeing Jake with uncertainty.

"Man, he caught her quick. That dickhead can run!" one teenage boy said as we passed them.

Jake's fingers tightened around my arm. All I could do was grin.

"How am I the dickhead?" he asked, tossing me a sideways glance. "You ran from a federal agent."

"Well, to start with, you tackled a woman. Or maybe it's *because* you're an agent. Take your pick."

When we stopped at the women's restroom, Jake glared at me. "All right, I want to hear you say it. No more surprises, right?"

"No more, I promise."

Jake was already outside the bathroom when I came out. Guess men do piss faster than women. Once we were in the vehicle, Jake turned the ignition and nearly jumped out of his skin. Music from the radio blared from the speakers, the windshield wipers screeched across the window at full speed, and the flashers blinked wildly.

He turned everything off and tossed a look my way as a vein on his temple bulged. "If you so much as crack a smile, I'm going to put you over my knee and spank you."

My brain told me to keep a straight face, but deep inside, I grinned my ass off.

• • •

"Would you stop?" Jake yelled, scowling at me.

"What?"

"You're tapping your fingers on the armrest."

"And…?"

"And you're driving me insane," Jake said. "First you were whistling, then humming, now tapping. Can't you sit still?"

"You aren't talking, and I'm bored."

"Well, at least if I bore you to death, you won't have to worry about Felts anymore. Find something else to occupy your time."

"I'm hungry," I told Jake. "Can we stop and get something to eat?"

"We'll eat when we get there. It's an hour away."

"Look, superhero, maybe you can do without food for an extended period of time, but I can't. I haven't eaten since yesterday. I could use some caffeine in my system."

"As fidgety as you are? You've got to be kidding."

"Can I drive, then?"

"No."

"Jeez, you have control issues."

"So do you." Jake glanced over at me. "You don't have *any*."

I narrowed my eyes. "I want to eat."

His eyes never left the road as my demand went unanswered.

"I don't appreciate being ignored, Jake."

"Yeah, right. Like anyone could ignore *you*."

"If I had something to eat, I'd be quiet."

He paused a moment, scrubbed at his face. "Fine. We can stop at a place in the next county. But you better be quiet afterward or I'm going to duct tape your mouth and handcuff you to the luggage rack."

I smiled. Jake could be a decent guy when he wasn't

being such an asswipe.

He whipped into the parking lot of Junior's Diner, which sat next to a Dairy Queen. I practically jumped out of the Explorer, excited by the notion of food. The diner resembled a big red barn, decorated on the inside with a western theme. Spurs and saddle blankets decorated the walls, along with some black and white pictures of John Wayne.

The waitress rushed past us carrying a pot of hot coffee and a tray of food. "Hi, y'all. Have a seat, and I'll be with you in a jiffy."

Jake chose a small booth in the corner away from the dozen other customers in the restaurant. The waitress came back with two menus in her hand.

"We don't need those," Jake told her. "Two cheeseburgers, two fries, and two large sweet teas, extra lemon."

The waitress hurried off to turn in our order before I had a chance to stop her.

"What the hell was that?"

"What?"

"Maybe I didn't want a cheeseburger," I said, raising my voice slightly.

"It's easy, and we're in a hurry. I don't want you parading around in public any more than you have to. You draw attention."

"No I don't!"

"Shhh!" Jake whispered. "See what I mean? You don't know how to blend in. You're a magnet."

"That's not true. Every time we have attention turned on us, it's because of something you've done, not me. I swear you do things to purposefully force me into having a reaction."

"Face it, honey. You're a drama queen."

The waitress came back with our iced teas and a small bowl of lemon wedges. I immediately picked up a slice, dumped salt all over it, and took a bite. Bitter juice splattered into my mouth as I sucked the lemon wedge clean. Instantly, my jaw clenched and my face puckered.

Jake watched me go for another before turning his attention back to the waitress. "Is Junior here? I need to talk to him."

"He's in the office going over numbers," she said. "I'll send him out."

Jake nodded a silent thank you to her and glanced back at me as she hurried away. "You have a lemon fetish or something?" he asked.

"Depends. How much do you have to like something before it's considered a fetish?"

A slight smile curved his mouth. "Are you going to let me have any lemon for my tea?"

"Probably not."

"Then it's a fetish." Jake peered over my left shoulder at something behind me. "How's it going, Junior?"

I turned to look and did a double take. In my mind's eye, I'd pictured Junior as a pipsqueak accountant, wearing dress pants and a tie. What I saw was completely different.

Junior was a tall, burly Native American with a thick braid of dark hair he swung over his shoulder. He wore western garb from head to toe, including a black Stetson hat, and a large buck knife hung from his side in a leather sheath. He had a bottom lip full of chewing tobacco and smelled sweetly of wintergreen.

The scent triggered a childhood memory of my father. He used to keep a candy dish of his favorite mints on the nightstand next to his bed. Whenever I'd have a bad dream, Dad would give me one, calling it a magic bean, saying it helped chase away fears. It always worked before. Knowing what a nightmare the last two days had been, I couldn't help but smile at Junior. His scent relaxed and comforted me as if my dad had handed me a mint.

"Heard you were coming home for a visit, Jake. About time."

"It's been a while," Jake said, shaking hands with Junior. He motioned to me as I took a sip of my tea. "Junior, this is my girlfriend, Emily Foster."

I choked. *Girlfriend?* When the hell did that happen?

Even in elementary school, the boys knew they had to ask if they wanted a girl to "go" with them. Of course, none of us ever knew where we were supposed to go. But at least they asked. Funny thing was, I didn't know where Jake and I'd go, either. Guess it goes to show that all I ever needed to know about boys I learned in elementary. They're stupid.

For a moment, Junior's eyes pierced mine. They were hard, golden brown, like a hawk's. Then he tipped his hat. "It's a pleasure, Miss Foster."

I let out a little cough to stifle the choking fit I kept at bay. "Please, call me…um, Emily." *God, I have to get used to this name.*

He nodded and turned back to Jake. "You want to try some of the new items on my menu? Fried alligator and rattlesnake jerky."

Jake looked at me with a sadistic grin, and I narrowed my eyes. "Nah, we'll pass," Jake said, chuckling. "Some other time."

A sign pointed to the restrooms. "Excuse me, gentlemen.

I'm going to go the ladies' room." I needed to throw up.

Jake rose, as if he were going to follow.

"No need to get up. I can plainly see where the bathrooms are, *sweetie*." I made sure to add some syrup to my voice.

He set his jaw and gave me a one word warning. "Emily…"

"I'll be right back. I promise."

The quick glance he gave his watch told me he'd be timing me. I could feel his eyes burning into my back as I strolled away. Man, no trust at all in this fake relationship.

The bathrooms were down a short hallway on the opposite side of the restaurant. I kept an even pace, afraid if I hurried, Jake might think I was making a run for it and tackle me again. And I was tired of ending up on the floor.

The tidy bathroom smelled pleasantly sanitary. I got straight to business, then washed and dried my hands thoroughly. Though I had been in the bathroom only three or four minutes, I imagined Jake having a small panic attack as he waited for me to come back. The thought made me smile. I turned to leave, but instead let out a blood-curdling scream.

Seconds later, I heard Jake on the other side of the door. "Emily? Are you in there?" He tried the door, but the door locked from the inside.

"Oh, my God! Jake, help! Please!"

"Emily, open the door!"

"I can't!"

"Damn it, Emily!" Jake pounded on the door. "What in the hell is going on in there? Open the door!"

I grabbed a weapon, but there wasn't much to choose from in a bathroom. "He won't let me!" I cried.

"Shit. Emily, I'm coming in."

I heard a loud bang as he kicked the door in, splintering the wood. Jake and Junior stood in the doorway as it swung on its hinges. Jake rushed in, pointed his gun around the small bathroom, and saw me holed up in the corner by the sink, holding a toilet brush.

"Where is he?"

"Behind the door!"

Jake looked at me strangely but checked, anyway. He holstered his weapon, stomped his foot, and stormed out. Junior stepped in and peeked curiously behind the door.

He turned back, his face serious. "You're damn lucky he didn't kill you."

"The big ass spider?"

"No. Jake. Of course, he still might once I tell him he owes me a new door."

• • •

There were no clocks on the wall in the restaurant. It didn't matter, though, because Texans seem to keep their own time. Guess it goes well with their lazy drawls. Jake hadn't said two words since he'd walked out of the bathroom. We finished our meal in silence and left as quickly as possible.

The late afternoon sun had faded fast, and a dark, glittery curtain blanketed the sky. I watched out my window as a black wall of trees whizzed past.

"Still mad?"

He gave me a frosty look. "No."

"You sure?"

"Not entirely."

I sighed lightly. "I didn't mean to—"

"You never mean to. That's the problem. We need to establish some basic rules. You know, like never cry wolf."

"Why are you so insistent about following rules all the time?"

Jake shrugged. "They keep people from doing stupid shit."

I wasn't sure, but I thought he was referring to me. "You mean like not warning someone before pretending she's your girlfriend?"

His mouth twitched with a tiny smirk.

"Want to explain?" I asked.

Jake glanced at me. "Don't freak out, okay? You and I are posing as a couple."

"What?" I shrieked. "That'll never work. Nobody's going to buy that when all we do is fight."

"Most couples argue."

"Not like us."

"We'll say we're passionate about each other. My uncle and aunt know the truth about you, but I don't want anybody else to know. We're staying in their guesthouse in the middle of the forest. It sounds better to say we're a couple while visiting."

"A guesthouse in the forest? Sounds fancy."

"It's got a pool." He smiled as if I missed a private joke.

"Who all knows where we'll be? FBI and U.S. Marshals?"

"No one. Last night, in the motel, I called Brockway while you washed up. I didn't tell him where we were heading. He wasn't happy about that, or that I disposed of the tracking device."

"Why?"

"The Bureau doesn't look kindly on disobedience. Or

their agents stealing key witnesses."

"You didn't *steal* me. I didn't have a choice but to go with you." I smiled when he glanced over at me. "Okay, maybe it sounds like the same thing. But you protected me, which I thought was the whole point of witness protection."

"My methods are unconventional. The FBI and the U.S. Marshals are not being supportive. Instead of winging it, they'd rather I had gone through the proper channels."

"Yeah, but that almost got us killed."

"True, but…never mind."

"Tell me." I waited, but he didn't say anything. "Come on, Jake. You can't start to say something and back down."

"Brockway thinks my motives are strictly personal."

That got my attention. "So is he right? Is this personal?" My heart surged at the thought.

"You can bet your ass it's personal. Frankie Felts will pay for everything he's done if I have to kill him myself. One day soon this will all be over."

Not that I wanted him to kill anyone, but Jake's words made me feel secure. He was serious about making Felts pay. "I hope so."

"Emily, I know it's hard to be isolated and cut loose from your own life. You feel caged in, but you don't feel safe." Jake glanced over at me. "Even after this ends, you'll always be looking over your shoulder."

"How do you know?"

"Because when I was younger," he said, looking back at the road, "I was in your shoes."

Chapter Six

Jake turned off the highway just past a sign marked LIBERTY COUNTY, TEXAS and veered onto a county road. "It's not much farther to my uncle's."

I gave him an incredulous look. "What'd you say?"

"I said it's not much farther —"

"No, not that. The other thing you said."

Jake kept his eyes on the road. "What?"

"The part where you said you'd been in my shoes before."

"It's not important. I wanted you to know that I understand what you're going through. I've been there. I know it's not easy."

"What happened? Why were you —"

"It doesn't matter. I don't want to talk about it."

"Jake, you can't say something like that and not tell me the rest of the story."

"Just forget it."

Quietly, I wondered what possibly could've happened to him that he would've needed witness protection when he was younger. The mystery was enough to drive my imagination wild. I let it go for the time being, but Jake had to know I wouldn't give up until I found out more. You can't dangle a carrot in front of this bunny's nose unless you want me to run away with it.

But I let it drop. Temporarily.

I thought the county road would go on forever, but finally we came to an intersection in the shape of a T. The sign across the road read TRINITY RIVER FLOOD ZONE. I looked over at Jake, but he was too busy turning left to notice.

"Flood zone?"

"Yeah, don't worry. My uncle said the river's down right now."

"Where's this forest you keep talking about? All I'm seeing is fields and pastures."

"Just ahead, a few roads over, where the tree line starts."

"Are you sure you know where you're going?"

"Of course, I do. It's easy. All I have to do is go left. It's eight lefts to my uncle's house."

"If you go left eight times, we'd be going in circles."

Jake laughed. "That only applies if you're talking about a city block. This is the countryside. Trust me when I say you can take eight lefts and not end up crossing your own trail. Look at it like a spiral rather than a square, as if we're circling our way into the forest."

"I'll take your word for it."

Jake crossed over some railroad tracks and veered left. There were more fields than houses, no streetlights, and the road got narrower by the minute. About five miles down, a fork in the road came into view, but Jake stayed left. At another stop sign, he swung another left, then continued down the road.

"See? Four lefts and we haven't crossed ourselves yet."

"Doesn't mean we won't," I said doubtfully.

We slowed down as we crossed an old one-lane, barrel-style bridge, then picked up speed until we neared the next curve. As we rounded the sharp left curve, Jake slammed on his brakes as two white-tailed deer darted across the road before us. I clutched my chest and drew in a deep breath.

"Scared?"

"I thought they weren't going to get across before you creamed one. Why don't you drive slower, Mario Andretti? This isn't a race, and I'm in no hurry to die."

"Everyone drives like this back here," he replied. "You'll get used to it."

"Please slow down. The trees are right at the edge of the road. I have enough people trying to kill me without the car reaching out to hug one."

Begrudgingly, he did as I asked. A few more miles up the road, he curved to the right sharply, then took another left.

"You went right back there," I said with a smug grin. "Guess it's not all lefts."

"Doesn't count."

"Why?"

"Because it's a curve. No other way to go."

"Yeah, but…"

"Doesn't count," Jake repeated.

"You always make up rules as you go along. Like you saying no family reunions, then heading to your uncle's house."

"Those were *your* rules, not mine."

After the next left turn, I spied an old pickup truck

sitting on the side of the road with its headlights shining on two men as they strolled out of the woods carrying a rope and a shovel. It was the first sign of life I'd seen in the last twenty minutes. The men reached the front of the truck and stood in the headlights as we passed. I craned my neck to get a better look.

One of them had no eye in his right socket, while the other stared straight at me and gave me a toothless snarl. They were filthy, as if they'd been rolling in dirt. It reminded me of something out of *Deliverance*.

"Jesus," I told Jake, swallowing a knot in my throat. "What the hell were they doing out there at night?"

"No telling. Probably hunting."

"With a rope and a shovel? I don't think so."

Jake grinned but didn't take his eyes off the road. "After this turn, I have to slow down.

"No! Keep going."

He chuckled. "Oh, *now* you want me to drive faster."

"Well, I sure as hell don't want you to slow down. Those creepy guys might be coming this way."

"Emily, I have to. Bonnie walks this road after sundown, and she's blacker than night. I wouldn't want to hit her. I don't know how many times we've all threatened to slap glow-in-the-dark stickers on her ass, but she won't stay off the roads."

"Jake, that's a terrible thing to say about someone."

He smirked at me. "Bonnie is Mr. Hensley's cow." Jake maneuvered the left turn, which landed us on a bumpy dirt road. "Look, I bet that's her up ahead. You can barely see her."

Sure enough, a shadowy blob moved in the darkness. As

we neared, the black cow stopped eating from the overgrown weeds at the side of the road, turned its head to look back at us, and switched its tail from side to side like a cat. I grinned as Jake maneuvered the Explorer around the living roadblock.

"Where does Mr. Hensley live?"

"House on the right with all the floodlights. He locks Bonnie up in a barn on the backside of his property, but he's never been able to keep her there."

Mr. Hensley's house was old, rickety, and neglected. Plagued with vines and rotting trim, it looked condemned— abandoned, at best. Large, orange-colored half-moons stained the sides of the house, and something resembling grass grew on the roof. I peered through the dark trying to see the barn, but the building I saw was too small for something as large as Bonnie.

"You're kidding me, right? Tell me that wasn't an out-house."

"Okay, it wasn't an outhouse."

I recognized his monotone for what it was. "Oh, Jesus! Where the hell have you taken me?"

"Calm down. Mr. Hensley's an elderly man who prefers to live by simple means. Where we're staying is more like the Hilton than Mr. Hensley's."

I breathed a sigh of relief. "Sorry, I thought…well, I'm not sure what I thought."

"Almost there. Another mile up the road," Jake told me.

I glanced over at his moonlit face and slanted an eyebrow. "Let me guess, it's on the left?"

He answered me with his silence and a wide grin.

When we turned into a long driveway, I snapped back to reality and had my first inclination that something wasn't right. A large wooden sign with faded black letters, which said MILLER'S BIRD FARM, leaned against the barbed wire fence at the end of the driveway.

Jake drove slowly up the drive, passing a workshop on the right, a vegetable garden on the left. He pulled up onto a large concrete pad next to an old blue pickup.

Two houses faced the concrete pad. A large white one before us—the main house, I assumed—sat high enough off the ground that you could drive a truck underneath it. The siding was unfinished, and the porch rails were likely to collapse any moment from the bowed and battered wood. Unlit Christmas lights hung from the eaves, though it was late March.

The much smaller guest house—something similar to a cottage—sat two steps off the ground, but wasn't in any better condition. Someone had scraped the old paint, but never got around to repainting the siding. Or maybe they preferred the weathered look. I wasn't sure, but regardless... *this* was the Hilton?

In that moment, all I knew was that Jake had brought me here under false pretenses, and I was pissed. Okay, it wasn't really false pretenses. After all, Jake did say it was a perfect place to hide me out. Nobody in their right mind would look for me here. Of course, that's only because I'd have to be out of mine to stay here.

He turned off the car and looked over at me. I gave him a menacing glare, hoping it filled him with as much dread as I'd felt when I realized where we'd be staying.

"Okay, Emily, I understand you're upset, but I think—"

"Upset? That doesn't begin to cover it, you...you... kidnapping asshole! You made it sound like we were going to be staying somewhere decent. Hell, I'd have settled for something livable. If you think I'm staying in that cardboard box, you can go get fucked."

A muscle twitched in the side of his jaw. Tension built in his shoulders as he gripped the steering wheel with tightly clasped hands. He tried to control his temper, but failed miserably.

"Kidnapping? I can't believe you're going to start that crap again. You're a royal pain in my ass. I've never met a woman this frustrating in my entire life. You're a rude, unappreciative spoiled brat!"

"Why? Because I don't want to spend my nights in low-income housing?" I asked with a sarcastic tone. "What's next? Are we going to share a sleeping bag in a tent out in the woods?"

"Either you can stay here or take your chances with Frankie Felts," Jake said matter-of-factly. "I'm offering you an alternative to death, but it's up to you. If you want to leave, I'm not stopping you."

A porch light flipped on upstairs and grabbed our attention. An older couple stepped out the front door and headed down the stairs.

"When you're done with your tantrum, you can decide what you want to do," Jake added. "All I ask is that you don't be rude to my aunt and uncle. They're good people."

I served him a sweet smile. "I'm sure I'll like them fine. It's *you* I don't like."

"Good. I don't like you, either," Jake said angrily, opening his door to get out.

He knew I wouldn't leave. Where else did I have to go? Nope, I was stuck with him, even after he called me all those names. The thing that bothered me most was that he meant them. Maybe I had reacted poorly to him misleading me, but he didn't have to be so harsh. I let the hurt feelings percolate through my system, then pushed them away. Mental note: send the FBI hate mail for saddling me with Jake.

I ran my fingers through my flat, lifeless brown hair hoping to tease it into better condition, but it was no use. After traveling cross-country, it wasn't going to look any better until I washed it. In fact, I wasn't going to feel better at all until I took a long, hot shower. Of course, that's assuming these people actually had hot water. My legs cramped, my back hurt, and my stiff muscles needed to stretch. Exhausted, I opened my door and stepped out slowly wearing cement shoes.

Jake shook his uncle's hand firmly, gave him a pat on the back, and then gave his aunt a big hug, lifting her completely off the ground. They were happy to see each other, which sent a small twinge of jealousy through me. I hated to break up their reunion, but introductions were necessary.

"This is Emily Foster," Jake said. "Emily, my Uncle Hank and Aunt Floss."

His uncle stepped forward to shake my hand with a slight hobble in his gait. Hank was probably somewhere in his late sixties with a head full of wavy silver hair and a neatly trimmed beard to match. He was tall, but round in the middle under his denim overalls. My first thought was he'd make a handsome Santa Claus. My second thought was he'd make an even better Kenny Rogers.

"You got a lot of baggage?" Hank asked with a drawl.

I shrugged and smiled lightly. "Does emotional count?"

He chuckled under his breath. "Well, I'd say it does, but

that's not something I can carry for you, young lady. I'm sure it's heavy, but you make sure you unpack that bag first," Hank said, giving me a wink. I couldn't help but love the man immediately.

Jake's aunt wore a cotton dress like a potato sack over her petite, slender body, with gray hair wound firmly into a bun on the back of her head. She grabbed me and gave me a kiss on each cheek. "Nice to meet you, dear. Are you hungry? I could whip up something. You look like you could stand to gain a few pounds." *Bless this woman!*

"Thanks, but no, we stopped and ate."

"Well, if you decide you want something, I stocked the guest house with a few snacks. Be sure to help yourself," she said.

I nodded and smiled a thank you to her. *Great. Now I feel like such a douche after the way I acted toward Jake in the car.* They both were kind, and I couldn't imagine it being that bad staying here, if only for a short while.

"I'm sure they're both worn out," Hank told his wife. "A shower would probably do wonders. I bet it's been a long day."

"You have no idea," Jake said, tossing me an ugly look. Guess he was still mad. "We'll get our showers and visit with you and Floss for a bit before turning in."

Hank nodded. "Let me help with the bags."

"It's just one bag. We left in a hurry," Jake explained. "Instead, why don't you get a fire going? You got beer, right?"

"Does a bear shit in the woods?" Hank grinned at Jake as he and Floss walked toward the house.

Jake grabbed our suitcase from the back and motioned

for me to follow him to the guesthouse twenty feet away. The thought of getting an actual shower put some pep into my step. As we got closer, something white lying on the small, darkened porch caught my attention.

"What's that?"

"Dog. Don't worry, he won't bother you." Jake stepped over him, but the animal never moved, never even lifted his head.

I stared at the dog closer. He had white fur, a few dark spots peppered over his floppy ears, and closed eyes. He didn't seem to be breathing. "Is he dead?"

Jake shook his head. "Nah. He's a lazy, old hound. You'll have to step over, or you're going to be there all night."

"What's his name?"

"Dog."

"I know what he is…I asked you what his name—"

"That's his name. Dog."

I gave Jake a strange look, then stepped over Dog. "Your aunt and uncle aren't very original."

Jake ignored me, opened the door, and flipped on a light switch. He held the door while I ducked under his arm and into the small cottage. "Home sweet home," he said. "I take it you decided to stay?"

I couldn't speak or move. I had expected less-than-perfect conditions, but the cottage was primitive at best. It obviously hadn't been used in some time and needed a facelift. The linoleum had cracks, the flowery wallpaper had peeled, and a yellow love seat with large brown flowers sat in the small living room. The room was clean—depending on your definition of clean—but I did spy a cobweb hanging in the corner of the living room. It was enough to give me the heebie-jeebies.

Jake steered me toward the bedroom where a double bed, covered by a quilt and decorated with green floral throw pillows, filled up most of the room. It would be like sleeping in a closet.

"So what are the sleeping arrangements?" I asked.

"You're looking at it," Jake said casually. "This is where we'll sleep."

"*We?* You're not French, and I doubt you have a mouse in your pocket."

"Nope, none in my pocket. But I'm sure you can find one hiding under the bed or in the closet if you look hard enough."

Jeez. Like the spider wasn't bad enough? I had to worry about mice, too. "Yah, we're sharing a toddler bed," I said sarcastically.

"Hank and Floss know we aren't a couple, but other people would wonder why I'm sleeping apart from my girlfriend. We're not teenagers. If I'm not nearby, I can't keep an eye out. We need to stay low-key, and I need to closely monitor the situation…or namely, you."

"What other people? We're out in the middle of nowhere."

"The neighbors stop by from time to time. I don't want anyone questioning our relationship. No one would believe I brought a woman home with me for a visit unless we're sleeping together."

I let out a sharp breath. "Fine, but we need to establish some bedtime rules. Otherwise, it could create more tension."

"Yeah, there's not enough of *that* between us," Jake said.

Okay, I didn't mind sharing a bed with Jake. In fact, my skin heated and my heart raced at the thought. But after he called me a spoiled brat, I wouldn't dare let him know I liked the idea of sleeping in the same bed as him.

"If you want, you can go first," he offered, pointing to the bathroom door. "Don't lock the door."

I grabbed some clothes and dashed into the bathroom. The water smelled funny, like rust or iron, but I stood under the blast of hot liquid, letting it pour over me as my sore, achy muscles loosened. I dried off with a ratty towel, dressed, and then tried to brush my teeth. I used the word tried loosely. I couldn't do it.

"Jake, I'm having a small crisis. I can't brush my teeth using this smelly water. It's…gross."

"You'll get used to it," he replied, brushing me off.

"I'm serious. Help me, or I'm not brushing my teeth the rest of the time we're here. And don't try to tell me it's not your problem, because if I accidentally turn over in the middle of the night and breathe on you, it will become your problem."

He rolled his eyes and walked out. A moment later, he returned with a bottle of drinking water. "Here, use this to brush your teeth with."

"Thanks. You're a lifesaver."

"So I've heard." Jake pulled off his T-shirt and unbuttoned his jeans.

"If you'll give me a minute, I'm nearly done."

"You've seen it before," he said, dropping his jeans.

I tried not to look—tried being the key word—while he dropped his underwear and stepped into the tub. Not much privacy in a one-bedroom cottage, but him showing his body to me freely, without sharing, was going to be a problem. It made me wonder how firm he stood on his no sex policy…

among other things.

My body drooped tiredly into the mattress. No television to occupy my time. I sat there waiting for him. Okay, so I hoped to get another peek. Sue me.

When Jake came out a few minutes later, he was shirtless and his jeans rested low on his hips. Water droplets spotted his back, and his muscles gleamed from the slick dampness of smooth skin. After putting on his shirt and shoes, we headed out the door.

"He's got to be dead," I told Jake, looking back at the lifeless white figure still lying on the porch. "I forgot he was there and accidentally stepped on his tail, but he still didn't move."

"Must not have hurt," Jake said.

I followed Jake across the driveway and up a trail of stepping stones in the dark, not knowing where we were going until I spotted Hank sitting in a plastic lawn chair next to a glowing fire. A two-foot tall stone border trimmed the outside of the burn pit, keeping the fire and ashes contained. Jake pulled up two more chairs for us as his uncle kicked a red ice chest over to us.

Jake cut his eyes over to me. "Emily, you want a beer?"

"Does a bear shit in the woods?" I said, watching Hank smirk. Jake twisted the top off my bottle and handed it to me. "Where's your wife, Mr. Miller?"

"Floss is upstairs grabbing some insect repellent. And, young lady, unless you want me to turn you over my knee, you'll call me Hank. You hear?"

I studied Hank's face, watching for signs of humor, but there weren't any, just a straight-lined mouth and serious eyes glaring back at me. Once I decided it wasn't an empty threat, I nodded solemnly, which made Jake take a turn smirking. What was up with the men in his family wanting to spank me?

"What's burning?" I asked. "It doesn't look like wood."

"It's not," Hank said. "It's a bag of garbage from inside the house. We don't get trash pick-up way out here. We separate our trash into three containers: burnable, unburnable, and glass. We recycle the glass, but once a month we haul the unburnable to a landfill."

"Oh," was all I could say. I tried not to make a face, but no wonder the smoke smelled weird. Who knows what all was in there? It was a trash can fire, and had it been contained in a barrel, we would've resembled a bunch of hobos.

A crackling noise directly behind me caught my attention. An electrical bug zapper with a blue, eerie glow hung from a small pole. It made a faint buzzing sound. Another bug flew into it, making it crackle, sizzle, and spit bug parts back out in all directions.

I ran my hand through the back of my hair, hoping I wouldn't feel anything resembling bug guts. Then I moved my chair.

Jake tried to stop me. "Emily, you might want to stay between the fire and the bug zapper if you want to keep the mosquitoes from eating you alive."

"I'm moving over here a little," I said, although my "little" was about ten feet away.

Once I was away from the fire, I could feel the slight breeze. How Jake could wear jeans and sit close to the heat was beyond me. He had to be hot. Hell, I was, and all I had on was a pair of shorts and a tank top.

Hank and Jake talked between themselves as I deposited myself back into my chair. I tuned them out and closed my eyes, listening to the sounds around me. Locusts buzzed, crickets chirped, and frogs croaked, lulling me into a trance. The most peaceful moment I'd had in the last few days.

A sudden stinging sensation nipped at my ankle. Not bothering to look, I reached down and slapped it away. Something bit my arm and I swatted at that, too. Then another and another. I jumped up, quickly checking my itchy legs, and realized mosquitoes swarmed me, launching a full-blown attack. For every one I killed, five more would take a bite out of me.

All the stomping, kicking, and slapping I did must've loosely resembled the German folk dance performed at Oktoberfest, because Jake busted into hysterics. Hank wasn't far behind him, but I wasn't amused. My legs would've been better protected if I had worn lederhosen.

Floss showed up and sprayed my arms and legs with a cool mist of insect repellent. "There you go, honey. It should help, but sit closer to the fire to keep the little buggers off you." She then sprayed Hank and Jake as well.

I moved my chair back to Jake's side and sat, crossing my arms. He had stopped laughing, but I wished he'd wipe the stupid grin off his face. We reeked of insect repellent, had bug guts thrown at us, and our skin and clothes were soaking up trash smoke. I leaned over and whispered, "What did we take showers for?"

He tipped his beer at me. "Welcome to country living."

• • •

An hour later, I cowardly clung to Jake's side as we made our way back to the cottage.

"For Pete's sake, Emily, they aren't going to hurt you."

"If you didn't want me to hang onto you, then you

should've let me keep thinking they were birds."

"Newsflash: birds don't fly around at night, unless they're owls. When was the last time you saw a robin or a sparrow after dark? Bats swoop over the lights and eat the insects."

We stepped over Dog and made our way inside the cottage. I headed straight for the shower. I tousled my wet hair with a towel as I came out.

Jake sat on the edge of the bed. "Feel better?" he asked.

"Yep."

He pointed to the spot next to him on the bed. "Sit."

"You could ask me politely. Do you expect me to obey your every command?"

"Yes. Now sit."

"Tarzan usually beats his chest," I said, walking past him.

Jake caught me by the arm and pulled me down next to him. He grabbed my ankles, shifting my legs into his lap, which made me fall onto my back. "I don't know why you have to be difficult."

Something cold touched my leg. "What are you doing?"

"I'm putting some medicine on your mosquito bites. Otherwise, you'll be scratching them all night in your sleep."

I propped myself up on my elbows. "I can do it myself."

"It's easier and faster if I do it," Jake said, rubbing another spot with a cold salve-laden finger. "Lay back. I want to get between your thighs."

My whole body tensed, making Jake's fingers stop. I looked at him, and he looked at me. We waited for the awkward moment of double meaning to pass. No doubt we were both still harboring sexual feelings toward each other and thinking the same thing, but I sensed his hesitation. He wasn't going to give in to temptation. At least not tonight.

Jake's finger dabbed my skin again as I lay back and closed my eyes. His light touch was torturously teasing, causing shivers to run the length of my body.

"Cold?"

"No, ticklish." And, apparently, easily aroused.

When he finished with my legs, he worked on my arms. "Okay, I'm done," Jake said. "I'm going to take a quick shower before bed. You don't have to wait up."

As usual, Jake left the bathroom door open. I slipped into the bed and closed my eyes. I tried to slide down the ladder of unconsciousness and into the black hole of slumber, but I got caught in the rungs. The light didn't bother me. The sound of running water didn't bother me. No, what bothered me was the naked man in the bathroom who refused to have sex with me but would soon be crawling into the same bed.

Yep. That was it. Jake definitely bothered me.

· · ·

I woke up shivering.

The window unit must've been really something, since I'd stolen most of the quilt from Jake, but was still as cold as an ice sculpture. The room wasn't chilly when I went to bed, which meant he knocked the air conditioner down to… oh, I don't know, below freezing. Good thing I didn't have to pee or I would've had to acquire a mush team to go to the bathroom and back.

Jake slept diagonally and commandeered an unreasonable chunk of the bed, probably to keep his feet from hanging off the end. He must've moved his leg closer because his toes were suddenly touching mine. They were warm, and the small

ALISON BLISS 111

amount of heat felt heavenly against my icicled nubs.

Quietly, I scooted toward him, hoping to soak up some of his thermal energy, but it wasn't enough. The warmth his body generated wasn't permeating my skin the way I'd hoped. I wasn't close enough.

His back was to me, and I could hear him breathing evenly. I reached over with my cold hand and lightly touched his back. I half expected him to jump with surprise or at least flinch away from my cool fingers, but he didn't. Actually, I jerked back, surprised by the feverish heat of Jake's skin. It felt pleasant under my slight touch, and I ached for more of his delicious warmth. I scooted closer until my entire body pressed against his back.

"Emily, we talked about this," Jake said, stirring from his slumber.

"You're awake?"

He groaned sleepily. "Wasn't that the point?"

"What are you talking about?"

"I already told you we can't. It's against the rules."

"Can't?" I paused in confusion. "Oh, wait. You thought I was trying to have sex with you?" I couldn't help but giggle. "Boy, are you *way* off!"

Jake wasn't amused. "Then what were you doing?"

"I'm cold."

"And…?"

"I poached your body heat, nothing more sinister than that. Besides, you had your chance with me and turned me down flat, remember? I doubt you'll ever get another. I don't take rejection well."

"No! *You*?" Jake said with a sarcastic tone.

"Hey, I tried to keep from waking you. It's not my fault

if you got the wrong idea."

"You snuggled up to my back and squished your breasts against me."

"So?"

"Like you said, you were cold. In the future, you might want to consider wearing a bra to bed." Jake turned his head to the side, as if he were trying to look at me. "Turn over," he ordered.

"Why?"

"Just do it."

I rolled over onto my back, while Jake flipped over to face me. He grabbed my hip and shifted me onto my side until I faced away from him. Then he wrapped his arm around my waist and slid me back into him until we were in a spooning position. His heat swaddled me.

Jake settled in behind me, getting comfortable, and his hips ground across my bottom. That's when I noticed the elephant in the room. Actually, it wasn't an elephant, more like the elephant's trunk, but nevertheless, it was present and demanding attention.

For a moment, we both lay motionless.

"What's poking me?"

"An involuntary reflex," Jake said. "Roll over at your own risk."

"Is it going to be a chronic condition?"

"God, I hope so. I'm too young to have those kinds of medical issues."

"I have a cure."

"What?" he asked. "Sandwiching a pillow between us?"

"Amputation."

"Never mind," Jake said grimly. "Problem solved."

Chapter Seven

Jake roused me from sleep by pulling the covers off me. "Rise and shine, sleepyhead. This is your wake-up call."

"Don't you have a snooze button or something? What time is it?"

"After seven."

"In the morning?"

Jake laughed. "Get up. My aunt will have breakfast ready anytime now. They're early risers."

I yawned sleepily and reached for the covers. "I'll skip breakfast."

"No you won't," Jake said, snatching the quilt away again. "Look, I know you're stressed out right now, and your life's been turned completely upside down. You didn't ask for any of this, and you don't deserve it, but neither do I. All I ask is that you make both of our lives easier by cooperating."

"Fine. I'll cooperate, but that doesn't mean you can force me to get up at the butt-crack of dawn." I rolled over onto my stomach and buried my face into a pillow. "I'm not going to breakfast. Deal with it."

"Deal with it, huh?" Jake shuffled around the room, but I didn't look to see what he was doing. Moments later, he yanked me to the end of the bed by my ankle, pulled me into a sitting position, and handed me some clothes. "You can put these on, or I'll do it for you." He stepped back and waited, as if he planned to follow through with his threat.

I crossed my arms and sat there, daring him. "You can't force — " I jumped up as he strode angrily toward me. "Okay, okay. I'll get dressed. Jeez, are you always such a grouch in the morning?"

While Jake put on his shoes, I stepped into the bathroom and put on the clothes — a white V-neck top and a pair of denim shorts. I brushed my teeth with the bottled water and ran a comb through my hair. When I came out of the bathroom, Jake was leaning against the wall waiting for me.

"It's my sexy, I-barely-had-any-sleep look," I said, slipping my feet into a pair of sandals. "What do you think? Hot, right?" Sarcasm oozed from my rough morning voice.

"It'll do." Jake said, pulling me out of the cottage door.

The sounds of birds filled my ears. Roosters crowed, turkeys gobbled, ducks quacked, geese honked. Other chattering noises, too, but I wasn't sure what type of birds made such weird sounds.

"Look," I said to Jake. "Dog is gone. I wonder where they buried him."

"I told you he wasn't dead, just sleeping."

"Lucky bastard," I mumbled under my breath. Maybe if I collapsed from exhaustion out here, Jake would step over me and keep going.

He caught me eyeing Dog's spot on the porch. "Don't even think about it."

Begrudgingly, I followed Jake up the stairs and into the main house. The inside was more appealing than I imagined. It had arched doorways, high ceilings, and décor colored in varying shades of brown with white woodwork around the fireplace and mantle. We traipsed farther into the house, stopping once we reached the kitchen. The dark plank floors looked new, complemented by the antique milk glass attractively displayed above the white cabinetry.

From the front door, I smelled bacon frying, but the aroma was much more intense in the kitchen. I instantly changed my mind about skipping breakfast. In fact, I was starving.

"Come on in and have a seat," Floss said, a smile beaming on her slender face as she cracked an egg into a frying pan. "Breakfast will be ready in two minutes."

We joined Hank at the kitchen table, where he drank his coffee and gazed out the window. "Morning," he said, turning to us. "Sleep well?"

"Yep," Jake said. "Always do when I'm here."

I shrugged. "Well, I didn't. Something kept poking me in the back all night long."

Jake glanced over at me with wide eyes and a flustered look, but then he composed himself. "Must be a broken spring on that side of the bed. I'll trade sides with you tonight."

"Yeah, like that's going to help—ouch!" Jake glared at me as he pinched my leg under the table. "What?" I said, rubbing my thigh.

Oblivious, Floss hummed to herself as she cracked

another egg into the frying pan, but Hank smirked over at me. At least one of them knew Jake was a big, fat liar.

. . .

I didn't walk away from breakfast unscathed. In fact, I wasn't sure I could still walk. At home, my normal morning fare consisted of yogurt and granola, maybe some fresh fruit. Today was different. I inhaled three fried eggs, a pile of grits swimming in butter, at least a half pound of bacon, and two fluffy homemade biscuits slathered with mayhaw jelly.

Though I'd never heard of it, mayhaw jelly was a kitchen staple around here. Being a Yankee, I hadn't expected to like the tart red jelly, but it tasted similar to a crabapple. Then again, all of the food was good. I couldn't stop eating, and I paid for it. Everything hurt. My chest. My stomach. My jaw hurt from chewing. I don't know what I was thinking. Well, actually I do. *God, I hope I don't burp egg all day.*

Floss put eggshells and wet coffee grinds into a bowl. She asked Jake to dump them on the compost pile while he showed me around the farm. Then she handed me a pair of mud boots. Guess I wasn't taking a nap.

Though it was early, the day was already heating up. The bright sun forced me to squint until my eyes adjusted, and the warm breeze touched my skin, leaving a slight sheen of perspiration behind.

I walked behind Jake, following him to the back of the house. The weeds got taller, and the air got smellier the closer we came to the compost bin near the fence line.

"Keep an eye out for snakes," Jake warned. "Bird farms attract a lot of them. If you smell something similar to watermelon, stop moving."

"Why?" I asked, releasing the hold I had on my nose.

"Water moccasins are known for the scent. If you smell it, then chances are, one is nearby."

I stopped moving. "I'll wait right here for you."

Jake kept walking. From a short distance, I watched him dump the bowl of scraps into a large bin before he headed back. Leading the way back through the tall grass, I hoped he'd clear the path of any lurking watermelon mines.

Hank and Floss stood outside the pole barn, where a lot of banging was going on. When we joined them, Jake handed her the empty scraps bowl.

"What's that noise?" Jake asked Hank.

"Our palomino colt. Come on and you can take a look."

We followed Hank into the barn, where I got my first up-close-and-personal whiff of horseshit. The pungent odor wafted up from the floor. I made an airtight seal over my nose with my shirt and fingers. Too bad horses don't smell like watermelon.

A lively white colt with bright blue eyes and wearing a red halter stood at attention, watching us warily. He stamped his hooves into the spongy ground and ran back and forth in his stall. He pawed the gate, but when it didn't accomplish anything, he kicked his back hooves against the wall, rattling the tin.

"What's wrong with him?" I asked.

"He's spirited and wild at heart. Had to separate him from his momma. She's due to foal again, and he refuses to wean. He's nothing but a momma's boy, but he makes an awful ruckus, doesn't he?"

"You plan on selling him?" Jake asked.

"I wanted to keep him, but the bastard's destroying the stall," Hank said over the loud beating and banging. "I need to move him to the back pasture, away from his momma. That way I can clean out his stall and replace the tin without getting kicked. Maybe you can help me, Jake."

"Sure. No problem," Jake said. "Emily, you might want to stand back when I lead him out."

Floss and I stepped away, leaning against a wood post near the hay storage. We watched Jake open the gate with a lead rope in hand. When Jake entered the stall, he was out of my field of vision briefly, but long enough for my palms to sweat. I breathed easier once Jake came out of the gate with the lead attached to the colt.

Jake led him toward the back pasture. They walked easily together most of the way, though Jake had to steady him a couple of times before he got the wiry colt through the back gate and released him.

Hank led another palomino, a large stallion with a flaxen mane and a calm demeanor, out of a stall nearby and passed him off to Jake. "This is his daddy. Put him in the same pasture," Hank said. "That should calm the colt down."

"Is that your trusty steed?" I asked, grinning.

"About as trusty as they come," Hank answered. "He reminds me a lot of Jake, strong and steadfast."

Jake released the stallion into the back pasture. He rubbed his hand slowly over the stallion's smooth neck, whispered sweet nothings to soothe him, and patted him roughly on his hindquarters to turn him loose. Then Jake turned, and our eyes met and held for several seconds.

Damn. Leave it to me to be envious of a horse.

When he got back to the barn, Jake slipped on a pair

of gloves, grabbed a wheelbarrow and a shovel, and pushed them into the colt's stall.

"I think they could use some lemonade," Floss said. "I have some upstairs in the fridge. Want to help me bring it down?"

"Sure, Mrs. Mill—" I stopped mid-word and wondered if she'd threaten to bend me over her knee. She was smaller than I was, though. I thought I could probably take her.

"Now, Emily, I don't call you Miss Foster. I expect you to return the favor," she said, walking casually toward the house. "If you refuse to call me Floss, then I'll refuse to feed you supper."

"Yes, ma'am," I said meekly. She turned to glare at me, until I corrected myself. "I mean, Floss." Yep. No doubt about it. That was definitely a verbal spanking.

I followed her into the kitchen and soaked up the air conditioning. The cool air was a relief to my senses, though Floss didn't seem to notice the difference. It would take me awhile to get used to this heat. Of course, that's assuming I'd ever get used to it.

"Is Floss your real name?" I asked her as she pulled out the lemonade.

"No, but Hank's called me Floss long enough, I don't much answer to Florence anymore. He always said I was skinny enough he could floss his teeth with me. Now, everyone calls me that. I reckon it's what they'll chisel on my headstone when I die."

Death wasn't a comfortable subject for me, so I shifted gears as quickly as I could. "May I ask what happened to Hank's leg? I noticed he limps when he walks."

Floss finished pouring lemonade into the four glasses

on the counter. "He got kicked by the colt a few months ago, which did a bit of damage to the cartilage and bone. Foolish numbskull needs a knee replacement surgery, but is stubborn as all get out. Keeps putting it off."

"Why?"

"He's a man, honey. Why do they do anything?" She picked up two of the glasses and motioned for me to grab the other two. "Hank's afraid to be laid up for a while. He'd feel helpless, which isn't a feeling he's fond of. Plus, there's enough stuff to do around here that he doesn't want to burden me with all of it."

"Jake could help out until—"

"It's the first time Jake's been back in over a year…since the funeral. I'll be lucky if I can get Hank to sit at all. He loves that boy as if Jake were his own son."

I went out the door first, then whirled around to look at Floss. "Funeral? Who died?"

She smiled lightly. "I'll let Jake tell you about that when he feels up to it."

Without another word, we walked down to the barn. I stopped outside the gate, but Floss walked into the stall where Hank hammered some tin. A shirtless Jake shoveled on the opposite side, but both men glanced up at the same time, set their tools aside, and came toward us.

"Thanks," Jake said.

He guzzled a long drink, working the muscles in his neck, while a bead of sweat trickled down the side of his face. When he lowered his glass, the only thing left was ice. I offered him my glass, which he grabbed with a slight hesitation. "You sure?"

"There's more upstairs," I said, shrugging. "Besides, I

drank some of it on the way out here."

"Trying to give me your female cooties?"

I leaned closer and whispered, "I've been trying to give you my female cooties for the last couple of days."

Jake looked over to his aunt and uncle, who pretended they hadn't heard us, then glared back at me with a hint of embarrassment. "Is there any conversation off-limits to you in mixed company?"

"No, I normally say whatever pops into my head."

"Yeah," Jake said in a low voice. "That's the problem. I should be mucking out your dirty mouth."

I laughed and started to say something else, but Jake stopped me. "If you say what I think you're going to, then I'm going to put my not-so-clean hand over your trap," he threatened, his face serious. "Jesus. You need to learn to control that mouth of yours."

"How's this for control?" I asked, giving him a sweet, angelic smile. "Muck you!"

Jake gritted his teeth.

"Emily, why don't I show you around the property before I start with the chores?" Floss interrupted.

"Sure," I said. "That'd be great. Can I help you do anything?"

Jake's eyes widened, clearly shocked by my offer.

Floss smiled at me. "Can you gather eggs from the chicken coop?"

"No problem."

"Aunt Floss, do y'all still have that big red cock?" Jake asked.

And he tells me to watch my mouth?

"Yep. He's a scrapper, doesn't like anyone messing with

his hens."

"Then I should get the eggs for you," Jake offered. "I don't think Emily would be able to do it."

My eyes narrowed, as if he challenged me directly. "Why, because of a measly rooster?" I asked. "God, Jake, have some faith."

"He's a fighting rooster. Very aggressive."

"I think you're taking this whole protection business too seriously. You make it sound like I'm going into a cage with a rabid pit bull. It's a stupid chicken."

"Okay, but I don't think you'll come back with any eggs."

"I don't know," I said with a laugh. "I'm pretty persistent."

"Stubborn is more like it. But if you're going in there, I want a front row seat. If you need any help—"

"I won't need your interference, Jake. This isn't one of your FBI missions."

Hank handed me a small white bucket and grinned, which worried me. Then, in true parade fashion, he led the way to the chicken coop next to the barn. Apparently, this would be a family affair.

The chicken coop was a large rectangular pen framed with chicken wire, had a rusted tin roof, and a door you opened by turning a small block of wood nailed to the outside.

I had never gathered eggs before, but it sounded easy enough. At least until they mentioned the killer chicken. I should've kept my mouth shut and let Jake do it. If it wasn't for the stupid power struggle going on between us, I probably would have. I didn't actually *want* to gather eggs. What I wanted was to prove Jake wrong. Hard to do when he was always right. The bastard.

"Watch out for the wasp nest in the back right corner,"

Hank said. "If you disturb them, you'll get stung before you can get out."

"Wasp nest. Back right corner," I repeated, trying to dig deep.

Jake opened the door to the large pen. Chickens of all sizes and colors ran toward the back, huddling against the wall. *Hell, this might be easier than I thought.* My confidence level shot upward, and I stepped inside without hesitation. The smell was disgusting. Tiny gnats were everywhere. I breathed through my nose instead of my mouth.

The hen boxes were located on the right side of the pen. I moved slowly, trying not to scare the chickens—or myself— any more than I had to. Most of the boxes held at least one egg. Some had hens still in them. No big deal, though. I'd grab the eggs and be on my way. And Jake thought I couldn't do it? What an idiot!

I grabbed an egg out of the first box I came to and carefully put it in the bucket. Simple. Then I reached for another in the next box. The chickens left their huddle in the corner and dispersed, though they still avoided me.

I spotted the rooster strutting nearby, but he looked as harmless as the rest of them. He was brightly colored with red, orange, and black feathers, but wasn't nearly as large as I had pictured in my head. He pecked the ground around him as he walked back and forth, never coming any closer than the hens did.

I shook my head, reached for another egg, and yelled out, "Jake, I think you're a weenie. This rooster is as tame as a—"

The rooster snared my attention when he threw back his head and crowed. It must've been his battle cry, because he launched himself at me in a fury of flapping wings and pointy beak. He was on me faster than I could run. I screamed like a girl and hit him with the bucket, knocking him against the chicken wire. He landed on the floor in a daze. I left the two broken eggs where they fell and ran.

Jake opened the door as I dashed out, practically knocking him over. "Are you all right?" he asked.

I held up my arm where a trickle of blood had formed. "That pecker bit me!"

After a serious pause, the three of them burst into hysterics. I wasn't the least bit amused. "What's so funny?"

Hank was the first to quiet down. "Honey, that's the same as saying a shark licked you. Roosters can't bite. They don't have teeth."

"Felt like a bite."

Jake examined my arm. "It's barely bleeding, you crybaby."

"Well, big man, then let's see your technique. You go get the eggs," I challenged, handing over the bucket.

He smirked as he stepped into the chicken coop. There was a moment of silence, a light rustling sound, and then the rooster crowed. Feathers flapped and Jake screamed, hitting a much higher note than I did. Then he ran out of the chicken coop.

"Holy shit!" Jake yelled, looking down at the scratches and a bleeding peck wound on his shirtless chest. "I agree with Emily—the damn nuisance has teeth!"

Jake looked frazzled from his humbling experience. None of us could hold back the laughter. We laughed until each of us was doubled over in pain from our aching bellies. It was a side of Jake I hadn't seen before. I'd seen him laugh and smile, but this was something different. He was more peaceful, more at home with himself.

"All right," Hank said, still chuckling. "Time to get back to work. We'll let the womenfolk tend to those eggs."

Womenfolk? Now I knew where Jake got the macho bravado crap—his uncle's an old-fashioned, sexist pig.

Floss accepted the bucket from Jake and disappeared into the chicken coop. Moments later, she emerged with a bucket of eggs. Guess we should've left the job to the professional.

I spent the rest of the afternoon with Floss. She walked me from pen to pen, pointing out the different types of birds they raised; pheasants, quail, guineas, white doves, and homing pigeons were some of the more diverse species. Together, she and I fed and watered all the animals on their property. Birds first, then horses, and then we went around the backside of the barn to feed the rabbits.

There were two of them in a large off-the-ground cage, one black with lop ears named Jack and one white with brown spots named Twitcher. Jack happily munched a carrot, but when I offered one to Twitcher, she growled and hissed at me. I didn't know rabbits could make sounds, but Floss said they could scream. It reminded me of *Watership Down*, and that movie always gave me the willies. I tossed the carrot inside and locked the cage fast.

The men finished the colt's stall and started stacking bales of hay. Afterward, they worked on the well pump together. Jake smiled a lot, as did Hank. I wasn't sure which one of them had the better time, but I saw a lot of respect and love between them.

I stood on the back porch eating an oatmeal raisin

cookie left over from lunch and watched Jake work. He was still shirtless. Easy on the eyes, but hard on the mind. Hank pointed across the yard at something, but I couldn't make out what it was. He said something to Jake that made him sprint across the yard and scoop it up.

Curiosity got the better of me, and I went down the back steps. Both men stood at the base of a large dead tree when I joined them.

"What are you looking at?" I asked, as Jake turned to face me. "Ooooh!"

He held a tiny duckling covered in brown downy feathers. "Here, Emily, take this one."

"There's another one, Jake," Hank said.

Jake jogged a couple of steps and scooped him up, handing that one to me, as well. "They're going to kill themselves," Jake said, looking up again.

I gazed up at the hollow in the top of the dead tree, at least fifteen feet off the ground. "They're coming from way up there?"

Hank nodded. "Our Muscovy duck had laid some eggs in the hollow last year, but they never hatched. Didn't think to check this year. Guess they laid some more and those hatched."

"Where's their mother? Shouldn't she be around here somewhere?"

"She's in the pond," Hank said. "Can't you hear her sloshing around in the water and calling them? She's trying to get them to come out of the tree. Jake, grab one of those five-gallon buckets in the barn and a ladder. We'll climb up and see if there are more in the nest."

While Jake got the ladder and bucket, two more yellow

ducklings jumped out of the nest, bounced off the ground, and were now resting in Hank's large hands. Their tiny heads poked out through his fingers and they peeped relentlessly. Jake leaned the ladder against the tree and climbed up. He came back down with six more ducklings.

The four ducklings we held reunited with their siblings inside the bucket by clumping together on one side. "Now what?" I asked.

"Now, we put them in a brooder box with a heat lamp," Hank said. "It'll keep them warm and safe from predators."

"What about the momma duck? Are you going to catch her?"

"Why would I do that?" Hank asked, looking at me strangely.

"How are they going to suckle?"

Hank and Jake looked at each other with astonishment and then chuckled. "Emily, ducks don't have nipples," Jake said.

"Or lips," Hank mumbled under his breath with a smirk.

I was confused. "Then why do the babies go under the momma's wings?"

"To get warm," Jake answered, trying not to laugh again.

My cheeks warmed. How was I supposed to know? It's not like I was raised on a farm.

Hank led us to the brooder box and opened the lid. There were two sides to the brooder, and one side already overflowed with colorful chicks. Huddled near the heat lamp, they all began peeping once disturbed. Hank plucked up a white chick and placed it gently in my palm.

One peek and I melted. "Aww," I said, cooing to the chick with the fluffy head. "It's so cute." Then it shit in my hand. "Ew, gross. Take this nasty thing."

Jake grabbed it and placed it back with the others. He didn't laugh this time, but the shit-eating grin on his face told me he wanted to. I rinsed off my hand with the nearby hose while Jake put the ducklings into the other side of the brooder box and turned on their heat lamp. Hank gave them food and water, which the ducklings walked through and made a mess of within about thirty seconds.

"Well, kiddos, dinner should be close to ready," Hank said, looking at his watch. "Let's wash up and eat. We'll work on the well pump more tomorrow, Jake."

As soon as we went inside, I stepped into the bathroom and washed my hands with soap. Twice. Then I headed to the kitchen. "Floss, can I help with anything?"

"Do you cook, dear?"

"Does boiling water or using a microwave count? I'm willing to learn, but my mom wasn't able to…uh…well, she wasn't around."

"Everything is about ready, but tomorrow I'll get you to help me with dinner."

"Sounds good." I sat next to Jake.

"Oh, and Emily, Junior called to say he was bringing over some clothes for you that belonged to his daughter. He's going to drop them off in the morning."

Jake gave Floss a look, but I couldn't grasp the meaning behind it and let it go. He probably wondered the same thing I did. How did Junior know I needed extra clothes?

"That's sweet of him," I said, taking a sip of iced tea. "What about you, Jake? Don't you need to go into town and buy a few things? You have fewer clothes than I do."

"I can pick up some things later."

"Actually," Floss interrupted. "You have clothes you left up in the attic, Jake." She smiled at me. "Every time Jake came in for a visit, he'd leave an article behind. I collected them in a box. Good thing, huh?"

"Yep, good thing." Jake smiled at her. "I'll go up and pull the box down first thing in the morning."

Minutes later, Floss had dinner on the table. She put ears of corn on each of our plates and went to tell Hank dinner was ready. He was still in the bathroom washing up. I inspected the corn, but my stomach rolled with a wave of nausea.

"Jake, I don't want to hurt her feelings, but I don't think I can eat it after what you told me about the dead bodies," I whispered. "I'd always wonder if it came from the same field."

"My aunt and uncle grow their own corn," he whispered back. "You're safe. No dead bodies."

I sighed with relief. "Thank God."

Hank and Floss joined us at the table, and we passed around the platters of food. When Jake handed me a platter of golden fried balls, I paused. They resembled hush puppies, but I wasn't sure about eating them.

"What are these?"

"Fish balls," Hank said, dipping one in tartar sauce and taking a bite.

"Seriously? I didn't know fish had—"

Jake clamped his hand over my mouth and politely excused us before dragging me away from the table. In the living room, he glared at me with exasperation. "What's your problem?"

"Mine? What's yours? I'm sure they've heard the word balls before. Hell, I bet your uncle even has a pair."

"Damn it, Emily. I don't want to think about my uncle's balls before I eat," Jake said, crinkling his nose at me.

"Well, neither do I, but I was making a point."

Jake shook his head. "Jesus Christ, you have an issue with censorship."

"No shit!"

"Next time, think about what you say before you open your mouth," Jake warned. "Didn't your parents teach you to respect your elders?"

"No, I'm sorry they didn't," I snarled. "They were too busy dying to bother."

Jake froze, realizing what he said. "I'm sorry. I didn't mean to…"

"Tell your aunt thanks for dinner, but I'm not hungry. I'm going to bed." Then I walked out the front door.

Chapter Eight

Jake found me sitting on the cottage porch an hour later, rubbing my fingers through Dog's white coat and scratching behind his speckled ears. Dog never moved, but his warm body suggested he was still alive. Barely. Maybe.

He disappeared during the day, but by the time the sun went down, Dog was back on the porch and dead once again, at least to the world.

"Taming the savage beast?" Jake asked as he sat next to me.

I grinned, but my heart wasn't in it. "He's blowing his image. Aren't country dogs supposed to be hunters? He might as well be mounted on the wall."

"Nah, the possums are big enough around here that we use them as coon dogs." Jake paused for a thoughtful minute. "I figured you'd be asleep by now. Having trouble winding down?"

I shook my head. "No, I needed some male action." Jake

raised one eyebrow. "Not that kind," I said. "There's a spider the size of a small horse in there. I wanted you to kill it. You know how I am about spiders."

A muscle twitched in his strong, angular jaw. I think he wanted to laugh, but refrained from it. Then his eyes turned to me, his face becoming more serious. "Emily, I'm sorry. I didn't mean to say…"

"It's okay, Jake. No need to apologize. I know it wasn't what you meant. Besides, there's some validity to what you said."

"But I shouldn't have brought up your parents. It wasn't right."

At the mention of them, tears stung my eyes, but I refused to let them fall. I hung from a cliff by my fingertips, and the emotional weight pulled at my feet. I managed to push back the sadness and smiled crookedly. His eyes locked on my trembling mouth. I nervously glanced away, gathered my hair at the nape of my neck, and braided it together.

"Floss told me she mentioned the funeral," Jake added. "She didn't know I hadn't said anything to you about it."

"You don't have to talk about it if you don't—"

"My parents died last year. At the same time, on the same day. It nearly killed me. It's part of the reason I haven't been back here." He swallowed hard, struggling with his speech. "They died because of me."

Minutes crept by silently. I didn't want to ask him to share anything he wasn't willing to. We stared up at the glass dome of stars while Jake marinated in his guilt.

Sometimes in life, you need to be able to throw something out into the universe, a rhetorical statement warranting no judgment from others. It's what I wanted to give to Jake because it's what I wished someone would've given to me when I thought the same thing about my own parents. *They died because of me.*

His dark hair was slightly disheveled, and his gray eyes drooped with weariness. The manual labor he performed under the sun had taken a physical toll, but the mental strain of his parents' death still weighed heavily on him. I understood that feeling well.

"Tired?" I asked, unsure how he managed to stay awake.

"I'm beat," Jake replied. "I'll go take care of your spider problem so we can go to bed."

My temperature rose slightly, thinking about snuggling into his warm, hard body. And he must've noticed the little smile gathering at the corner of my mouth.

"Emily, I don't think either of us got much sleep last night with the…uh…tension in the room. Unless you want a repeat, we're going to have to pretend there's a crossing guard between us tonight."

"A *ménage à trois*?" I said with a teasing laugh. "Might be interesting."

Jake paused. "Shit."

• • •

It took me forever to fall asleep, but I must've finally dozed off, because when I opened my eyes, Jake was asleep next to me. Actually, he was under me. I had draped myself across his chest, capturing his body heat. It was like cuddling with a high-temperature furnace. As cold as it was in the room, the cottage could've been easily mistaken for a cabin in Alaska.

It was five o'clock when the stupid rooster started

crowing relentlessly, robbing me of my sleep. The sun hadn't even risen yet. Dumbass bird should be on Prozac.

I shifted slightly against Jake to get more comfortable. His body tensed as his muscled forearms tightened their grip around my back, pulling me further in to him. A knee slid up between my thighs. His warm breath quickened, blowing against my neck. Suddenly, the room changed from cold to hot, like Jake was a sunray burning into my skin. Flustered, I considered cranking down the air conditioner in the room before I melted.

When something hard pressed heavily into my pelvis, I knew Jake was awake. I leaned my mouth closer to his, brushing my lips lightly over his. "Jake…"

"We can't," he whispered, sounding painfully unsure of himself. "Stop before this goes any further."

"I don't want to stop," I said softly, letting my tongue flicker across his briefly. "I want to feel you inside me."

A definite pause on his part. Then he dumped me back onto my own side of the bed. "Jesus Christ, Emily. I'm a man. You can't say that sort of thing to a man and expect him to maintain any sense of self-control."

I narrowed my eyes and pursed my lips, stopping myself from saying, *Duh. That's the point, dipshit!* "You don't have any problems with self-control. In fact, you're good at pushing me away. Must be all the practice you're getting."

"Don't give me a hard time."

"I'm not. What I want is for you to give *me* a hard time."

He sighed wearily, throwing his head back onto his pillow. "Once the trial is over we'll be able to—"

"The trial could be months or even a year away. You're crazy if you think I'll wait that long for something that's not a sure thing." Okay, so it was a lie. I'd wait for him if I had to, but I wasn't stupid enough to tell him that. At least not yet.

"Oh, it's a sure thing," he said with a sardonic laugh. "When I do finally get inside you, you're going to wish you hadn't teased me the way you have." Then he raised his eyebrows and lifted the corner of his mouth in a smirk.

I wanted to respond, but the words caught in my throat. After a moment, all I could say was, "God, I hate you sometimes." Then I rolled to my side, facing away from him, and went to sleep with hard nipples.

And he thinks I'm a tease?

• • •

Two days went by, and I was bored out of my mind.

Hank found me sitting in the backyard on an old, rickety bench overlooking an aboveground pool filled with cloudy, urine-colored well water, littered with bug corpses and dead leaves. At least I think it was a pool. It looked more like the horses' watering trough.

"You okay, honey?"

I nodded. "I don't have anything to do, so I'm watching the squirrels."

"I hate those damn things," Hank said, scowling up at the tree. "They get up in the attic, build nests in the insulation, and shred everything up. I've been battling them ever since Floss planted a pecan tree and it produced nuts."

"How do you get rid of them?"

"Shoot 'em."

I gasped. "Hank, that's mean!"

He grinned with amusement at my reaction. "Last

squirrel I shot had its nuts still in its mouth when it went down."

That made me laugh. "Didn't want to let go, huh?"

"Came down to a choice—its nuts or its life. Damn squirrel chose to keep its nuts." Hank nodded toward Jake, walking toward us from across the yard. "I reckon most men would do the same."

I wasn't sure what he meant, but somewhere in his words there was bound to be a pearl of wisdom. I had a few choice comments, but I didn't say anything, figuring Jake would get mad at me again.

"I'm burning the last of the brush pile from the back of the property," Jake said to Hank. "What do you want me to do now?"

"Take a break," Hank demanded.

"I'm fine," Jake said. "I'll rest after the work's done. I'm trying to keep you off your bum knee as long as I can, old man."

"I'll make you think old man, you piss ant." Hank glared at Jake, but the taunting smile on his face led me to believe he wasn't serious. "If you want something to do, why don't you take the culled birds down to the pond? Take Emily with you. She's bored. It'll give her something to do."

Jake started to argue but decided against it. "Come on, Emily."

We strolled to the barn, where Jake picked up a bucket covered with a lid and continued toward the pond. Almost there, we heard the sound of a truck rumbling down the driveway. Jake tensed for a moment and reached for my arm but relaxed as three young men and a pretty blond woman slid out of the tan Ford. All four of them waved at Hank, then walked in our direction.

"Can't say I'm surprised to see them," Jake said, undeterred from his mission.

I stumbled after him but curiously glanced back at the new arrivals in the distance. "Who are they?"

"Friends of mine," Jake said, stopping next to a moss-covered tree and removing the lid on the bucket.

The pond sat closer to the back of the property, surrounded by red oak and cypress trees. A green scummy film of algae floated on the surface around the lilies, and small turtles rested on a log within the cattails at the water's edge. Between the thick, stinky black mud on the shoreline and the green climbing vines and weeds, the pond resembled a cross between a jungle and a swamp.

I leaned over to check out the contents of the bucket and saw nothing but dead birds. "Oh, gross! Why are there dead birds in there?"

Jake picked one up and threw it in the pond. "Got to get rid of them somehow."

"How'd they die?"

"Disease or sometimes gnats. Most of these were already dead," Jake explained, picking up another. "Well, except for this little guy right here. He was on his deathbed. Hank pulled his head off this morning."

My God! First squirrels and now his own birds? If Dog wasn't already dead, I'd worry about his safety.

"This is disgusting," I said, openly disapproving of Hank's methods. "I'm not going to stand out here in the weeds, watching you throw dead birds into a smelly pond."

I turned to walk off, but a dragonfly flitted past my nose. Flustered, my right heel caught on a cypress knee, and I stumbled backward into the pond. I was surprised at the depth. No shallow area to stand in, just a sheer drop-off into deep water. I broke the surface of the water, used my hands as a squeegee to wipe the slimy film from my face, and thought about crying.

Hank peered over the old tractor he tinkered with and laughed. "What you doing in there, honey? Checking to see if those fish have balls?"

Jake grinned as he continued throwing dead birds into the pond. Three young men ran out to join Jake on the bank, but no one appeared overly concerned about my situation.

One wearing a white straw cowboy hat asked Jake, "You going to fish her out?"

"Nope."

"Mind if we do?"

"Have at her," Jake said, throwing the last dead bird into the pond.

I waited for one of them to produce a rope or lean down on the bank and offer me a hand, but nooo…the morons stripped off their shirts, hats, and boots, then jumped in.

"Might want to hurry," Jake told them. "Charlie's lost interest in the birds."

I splashed some floating algae away as the man who wore the cowboy hat reached me. "Who's Charlie?" I sputtered, clueless.

The man grinned. "Hell, darlin', he's the gator you're sharing this pool with."

I shrieked and flailed my arms, trying to grab anything I could on the side of the bank to pull myself up. The man grabbed me and hauled me quickly toward the side of the pond as the other two men swam next to us. I screamed all the way there.

"Sweetheart, I'm starting to go deaf. Now, stop thrashing around before you drown both of us." We reached the side where the slope of the bank wasn't as severe, and he dragged us both out of the water, dropping me on the muddy bank. "See, you're fine. That hissy fit you threw was uncalled for. God always takes care of helpless creatures."

Yeah, sure. Tell that to the squirrels and the birds.

Once the other two men crawled out of the pond, the man who saved me pulled me to my feet. "You must be wearing lotion or something. I've caught salamanders in here that weren't as slippery as you," he said, making me want to roll my eyes. Sure, it had nothing to do with the green slime clinging to me. "You all right now, sweetheart?"

"Yes, thank you." I glanced over at Jake, who casually talked to the pretty blonde with the overinflated chest. She walked up and hugged him, which made my eyes narrow. "Excuse me for a moment. I have to go borrow a gun from Hank."

I stormed past the man, but he grasped me firmly by the arm and threw me over his shoulder. "Oh, no you don't, Tiny. I haven't seen Jake in over a year. You can't kill him until I'm through with him. Now, let's go get you cleaned up."

The man carried me up to the house before putting me down. He turned on the hose and sprayed me from head to toe. The well water sprayed out warm at first, but quickly changed to freezing cold. I shivered.

"Cold?" he asked.

"F-f-freezing."

He pulled me to his chest and kept his arm around my waist as the hose rained down over the both of us, rinsing off the green algae. I tried to move away, but he tightened his grip.

"Stay still, darlin'. I'm trying to keep you warm."

I wasn't sure how I felt about some strange guy—especially a friend of Jake's—holding me against his shirtless, nicely toned body. That is, until the others walked closer to the house, the blonde's arm looped through Jake's and her right breast resting comfortably against his bicep. They were deep in conversation, smiling at each other, and…and well, it pissed me off.

I did the only thing I could in this situation. I leaned into Jake's friend and wrapped my arms around the back of his neck. His green eyes sparkled like emeralds and the color deepened. My lips were close to his as I breathed out, "Is there anything I can do to thank you?" I purposefully made my tone sultry.

Jake's mouth hinged open, followed by the mouths of the men and the woman on Jake's arm. The only one who didn't look shocked was the man holding me, though his breathing was a little ragged. He turned the hose on himself and sprayed his chest, letting the ice cold water run down his front. The ridge in his pants led me to believe it wasn't the algae he tried to do away with.

"Oh, daaamn. I wanted to hose her down," the biggest guy said. "Why does Cowboy get to have all the fun?"

I looked back at the man with the hose, knowing Jake was walking toward us. "Cowboy, huh? That's a strange name." Cowboy winked at me and grinned. My eyes scanned to the swell in his jeans. "So, Cowboy, is that a kink in your hose or are you just happy to—"

A hard hand bit into my arm, turning me around. All

I saw was Jake's intense glare. He didn't say anything, but dragged me off toward the cottage.

He wrangled me into the bathroom, turned the water in the shower on, and yelled at me. "What the hell was that?"

"What?" I asked innocently.

"You're supposed to be my girlfriend, remember? Do you always hug up on strange men like that?"

"The water was freezing, and I was covered in slime." I stepped into the shower, closed the stall door, and stripped out of my wet, nasty clothes. "No thanks to you, of course."

"It's not like I pushed you in."

"Well, you sure the hell didn't pull me out. You left me in there with an alligator. A fucking alligator! I could kill you."

"You know, it's against the law to threaten a federal agent," Jake warned, his tone lightening with amusement.

"Are you going to arrest me?" I asked, my tone bordering on a dare.

"No."

"Good. Fuck you, then!" I threw my bra and panties over the rail, hoping they smacked him in the face, but he just laughed. I stepped under the spray, splashing warm water on my face and letting it run over my hair, warming my cold body as it trailed down. "Who's your friend?" I asked, trying to lighten my harsh tone.

Jake paused before answering. "Look, Cowboy may be a friend of mine, but I don't want you to —"

"Not him. I'm talking about the blond chick."

"Oh, you mean Bobbie Jo?"

"Bobbie Jo? Isn't that a boy's name?"

Jake chuckled. "Not around here it's not. It's her name. She and I go way back. You'll like her. Sweet girl."

My eye roll was lost on him through the steamed up shower door. "Oh, yeah. I'm sure we'll be besties."

"Finish up in here. Then I'll give you a proper intro-duction—one where you shake hands instead of rubbing against each other's body parts."

"Funny," I said, though I heard the door shut and realized he was already gone.

I got dressed, blow-dried my hair, and dabbed a little makeup on before returning outside. It wasn't hard to find them, since I could hear the sounds of them clowning around in the backyard. When I walked up, they were throwing back beers and laughing, though Cowboy was no longer with them. That was probably a good thing.

Jake motioned to the others one at a time. "Emily, this is Bobbie Jo." The thin, pretty blonde with the perfect glowing complexion and large boobs smiled and waved politely, as Jake motioned to a little guy next to her. "And this is Ox."

"Ox? Does anybody here have a normal name?" The dig was meant for Bobbie Jugs. I mean, Jo. *God, why do I do that? I don't even know the poor girl. It's not her fault Jake has me so tied up in knots.*

Laughing, Ox stepped over and shook my hand. His earsplitting, boisterous laugh seemed out of place with his little body. "Judd does," Ox said. "And Jake, of course."

I looked over to Judd, who was squeezing superglue into a cut on his leg, and reveled at his size. He was a big boy—not fat, but big. Everywhere. He had a large barrel head, broad shoulders close to three feet wide, and bulges in places that were unnatural. He gave a quick nod and went back to what he was doing.

"What happened, Judd?"

"It's no big deal. I banged my knee against a root or something when I jumped into the pond. Must've gashed my leg open."

I stepped closer for a better look. "It looks like it needs stitches," I said, appalled by the angry-looking laceration. "And the pond water is probably crawling with bacteria. You might want to get it checked out."

Everyone around me burst into laughter.

Jake shook his head at me. "He'll be fine. Each of us has stepped out of the pond at some point with a knick on us."

A knick? Was he kidding? That's like saying the scar left after open-heart surgery resembled a cat scratch. Jesus. They were all fucking nuts.

"Good thing you didn't get hurt, Emily. You probably would've cost me a trip to the emergency room," Jake said, suggesting to everyone I was a wuss.

"Actually, I hurt my finger when I tried to climb out. I think I broke it."

"No you didn't," Jake said, resting his arm on the bench behind Bobbie Jo. "You probably jammed it."

I gritted my teeth but held my ground. "No, I think I broke it. Besides, how would you know? You haven't even seen it. My finger could be mangled and twisted into some weird shape."

Jake sighed. "All right, you big baby, let me have a look at your finger." After a silent pause, his friends chuckled. "Not that one, smartass."

Somebody approached me from behind, and I turned to get a better look. Cowboy stood there in all his handsome perfection with an incredible smile flattering his already-gorgeous face.

"Emily, this is— "

"We've already met," Cowboy said, interrupting Jake as he lifted my hand to his lips, kissing it lightly. "Intimately," he added, his smile widening.

"Briefly," I corrected, pulling my hand from his.

"Jake takes all the fun out of everything." Cowboy's glittering green eyes playfully probed mine. "Most of my encounters with women are not nearly as short-lived."

My mouth twisted with sarcasm. "Do women agree with that statement, or is that just *your* perception?"

"Holy shit!" Ox said, laughing. "Where'd you find this girl, Jake?"

Cowboy's jaw tightened, as if I had issued a challenge. He lowered his head to my ear and whispered, "Why don't you take a test drive and find out for yourself?" He didn't wait for an answer before walking over to grab a beer from the cooler.

I doubted many women turned him down. If ever. He had a confident, loose-hipped gait and was the most genetically perfect specimen I'd ever laid eyes on. But I decided right then he had a flaw. He was too perfect. No one is that handsome, that confident, or that charming. Definitely something wrong with him. I mentally giggled to myself as I considered he had a small endowment. The universe does have to keep a certain balance in the world, after all.

"Jake," Bobbie Jo said, "I need to get going, or I'm going to be late picking up my mama. Can you give my guys a ride home? I'm sure they all want to stay awhile longer."

"Yeah, no problem." Jake reached over and gave her a big hug and a kiss on the cheek. "Stop by again when you get a chance. We'll catch up."

"I will. You don't know how much I've missed you," she said, her eyes glimmering.

Oh, jeez. I think I just threw up in my mouth.

By the time she drove away, the sun dipped behind the trees and mosquitoes invaded the backyard. We took refuge near the burn pit.

"So what are you boys doing here?" Jake asked.

"Had to see if the rumor was true," Judd replied.

"What rumor?"

Judd grinned widely. "The rumor about you being engaged."

Jake's eyes widened and his mouth fell open. "What? Who told y'all that?"

"Ran into Junior at the hardware store. He said you were going to marry this one."

I couldn't help but smile since I figured Bobbie Jo probably heard the same rumor.

Jake's eyes flitted to me and back to Judd. "She's my... girlfriend. That's it." He wasn't a good liar. Even I sensed his hesitation to answer.

Cowboy leaned over toward me. "Pregnant?"

"Of course not," I replied, shocked by his assumption.

The corner of his lips curled upward, and his voice grew huskier. "Want to be?"

"Does that approach render most females helpless?"

"It's been known to light a few fires," he said, winking. "Lucky for you, I'm a fireman."

"You're a fire fighter?"

"Yes, ma'am." He waited for me to be impressed.

"Well, Cowboy, if my pussy is ever in need of being rescued, then I'll be sure to give you a call. Until then, you'll just have to play with your own hose."

Jake's three friends stared, slack-jawed and silent, as he shook his head. "You'll get used to it," Jake told them. "Emily has a bad habit of using colorful language."

"Fuckin' A," Ox said with surprise. Then he turned to me and said, "We don't normally hear that kind of talk from women. They tend to mind their Ps and Qs around here."

"She isn't a southern belle," Judd said, smiling. "That's for damn sure."

"I like it," Cowboy said, shrugging his brows at me. As if that surprised me.

I rolled my eyes. "You mean to tell me Bobbie Jo doesn't use bad language? Ever?"

"Bobbie Jo was head cheerleader, as well as valedictorian," Jake said in her defense. "She always set a great example of a lady, and the other girls admired her for it."

Damn. Miss Perfect was getting on my nerves, and she wasn't even there. "Yeah right, and I bet all the guys admired her oversized pom-poms."

"Emily, don't be crude," Jake said, scrunching his nose. "She hasn't done anything to you. She's a good person, and you'd like her if you gave her half a chance." He stood and walked away, mumbling something about getting more beer.

Ox and Judd set off after him, leaving Cowboy alone with me. Great. Smart move, guys. Then again, I was being a little bitchy. Bobbie Jo didn't seem so bad. Maybe I should spend some time getting to know her. And who knows? We might even end up friends.

"Don't worry," Cowboy said. "He'll get over it. Jake's a little overprotective when it comes to her."

"And why's that?"

Cowboy leaned back in his chair and stretched out his

long legs, kicking one scarred boot over the other. "Jake dated Bobbie Jo in high school. They took each other's virginity."

Now, I had to compete with the virgin he deflowered in high school?

Fucking great.

Chapter Nine

Floss invited Jake's friends to stay for dinner and wouldn't take no for an answer. She tempted them with promise of roast beef, mashed potatoes and gravy, and fresh green beans from the garden. Homemade apple pie was the clincher, though.

After dinner, Hank and Floss decided to turn in early. We said our good nights and the five of us headed back down to the burn pit with the intention of polishing off the rest of the beer. After all, there were only two things to do out in the middle of the sticks—have sex and get drunk. Since Jake continued holding out on the first thing, I accompanied the boys on the other.

Cowboy opened another beer and passed it to me with a sly, sexy smile. "You doing okay, darlin'?"

I nodded lazily, my brain buzzing with alcoholic contentment. "It's not oil," I slurred, pointing at the fire.

He cocked one eyebrow. "Oil?"

"We're burning the midnight trash," I mumbled, before bursting into hysterics and falling out of my chair.

Jake caught my arm, righted me, and snagged the beer from my hand. "Okay, slick, I think you've had one too many."

I pushed my lip out, pouting. "Oh, Jake, you're no fun."

He tipped the bottle back and guzzled my entire beer. "Well, that was fun," Jake said smugly, making the other guys laugh.

I leaned over to Cowboy, though my head tilted too far to the right and I had to correct it. "So what's with the name? Why do they call you Cowboy?"

"Because I always rounded up the most cattle."

"That's it?" I asked, unimpressed. "I thought for sure there'd be a better reason for it than that. You should try something like, *'because I can stay on longer than eight seconds, which is more than most men can.'* It would've done more for your image."

He chuckled under his breath. "Not when the cattle we're referring to *are* women."

"Oh, jeez," I said, looking over at Ox. "Well, what about you? Why Ox?"

Jake, Cowboy, and Judd all broke into chorus, "Because he's hung like an ox." I swear all three of them reached down and self-consciously rearranged their balls at the same time.

"No freaking way!" I laughed giddily, though I was the only one doing so. I looked to Jake for confirmation, and he nodded solemnly. My eyes widened and found their way back to Ox, who displayed a proud grin. "You've got to be shittin' me." I surveyed his pint-size frame and shook my head with disbelief. "No way!"

Ox smiled wider. "Want me to prove it?"

"Yes!"

"NO!" the men said in unison.

"Oh, come on, guys. He has to. There's no way I'll believe it until I see it for myself. You may as well have said he had the legendary Bigfoot dangling between his legs."

"He practically does," Cowboy mumbled under his breath.

Jake stood. "All right, I think it's time to call it a night." He tossed Cowboy the keys to our commandeered Explorer. "You can bring it back tomorrow."

"That'll work," Cowboy said in agreement.

"Come on, Emily. It's bedtime," Jake said, as if I were his child.

"I'm not going inside yet." Even if I did feel a little loopy.

He glared at me. "Well, you're not staying out here alone."

"You can't boss me around. I'm capable of making up my own mind. If I want to stay out here then you can't stop—"

Jake took two long strides, threw me over his shoulder, and carted me off toward the cottage. Damn Neanderthal. It would have served him right if I puked on him.

The guys laughed as they walked behind us toward the Explorer.

"You two fight like you're already married," Ox said to us. "You should go ahead and make it official."

"We probably would if Emily didn't have commitment issues," Jake replied, hamming it up by slapping me on my butt. "All she wants is sex."

God, I wanted to blow his stupid cover right then and tell them how Jake acted like a virginal schoolgirl who refused to part with his panties, but I didn't. I couldn't. And he knew it.

All evening I'd been helplessly drowning in male testosterone. I don't know why I expected anything different at this point. If this was any indication of how Smurfette felt, she should've left Smurf village a long time ago and begged Gargamel to kill her estrogen-laden ass.

"*I* have commitment issues?" I said to Jake. "You're a man, right?"

"You should know, *honey*." Then he smacked my ass a second time.

I growled under my breath, "If you do that again, you're going to have to sleep with one eye open tonight."

• • •

I came out of the shower as mad as when I went in.

Jake pulled back the quilt on the bed. "Still upset with me?"

"Eat shit."

"Guess so," he said, shrugging. A brief silence passed before he spoke again. "Okay, I know I'm going to regret this. Tell me what the problem is."

I glared at him. "You keep bossing me around. I'm starting to think Cowboy is right about you. You're no fun."

"We're not here to have fun. I brought you here to hide you and keep you alive. Those are my two objectives right now. You want fun, go to Disney World."

"Doesn't mean you have to be boring. I have all this idle time to do nothing, yet I annoy you more when I'm left to my own devices. I can't win."

Jake closed his eyes briefly and sighed. "Okay, tell me

what I can do to make this less boring for you and less infuriating for me."

I grinned from ear to ear as I crawled into bed with him. "You know that's a loaded question, right?"

"Something besides *that*," Jake said.

"Afraid I might tarnish your precious halo?"

"Nope. I want to channel your energy into something else, in hopes you'll behave yourself from now on."

"A reward for good behavior?"

Jake nodded. "Sure. What do you want?"

I considered my options, though I didn't have many to choose from. But there was one thing I truly wanted. Well, besides *that*. "I want to go somewhere. I'm tired of sitting around here."

"Nope. Not going to happen. Pick something else."

"Come on, Jake. I'm like that colt in the barn. I need to be able to stretch my legs, but you keep fencing me in. I need to get out of here, even if it's only for a little while."

He thought about it for a second, then let out a hard breath. "Okay, fine. God, I hope I don't regret this," he said, running a hand through his hair. "Tomorrow evening, I'll take you out."

"Really?"

He nodded. "Yes. But not for long, and we have to stay low-key. Is it a deal?"

"Deal," I said, grinning. "Wow, your halo is really glowing tonight."

Jake flipped off the lamp. "Yeah, yeah. I'm a regular angel."

"Well, it's better than acting like a nun," I said, before pausing to roll my mind over a drunken thought. "Wait a minute. Do angels have sex?"

"Go to sleep, Emily."

• • •

Earlier in the day, Jake called Cowboy and arranged for him to bring the Explorer by before dark. When I heard him pull in, I figured we'd be leaving soon. I dabbed my lips with shiny, clear gloss and misted myself lightly with perfume. I wanted my outing with Jake to be memorable, and the last look in the mirror had brought a smile to my face.

The flowery halter dress had a vintage, romantic feel, but paired with white strappy heels and a wide belt cinching my waist, the dress transformed into a traffic stopper. Junior's daughter had great taste.

Jake poked his head in the bedroom door. "Are you ready—" He stopped and stared with a stunned expression. "—to go?"

"Yep." I moved past him toward the cottage door. His head turned to watch me, but his feet stayed planted. "Coming?"

"Uh...yeah, of course." Only then did he move to the door. He opened it, but paused. "Emily," he said, hesitating again. "You...uh, look great."

I smiled. "Thanks. You, too."

His blue plaid shirt wasn't anything fancy, but it brought out the blue coloring in his gray eyes. His denim jeans emphasized his long, muscular legs and were tight on his ass. What more could a girl want?

Jake held the door for me, and I stepped out onto the porch. A shrill wolf whistle pierced the air. Cowboy leaned against the fender of the Explorer wearing faded Wranglers, a white muscle shirt, old work boots, and his white straw hat. He motioned his finger in a circle, wanting me to spin. I happily obliged.

He looked me up and down. "Mmmm-mmm." He didn't need to give me a verbal compliment. The fiery spark of desire in his eyes, as well as a hint of the green-eyed monster when he glanced over to Jake, was compliment enough.

I hadn't seen desire in Jake's eyes when he came into the bedroom. If anything, he looked more like a scared bunny crossing paths with a hungry coyote. What happened to him being the big, bad wolf? I chalked it up to the fear of going into town with the woman he stole from witness protection—it's bound to make anyone a little nervous.

Jake drove and I sat in the front passenger seat, though I don't know why, since I wasn't alone. Cowboy said he'd sit in back, but he spent most of his time leaning over my shoulder, breathing on my neck. I think he was looking for a mountain view, but with my average-sized chest, he was sorely disappointed. Most he could hope for was a glimpse of the twin peaks.

Once we dropped Cowboy off at the fire station, Jake drove the back way toward Liberty County. I thought it was funny, since *all* the ways were the back way to me, especially when surrounded by thickets of trees.

"Your friend is flirtatious."

"And persistent," Jake added. "I think you've caught his attention."

"What do you mean?"

Jake shrugged. "He's never met a woman he couldn't have before."

"Quantity over quality, huh?"

"I don't know if I'd go that far," he said with a smirk. "The women he's been with have never complained about quality control. It's more like he's an avid hunter, and it's open season year round...as far as women go."

"Oh, I get it. He's all about the bag and tag...but with no limit?"

"That's right," Jake said, laughing. "Cowboy needs a woman who challenges him. Most of them tend to fall over with their legs in the air. It's no fun hunting if the game comes to you and commits suicide at your feet." Jake glanced over at me as he drove. "Is he bothering you?"

"Cowboy? No, he's harmless...I think," I said with a laugh. "Is he bothering you?"

He grinned. "Did he hit on me and I didn't know it?"

"No, I mean, does it bother you that he's hitting on me?"

Jake didn't hesitate. "Not at all."

Ouch. That stung. I wanted to ask him why he wasn't jealous, but I couldn't bring myself to do it. Valuable lesson of the day: don't ask questions you might not like the answers to.

Jake turned down an unpopulated county road, and I spied something ahead. It had already gotten too dark to tell what it was from a distance, but when we got closer, I saw four large skeletal remains hanging from the barbed wire's wooden posts. Jake didn't bat an eye as we drove past, but I remembered the men who crept out of the woods the night we arrived.

"Oh, my God. What the hell were those...*things*?"

He glanced in his rearview mirror. "Alligator gars."

"What?"

"Alligator gars. They're a type of fish."

"There's no way. Those things were too big to be fish. They were longer than me."

Jake smirked. "Trust me, they're fish. Gars can get up to ten feet long."

"Why are their skeletons hung up on the fence? That's creepy."

"You don't want to know."

I gave him an impatient look. "Tell me."

"All right. Well, some people around here believe in voodoo."

Just what I need. Something else that gives me nightmares. "Never mind. You're right. I don't want to know."

We drove silently while I tried to erase the disgusting skeletal creatures from my mind. Darkness crept forward and encompassed everything around us. I had no idea where we were until Jake pulled out onto the highway. Junior's Diner was on this same highway, so chances were good that Jake was taking me to dinner. Junior would love that since I made such a lovely scene in the bathroom the last time I visited his place.

Jake slowed and turned his blinker on, but he passed the diner, pulled into the Dairy Queen parking lot, and got in line at the drive-through. I didn't understand what he was doing, so I held off on reacting. Something must've got lost in translation. I was still trying to connect the dots when we arrived at the microphone.

Jake leaned out his window. "Two small vanilla cones," he said into the speaker.

Too stumped for words, my lips couldn't form any clear communication. My face began to feel hot. I rolled down the passenger window to let the cool night air in and closed my eyes. This couldn't be real. Somehow, I had convinced myself Jake was taking me on a romantic outing, but all he had planned was ice cream at the Dairy Queen drive-through. Talk about an insulting buzzkill.

As if that wasn't bad enough, he didn't even ask me which flavor I wanted. He assumed I'd take whatever he'd give me and be happy with it. Don't know why I was surprised. He'd been doing it since I met him.

Jake pulled around to the other side of the building where the window was. The car in front must've gotten ice cream as well because they'd already pulled away. The freckle-faced teenage girl at the window smiled flirtatiously at Jake as he handed her a ten-dollar bill. She handed him his change and some extra napkins. A plump, older woman walked over with two vanilla cones and handed them to the teen.

She passed the first ice cream cone out the window to Jake. Then Jake passed it to me. And, with no hesitation, I passed it right out my passenger window. It splattered on the pavement, cone and all.

"What the hell are you doing?" Jake asked.

"Maybe I preferred chocolate, you prick!"

"If you wanted chocolate, all you had to do was say something."

"I didn't want…never mind. Just forget it." With that, I opened my door and got out of the Explorer, noticing two other vehicles had pulled up in line behind us.

Jake was genuinely confused. "What's your problem?"

"This is where you chose to take me? Seriously?"

"What's wrong with Dairy Queen?"

"Nothing!" I marched toward Junior's Diner with my feathers more ruffled than before.

I could hear the people in the other cars laughing as Jake pulled out of the drive-through line, parked, and got out. "What are you whining about now?" he asked.

"Whining about?" I said, spinning on my heels and pacing back in his direction. "Are you kidding me?"

"Emily, you're making a scene."

"Well, you might be in for one hell of a shock, but I don't fucking care!"

"I don't get it. You didn't throw a tantrum last night."

"Because I didn't know where you were taking me last night!"

"I didn't, either," Jake said. "Is that why you're so pissed?"

"God. All you men are liars!"

A trashy-looking woman from one of the drive-through cars hung out her window and shouted, "You tell him, girl!"

"Hey, women lie, too, and not always on their backs," a young man yelled from the other car in the drive-through, then followed it with animated laugh.

Jake's steely gaze bore into mine. "Are you done being hysterical yet?" he asked in a low, rough voice.

"Not. Even. Close." I squeezed past him and walked between two parked cars.

Jake followed, not allowing me to escape his field of vision. He was thoroughly pissed off. "You know, I wondered when the next storm would hit," he said angrily. "We should have named you Hurricane Emily. It's more fitting."

"Sure, Jake. Throw more gas on the fire."

"You know what your problem is? I'll tell you. You're an overindulged, entitled baby who is prone to outbursts and too wrapped up in yourself to care about anybody else."

The woman from the drive-through car yelled, "Honey,

I wouldn't take that shit."

The young man in the other car didn't appreciate the woman's comment and honked his horn. "Hey, bitch, why don't you shut your pie hole and mind your own business?"

"Look who's talking, jackass!" the woman hollered back.

Jake shook his head. "Jesus Christ. Are you trying to start a riot?

"Now it's *my* fault the people in the drive-through are arguing? I guess everything's my fault, right?"

Jake grabbed my arm. "We need to go before someone calls the cops."

I shook him off and tilted my chin up. "Let them. I'd rather be arrested, handcuffed, and loaded in the back of a cruiser than to get in the vehicle with you again."

He glanced around and lowered his voice to a whisper. "If they run your fingerprints, you'll be put in the system and Felts will find you."

His attempt at forcing me to maintain a healthy perspective didn't work. I was too far gone and still lashing out. "What do you care, anyway? You'd be rid of my *overindulged, entitled ass*."

"Emily, get in the car."

"There you go, telling me what to do. What are you going to do if I don't…kidnap me again?" I stood there with crossed arms, tapping my foot, and watching anger flicker like fire in his eyes.

"Would you knock it off, you spoiled little…" He stopped himself from continuing his train of thought.

I didn't care. That got my blood pumping, coursing through my veins at the speed of light. I had to get away from him before I punched him. "Oh, I give up!" I tried to step around him, but he blocked me from leaving.

"No, that's exactly your problem," Jake said, his nostrils flaring. "You *don't* give up. Ever. In fact, you don't ever shut up, either."

Don't do it. Don't say— "It's not my fault the average intelligence level around here is a big whopping three. I didn't ask to be held captive in Hicksville or for us to sit around playing Duck, Duck, Goose, either. If all of you want to sit around licking windows and eating crayons with googly eyes and missing teeth, then be my guest. My ass will be on the next bus back to Chicago." *Damn, I said it.*

Looking into Jake's eyes, I knew our unpleasant battle of wills had become more personal than I meant it to. *Me and my big mouth.* His body swelled with rage as I pushed him to his breaking point.

"Get back in the car," he growled.

I couldn't move my feet. Regretting my words, I wanted to apologize, but didn't know how. He regarded it as a sign of rebellion and snapped.

Jake gripped my arm, making me yelp, and manhandled me toward the Explorer. Out of the corner of my eye, I caught a glimpse of Junior standing under a security light in the parking lot of his diner, watching the entire scene. He grinned at me and stepped back into the shadows.

"That's right, bubba," the young man in the drive-through yelled out. "You show that bitch who's the boss!"

Jake glared at him. "Shut up, dick!"

. . .

He was silent on the way home, spending half the drive

gripping the steering wheel with such pressure I was sure he'd break his knuckles.

A hard lump formed in my throat, forcing me to choke on any words of apology that wanted to make their presence known. *I shouldn't have let things get so out of hand.* I felt terrible about implying his friends and family were uneducated hicks, especially since they'd been nothing but kind to me. He was never going to forgive me. It would serve me right if he abandoned me on the side of the road.

Jake pulled off onto the shoulder and stopped the car. Oh, shit. Was that what he was doing?

"Stay here," Jake ordered, his voice calmer than before.

I nodded and stared out the window. Jake walked around the back of the Explorer, crossed the ditch, and disappeared into the forest. He probably planned on leaving me here alone and never coming back. I'd never be able to find my way back to his uncle's house on my own. Hell, I'd be lucky if I made it back to the highway.

A minute later, Jake stepped out of the trees and walked back to the car. Once he got back in, I asked him, "Checking to see if someone followed us?"

"No, I took a leak."

"Oh."

He let his eyes rest on me for a moment. "I want to talk about what happened before we get home."

"Jake, I don't want to fight." I propped my head against the seat. "I'm sorry about what I said, all of it. I didn't mean any of it, and I don't know why I reacted poorly. I just thought—"

"You thought this was a date." He didn't form it as a question.

My cheeks felt feverish as the embarrassment and fear of rejection pressed forward, but I didn't answer him. I couldn't bring myself to admit I read into it more than he did.

"I didn't understand why you were mad, but it's because you weren't mad," Jake said sympathetically. "You were hurt."

I didn't want him to know how foolish I felt. "No, I was mad."

"No, Emily, you got hurt and *that* is what made you mad. There's a difference. You don't lie down and die when you get hurt like most people. You come out swinging." He smiled and his eyes glittered in the darkness. "I didn't mean to hurt your feelings. I care about—"

My head snapped toward him. "Don't say things you don't mean."

He reached for my hand and pulled it into his. "Damn it, Emily, I do care. As much as I don't want to, I do." He gazed deeply into my eyes. "You infuriate me more than anyone ever has, but for some strange reason, I keep coming back for more."

I shook my head. "Jake, do you expect me to believe that? You left me in the pond to get eaten by Charlie."

"He wasn't going to eat you. I wouldn't have let it happen. If I thought for one second you were in any danger, I would've gotten you out."

Jake sounded sincere, but I still had to wonder. "You also said it didn't bother you that Cowboy hit on me."

"It doesn't." Jake chuckled at my puzzled expression. "Look, it's the way he is. I'm used to it. He's a womanizer, but he's one of my best friends. I trust him. Even if I didn't, he doesn't want to get into a pissing match with me because he knows he'd lose. Besides, I trust you. Though we haven't labeled this thing between us, I think our intentions are clear."

"And Bobbie Jo?"

Now it was his turn to look puzzled. "What about her?"

"Cowboy said you two dated in high school."

"That was a long time ago. We're just friends now."

"But you took her virginity."

His head snapped back to me, surprised I knew as much. "Yes. And she took mine. So what?"

I shrugged. "I'm not a virgin, Jake."

He lifted his eyebrows at me. "Good thing, because I'm not either."

"Very funny. I'm being serious here. She gave you something…well, I can't give you that. I'm sure it still means something."

Jake coiled his fingers around mine and squeezed. "Look, two virgins having sex—when neither knew what they were doing—was awkward and clumsy, not romantic. Trust me, it's an experience I'd love to forget, not repeat."

"I think some people have a different view on those things," I said. "Women, especially. They don't forget their first time."

"So should I worry about the guy who took your virginity?"

"Oh God, no," I said with disgust. "Don't be silly."

He ruffled my hair on top of my head, like I was a child. "We'll talk more later. We need to get back to the house. Floss is saving dinner for us."

Jake let go of my hand and shifted the car into drive. I rested my hand in my lap, but he reached for it again. He held it as he drove us home.

"I'm going to go to bed earlier from now on," Jake said, grinning. "Fighting with you is exhausting."

Chapter Ten

After dinner, Hank and Floss invited us to sit with them downstairs around the fire. I thought they had more trash to burn, but was pleasantly surprised when Hank lit a fire using actual logs from a dead tree Jake had cut down earlier in the day.

"So, Emily," Hank began, "What'd you think of dinner?"

I smiled. "It was…interesting. When Jake said we were having pie for dinner, I thought I'd died and went to heaven."

"I didn't say pie, I said Frito pie. You have selective hearing," Jake said.

The memory of Floss slicing down the side of a grab bag of corn chips, then adding canned chili, grated cheese, and diced onions was comical. Jake had handed me a spoon and the meal-in-a-bag and said, "Don't make that face. Try it. You'll see." He's lucky I'm adventurous, and I'm lucky it tasted better than it looked.

"I'll never look at a bag of Fritos the same way," I told

them.

Floss reached into a paper bag she had brought with her from the house. "Ready for dessert?"

"Is it pie?" I asked, making them chuckle.

"Roasted marshmallows," Floss said, turning her attention to her husband. "Hank, we need some utensils."

"I'm on it," he responded.

Hank walked around, his eyes searching the ground, until he found four long, thin branches. He returned to his chair, flipped open his pocketknife, and scraped the bark off the end of each stick. Then he passed them out.

Jake put a large marshmallow on the end of my stick for me. "You know how to do it?"

"Is there a trick to it?"

"Depends on how you want it. Slightly warm or scorching hot?"

I leaned toward him and whispered, "Are we still talking about marshmallows?"

He grinned as he turned his marshmallow in the flame, caught it on fire, then brought it to his lips to blow it out. "With you? Somehow I doubt it."

A while later, Hank and Floss retreated upstairs, leaving Jake and I to finish off the bag of marshmallows.

I held my stick out over the fire and watched the flames lick the underside until a hot flash caught hold and wilted my marshmallow into a black, boiling blob. Quickly, I vanquished the flame with my breath, but continued to blow on it to cool it down. Jake watched as I pulled the blackened marshmallow off the end of my stick, held it between two fingers, and took a bite. It was hot and gooey on the inside and melted onto my fingers. I licked the white ooze from my sticky lips.

He watched. He waited. Hell, I think he jotted down mental notes. "Are you enjoying yourself?" Jake asked, uncomfortably readjusting his sitting position.

"Mmmm." The sound effect was more for him than the marshmallow. "Uh-huh."

His smile melted me, as if he had skewered me and held me over an open flame. "Keep poking the bear, and one day the bear is going to poke back," he warned.

"I'm counting on it."

With a giggle, I rose to throw my stick into the fire and caught a glimpse of something in the back pasture. Hundreds of emerald-green twinkling lights danced around a wooded-themed ballroom made up of shadowy trees and glistening pond algae. I watched in amazement as the uninvited guests danced around the forest floor uninterrupted.

"Ready to go inside?" Jake asked.

"Not yet. Just a few more minutes. I'm watching the fireflies light up the pasture. They're different from the ones in the Midwest."

"Southerners usually call them lightning bugs."

"Well, it comes to my attention your lightning bugs have asses that glow green, whereas our fireflies glow yellow. Strange, huh?"

"I'd rather have your attention elsewhere at the moment." Jake grabbed my waist and pulled me into his lap.

"Well, well. What brought this on? You're awfully playful tonight. I should fight with you more often."

He tightened his grip and rested his head against mine. "I've wanted to hold you like this for a while now. Is that all right?"

"Just an observation. I'm not complaining."

The fire dwindled on its own, though I barely noticed anything other than Jake holding me in his arms, stroking my hair lightly between his fingers. It should've been pleasant. It was pleasant. But part of me wanted him to stop, and I didn't know why. Then it hit me.

My vision blurred, misting over with sorrow. I turned my head away to keep him from seeing the tears, but it was too late. He placed one finger under my chin, gently coaxing my face back to his. "What's wrong?"

I couldn't talk. I didn't even try to, which worried Jake more. I buried my face into his shoulder. Sobs exploded from my chest, shaking me from the inside out.

Alarmed by my sudden crying jag, Jake's body tensed under mine. He held me, rubbing my back with gentle, soothing hands. "Emily…?"

I clutched at his shoulders, holding myself closer, as I got myself under control. "I-I'm sorry."

"It's okay." Jake pushed a strand of my hair back, tucking it behind my ear. "Tell me why you're upset. Is it about earlier?"

If I could've folded myself up small enough, I would've crawled into his pocket to hide from the embarrassment. I blew out a deep breath. "No. It's…how you're holding me. It reminded me of…someone else."

Hurt and anger flashed in his eyes. "Who?"

"The last man who held me…" I swallowed hard, trying to keep my voice even. "He wrapped me in his arms and had these big hands that stroked across the back of my hair…"

"I don't want to hear about you with some other guy."

"No, you don't understand, Jake. He was a grown man,

and I was only fourteen."

"Fourteen? Are you saying he raped—"

"Oh God, no! Nothing like that. Nothing sexual about it."

Jake was confused. "What, then?"

"He was the policeman who told me my parents died." A tear squeezed out and rolled down my cheek.

"Emily—"

"Wait. Let me finish." I sucked in a deep breath to maintain control of the pressure building in my chest. "That policeman showed me compassion and kindness, letting me cry until I thought I'd die myself. He never asked me to stop, or be brave, or anything else I imagine you'd tell a young girl who had lost her parents. He wrapped his arms around me and didn't let go. I had no one else, Jake, but he didn't let go. He promised everything would be okay, and I believed him. Then Child Protective Services showed up and practically tore me from his arms. But no matter what, he wouldn't let go. Another officer held him down and pried his fingers off my wrists. They shoved me in a car, kicking and screaming. He fought to get to me, but they drove me away."

"He was a friend of your parents?"

"No."

"Had you ever met him before?"

"No."

"Emily, did you even know his name?"

"No, Jake."

His eyebrows knitted together. "I don't understand. Why did he not want to let go? You were strangers."

I cleared my throat and looked directly into Jake's eyes. "The night I met you, I felt something. A connection between us."

"Yeah, I thought so, too. But what does it have to do with—"

"When that policeman came to talk to me, we had an instant connection. I didn't know what it was at the time. His partner held him down as they yanked me away. He kept telling him *'She's not your daughter.'* I remembered hearing about a cop's daughter who died a few weeks before. She was close to my age, but I don't believe we went to the same school. Afterward, I knew why he'd reacted the way he did and why I felt connected to him. We both were grieving for the family we'd lost."

Jake shook his head in disgust. "Just to have him ripped away, too. Jesus. No wonder you have a hard time trusting people."

"I didn't want to ever let anybody else get close to me again. Somehow, Dale and Gina snuck under my radar. Still, I kept them at arm's length. They asked me to move in with them, but I couldn't. I'm afraid to let them in, though they're my best friends. It's why I couldn't say good-bye. I can't stand the thought of losing anybody else, including you."

"I'm not going anywhere."

It was now time to fess up to the embarrassing part, the part I never thought I'd have to explain to anybody. "I know it's going to sound stupid, but there's a reason I keep forcing the sex issue."

Jake looked at me with an intrigued expression.

"I wanted it to be sex, and only sex, between us. Keeps it impersonal, allows me to stay detached, and…"

"Easier to walk away?" Jake guessed.

I nodded. "I don't sleep with just anyone. In fact, there

haven't been many. I can still count them on one hand," I said, giving him a weak smile.

Jake smiled back. "That doesn't matter to me."

"Well, it matters to *me*," I said, sitting up straighter in his lap, with a tight laugh. "I bet you can't count your partners on one hand."

Jake raised an eyebrow.

"Two hands?"

"How about I see your two hands and raise you a foot?"

"Why so many?"

He shrugged. "Men are despicable creatures."

I managed to laugh. "Trying to make me feel better?"

"Is it working?"

"Yes," I said, yawning. "I'm tired. We should get ready for bed." I climbed off his lap and walked toward the cottage.

"Hey, Emily," Jake called. "So about this whole promiscuous act…"

"You thought I was promiscuous?"

He shuffled his feet nervously. "Well, yeah…uh, no… shit. Forget it."

"Jake, I'm not a slut because once in my life I wanted to shag a hot stranger. Jesus. I do have morals."

He smiled wide. "You think I'm hot?"

That's all he got from what I said? *Guess I'm not the only one with selective hearing.*

• • •

Jake stood behind me, trailing his hands slowly down my arms as his stubble scoured my shoulder. His warm breath blew onto my neck. I felt his hard-on pressing into me from behind.

My hands shook, and though I closed my eyes, I was unable to concentrate. With his every touch, I vied for control of my senses. His hand-eye coordination was much better than mine, but that only comes with experience. And I didn't have much.

"Maybe we should wait," I whispered to Jake.

"Grab it, Emily."

I wrapped my hand around it, feeling the textured ridges under my fingertips as my pulse raced. "Now what?"

"Open your eyes."

Laughter escalated from behind us. I opened my eyes to toss Cowboy, Ox, and Judd a go-to-hell look.

"Ignore them," Jake said. "Concentrate on the target."

"I can't concentrate when you're this close."

Jake's cheek rose against mine. The jerk was smiling. I guess no one deemed this serious, except me. I stepped away, lowered the small .22 caliber pistol he had given me from his ankle holster, and gave him a withering stare.

Jake pulled out the 9mm semi-automatic pistol resting in his shoulder holster. "Want me to demonstrate again?" He pointed it at the hay-stuffed scarecrow he nailed up on the tree thirty-five yards away. I prepared for my body to flinch the way it did every time he pulled the trigger. For me, gunfire didn't hold pleasant memories.

"Hold on, Jake." Hank walked up and leaned against the wooden fence post. "I need you to drive to the feed store and pick up the order I called in."

Jake stepped over to him and lowered his voice. "I can't leave her alone that long. I'll be too far away if something happens."

Hank looked insulted. "What am I, chopped liver?"

"I'll send the boys in my place. It's going to take me all day to teach Emily how to shoot. We've been out here half an hour already, and I just now got her to hold the gun."

"I'll work with her while you're gone," Hank offered. "It'll take an hour for you to get back. She'll be shooting like a professional by then."

"The boys won't mind. They have nothing better to do."

"I didn't ask your opinion, Jake. That was an order."

"But I—"

"Son, unless you want me to jam that 9mm of yours up your ass and kick off the handle, I suggest you get going."

Jake knew better than to hang around any longer. He and the boys loaded into the pickup truck and shot down the driveway without another word. When Hank says jump, you shut your mouth and put your parachute on.

"Was there any particular reason you didn't want Jake teaching me how to use a weapon?"

"Yep."

I scowled at him. "It's not one of those male bravado things about women shooting guns, is it?"

"Honey, my wife shoots better than most men I know." He stepped over to me and smirked. "That boy tried to teach you how to use his weapon, all right. But it had nothing to do with the gun in your hand. If I'm going to get any work out of Jake, then I thought it best I step in before his so-called private lessons got any more explicit than the tent in his pants."

"Oh God." My cheeks reddened.

"I'd go to church to pray for you both, but I doubt it'll help your situation any," Hank added with a laugh. "Now let's get to work. I'm going to give you a crash course in target practice. Before long, you'll be outshooting Jake."

"But Jake hits the bull's-eye nearly every time he shoots."

"Then he's almost as good as me," Hank said.

"Okay, what do I do?"

"Point, shoot, and hope for the best."

"I thought you said I'd be shooting like a professional in an hour?"

"The hour's not up, honey. It's easy. Point and shoot. You can't mess this up," Hank said, watching as I lifted the gun and aimed. "Wait, that's not how you do it."

By the time the boys came back, Hank and I were sitting in the shade drinking some iced tea Floss had brought down. I was more confident with the gun and wasn't flinching anymore at the sound.

Jake strolled up with an acidic grin on his face. "We were going to unload the truck first, to give you some extra time to practice, but since you don't seem to need it…" he trailed off. "I want to see what you got."

That prompted a chuckle from Hank. "She's a natural. Damn good shot."

"Emily can't hit the broad side of a barn," Jake said, grinning at the other men. "In fact, I'll bet fifty dollars she can't hit the scarecrow in three shots or less."

"So you're a betting man now, are you, Jake?" Hank asked, eyeing them all. "Any of you other boys want to get in on the action?"

Unreassuringly, they all jumped at the chance to bet against me.

"Can't wait to see this," Jake said, walking ahead toward

the target with his tight-knit group. They chuckled and bumped fists in a show of macho posturing.

It made me regret letting Hank bet on me. "Hank, I appreciate what you're doing, but you know you're about to lose some money, right?"

"Emily, I have faith in you. Get your adrenaline pumping and focus. It'll be like second nature. You're the minority, and you have a temper. It won't take long before these guys light a spark under you. You'll do fine."

Once I was standing there, lining my sights on the target, I knew Hank was on the wrong side of the betting pool. The pressure of performing like a seal with a ball on my nose got to me.

Jake glared at me, waiting for me to mess up my first shot, which wouldn't be a problem since I was genetically programmed to short circuit around him. It didn't help that the others heckled me.

I squeezed the trigger gently, and my first shot went wild, not coming close to my target. All the boys laughed.

"There's one," Jake said.

"Glad you can count," I replied icily.

When I shot for the second time, a piece of the bark flew off the tree, but the scarecrow remained untouched.

Jake had a smile plastered on his face. "There's two. Maybe Hank should've made a sticker chart for you."

"At least I hit the damn tree. He said the more I practice, the better I'll get," I said, shrugging off his comment.

"Or the luckier she gets," Jake muttered to the guys, making them laugh more.

"You're all a bunch of comedians, aren't you? I've been shooting for only an hour. Heaven forbid you pass a compliment my way. It's nerve-wracking enough shooting while you're all staring at me as if I were standing here in my underwear."

Cowboy spoke up. "Darlin', if you were in your underwear, none of us would *care* if you hit the target. Hell, I doubt we'd even notice you missed. Might be worth fifty bucks to watch you shoot in your panties."

The male chauvinist attitude pissed me off. Call me oversensitive, but their remarks left me motivated to hit my target more than ever. On a whim, I lifted the gun, barely aimed, and squeezed off another round, working more on instincts.

My third shot hit the scarecrow in the crotch, blowing a hole in the target's pants. All of the men winced and let out a collective groan. I doubted it had anything to do with the money they'd lost.

Hank walked up, tickled with my shot, and slapped Jake on the back. "That girl sure knows how to twist the knife, doesn't she?"

"Jake, maybe you should get Emily to show you a few things about shooting," Judd said, laughing. "She must have a knack for it if she can make a shot like that."

I smiled proudly at my win. Men are such pushovers.

Cowboy, Judd, and Ox all dug out their wallets and slapped cash into Hank's hand. Jake was the only one who hadn't paid up. He reviewed the target, probably wondering how I made that shot. Hell, I wondered the same thing.

I couldn't help but gloat, though. "Man up, Jake. It's not every day you get shown up by a girl."

Jake was irritable, but I never expected him to react the way he did. He pulled the 9mm out of his shoulder holster and unloaded the entire clip into the scarecrow. Apparently,

I wasn't the only one with a temper. About three seconds after he put away his gun, the scarecrow fell off the tree. Show-off.

He grabbed the gun from my hand and shoved it into the waistband of my shorts. "Keep this somewhere accessible in case you need it."

I didn't like the feeling of a loaded weapon pointed at my crotch. At least not one of the metal variety. "You think my pants are accessible?"

"For the gun, no. For me? Oh, yeah." He grinned, then walked over and handed Hank fifty dollars from his back pocket.

Hank pocketed his money. "As lucky as that girl is, we should take her with us in the morning."

Jake gave him a *yeah, right* look. "Emily? Hunting? You're kidding, right?"

His comment bugged the crap out of me. It was bad enough he'd called me promiscuous. He was lucky I didn't shoot him for that alone. Now, I had a good mind to pistol whip the bastard. No need, though. Jake had given me all the ammo I needed to get even. So he doesn't want me to go hunting and thinks my pants are accessible, huh?

We'll see about that.

· · ·

Jake slid under the covers. "You're not going. End of discussion."

"I *am* going. Hank said I could."

"And how did you talk him into that?"

"By winning him two hundred dollars in your stupid bet. Guess he felt like he owed me. What does it matter? You said yourself that you should be close by if something happens."

"I'm not going to be far," Jake said. "Floss will be here, and she knows how to shoot a gun. Besides, no one will find you here. It's the last place they'd look. You're safe here."

"Maybe, maybe not."

"You're still not going," Jake said, glaring at me.

"We'll see what Hank says about that. Of course, it might hurt when he kicks the handle off your gun while it's in your ass."

Jake clenched his teeth. "Stop being pigheaded. Why would you want to go sit in a deer blind? It's not going to be any fun."

"Oh, I don't know about that," I said with a wicked grin. I was having lots of fun annoying the hell out of Jake right now. "Besides, it'll break up the monotony."

"Are you going just to irritate me?"

"Who, me?"

Jake looked exasperated. "You're getting even with me about earlier today."

Before he could catch me smiling, I rolled away from him and flipped off the bedside lamp, plunging us into total darkness. "I don't know what you're talking about."

There was a moment of silence.

"You're going to get cold and end up snuggled up to me in the middle of the night. Might as well come over here now."

My heart skipped a beat, but I stayed put. "No thanks."

"Want me to spoon with you instead?"

I held the mattress in a death grip, forcing myself to stay on my own side of the bed. My attempts at torturing Jake had mixed results. I needed to rewire my own brain to alter its responses to him if I was going to have any luck driving him crazy.

"That's okay. I'm fine," I lied.

Jake sat upright in bed. "Okay, what's wrong with you?"

"What do you mean?"

"I'm waiting for one of your snide sexual remarks."

"Too tired. Plus, we have to get up in a few hours. Maybe tomorrow night I'll feel up to it."

I couldn't see him, but I imagined him glaring at the back of my head with brows furrowed into the bridge of his nose and his mouth tightened into a thin straight line. If anything, his silence reeked of confusion. It surprised me how fast he gave up and lay back down.

After admitting he cared for me, I was positive he'd become the sexual aggressor. I hadn't counted on Jake's resilience and patience, as well as my lack thereof. To drive him bonkers, I'd have to rethink my strategy and start baiting him to keep him involved, like a sexual game of tag.

"Oh, Jake…" I paused for a moment. "Did I ever tell you I don't have a gag reflex?"

He groaned. "Damn it, Emily. You make it hard to be a gentleman sometimes."

Gotcha! You're it.

Chapter Eleven

Okay, maybe it wasn't such a great idea after all. What moron gets up at five o'clock in the morning to go hunting? Me, that's who. And I only did it to get Jake's goat. If I was smart, I would've let him keep his damn goat and gone back to bed.

"That's not camouflage," Jake said.

I looked down at the T-shirt I got from Junior's daughter. "What do you mean?"

"It's pink."

"So. It still has the same pattern as your shirt does."

"Yeah, but mine is the color of dirt and leaves. Only thing you're going to blend in with is a piece of bubble gum. Here, wear this." Jake peeled off the long sleeve camouflage shirt he wore over a black T-shirt. He put it on me as his uncle came out of the house.

I pointed to Hank's bright orange hat. "Why does he get to wear color, and I don't?"

Jake glanced over at his uncle and shook his head. "Because

his hat is that color for safety reasons. He won't get mistaken for an animal and accidentally shot walking through the woods."

I slid Jake's shirt off and tossed it back to him. "Well, unless someone is hunting bubble gum, then I should be fairly safe."

Jake grunted, glaring at Hank. "You said she could come; you get to deal with her." Then he grabbed a flashlight and stomped off toward the back of the property.

"Who crapped in his oatmeal this morning?" Hank asked.

"I guess that would be me."

Hank grinned and turned on his own flashlight. "Let's go."

We caught up to Jake on the back side of the pasture near the barbed wire fence. Jake pushed the bottom wires down with the weight of his boot and picked up the top wire to create an opening. Hank went through first and I followed, before turning to watch Hank do the same for Jake.

Jake led the way on the walking trail with his rifle leaned over his left shoulder as we followed. Hank kept his rifle in his left hand, opposite of me, and pointed to the ground. "You need to keep watch for wild hogs," Hank warned me. "They hang out near the deer feeders usually, but we sometimes cross them on the trails. They're dangerous."

"A pig, dangerous? You're kidding, right?"

"These aren't domesticated pigs. They're wild hogs. Mean little bastards. They'll rip you open with their tusks if they get a chance. I'm not kidding about that. I've got an eight-inch long scar on my calf to prove it."

"I thought we were supposed to be the hunters. Now you're telling me the animals can attack us?"

Hank chuckled. "Anytime you corner an animal, you run the risk of it turning on you." He shot a look at Jake's back. "Same goes for people."

"Another pearl of wisdom?"

"An observation," Hank corrected.

"Good eyes."

The trail ended, and we walked through the long, deep grass until the sticky ground got mushier where it had rained earlier in the night. Hank told Jake to cut through the scrub brush to avoid the mud, then sandwiched me in between them. I followed Jake's flashlight as he cleared the path ahead.

After a few minutes, Hank tapped me on the shoulder. "Emily, do you know what they call a bunch of deer?"

"Herd."

"Heard what?" Hank said, grinning at his dumb joke. "You know what you call a deer with no eyes?" Hank asked, pushing through the brush behind me as I shrugged. "No-eye deer," he said in a corny voice and then chuckled.

I laughed at that one, and Jake shot us an ugly look. "If you two don't zip it, you're going to scare off everything within a ten mile radius."

"Put a lid on it, Jake." Authority colored Hank's tone, and Jake wasn't dumb enough to push the issue. We walked in silence the rest of the way.

The deer blind—a green wooden structure with rectangles cut out for windows—was elevated off the ground and had a ladder attached. Jake climbed up, opened the door, and shined his flashlight inside.

"All clear," he said, knocking a cobweb away from the door.

"You two go on in," Hank said. "My neighbor isn't hunting this morning. I'm going to go over and sit in his deer blind. Bubba said he didn't mind."

"When did you talk to Bubba?" Jake asked.

"Last night." Hank grinned and turned to walk away. "I'll be back for you two around nine o'clock."

Jake shook his head with disgust and motioned for me to climb up the ladder. Silently, I did as asked. Once inside, Jake slid an upside down milk crate over to me and plopped down on one himself. He leaned the rifle in the corner and propped open two of the hinged windows, letting in the slight breeze and a small amount of blue morning light.

"What's the deal with Hank?" I asked.

"The old man doesn't know how to leave well enough alone. I guess he thought we needed some alone time."

"What kind of *alone* time?"

"The kind when there isn't another person around," Jake said, unable to keep from smirking.

"You've got to be kidding." Hard to believe Hank considered a shoddy, musty-smelling box in the middle of the woods romantic.

"If you keep talking, we won't see anything. Sound carries, and the deer spook easily." Jake checked his watch. "The feeder's on a timer. We've got twenty minutes before it starts throwing corn."

We sat in silence—boring, painful silence—until we heard the whir of a machine in the distance as the feeder dropped corn. Deer must have a built-in clock because moments later Jake put his fingers to his lips and motioned for me to look out the window.

A small white-tailed buck with a modest rack approached

the feeder, peacefully nibbling the corn beneath his feet. A doe trotted up behind him. I watched them for a few minutes, but my legs fell asleep from the way I squatted near the window. I reached for my milk crate and slid it closer, grating it across the wooden floor. The noise was enough to scare off our company.

Jake gave me a stern look, but all I could do was shrug and mouth "sorry" to him. I settled in next to the window and picked dry mud out of my sneakers with a twig. I practically fell asleep leaning against the wall when Jake touched my arm and whispered, "Deer."

I swept my eyes back and forth over the area. "Where?" I whispered. "I don't see a deer."

"To the left of the feeder, standing on the other side of the bushes."

Either Jake lost his mind or I was gullible. Probably the latter, but I still didn't see anything. Jake grabbed the rifle and carefully stuck it out the window. He peered through the scope until he found what he was looking for and then held the gun steady for me. "Look through the scope. You'll see him."

Seconds later, I caught the movement of brown fur through the thick cover of greenery. A large buck with an impressive display of antlers stepped out from behind the bushes and into the open area beyond the feeder. Alert, he stopped and lifted his large head, turning it back and forth and twitching his ears as he listened for danger. His nostrils flared, taking in the surrounding scents, before he shook his head and went back to grazing.

I pulled my eye back from the scope and tried to give the gun back to Jake, but he shook his head. "He's all yours."

"Damn it, Jake. He's not going to stand still and let me shoot three times before he runs," I said in a low voice. "You do it."

"Man up," Jake whispered, grinning from ear to ear. "Isn't that what you told me? Now it's your turn."

I don't know why I always felt like I needed to prove something. "Fine, then. Move over," I whispered back.

I aimed the rifle to the buck and watched him through the scope with a twinge of sorrow. He was divine. Completely unaware of how fragile his life was. How shaky the ground was that he walked on.

It was hard to fathom destroying a majestic creature. Only time I ever thought I'd shoot an animal was when I had a camera in my hands, which of course would be painless for the animal. And for me.

"Aim for the neck, just behind the jawbone, at the base of the ears," Jake told me in a hushed voice. "It'll break his neck bone and drop him where he stands."

"Do I have to keep my eyes open?"

Jake gave me a stern look. "Couldn't hurt."

I steadied the rifle against my shoulder, aimed carefully, and let my finger linger over the trigger. When I glimpsed a movement in the nearby brush, I adjusted a little to the left.

A small nimble doe stepped out into the open and walked toward the buck. A fawn, still covered in spots, pranced up alongside her and the two of them joined the aloof buck in eating the corn.

Not only did I feel sorry for the deer, but I felt like a monster for what I was about to do. Maybe it was a biological response. Or maybe it was my conscience swooping in to complicate matters. Either way, I had a hard time tuning out the voices in my head.

"I can't do it," I said. "I can't pull the trigger."

"Yes, you can. I'll help you." Jake put his finger over mine and I froze.

I peered at the three deer and watched the trusting, innocent fawn dance happily around its mother. My pulse quickened as I trained the rifle on the massive buck that was moments away from falling to the ground with nothing left to show for his life except a fresh, bloody wound.

Don't think about it. Just do it.

But I couldn't because my hands shook. I broke out in hives over my deep-seated guilt complex brought on by my own mortality and attachments to the people I had lost. My dad. My mom. My policeman. All severed from my life by one thoughtless act carried out by someone else. Now, I was that someone else.

Jake steadied the rifle and tightened his finger over mine. "Take a deep breath and let it out as you pull the trigger," he whispered into my ear.

A wave of emotion swept over me as my chest involuntarily swelled with air. I held my breath, keeping it inside, knowing when I let it out Jake would coordinate it with one ruthless pull of the trigger.

It felt like senseless killing, but I couldn't hold my breath any longer. Jake slowly squeezed my finger and the air from my lungs screamed past my lips. The crack of the rifle drowned me out as I felt the power under my hands and against my shoulder. Jake fell backward in shock but recovered in time to see what I was looking at. With a flash of their white tails, the three deer scattered into the forest.

"What happened? Why did you scream?" Jake asked,

grabbing the rifle and looking out the window for signs of life. When I didn't answer him, he grabbed my shoulders and turned me toward him. "Emily…?"

I didn't want him to know I couldn't do it. If I could concoct a reason for why I screamed, then maybe…he wouldn't have to know. But the tears came. Big traitor tears trailed down my traumatized face, tattling on me for my weakness. I was a wreck.

Jake knew why. "You gotta be shittin' me. Jesus Christ. You're such a girl." He slammed his hand against the plywood wall as he opened the door and jumped out, letting the door swing shut behind him.

I watched from the window as he threw a dead branch and kicked into the air, blowing off steam. It was an inappropriately handled and irrational display of male arrogance, but I had predicted this reaction.

Jake was a man's man, one accustomed to being the master of his domain. He wanted control—to be the one in the driver's seat—but I pulled relentlessly at his wheel. Even while he patiently colored inside the lines, I consistently scribbled outside them. He needed rules to keep his life balanced, but my reckless, unpredictable behavior constantly tipped the scales.

When the door opened, I wiped at my runny nose and tried to stop the sniffling, but a dry heave shivered across my shoulders. Jake kneeled beside me, but I couldn't look at him.

"Emily…?"

Shit. I knew this was coming.

"Look at me."

"No."

I stayed put, but Jake touched his hand to my cheek and turned my face toward his. He took in the sight of me, which was probably pretty rough. "Oh, hell. I'd like to choke you."

"Why don't you, then?"

"Because I'd rather do this," he said, placing his mouth over mine.

The potency of his kiss threw my senses off, making me tingle from head to toe as my breath bottomed out. He was kindling for me — one tiny spark and I was on fire. His tongue explored my mouth, feeding the flames growing inside me, burning me from the inside out.

Jake pulled off my pink camouflage shirt, tossed it aside, and his gaze fixated on my breasts as if surprised by my lack of bra. I couldn't take my eyes off him as he touched my neck and ran his hand slowly down my chest, making my breath catch in my throat. He stripped off his open camo shirt and laid it on the ground before maneuvering me onto my back. His shirt separated my soft skin from the hard wooden floor.

Wandering eyes and hands feasted on my exposed skin, taunting me with every touch until I was limp and pliable. The torture was too much. I reached down and unsnapped my jeans, inviting him to go further. He stripped off his black T-shirt, revealing his tanned muscular physique. Making quick work of it, Jake yanked the jeans from my hips and slid them off, along with my shoes. It left me completely nude.

"I'd swear you planned this," he said, grinning.

I shrugged. "It's laundry day." And I never saw much point in wearing only half my underwear. After all, isn't that why they make matching bras and panties?

Jake leaned over me and put his mouth on my neck while I traced my fingers over the muscles on his back, feeling them bulge and tighten under my grip. He moved up my throat, kissed my chin, then trailed his tongue back into my mouth where the sexual tension between us exploded.

Without words, he kneed my thighs apart and fumbled with the button on his jeans. Then he stopped. A pained expression seized his face. "Damn it," he whispered, looking at his watch. "Hank's back early."

"How do you know?"

"I can hear him whistling in the distance." Jake shoved my clothes at me. "Hurry and get dressed."

We slithered back into our clothes as quickly as possible and made it outside as Hank walked up. We were both still rearranging and smoothing, making sure our clothing was in order. I could imagine how bad it looked.

"I heard the gun shot. You two get any action?"

Hank caught the uncomfortable look Jake and I exchanged, and although he didn't say anything, he barely kept a straight face. I'd swear he'd done it on purpose.

"Don't ask," Jake grumbled.

• • •

At dinner, Floss announced she'd invited some of the neighbors for a barbecue the next afternoon. The idea of being around new people excited me, like a prisoner allowed her first visitors. Or maybe it was more like I was given privileges after serving time with good behavior. Okay, that was pushing it.

It was supposed to be potluck, but Floss still had a list of foods she wanted to prepare. Ox and Judd volunteered to set up tables and chairs downstairs, Cowboy offered to clean the pool, Jake would mow using the tractor, and Hank would fire up the large barrel smoker he had proudly welded himself.

"Well, what about me? What can I do to help?"

Floss smiled. "You can pitch in anywhere you see fit."

It was barely a step above "stand around and look pretty," but I accepted it. No one thought I could do anything right. I may not be a country girl, but at least I tried to help. Floss wasn't trying to hurt my feelings, but I still wanted an E for effort.

I swallowed another bite of my dinner and smiled. "I've never been one for stew, but this chicken is great, Floss." All three of them looked up from their bowls and stared. "What? Do I have food on my face or something?"

"Never seen a chicken with four legs before," Hank said.

A surge of panic shot through me. "What the hell am I eating, then?"

They chuckled as Jake wiped his mouth with a napkin. "Rabbit stew. It's good, right? Want some more?"

I pushed my bowl away. "I'm full, thank you." My legs shook as I weakly stumbled toward the front door.

Jake yelled out after me. "Mind over matter, Emily! If you don't mind, it don't matter." And the three of them laughed some more.

Nauseated, I could've easily crawled into bed and gone to sleep, but I had to check something first. I was tired, but there was no way I'd be able to go to sleep without knowing. I grabbed a flashlight and headed for the backside of the barn.

Halfway there, I heard the front door open on the main house. Jake was probably heading to the cottage. He'd be surprised when he realized I wasn't there and hadn't told him where I went. Good. I smiled, thinking how it served him right. Let him worry for five minutes. It won't kill him.

Approaching the cage, Jack hopped around gleefully at the sight of me, hoping for a carrot. Twitcher stayed in the back corner, sizing me up and growling like a guard dog. I was relieved Jack was okay, though Twitcher stew wouldn't have bothered me much.

Jake's voice came from behind me. "I knew you'd be out here."

I shone my flashlight on his face on purpose as he shielded his eyes with his hand. "Congratulations, Scooby. I guess you solved the mystery."

"You're mad?"

I sighed. "I'm too tired to be mad. And it was good stew, before I realized we were eating bunnies."

Back at the cottage, we stepped over the lifeless dog on the porch and went inside. I collapsed onto the edge of the bed and pulled off my shoes. Jake stood at the door, watching. As soon as my shoes hit the floor, he moved forward and leaned over me, as if his body were willing mine to lie back on the bed.

Jake's eyes were expressive, his face intense. "We have unfinished business," he said, crawling onto the bed and overwhelming me with his presence. I moved farther back, but he followed. "So how tired are you?" he asked in a hushed voice, his face close to mine.

My brain turned to mush. "W-who said I was tired?"

The corners of his mouth lifted slightly. He leaned into my hair and nibbled my ear. "You did," he said, breathing on my neck.

Chills ran over my skin. "Well, I was wrong."

Jake stopped kissing my neck. "So far, that's the sexiest thing I've heard you say."

Jake placed his mouth over mine. His warm hands worked their way under the edge of my T-shirt. He trailed them to my breasts, molding and cupping them in his palms. I was practically purring by the time he pulled away and told me to lift my arms, snatching the shirt from my body. He held my wrists above my head.

I leaned up slightly and kissed his neck, trailing my tongue softly along his throat and kissing down his jawbone.

He grunted at first and squeezed my wrists tighter, but then got quieter. "Uh...Emily..."

I groaned. "If you stop this now, I'm never going to forgive you." He closed his eyes, and I got the hint. "Jake, you've got to be kidding me. Let me guess. You don't have a condom."

"No, that's not the problem."

God only knew what was going through his mind. "Then what?"

"You aren't going to freak out, are you?"

"Why would I freak out?"

"Because you have a tick embedded into your armpit."

"What?" I jumped up, screaming. "Get it off me! Oh God, get it off!"

Jake chased me around the room until I stopped moving. Then I did the gross-out dance, where your feet run in place and you shake your hands constantly. As if it does any good.

He ran into the bathroom and got some tweezers. "Hold still, Emily. The head is still inside you. I have to pull it out carefully."

Once he removed it, he threw it in the toilet and flushed it, while I gagged.

"Thought you said you didn't have a gag reflex?" Jake said, laughing.

"I lied," I said, dry heaving again. "That's sooo disgusting!"

Someone knocked on the cottage door. "Hey, Jake?"

Jake went to the door while I pulled out some alcohol and sterilized my armpit. But I overheard the conversation at the front door. "Yeah, Hank," Jake said, opening the door.

"Is everything okay? I was lugging some trash down to the burn pit and heard Emily screaming."

"She's fine. She had a—"

"That's okay, son. I don't want to know what the two of you were doing. Some things are better left unsaid."

Jake chuckled as he shut the door. He stepped back into the room where I lay curled on the bed in my robe, holding my stomach. "You okay?"

"No. I don't feel good. I feel…contaminated."

Jake smiled. "Didn't you check yourself for ticks when you took a shower after hunting this morning?"

"I didn't know I was supposed to."

Jake rubbed at his face and sat on the bed. "Come here and put your head in my lap. I want to check your scalp to be sure you don't have any more on you."

"Oh God. You think there're more?" My stomach churned as I crawled across the bed and placed my head on his leg, resisting the urge to puke. "Why couldn't I just have carpet burns or something? I'm going to need therapy after this."

Jake poked through my hair, lifting and moving a section at a time. "Stop whining and being melodramatic. You won't need therapy."

"Oh, you don't think so? I had a waxing once that left me needing post-traumatic stress counseling afterward."

Jake laughed and ran his fingers through my hair again, showing off his fine motor skills and making my scalp tingle. His touch was heaven. Soft. Soothing. Sleep inducing.

I slipped out of consciousness and could do nothing to stop it.

Chapter Twelve

I wanted to kick myself.

Why did I have to fall asleep? Stupid. Stupid. Stupid. God, I'm an idiot. Apparently, Jake was too, since he didn't bother waking me. He must've snuggled around me and went off to dreamland himself.

He lay next to me, breathing deeply, all warm and hard. Yep, definitely hard. As easy as it would be to turn in his arms and wake him, I knew Hank would interrupt us soon. That alone made the option unappealing.

With the barbecue this afternoon, it would be a busy morning, though technically, I didn't have anything to do. No one trusted me to handle anything on my own. I guess I'd follow the boys around and try to help with what I could. It embarrassed me that nobody had any faith in me and spoke volumes as to what kind of character they thought I had.

I wanted to show some usefulness but couldn't think of anything to do offhand. Then the idiot rooster started crowing, which gave me an idea. What the hell, it was worth a shot.

Jake didn't feel me leave the bed. I threw on some clothes and quietly scuttled out the door. The sun had barely risen, but I figured Floss was already awake and brewing the coffee. Hank would be up, too, but he was probably still in the bathroom—his early morning ritual.

Close to the barn, something round and dark blocked my path. At first glance, it resembled a pile of horse manure. As I got closer, I realized it was alive and moving. A splotchy black snake with reddish-brown swirls coiled itself into a tight ball, daring me to come closer. I couldn't tell how long it was, but it had the impressive thickness of a banana. I stayed back, sniffing the air, but didn't smell watermelon like Jake had said. Maybe I wasn't close enough, but I wasn't about to get any closer. Either this snake was unscented, or it was of the scratch-and-sniff variety.

My instincts told me to ask for help, but I didn't want any of them to think I couldn't handle the situation on my own. Sure, I *could*. I just didn't necessarily want to. But running to Jake would be the spider-in-the-bathroom incident all over again. He would roll his eyes at me and consider me pathetic.

Nope. I refused to get his help this time. I wanted to prove to him—and myself—I was capable of handling this.

Keeping my eye on the snake, I maneuvered around it at a safe distance and grabbed a shovel from the barn. I distinctly remembered hearing Judd say if you cut off a snake's head it would die. Carefully, I kept my feet and butt pushed back, leaned over, and with a hard jab, I chopped off the snake's head.

Then I ran.

Holy shit! It didn't work at all. The fucking snake was still moving. My God, how is it still alive without its head attached? Snakes must be similar to cockroaches, which can live for days without their heads. Damn you, Judd! The dipshit didn't mention that part.

I searched for another weapon until I spotted a large jug of diesel near the burn pit. Hank used it to burn the trash daily. I remembered where he put the matches, as well, so I grabbed both and ran back to the snake. It continued to toss and turn on the ground, slithering and wrapping around itself.

Staying as far back as I could, I poured diesel on the snake and threw a lit match. The fire caught instantly, but the snake continued to wiggle and squirm. Jesus Christ. What the hell did it take to kill one of these bastards?

Enough was enough. I ran back to the cottage, silently ducked inside, then found myself standing back over the snake with a .22 caliber pistol.

Pow. Pow. Pow.

Even at close range, I hit it only once. The snake rolled, curled onto itself, and finally went completely still. Jake ran out of the cottage, barefoot and shirtless, with a gun in his hand, while Hank and Floss stood on the back porch, grinning.

"What the hell are you doing?" Jake said, panting and staring at the snake's burning corpse. "You scared the shit out of me! I thought some nutcase was out here shooting." He waved his hands in the air angrily. "When I woke up and you weren't in bed, I thought Felts had found you. But I guess my original assumption was correct. A nutcase *was* out here shooting."

"Jake, I was…"

Hank and Floss had made it down the back steps and came over to us. "She killed the shit out of that snake," Hank said, laughing. "Chopped off its head, set it on fire, then shot it."

Jake looked at me as if I were crazy. "A little overkill, don't you think?"

"It wouldn't stop moving."

Hank chuckled again. "They do that, honey. It's their nerves twitching in their bodies. They'll stop after a while."

"What the hell were you doing out here this early, anyway?" Jake asked, his tone still slightly on the rough side.

"I wanted to help Floss by getting the eggs for her this morning. I figured it was the least I could do since nobody thinks I can do anything else. I'm useless and in the way all the time. I went to gather eggs, but ended up stumbling across this snake instead."

"Damn it, Emily, you can't—"

"Now, you watch your tone with her, Jacob Ward." Floss stepped over toward me and glared at him. "Her intentions were good, and that's all that matters."

"But she can't go around shooting—"

Floss raised her hand to shut Jake up. "I've said my piece, and I don't want to hear nothing more about it. Emily, dear, as soon as you can get me those eggs, I'll start breakfast."

I smiled, grateful she'd give me a chance to prove myself. "Coming right up!" I set out for the barn, but Jake grabbed me by the arm to stop me. "What now?"

He held out his hand. "The gun. Unless you plan on using it to get to those eggs?"

I slapped the pistol into his hand, went to the barn to

grab a small bucket, and marched straight for the chicken coop. From the moment I stepped inside, I was on high alert. The rooster huddled with the hens at the back of the pen as I made my way toward the nesting boxes. Like before, the hens scattered and the rooster strutted closer, nonchalantly pecking the ground, puffing out his feathers. From previous experience, I knew this behavior was similar to a dog's warning growl before the actual bite.

But I didn't wait for him to charge. Instead, I reached out, grabbed him by the neck, and slung him away. He jumped to his feet and came back for more. I raised the bucket in warning and yelled, "Rooster, I'll fuck you up!"

He spread his wings wide, flapped them lightly, and then folded them back to his body. Feathers around his neck ruffled as he shook his head and began to groom himself. I kept an eye on him, but he didn't give me any more problems as I filled the bucket with eggs.

When I came out of the chicken coop, I realized I had company. Floss gaped at me in shock, Hank snickered, and Jake shook his head in disbelief. "What?" I asked.

Hank patted my arm, grinning. "Honey, you may have the face of an angel, but that halo of yours is awfully crooked."

. . .

After breakfast, Jake and I followed Hank downstairs to get ready for the barbecue while Floss went to the grocery store. Cowboy, Ox, and Judd showed up soon after.

"Hey, beautiful," Cowboy said, as he took a turn behind Judd and Ox, hugging me and kissing me on the cheek. "Are you helping out?"

"If someone gives me something to do."

"I've got to clean the pool. Think you can handle getting wet?" Cowboy shrugged his eyebrows suggestively, and although his open flirtatiousness didn't surprise me, the look on Jake's face did. He was irritated.

"I don't have a swimsuit."

Cowboy's face broke into a smile. "I don't mind if you—"

"She's helping me today," Jake cut in. "You're on your own with the pool."

"But aren't you mowing with the tractor?" I asked. "How am I supposed to help you with that?" Cowboy, Ox, and Judd waited for Jake's answer as well.

"You're going to learn to drive it."

"What? You wouldn't even let me drive the Explorer," I said, suspiciously. "So what changed?"

Jake smiled lightly. "You said you wanted to do more around here, right? After the initiative you showed this morning, I figured…"

"What'd you do this morning?" Cowboy asked me.

"I choked a chicken."

The boys all laughed, and then Cowboy looked at Jake and said, "You dog!" They threw some fake punches at each other and playfully wrestled into the middle of the yard.

Judd and Ox grinned, but I was flat-out confused. "What'd I say?"

"Choking a chicken is an old slang term. You just told us you performed sexual favors on Jake this morning."

"I wouldn't mind having a girl with that kind of initiative," Judd added.

I couldn't help but laugh at my mistake. "That's not what I meant. Maybe I should've said I bullied a cock into surrendering."

"I'm afraid it doesn't sound much better," Ox said.

"Jacked up a rooster?"

Ox smirked. "The mental image is already there. Sorry, no dice."

I laughed. "I set a snake on fire."

"Damn, girl! What *did* you two do in bed this morning?"

"Let's just say I got up really early," I replied.

Jake broke apart from Cowboy and headed for the tractor next to the barn. He motioned for me to follow. Jake said the tractor was a 1953 Ford Jubilee, which I guess was supposed to mean something if you knew anything about tractors. Obviously, I didn't. All I saw before me was an old grayish-white tractor with a red belly, big back tires, and a lot of rust.

I watched as Jake climbed into the seat. "Where am I supposed to sit?"

He leaned on the steering wheel, with his mirrored aviator sunglasses pulled down over his eyes. He looked hot, but it had nothing to do with the sun or the heat. "God made laps for a reason." Jake said, grinning.

He offered me his hand, and I climbed into his lap as Hank came out of the barn. "Jake, when you're done mowing, I want you to caulk something for me."

I placed my lips against Jake's ear. "Should I tell him to get in line?"

Jake gave me a stern look. "*C-A-U-L-K*. Get your mind out of the gutter," Jake said. Then he cranked the tractor.

Yeah, like sitting in Jake's vibrating lap would make me think pure thoughts.

...

By lunchtime, Floss had returned and flagged us down to get our attention. She said Hank and the other boys had to run into town to pick up some parts for the pool pump. Floss handed us a basket of goodies she'd packed up and told us to find a shady place for a picnic. She gave me an exaggerated wink before walking away. Floss was my kind of woman.

Jake and I found a breezy spot under a large mesquite tree in the pasture where we could watch the horses graze. He spread a blanket in the patch of shade among the wildflowers and we sat, facing each other, while we ate. Floss had wrapped up some sandwiches, fruit, cookies, and a couple bottles of water.

"I'm surprised she didn't cut our sandwiches into triangles and give us juice boxes," Jake said.

"Oh, I think it's sweet. It reminds me of when my mom made my lunches, except she'd put weird stuff in my lunchbox."

"Such as?"

"Boiled eggs, dinner rolls, and probably the worst one ever, sardines." Jake laughed, so I hit him. "It's not funny. Didn't your mom ever do anything strange?"

He thought for a moment. "Yeah, but I'll have to show you." He leaned off the blanket, plucked a couple of dandelions from the ground, and tucked one into my hair above my ear.

I grinned. "That *is* weird. Did she put pink bows in your hair, too?"

"No, smartass, not that." Jake held the other dandelion and placed it under my chin. "My mom would hold one of these underneath and if the yellow shined on my chin, she'd say *'you like butter.'"*

"What does it mean?"

"Beats the hell out of me," he said, shrugging his shoulders. "I never thought to ask. I guess I figured I had all the time in the world to. I had always pictured her doing the same thing to my children one day. But now that'll never happen." Guilt darkened his gray eyes. "I guess the least I could've done was ask her what it meant."

His regrets pulled at my heartstrings. I knew how he felt. Though I'd had years to come to terms with my parents' deaths, the clouded memories of the past still haunted me. But he reeled from a trauma that happened just last year.

"I'm sorry," Jake said. "I didn't mean to bring up the past."

"It's okay. I liked hearing about your mother."

"Yeah, but it's not fair. You've spent half your life without your parents. Knowing that, I feel bad talking to you about my own."

"I don't mind, Jake."

A noise startled me and I turned my head to see Hank and the three boys unloading some parts from the truck. I guess we were too deep in conversation to hear them pull up, though I don't know how, since they were all whooping and hollering. Then Ox smacked Cowboy on the ass.

"Why am I starting to feel like I'm in one of those cowboy butt-sex movies?"

"Come on," Jake said with a grin. "Let's wrap this up. I think the heat is frying your brain cells."

• • •

Jake didn't have time to bathe before a whole slew of neighbors showed up and cornered him into chatting with them. Since I didn't know anyone, it was easy for me to slink back to the cottage and wash off the stink.

I dressed in a pair of green belted cargo shorts, a white knit top, and my stretch canvas sneakers. My melt-proof makeup consisted of cream blush, mascara, bronzer, and a touch of lip gloss. I finished my hair and had just turned off my flat iron when Jake stepped into the bedroom.

"Where'd you get that thing?" he asked.

"This *thing* is called a flat iron. Floss picked it up for me at a garage sale. She got a good deal on it—two dollars—and it works great."

He picked up a section of my hair and examined it. "I don't get it. Why do girls straighten their hair when it's already straight?"

God, men know nothing. "Do you really want me to explain?"

"Nope," he said, dropping the section of hair. "It was more of a rhetorical question." Jake motioned to the door. "Ready to face the firing squad? Everyone wants to see you."

"See me?"

"Yeah, they all want to get a look at the girl I brought home. You're the first, you know."

"Considering the circumstances under which we came here, I'm not all that flattered."

"I guess I understand, but none of them know about that. They all still think you're my girlfriend, remember?"

"I'm nervous. What if everyone gawks at me?"

Jake kissed my temple and squeezed my hand in his.

"Then it won't be any different from any other day."

We barely made it out to the yard when Floss stopped us in passing. "There you two are. Momma Bell is here," Floss said, pointing across the yard at an elderly woman. "I told her all about Emily and she's dying to meet her. Be sure you go over and introduce her."

Jake rubbed at his forehead. "God, maybe we could hide inside for a while, just until it's past her bedtime and she leaves."

His callousness toward a little old lady appalled me, though Floss wasn't the least bit surprised. "Momma Bell may be overbearing at times, but she means well. Say hello to her, Jake. It won't kill you. But if you don't, I might," Floss threatened as she walked away.

"Yoo-hoo! Jakey, over here," Momma Bell said, waving.

He plastered on the fakest smile I'd ever seen and waved back to her.

"Aww. Look at her. She's fond of you...*Jakey*," I said, laughing.

"Don't start," Jake said with a serious face. "You don't know her. She's a pushy pain in the ass."

"She seems delightful. With a name like Momma Bell, how could she not be?"

"Her name is Maebelle, but she constantly mothers everyone, hence the name. I wish the old bat would've had kids of her own before her husband died. Then she would've left all of us alone. She adopted us the same way a kidnapper adopts a child...against our will."

"Oh, that's a terrible thing to say. Maybe she's lonely. You wouldn't know anything about it since you have family, but I know how she must feel. I've been alone for years." I glanced back to the elderly woman chatting with Hank and couldn't help but feel sorry for her. "Let's go say hello," I said, starting in her direction.

He grabbed me and yanked me back. "Before I go anywhere near that woman, I need a beer. In fact, you do, too. You just don't know it yet."

"Jake, knock it—"

"Emily, I'm telling you, if I have to hang out with her for more than five minutes, I'm hitting the hard stuff in my uncle's liquor cabinet." A bead of sweat ran down the side of his face.

"You'd think she's the devil the way you're acting," I said. His eyebrows rose as if to confirm the accusation. "Fine, we'll get your beer first, you chicken, but then you're going to say hello, or I'm going to tell Floss on you."

"Oh, real mature," he said, guiding me toward the coolers his friends congregated around.

"I need a beer," Jake said. "Possibly two." Cowboy pulled two bottles out of the ice, handed one to Jake, and then opened the other, passing it to me with a wink. That annoyed Jake more. "I meant two for me, numb-nuts."

A smile spread across Ox's face. "If you're double fisting, then it can mean only one thing, huh, *Jakey*?"

"Jakey! Jakey!" the three men chanted.

Jake showed them all an up-close view of his middle finger and pushed me in Momma Bell's direction. "Let's get this over with."

We approached the elderly woman from the side, but she didn't notice. Momma Bell sat in a plastic lawn chair with her pudgy hips sticking out the sides along with her flowery sundress. Her fluffy white hair reminded me of the baby chicks in Hank's brooder box.

Floss motioned to us and gave the introduction. "Momma Bell, you remember Jake. And this is his girlfriend, Emily."

Momma Bell wrenched herself out of her chair, pinched Jake's cheek lovingly, and then slapped him in the back of his head. "Jakey's all grown up, but obviously didn't learn any manners," she told me, before looking back at him. "You took long enough getting over here."

"Sorry about that, Momma Bell. How have you—"

"Jakey, put a sock in it. It's time I met my newest granddaughter. Why don't you leave us girls alone to get acquainted?"

As big a smile as Jake wore, you would've thought the guy had just gotten laid. Blissfully happy, he didn't argue or waste any time making tracks back to the ice chests for another beer.

I turned back to Momma Bell to meet the granddaughter she spoke of. That's when I realized she was referring to me. Granddaughter? I just met the woman. And Jake wasn't her grandson, nor did he wish to be.

Momma Bell grabbed me in a bear hug, practically squeezing the life out of me. For a second, I wondered if Frankie Felts had put her on his payroll. Seconds before I passed out, she released me. But that wasn't the extent of the torture. She felt me up, from my shoulders all the way to my hipbones.

"You're too scrawny, girl. Need some meat on your pitiful bones. Floss, you go get this girl a plate of food, and pile it high. I'm going to see to it she eats every bite."

"Oh, no, that's okay. I'm not hungry."

"Nonsense," Momma Bell argued. "You're going to eat or we're going to have one of them there telethons for you.

You'll make yourself sick being so skinny."

Floss smiled at me before changing the subject. "I need to check if Hank watered my garden. He sometimes forgets."

Momma Bell looked beside herself. "Men these days. They don't pay attention. Why, if my Earl had ever done that, I'd have cooked his goose."

"Earl is Momma Bell's late husband," Floss explained.

I nodded. "Jake mentioned him earlier."

Momma Bell patted the chair next to hers as Floss walked away. "Sit, girl. I'm going to tell you all about Earl."

Floss cut out after the first five minutes and never came back. And to think I used to like that woman. I glared across the yard, giving Jake a *help-me* look, but he just shrugged and tipped his beer at me. I returned a look, promising retribution, and resisted the urge to rip out my hair.

I tried to be polite, but an hour later I found myself scooting away like a coward. "Nice to meet you, Momma Bell."

"I'm not through with you, young lady. You come back and visit me."

"Okay," I said, forcing my mouth to curl into a smile. What I really thought was *right after I commit suicide, you crazy loon.*

I couldn't find Jake, but saw Cowboy standing near the coolers. "If Jake ever leaves me alone with that woman again, I'm going to borrow her pitchfork and stab him with it."

He grinned. "What happened?"

"That crazy ass woman put a dip of snuff in her mouth and made me hold her spit can. Then she pulled a jar from her purse and made me take a drink. I think it was poison."

"Moonshine," Cowboy corrected with a chuckle. "Why

didn't you refuse?"

"The woman carries a gun in her purse. I'm not nearly as crazy as she is."

"Now you know why *Jakey* avoids her."

I blew out a breath. "No kidding. I'm surprised Jake hasn't fed her to Charlie yet. Where is he, anyway?"

"He's…uh…well, he's…" Cowboy looked around, as if he was searching through the crowd. "Um…I don't reckon I know."

"What a crock of bullshit," I said, which made his head turn to me with wide eyes. "Since the day I met you, you've never been at a loss for words, Mr. Smooth Operator." My eyes pierced into his with an unnerving stare. "Now, let's try this again. Where's Jake?"

Cowboy sighed. "He didn't want me to tell you."

"Tell me what?"

"He went to the barn with Bobbie Jo."

First, I was shocked. Then hurt. Then enraged.

"Hey," Cowboy called after me. "Where are you going?"

"To the barn. Where else?"

Chapter Thirteen

The thought of Jake and Bobbie Jo in the barn alone was unbearable. Him asking Cowboy to keep it from me only worsened the feeling.

I made it to the barn as they came out. Her face reddened and her eyes wouldn't meet mine. Signs of guilt—all the confirmation I needed. Jake, on the other hand, didn't look embarrassed or guilty. Surprised, maybe, but definitely not guilty. Fucking jerk.

"Hello, Emily," Bobbie Jo said solemnly, keeping her gaze lowered. "I'm sorry I borrowed Jake for a few minutes. He helped me figure something out."

"Well, did you get it fingered…er, figured out?" My icy tone matched the look I gave her. Jake wrapped his hand around my wrist, tightening his grip as a warning.

Bobbie Jo gave him a slight smile. "Thanks for your help. I'll leave you two alone now."

Jake nodded as she turned to walk away. "Sure thing,"

he said, letting her get out of earshot before he turned back to me. "Got a problem?"

I shrugged nonchalantly. "Who said I have a problem?"

"Don't play games, Emily. If you're mad, just say so."

"What's there to be mad about? If you want to sneak out to the barn with another woman, then that's your business. After all, I'm just your pretend girlfriend, right?"

"Stop it. It wasn't nearly as scandalous as you imagine it to be. She needed to talk."

"About…?"

"It's personal."

"I thought *we* were personal. Guess I'm the only one." I tried to walk away from him, but he wouldn't turn my wrist loose.

He dragged me back and held me by my shoulders. "Don't walk away from me. It didn't have anything to do with you. I asked Cowboy to keep his big mouth shut only because I knew how you'd react." He breathed out as if trying to control his temper. "Look, I can't tell you what we talked about because I'm not going to break her confidence. Bobbie Jo is still a good friend of mine, but it's no reason to be jealous."

"I bet she is. I know I always sneak off to barns with my good friends."

"Jesus. You don't trust men at all, do you?"

"Why bother? They all disappoint sooner or later."

"Get over yourself, Emily. Not everything is about you. God. Maybe you're right, after all. You *do* need therapy." He let go of my arms and stormed toward the house.

I stood alone, wondering how in the hell it happened. How was it possible I found him with another woman, yet I ended up feeling bad? Jake wouldn't have been Mr. Understanding if he caught me alone in the barn with Cowboy.

Annoyed, I followed him, but stayed far enough away until I could control the frustration burning behind my eyes. Once I pushed it back to a manageable level, I sat on the edge of the picnic table and quietly processed what he had said. Jake lingered nearby but didn't say anything directly to me. He didn't have a problem talking to Ox or Judd, though.

Bobbie Jo walked around the yard saying good-bye to everyone in the safety zone—ideally anyone who wasn't near me. Her radiant blond hair hung past her shoulders and flipped out at the ends. Her boobs bounced in her top as she leaned over to hug someone's child. She was well liked by everyone here. A little too well liked for my taste. *God. Why am I so insecure?*

She waved at Jake and he smiled at her. *Oh, yeah, that's why.* It made me want to rip every strand of her shiny, bleached blond hair out of her scalp. Instead, I crossed my arms and blew out a large breath, showing my irritation.

Ox looked over, puzzled by my expression. "What's wrong with her?" he asked Jake.

"Who knows? She's moody. Maybe it's Mad Cow Disease," Jake answered, unfazed.

A loud gasp came from behind him, and everyone around us stopped moving. Jake froze in place, closed his eyes, and let out a silent curse. Momma Bell stood there, giving Jake the stink-eye with her fists balled up on her plump hips. Reluctantly, he turned to face her.

"Why, you little shit. Don't you dare talk about her like that. Why, if my Earl had ever said that about me, I'd have blasted him between the eyes." Momma Bell stuck her gnarled finger in his face. "Now, you apologize to her or I'm going to tan your hide. I don't care if you're nearly a man."

All irritation left my body as I swallowed a giggle. Nearly a man? At thirty years old? Jake's a late bloomer.

"Aw, Momma Bell, Emily knows I'm kidding," Jake said, taking a swig of his beer.

"Jakey, I mean it. You apologize to that girl," Momma Bell ordered, her harsh eyes glaring at him. "My Earl wouldn't have hurt my feelings for nothing in the world."

"Okay, fine." Jake had to will himself to do it. "Emily, I'm sorry."

I smiled, but more out of sympathy for Jake. Everyone watched and listened as Jake apologized to me. It was almost comical, since I should've been the one offering an apology for how I acted at the barn.

Momma Bell wasn't satisfied, though. "You two having a spat, are you? Jakey, kiss that girl and make up with her. Don't you know anything, boy?"

Jake and I stared at each other. Neither of us wanted to be in that position. He tried to finagle out of it, but no one could tell Momma Bell no. The lady didn't take no for an answer. The crowd watched as she pushed Jake closer to me, stood off to the side with her arms crossed, waiting, as Jake and I faced each other awkwardly. Everyone whispered amongst themselves, making me wonder if they'd placed bets on whether we'd follow through. Hell, if they were smart, they'd bet on Momma Bell.

Humor twinkled in Jake's eyes. "Should we try to make a run for it?"

"Momma Bell's packing," I warned him.

"I guess we don't have much of a choice, then."

The crowd watched intently as we stood there like idiots.

"Maybe we should ask for a drum roll or something," I suggested.

Cowboy walked closer and planted himself next to Ox and Judd. "I'd be happy to stand in for you if you're not feeling up to it, *Jakey*."

Jake gave his friend a wicked grin. Only then did I understand the sensible, if not mundane, kiss I'd expected wasn't going to be as mild as I'd thought. Cowboy issued a dare, and Jake never did anything half-assed.

I refused to let Jake put on a show for his friends. Resentfully, I dug in my heels, hoping to keep the kiss polite and viewer-friendly. But before I could stop him, Jake ratcheted me into his arms and drew his mouth over mine. I forced my body into rigidity, as if I were a wooden puppet. Unfortunately, my strings were attached to my heart. Jake's tongue demanded my lips to part, and I responded as if he were my master. It was ravenous and indulgent and no longer just a kiss. In front of everyone, Jake made love to my mouth, and I forgot he was using me to prove something.

"Ahem." The sound cut the air around us as Momma Bell cleared her throat. We stopped kissing and saw everyone standing there, watching, mouths opened in awe. Or possibly disgust.

"That was a real doozy of a kiss…almost as good as the potato salad. Why, my Earl never gave me a saucy kiss like that." She leaned over and whispered, "My Earl was a real flash in the pan, if you know what I mean." Then Momma Bell winked and walked away, still mumbling to herself.

Jake and I traded glances with each other and then

moved farther apart, as if we were afraid the closeness would trigger another attack on one another's sexuality.

Out of the corner of my eye, I saw Junior stand and take a pouch from his back pocket. He twisted his hand inside and pulled out a large wad of chewing tobacco. It was a disturbing thing to watch. I'd seen people reach into salad bowls and come out with less than what he stuffed into his mouth. When he stepped over to me, the faint scent of wintergreen drifted into my nose.

I couldn't help but smile. "Hi, Junior."

"Emily," he said, nodding and tipping his black Stetson.

"I haven't had a chance to thank you for the clothes you brought over the other day. Almost everything fit. Are you sure your daughter doesn't want to keep them? There were some cute outfits in there. She has excellent taste."

The corner of Junior's mouth lifted. "I'm sure she's glad you're able to get good use out of them."

"How'd you know I needed clothes, anyway?"

"Before opening the diner, I spent a great deal of my life as a tracker. I'm used to spotting things invisible to others."

"Good guess, in other words?"

He tossed his head back and a deep, bellowing laugh came out. "Something like that," he said as he walked away.

Jake strolled over. "What'd you say to him?"

"Nothing. Why?"

"You made him laugh. I don't think I've ever seen him laugh before. Most people are usually afraid of him."

It struck me as odd, since I found Junior to be a kind, considerate person. He came off as a hard man who probably lived a hard life, but in his presence I felt safe, protected even. Nothing bad would ever happen as long as Junior was around. Probably because he smelled of wintergreen and the scent reminded me of my own father. But either way, I wasn't afraid of him. In fact, I was quite fond of him.

A few minutes later, Floss announced it was time to eat, and the crowd zipped over to form a line as the feeding frenzy began. I headed to the back of the line, but as I passed Jake, he grabbed me and slid me in front of him.

"We're taught in elementary school not to cut in line."

"And you say I never break the rules," he said teasingly, handing me a foam plate, plastic fork, and a napkin.

"Never any that matter."

We made our way down the line, and our plates got heavier with brisket, jalapeno sausage, potato salad, baked beans, carrot-raisin salad, and ambrosia. Floss offered some pickled quail eggs, but I passed, managing to grab one of the last deviled eggs.

"Here, Emily, try this," Cowboy said, shoving a piece of meat under my nose.

I picked it up with my fingers and gave it a sniff. It smelled okay, but I was leery of anything attached to telltale words like "try this." I nibbled on a tiny piece until Jake grinned.

"Okay. What is it?" I asked, not sure if I wanted to hear the answer.

"Fried backstrap," Cowboy said. "Don't worry. It's nothing weird."

I finished chewing and swallowed. "Then why are you smiling, Jake?"

Jake laughed. "It's deer meat." I closed my eyes and breathed out of my nose, but didn't say anything for a full minute. "Are you going to be sick?" Jake asked.

I opened my eyes and glared at both of them. "No, I'm

trying to decide which of you I'm going to kick in the balls first." Obviously, they weren't too concerned, since both of them laughed.

"Shit, it's nothing," Cowboy said. "Judd is over there right now eating a bowl of squirrel stew."

I fought the urge to gag. "Do you people kill and eat anything that moves or has a heartbeat? God, I hope a homeless guy doesn't wander onto the property."

They all smirked as we sat at the end of a picnic table. Ox offered to get me some pink lemonade and brought it back to me in a clear plastic cup.

"No opossum blood or anything strange in it, right?"

"No, ma'am, not unless you think vodka is strange."

I peered around at the other tables and saw some young children drinking pink lemonade as well. My eyes enlarged to the size of dinner plates. "Don't tell me…"

"No," Ox said, laughing. "I added it to your cup, not the pitcher. We don't start off that early around these parts."

"Thank God."

• • •

After sunset, the party continued.

Hank turned on the outside lights to the barn to light up the pool and threw some logs in the burn pit to ward off the mosquitoes. Kids swam tirelessly, women stood around chattering like a flock of hens, and the men took turns telling stories and picking on a guitar around the fire.

Jake found me lying on the top of the picnic table away from the crowd, looking up at the stars. He leaned over me, blocking my view. "Hey, I've been looking for you."

I peered around his big head. "I've never seen this many stars before."

"Yeah, they don't have starry skies in Chicago," Jake replied dryly.

"No, that's not what I mean. The atmosphere is different here. No honking horns, no cars, no city lights—just the sounds of nature. It's quiet, like I'm the only person in the world seeing this."

"You might be cut out for country life, after all."

I laughed and sat up. "I wouldn't go that far."

"Well, I was looking for you because Big Jim and the twins haven't met you yet."

"Excuse me?" I nearly choked on the saliva in my mouth.

Jake stepped to the side and pointed across the yard to a large man with a beard standing next to two toddlers. "His wife, Amy, talked to you earlier and wanted him and the twins to meet you before they left. It's past their bedtime."

I stifled my giggles while we talked to them, but every time Jake called him by name and referred to his twins, the laughter bubbled in my throat. I'd met too many people to remember all of their names, but some stood out more than others. Big Jim was one of them. Then again, I wasn't bound to forget Catfish or Slick, either.

After making our rounds to say good night to the guests who were leaving, Jake ended up back over near the ice chests with his boys. I gathered empty beer bottles from a neighboring table.

"Hey, Jake, everyone's leaving. Why don't we all go down to The Backwoods for a few drinks?" Cowboy suggested. "They have a live band tonight."

Jake's back was to me, but I saw him give Cowboy a

noncommittal shrug. "Nah, that's okay. It's been a long day. I think I'm going to take a shower and turn in."

"Come on, Jake. It's been a long time since we've all been out together."

"Emily's a homebody," Jake argued. "She wouldn't want to go."

They all looked at him as if he was crazy, but Ox spoke up. "Your girl? You're kidding, right? She has party written all over her. What's the real reason you don't want to go?"

"Look, guys, Emily can't—"

"I had a headache earlier," I said, approaching from behind. "But it's gone now. Why don't we go, Jake? It sounds like fun."

Jake shot me an unappreciative look. "No." His definite tone meaning "end of discussion" was easily deciphered.

"Why?" I asked. "I wouldn't mind—"

"I said no, and I meant it," he snapped, rubbing his hand through his hair with irritation. Then he got up and stomped off.

My blood boiled, driven mad by the injustice, though I pretended to blow it off when Judd asked, "Anyone else notice how strange he's acting?"

They all looked to me for an answer, but all I could do was turn my hands up and shrug. "He's probably just tired."

"Well, then we should get going, let him get some beauty rest," Cowboy said. "He knows where we'll be if he changes his mind."

• • •

There were a few stragglers left when Jake and I went to the cottage. He wanted to shower, and I got ready for bed. At least that's what Jake thought.

After his friends left, I had asked Slick for directions to The Backwoods. He was thoughtful enough to draw me a map on a napkin and told me which landmarks to look for. Guess he's not the only one who's slick.

I sat on the bed and kicked off my sneakers. Jake stripped his clothes down to the dark gray boxer briefs riding up his legs. I don't know how I'd never noticed before, but Jake had a small round scar on the front of his thigh. Guess when he was naked, I was looking at something other than his leg.

"What happened?" I asked, blatantly staring.

"It's nothing," Jake said, unwilling to elaborate. He stepped into the bathroom and turned on the water.

As soon as the sliding glass door closed behind him, I threw on the little red off-the-shoulder number given to me by Junior's daughter. I grabbed my heels, my fake identification, and the keys to the Explorer before sneaking out the front door.

Maybe I went haywire by blindsiding Jake, but it was the only way to get out the door hassle-free. I didn't waste time formulating a plan. One hour. It's all I wanted. Then I'd return and face Jake's wrath. I'm sure it would be in full swing by then. Minor thrills always have major repercussions, but the long-term boredom and monotony was getting to me.

I barely made it to the Explorer when someone behind me said, "Going somewhere?"

"Holy shit!" I said as Junior stepped out of the shadows. "Don't do that. You nearly gave me a heart attack."

He grinned, then lifted his head toward the cottage. "Where are you off to by yourself?"

I raked my fingers into my hair, giving it a nervous flip. "I'm going to The Backwoods."

"Jake know?"

It was my turn to grin. "Cowboy and the others will be there," I said, avoiding his question.

"You know I have to tell him."

"Oh, come on, Junior." He gave me a *yeah right* look. "Okay, well, how about giving me a head start?"

"Woman, you're asking for trouble."

"Pleeeease?"

His face softened, though his eyes stayed as bright and rock-solid as ever. "Two minutes."

"Two minutes?" What the hell is up with these people and giving somebody only two minutes? You can't do shit in two minutes!

"Take it or leave it."

I threw my arms around him and hugged him, though he didn't hug me back. He seemed more surprised than anything. "Thanks, Junior." I got into the Explorer, but turned back to him. "Hey, uh…one more thing. Do you know how Jake got that scar…the one on his thigh?"

"I'll let Jake tell you."

"I asked, but he didn't want to talk about it."

"Give it time. Scars need a lot of time to heal. You of all people should know that."

"But I don't have any scars."

"Some scars can't always be seen with your eyes," he said, "Doesn't mean they aren't there." He gave me a terse nod and glanced at his watch. "Two minutes," Junior reminded me.

• • •

The Backwoods was packed and just what I needed—an adult's playground—even if I hadn't acted like much of an adult sneaking off without telling Jake. By now, Junior had surely ratted on me. I pictured Jake punching the air with his fists until a vein popped out on his temple. It made me glad I wasn't there when it happened, though I doubted he'd be much calmer by the time I got home.

I stood at the bar, waiting for the bartender to look my way, when Cowboy slung an arm around me. "You are one big bucket of crazy, you know that? No, actually, crazy doesn't begin to cover you."

"Did you see me come in?"

"No. Junior called to let me know you were on your way here. He was about to do the same for Jake when I hung up with him." He smiled wide. "You're going to get the whooping of your life when Jake finds out. Hell, I've got half a mind to do it myself," he said with a wink. "I'd probably enjoy it too much, though."

"I'm surprised they don't call you Playboy instead of Cowboy."

"Some of my female friends do." He motioned across the room, where Judd and Ox sat at a table. Ox gave me a thumbs-up. "We had a bet on whether you'd come tonight— with or without Jake," Cowboy said. "Ox won. I'm buying the next round."

"You didn't think I'd come?"

"No, I didn't think you'd come without Jake knowing. That's suicide, darlin'. Now, whatcha drinkin'?"

I grinned. "Whatever you're buying."

Cowboy sent me to the table and joined us a few minutes later with a handful of shots. He doled them out to each of us.

"What is it?" I asked, eyeballing the golden brown liquor.

"Ass."

"Excuse me?"

They all chuckled. "It's a shot of ass," Cowboy explained, wearing a shit-eating grin. "It's a combination of three liquors, none of which will keep you from taking off your clothes."

I swigged a small sip and coughed. "Eww. This does taste like ass." They all laughed as I downed the rest of it and made a face. I laughed, too, but stopped when my eyes snagged on something across the room.

"Oh, damn. I think I need another drink."

The boys followed my gaze with their eyes, and then three shot glasses slid across the table simultaneously.

Unlike Elvis, Jake was in the building.

Chapter Fourteen

I couldn't down the three amber-colored shots fast enough.

Ox grimaced. "Shit. The warden's here."

Jake strode over, his eyes flicking to each of his friends as disapproval colored his face. "You bought her a drink?" he asked, disbelief rooted strongly in his tone. "Never figured you three for traitors." Jake gave them a harsh, cold-eyed stare that made my heart pound against my rib cage.

"Glad you could make it," Cowboy said with an unconcerned smile. "About time you got here."

"Had some catching up to do," Jake replied, still looking at me.

I glared over at Cowboy. "You knew he was coming!" It wasn't a question.

"Are you kidding? Have you met Jake?" Cowboy looked back at Jake. "How'd you get here, anyway?"

"I borrowed Hank's pickup. I'll need you to bring the Explorer back tomorrow. I'm driving Emily home in the truck."

"God, Jake. You're such a buzzkill."

"And you're a sneaky little—"

Cowboy got up, scraping his chair on the floor. "We'll give you two a few minutes alone." He motioned to Ox and Judd to follow him toward the bar.

As soon as they left, Jake started in on me. "I can't believe you lied to me."

"I told you I wanted to go out. I was honest...ish."

"Are you hardwired to drive me insane? If so, you're doing a damn good job of it. I've never seen a grown woman act like such a thoughtless, thickheaded, temperamental, tantrum-throwing toddler."

I could almost admire the alliteration of his words if it hadn't been meant as an insult. "Jeez, Dr. Seuss, tell me how you really feel."

Jake gripped the edge of the table until his knuckles turned white. "Why do you have such a lack of commitment to your own safety?"

I sidestepped his question with one of my own. "Why does your concern feel more like control?"

"Because you can't seem to restrain yourself from giving in to impulses."

"God, you don't know how to have fun, do you?"

"Sure I do. I'll show you how much fun I'm going to have dragging your ass back to the house," Jake said, pulling me out of my chair. "Come on, we're leaving."

I drew back from him. "No. I just got here."

He tightened his grip on my arm and shook me. "You don't want to go there. I'll throw you over my shoulder and force you if I have to."

A big guy at the table next to us stepped over, sizing

Jake up before his eyes settled on me. "Is there a problem?"

The cords in Jake's neck muscles tightened, but he let go of my arm. Jake was itching for a throwdown and obviously had the urge to punch something. Since I knew he wouldn't hit me, I worried he'd just found his target.

"No, no problem," I told the big guy. "Right, Jake?"

Cowboy, Ox, and Judd must've been watching from a distance. Suddenly, they stood next to Jake, awaiting the showdown brewing in the air. Or maybe they just wanted to take part in it.

"You need any help getting her out of here?" Cowboy asked, tauntingly eyeing the overgrown man next to me.

"Nope. She's stubborn, that's all," Jake said, making his friends grin, and me roll my eyes.

The big man wasn't keen on the idea of fighting once he became outnumbered. He backed off and sat in his chair without another word.

"Yeah," Cowboy said with a triumphant grin. "She does offer a unique set of challenges, doesn't she?"

Jake closed the physical space between us and wrapped his arm tightly around my waist. With a commanding presence, he tried to maneuver me toward the door.

I planted my feet firmly on the floor. "Jake, if you try to pull me out the door, I'm going to scream. I'll cause an even bigger scene than I did at Dairy Queen."

"You wouldn't dare," Jake said, eyeing me.

I tilted my head to the side, crossed my arms, and lifted my eyebrows, daring him to try me. We glared at each other in silence, both of us trying to will the other to back down. Meanwhile, the other boys talked amongst themselves, though we heard every word.

"Oh hell, they look like two bulls with their horns locked," Ox said, laughing. "Who do you think will win this round?"

"If I know my boy, Jake's got this one," Cowboy said with certainty.

"I don't know. She's smooth," Judd said. "Jake may have finally met his match."

Jake didn't care for Judd's remark. "She's not smooth… she's stubborn. There's a difference. She's not any worse than a stubborn heifer that doesn't want to be loaded into a stock trailer, and I've dealt with plenty of them. That's what cattle shockers are for."

"Twice today you've referred to me as a cow," I said, narrowing my eyes. "Once more and I won't speak to you for a week."

Jake grinned. "Promises, promises."

I grinded my teeth together, but thought it would be better to offer a solution. "We'll compromise. One hour, then I'll go willingly."

"That's not a compromise. That's you getting your way," Jake argued. "Besides, I don't have to compromise. I can force you to go now."

"Not without a scene, you can't." I smirked, knowing the last thing he wanted was to draw more attention. Then I stole a note from Junior's book. "One hour. That's the deal. Take it or leave it."

"Emily…" Jake glimpsed around at the packed bar and swore under his breath. "One hour," he agreed. I cracked a smile, but he pulled me roughly against his chest. "But the next time you pull this crap, I'm going to call you on your bullshit and see just how far you're willing to go to put yourself in danger."

Once he let go, I rubbed at my side where Jake's fingers had dug into my flesh.

Cowboy grinned. "So, date night, then?"

"Yeah, whatever," Jake said, stopping a waitress and asking her to bring him a bottle of water.

"Water?" Judd asked. "What's up with that?"

"Someone needs to be the responsible one. Besides, the best part of being the designated driver is figuring out who's drunk and who's stupid." He said, tossing a look my way.

"So now I'm fat *and* stupid?"

Cowboy, Ox, and Judd bit their lips.

"I'm not taking back the stupid comment," Jake said, "But I did *not* say you were fat."

Barely paying attention to him, I rambled on. "It's because my cheeks are chubby, right? Squirrels aren't fat, but they have chubby cheeks."

He shrugged. "You could pack a few nuts in there…"

I gave him a warning look. "I'm going to pretend you didn't say that."

Jake sighed. "You're not fat."

Cowboy patted Jake on the shoulder and threw his arm around my shoulders. "Jake, pull your foot out of your mouth and tell Emily how beautiful she looks tonight."

Jake's eyes touched upon my curve-hugging, off-the-shoulder dress. "Where'd you get the gown?"

"It was in one of the bags Junior brought over for me. It fits, but it's a little tight," I said, adjusting my breasts as Cowboy's eyes slid down my chest.

"A little?" Jake said with disbelief. "It's practically painted on your ass."

"Aw, Jake. It can't be that damn tight," Ox said, trying

to be the voice of reason. "It doesn't even show her panty lines."

I smoothed my hands down my dress and laughed. "Who said I was wearing any?"

Their heads whipped toward me. They all looked stunned, including my so-called hero sitting at the table next to us. With as large of a breath as they each sucked in, I was surprised there was any oxygen left in the room.

"Damn, woman," Cowboy said, looking me up and down with his tongue practically hanging out of his mouth. "You have to stop saying shit like that. Men aren't corkboards you can keep pinning messages to." His eyes smiled at me as he tightened his grip, pulling me closer.

Jake watched closely as I rubbed a finger down Cowboy's lips. "Now, now," I teased. "You know what they say about coveting your neighbor's—"

Cowboy didn't allow me to finish. "They also say 'do unto others as they do unto you'…and damn, girl…you don't know what the hell you're doing to me."

That comment prompted Jake to speak up. "Look all you want, but keep your hands to yourself."

Cowboy frowned. "You're no fun at all."

"I wasn't talking to you," Jake said, nodding toward me.

His friends laughed and I couldn't stop myself from joining in.

"Well, if I can't touch them, then I guess that means you're dancing with me."

"I'm not in the mood right now," Jake replied. "Get one of them to twirl you around the dance floor a couple of times."

"Performance anxiety?" I asked, making his friends

smirk. I grabbed Judd's hand. "Come on, Judd. Dance with me." Reluctantly, he let me lead him to the dance floor.

Judd put his hand nervously on my waist and moved me around the floor. "I'm not a good dancer," he said. "The other guys say I can't walk over a painted line without tripping."

"Why do they say that? I think you're doing fine," I lied, stumbling around the dance floor with him.

"I've got fifteens," Judd explained.

My face bent with confusion. "Are we talking about tires?"

"No, we're talking about the size of my boots," he said with a grin. Then he stepped on my foot.

"Ouch." I stopped to rub my foot and caught Jake watching us from a distance with a grin.

"Sorry. See, I told you I wasn't good at dancing."

I smiled up at Judd, trying to make him feel better. "Hey, I don't know how to two-step either. We'll pretend we know what we're doing. Besides, I'm sure you have plenty of other things you're good at. Every girl knows what they say about the size of a man's feet…"

Judd's face lit up with the compliment and he hugged me closer. He spun me around the floor until I was dizzy. I'd swear my feet never touched the ground.

After two awkward dances in a row, Judd offered to get me a drink. I made my way over to Jake and Cowboy, who sat in a dark corner of the bar with their backs to me and away from everyone else. As I approached, I overheard my name and eavesdropped on their conversation.

"I know what you told me earlier," Cowboy said, keeping his voice low. "But I still can't believe she's one of your cases. So the girlfriend bit was…"

"Me keeping up appearances until we figure out who's releasing information," Jake said coldly, as if he had the emotions of a popsicle.

"She's a feisty little thing. You've got your hands full with that one," Cowboy said, laughing.

Jake shook his head in agreement. "She's an acquired taste."

"Sounds like you two need to go ahead and bang it out," Cowboy suggested. "That'll let the air out of her sails and keep her on course."

My heart wrenched in my chest, and I couldn't stand to hear any more. I was pissed Jake told Cowboy the truth about our arrangement, but also confused by Jake's callousness. I wound up inside a bathroom stall unable to swallow and sniffling so much snot that I was sure the lady in the stall next to me thought I was an addict. I blew my nose and wiped my wet cheeks, but not necessarily in that order. No doubt about it: men are jerks.

It was bad enough Jake fooled me into believing he actually cared, but I resented him for allowing me to fall in love with him. Oh God! I loved him. That's why I was upset and sniveling like a wiener. I was in love with Jake.

He was mad I blindsided him by sneaking out, but he had fooled me in much the same way. Except, emotionally, he was never there to begin with. He just pretended to be. And, stupid me, I believed him when he said he cared about me. Damn him.

After straightening my face, I came out of the bathroom and looked for Jake. I picked him out of the crowd on the dance floor where he two-stepped with a pretty blonde with big boobs. Bobbie Jo. That sonofa—

Arms wrapped around my waist from behind and I turned around quickly. "I've been looking for you," Cowboy said. "I requested a fast song. Want to dance?"

"Ask one of your groupies," I told him, acid leeching into my voice.

His face twisted. "Something wrong?"

"If you have to ask, then you're even more naïve than I am."

Cowboy gazed over at Jake dancing with Bobbie Jo. "That's why you're upset? Hell, sweetheart, Bobbie Jo is our friend. None of us are romantically involved with her, including Jake. Do you think he would've kissed you in front of everyone earlier if he had feelings for her?"

"Just a kiss," I said, shrugging, minimizing how I felt.

"Just a kiss?" He blinked with surprise. "Both of you were on the verge of losing your clothes."

"And you boys think *I'm* melodramatic?"

The song ended, and the music changed to a fast rock beat. "Why don't we go out there and show them how it's done?"

I considered it for a moment. Determined not to let Jake ruin my good time, I accepted. Cowboy pulled me out to the dance floor and started shaking his ass. I laughed, which made me feel better. Then I saw Jake and Bobbie Jo sitting together at the bar watching us intently. I wasn't sure which of them I wanted to put on a show for, but the next thing I knew, I had one of Cowboy's legs between mine as I ground my hips against his. Cowboy had less scruples than Ox and Judd. I wasn't surprised when he grasped my hips and grinded back.

I shimmied and squirmed up and down his nether

region, hoping Jake watched every suggestive move I made.

Cowboy's eyes widened. "Damn, sweetheart, Jake's done gone and got himself a live one."

Turning around and shoving my ass against him, I threw my head back onto his shoulder and turned my face toward him. "I hope I'm not getting you into trouble."

"Nah. Jake's all bark, no bite." Yeah, no kidding. That's been the problem all along. "Is that what you're doing? Trying to make him jealous?" Cowboy asked. I chose not to answer because I didn't want to lie. "It won't work," Cowboy said, still moving against me. "Jake knows I'd never make a move on his woman."

Surprised, I turned to face him. "But I'm not his…"

"I know. Jake told me already. But I know him better than anyone, and you're definitely Jake's woman. You two just don't know it yet."

"You're wrong about—"

"Darlin', I'm *never* wrong about women."

After the dance ended, we headed over to Jake and Bobbie Jo. Cowboy ordered me a drink, but I didn't plan on hovering. Last thing I wanted to do was schmooze with the two of them. It required everything I had to control the chaos raging inside me while we waited for the waitress to bring our beers.

"Your hour is almost up," Jake said, checking his watch.

"What do you care? Don't you have your hands full?" I said, blatantly staring at Bobbie Jo's large breasts, barely covered by her white top. "Or are you bored with her… again?"

Bobbie Jo swung her head toward me. "Wow. You can be a bitter pill to swallow."

Some of it may have been the booze, but her sheer presence grated my nerves. The model behavior I promised Cowboy flew right out the window. "Somehow I doubt that's the only thing you've ever swallowed."

"Emily!" Jake grabbed my arm. "Don't talk to her like that."

"Sure, Jake, take up for your ex-girlfriend. If she doesn't want anybody to think she's a slut, maybe she shouldn't be sneaking off with someone else's boyfriend."

Bobbie Jo came off mousy, but she struck back with the accuracy of a snake. "It's okay, Jake. When little Miss Know-It-All gets through divvying up her time among all of my boys, maybe she'll have some left over for you." She got up to leave, but turned once more. "And if I'm the slut, then how come you're the one not wearing panties?" She smirked as she walked away.

I tried to go after her and grab her by the back of her fake-ass blond hair, but Jake wouldn't let go.

Cowboy positioned himself in my path. "No catfights."

"Oh, now she needs both of you to protect her?"

"It's not *her* we're protecting. She would've wiped the floor with your ass. You're lucky she walked away when she did, or we'd be pulling her off you right now."

I rolled my eyes. "Yeah, right! What's she going to do? Steamroll me with her tits?"

"Enough, damn it!" Jake squeezed my arm tighter, showing me he was serious. "She knows people in here and you're not going to embarrass her, or yourself, by acting like this."

I wrenched myself from his grip and walked away, ignoring him when he called after me. I sat at the bar. I hadn't meant to take my anger out on Bobbie Jo, but my tolerance level for being around Jake without bringing up what I overheard him say to Cowboy had peaked the moment I came face-to-face with him. He didn't care about me, just his stupid case. That was why he kept me at a distance. It all made sense now. I didn't have anything else to say to Jake. If he wanted me to talk to him, then he'd have to break the silence.

After about ten minutes, Jake strode briskly toward me. I held my composure, pretending not to notice him. He stopped next to my seat. My eyes hovered somewhere around knee-level, waiting for him to speak. Instead, he snagged me by my elbow, ripped me out of my seat, and manhandled me across the room. I got a reaction out of him, but it wasn't the one I wanted. Guess I'm not the budding genius I thought.

"Where are you taking me?" I demanded, unable to pry his fingers loose.

He shoved me into the bathroom, shutting and locking the door behind us. "All that because you were jealous?"

Knowing Cowboy opened his big mouth, I crossed my arms and turned away from him.

"Emily, I can't read your mind by looking at your ass. Bobbie Jo is my friend, nothing more. I've told you already. I don't understand why—"

I whipped around to face him, my eyes burning with heated fury. "I'm just one of your cases, right?"

"What?"

"It's what you told Cowboy...that I was one of your cases."

"I don't know what you think you heard, but—"

"Don't embarrass yourself by denying it. I know what I heard." Then I tried to master Cowboy's tone as I said, *"You two should bang it out."*

"You didn't hear the rest of the conversation, did you?"

"I heard enough—"

"Woman, get your head out of your ass," he yelled in a holier-than-thou voice. "You don't ever shut up and listen. Your mouth is like a runaway train—no fucking brakes."

"Up yours, Jake! Who do you think you—"

He grabbed my waist and covered my mouth with his. My hands went straight to his chest to force him away, but I might as well have been pushing against a statue. When his tongue nudged its way into my mouth, I couldn't deny him access. Wasn't much coaxing involved, anyway. It was an unguarded moment. I wasn't prepared for the warmth of his lips or the heat of his hands.

Jake kissed me deeply, tracing my lips with his. He pressed his body into mine until he had me aching for him. I ran my fingers through the back of his hair, then down to his sleek shoulders, as he pulled his mouth from mine.

I swayed to the left, intoxicated more by his kiss than the alcohol. He steadied me, resting his velvety fingers against the pulse on my neck. I tilted my head back to look at him, reveling in my guilty pleasure and the intensity of his gaze.

He smiled lightly. "Do me a favor?"

"Mmmm," I murmured, my head flopping lazily onto his shoulder.

"Apologize to Bobbie Jo."

Moments before, my heart was in freefall with sixty seconds of pure bliss, but his words snapped me back to reality like a bungee cord. "Do what?"

"She's forgiving," he said.

"Screw her and her forgiveness. That's why you kissed me? Because you wanted me to say sorry to your old flame? You're crazy if you think that's going to happen."

I unlocked the door to the bathroom and marched out. Jake didn't try to stop me, which bothered me more. Tears sprung from my eyes as I made it to the bar. I wiped them away, but more surfaced in their place.

Ox sat beside me and handed me a napkin. "Here, dry your eyes," he said softly. "Want to talk about it?"

"No, I just…I cry when I drink."

"Don't we all," he said, smiling, rubbing his hand on my back. "How about a dance? I haven't got you out on the floor yet."

I wanted to decline, but he didn't give me a chance before he hauled me to the dance floor. I didn't know how to two-step, but within minutes, Ox had me two-stepping almost as well as him. It wasn't as hard as I thought, and after a moment, I wasn't required to concentrate on my movements anymore.

"I'm a mess, aren't I?" I asked him as he wiped mascara out from under my eyes.

Ox smiled at me as he pulled me closer, rubbing my hair to console me. "I think you're cute." Something hard in his pants brushed across my thigh, making me pull away from him. "Calm down, it's a roll of quarters," he said.

"Yeah, that's what they all say."

To prove me wrong, Ox dug in his bulging pocket and pulled it out. "It's for the pool table."

"Oh, shit, it *is* a roll of quarters," I said, laughing.

"I like you, Emily, but I'm not the least bit attracted to you," Ox admitted gently. "Sorry, honey, but you're not my type. You're cute, but you ain't that cute."

"Most guys won't say something is cute," I told him. "In fact, I've only known one guy who ever—" Jake walked past us outside the dance floor. He glanced over at me as he took a seat at the bar next to Cowboy. "God, I'm starting to feel like I have leprosy or something. What's wrong with me?"

"What's the problem with you and Jake?" Ox asked. "He has it bad for you."

"I think you're wrong. Every time we start to get…uh… close, we end up throwing sparks."

"Shit, girl, even electric eels can mate without stunning each other."

"Yeah, but how?"

"That's for you to figure out. If I were you, I'd take a more proactive approach with Jake. He can be a little slow out of the starting gate on a relationship, but you're one of them high-spirited fillies that jumps the gun. You have to find something that'll elicit a reaction from him. You know, make him catch up. I'd tell you to slow down, but that'd be like trying to stop a fast-moving train with my bare hands, and I'm no Superman."

I gave him a quick peck on the cheek. "With you, Ox, who needs a therapist?"

A guy wearing a Mossy Oak camouflage hat bumped into Ox's shoulder as he passed by. "Sorry about that, shrimp. Didn't see you standing there," he said, laughing as he walked away.

"He did it on purpose, didn't he?"

"Yeah," Ox said. "He's a spineless dick. Steer clear of him."

"Who is he?"

"That's Germy."

"Germy? You mean Jeremy?"

"No, I mean Germy. That guy dips his stick into any available mud hole. Probably thinks the clap is a round of applause."

I made a face. "Eww."

"Yeah, none of us can stand the asshole. He and Jake played football on opposing teams. They've hated each other for as long as I can remember."

"Really?" I smiled, feeling inspired.

Hmm. The jealousy thing didn't work when I danced with Jake's friends. He wasn't concerned because he knew none of them were trying to pole-vault into my pants. But I might have set the bar too high. Maybe I need to rethink my approach.

Ox read my mind. "Girl, you better banish that thought. Toss it out right now. That's playing with fire."

"You told me to elicit a reaction."

"Yeah, but I didn't say cause an explosion. There's bad blood between them. You're going to incite a riot if you go there."

"Oh, it won't be that bad," I said. "I'm just going to dance with him."

"Jake hates that prick," Ox said. "And…well…you know how a male dog marks his territory?"

"What does that have to do with anything?"

"You're Jake's smitten kitten," Ox said, smiling. "And he can be territorial. I don't want you to get pissed on."

"Oh, come on. Jake didn't consider my feelings when he danced with Bobbie Jo. It shouldn't matter who I dance with." The song ended, and I shuffled off toward Germy…

uh, Jeremy.

Ox laughed and called out, "When you come back with crotch critters, don't say I didn't warn you."

Jeremy stood talking to two other men at the bar. All three watched me approach. Silently, I squeezed in between them and sat on a barstool. Jeremy's eyes traveled up my legs, reminding me to lock my knees together.

"Hey, sweetheart." He motioned for the bartender. "Can I buy you a drink?"

The bartender smiled at me, probably recognizing a woman who'd never paid for a drink in her life. "Anything with a cherry," I told him. Seconds later, he slid a drink toward me with a plump red cherry on top.

I picked it up by the stem, pulled it into my mouth with my teeth and ate it. Then I popped the stem in my mouth as Jeremy and his friends watched. Seconds later, I pulled the stem out and held it up, showing the neatly tied knot in the middle.

For some reason, forwardness always catches men off guard. That's why Gina, Dale, and I once went through a whole jar of cherries practicing that move. I always beat them. They would've been proud at how fast I tied this cherry stem with my tongue. Worthy of a gold medal.

"Neat trick," Jeremy said. "What else are you good at?"

I goaded him with a puckish look. "Lots of things."

"Dancing?"

"Sure," I said, knowing men can't resist a challenge. "If you think you have the stamina to keep up."

Jeremy grabbed my hand and led me through the crowd. We two-stepped to a country song, then the band played rock. Jeremy cinched my waist with his hands and pulled me to him. I slithered against him with slinky, sexually explicit moves that bordered on stripper. Jeremy wasn't well behaved either, pawing at me with grabby hands and polishing the front of his jeans with the back of my dress. It did nothing for my ego.

I nonchalantly glanced over to Jake, whose brows lowered toward his eyes, and his mouth tightened into a hard line. He wasn't enjoying the view. In fact, Cowboy, Ox, and Judd didn't like it either. The rapid-fire succession of dirty looks they gave Jeremy made me nervous. They circulated the room, staying in my general vicinity, ready to pounce with the slightest signal from Jake.

"So you and Jake an item?" Jeremy asked, grinning smugly.

I shrugged. "Why do you say that?"

"It's not rocket science. He's watching both of us like a hawk, and he doesn't look very happy I'm dancing with his girl."

"He'll get over it."

"That's the thing, honey. I don't *want* him to get over it," Jeremy said, planting his mouth over mine.

Chapter Fifteen

I tried to dodge Jeremy's lips and whacked him in the chest. Unfazed, he tried to shove his tongue in my mouth. I pushed him away from me, and he flaunted a mischievous grin.

"You know, ever since you walked through that door, I wanted to make love to you really bad," Jeremy said, winking.

I wiped my mouth with the back of my hand. "Judging by the way you kiss, I wouldn't doubt that's *exactly* what would happen, you slimy — "

"What's wrong, princess? Your tiara bent out of shape?"

"Why don't you go tip a cow, you bastard?"

"Because teasing the bull is more my speed." He peered over my shoulder. "Oh, look, here comes your boyfriend."

His bull reference nailed it. Jake, red-faced with flaring nostrils, charged through the crowd with a powerful gait. He practically bucked Cowboy, Ox, and Judd off as they tried to stop his forward motion.

By the time Jake trampled past me, the boys had a firm hold, not allowing him to get close to Jeremy, who had taken a few steps back. I worried what would've happened if Jake's matadors had not intervened.

Jake must've realized everyone in the bar had stopped and watched. The feral, inhuman look left his eyes. His posture relaxed, as if he flipped a switch and forced himself to calm down.

"I'm fine," he told his friends, wanting them to release their grip. They must've believed him since they let him go.

"Problem, Jake?" Jeremy asked smugly.

"You mean besides you not keeping your hands or mouth to yourself?" Jake replied in an even-tempered voice. "She's with me. You keep your damn hands off her, or I'll break them. Same goes for your mouth."

Jeremy's eyes lit up with the challenge. "My mistake. I thought she was a hooker."

"You sonofabitch!" I reared back and punched him in his nose, which hurt my hand.

Jake grinned with only a small amount of satisfaction. "How'd that feel?"

Jeremy shook it off, though his eyes watered slightly. "She hits like a girl," he mumbled.

"I *am* a girl, you douchebag!" I shouted, still rubbing my knuckles and shaking my hand in the air.

"You always let a woman do your fighting for you, Jake?"

"Hey, you called her a hooker," Jake said with a shrug. "What'd you expect? You should apologize to the lady." It was more a demand than a request, but I didn't like how I got edged out of the conversation.

"You're kidding me, right?" Jeremy laughed and said in a crass tone, "Lady, my ass. She isn't even wearing any panties."

Impulsively, I launched myself at him. Jake caught me around the waist with one arm. I wriggled out of his grip, but he yanked me back and handed me off to Cowboy. "Here, hold her for a second," Jake told him.

Cowboy shoved me behind him, keeping one hand resting on my hip, making sure I stayed put. It was a defensive move rather than conflict management. Jake expected trouble and wanted me out of the way. Things were about to turn sour.

"You're going to apologize to Emily right now, or I'm going to break your jaw," Jake threatened, his fist already clenched at his side.

"I'll do you one better," Jeremy said, laughing. He tossed a wink over Jake's shoulder directly at me. "Sweetheart, why don't you come home with me? I'll spend the entire night apologizing to that sweet little ass of yours. After all, another man's trash…"

It was all Jake needed.

In an impressive display of male bravado, Jake's fist struck Jeremy in the jaw with a cracking sound that made me cringe. Jeremy's two friends jumped on Jake, double-teaming him, prompting Cowboy, Ox, and Judd to step in. Instead of stopping the fight, everyone in the room bum-rushed the dance floor and a riot broke out.

Caught in a snarl of flying fists and broken beer bottles, I scrambled to get off the dance floor. Not knowing where the others were, I grabbed the keys to the Explorer from our table. Then Jake and Cowboy elbowed their way through the crowd. As they reached me, I got a good look at their faces and gasped.

Jake's cheek was red and already bruising, his right eye almost swollen shut, and his knuckles on both hands were bleeding. Cowboy looked worse. I'd swear his nose hadn't been that flat before, and he had blood splatters on the front of his shirt.

"Are you okay? Hey, wait—"

Jake scooped me up and dragged me out, kicking and screaming. When we reached the parking lot, he dropped me—literally—on the ground. He jerked the Explorer keys from my hand and tossed them to Cowboy.

"Walk it off," Cowboy said to Jake. "Tar and feathers are your best option." Then Cowboy got into the Explorer and drove away.

Jake paced as I got up and dusted myself off. "What the hell is your problem?"

He stopped and leaned into my face, his crazed eyes chock-full of anger, his voice cold as ice. "Shut. Up."

My eyes widened. "Excuse me?"

He put his hand over my mouth. "Stop talking." With a bruising grip, Jake pulled me to the side of the building where he'd parked and crammed me into the old pickup, slamming the door. The window was down, so I heard his frustration as he grumbled and kicked the fender. I tried to get back out, but he pushed the door closed again. "Emily, you don't want to test me right now. Keep your ass in the truck."

"Jake, this is stupid—"

"Damn you, Emily! I've never put my hands on a woman before, but you have me very close to doing it. Stay in the truck and shut your fucking mouth!"

The enforcement in his coarse voice shocked me. I guess

now I know what Cowboy meant by tar and feather being Jake's best option. I crossed my arms as he paced some more. Okay, so I pushed him too far this time. I hadn't meant to, but I had a hard time controlling myself where Jake was concerned. No matter how good my intentions were, I always seemed to screw everything up.

Ten long minutes later, he decided to get in the truck. I sat in silence, thinking he'd apologize for the way he spoke to me. All he said was, "Buckle up."

It was probably the alcohol talking, but my irritation came out full force. "Are aliens going to snatch me if I don't?"

Though I wasn't sure he would, he kept his cool. "It's the law."

"You going to arrest me?"

He gritted his teeth. "Goddamnit. You should've come with an instruction manual. For once, take responsibility for your actions, stop being difficult, and buckle the damn seatbelt."

"If you want it buckled, do it yourself."

Jake catapulted across the seat, grabbed my shoulders, and shook me. His lightning fast reflexes and the strength of his hands made my body tremble violently. He focused on me with eyes of a predator. I froze in place, like a skittish bunny, not sure if I should run like hell. He was dealing with his demons, and this was a side of Jake I hadn't seen before.

Slowly, he loosened his grip and his mouth softened. "I'm sorry. I didn't mean to scare you."

His words had softened, but the intensity of his gaze confused me. It wasn't guilt, but something else. I was clueless to know what Jake was thinking, but the visual cues were there. He wasn't trying to defuse the situation any longer.

His eyes were those of an aggressor.

A sexual charge pressed into the air around us, making it harder for me to breathe. I gulped shallow breaths, savoring them as if they were the last bits of oxygen I'd receive before Jake smothered me with his overwhelming male presence.

He gave no warning. Jake captured my waist, pulling me closer, only to shove me onto my back before positioning himself between my legs. I should've been frightened, but how he handled me was wickedly sexy. Instead of fear, my stomach fluttered with anticipation.

He took my lips forcefully, bruising them. With intense carnal gratification in mind, he yanked the front of my dress down to my waist and cupped my breasts with rough hands. Jake moved lower, my nipples hardening in his mouth. My body responded in a frenzy, arching under him, twitching with pleasure.

Jake sensed what I wanted, giving it before I asked. No words of passion, no gentleness in his eyes, no softness in his touch. Like being tickled too hard—it might hurt a little, but you can't stop laughing with enjoyment. Even if I had wanted to, it would've been impossible to resist.

A low moan escaped my lips, pushing him over the edge. Grunting, Jake fumbled to loosen his zipper with quivering, unsteady hands. He was ready to unleash the primal urge building inside him. The stingy, inadequate foreplay didn't matter. To him, or to me. I wanted him to take what he needed and would ask nothing in return.

Fully aware of the alignment issues, Jake pulled off my heels and threw them onto the floorboard. He sat upright and repositioned, pulling me astride. Having sex in the front seat of a pickup is like trying to get a cushion cover back on the couch pillow after it's been laundered. It's a tight squeeze with a lot of grunting, but not impossible.

His fingers dug into my back with need and fervor. His rock solid erection pressed into my inner thigh, throbbing and hot. His tongue found its way back into my mouth with unstoppable passion.

So you can imagine my surprise when he did stop.

People were talking as they came out of the bar, but I was the only one who ignored them. Jake let his head rest on the back of the seat and blew out a breath. "Emily…"

"You're thinking," I breathed into his ear. "Stop it."

Jake's bottom half was definitely there, but his top half was only semi-present and still contemplating. Eager to finish what he started, I trailed my tongue down his neck and kissed him. His hands worked their way under my dress and up the back of my thighs.

Then I heard a sound bordering on a laugh. "You liar."

"It's a thong," I said, still kissing his neck. "I never said I wasn't wearing any panties. I only *suggested* I might not be."

His hands stopped moving as he swore under his breath. "Emily, I…"

I pulled back to look at him. "God, Jake, don't do this again. I'm horny and shitfaced and—"

"That's why we can't. I feel like I'm taking advantage."

"By all means, take advantage!"

"You know what I mean. I feel like I'm in a wading pool, and it's getting deeper and deeper."

I nipped his bottom lip with my teeth and whispered into his mouth, "Isn't that the point…to go deeper?"

The seconds stretched on indefinitely.

"Not when you're drunk," he said. "Alcohol fuels bad

judgment. I don't want you to regret this."

"What are you…a human Breathalyzer? Jesus, Jake. We've nearly had sex dozens of times in the past week and I was sober each time. Why do you think I'd regret it now?"

"Emily, I told you before…I don't do meaningless sex."

"It won't ever mean anything as long as you keep stopping it from happening. My God, Jake, virgins safeguard themselves less than you do."

"Cue the violins. Poor Emily didn't get laid," he said sarcastically.

"Don't turn this around on me. Maybe you shouldn't start something you obviously can't finish."

"This *is* about you. You have a habit of making bad choices. I can't help it if I don't want to be one of them."

"Oh, fuck me." I pulled my dress up to cover my breasts and climbed back into the passenger seat.

"Sweetheart, if a frolic is all you're wanting, then you should have ridden home with Cowboy," Jake said, buttoning his pants. A brief but tangible silence followed. "You actually considered it for a moment, didn't you?"

I propped my arm on the door and looked at him, realizing he was serious. "You think all I care about is sex?"

"If the shoe fits," Jake said, shrugging as he cranked the old truck.

For a moment, I sat in stunned silence, then my temper flared. "If that's what you think of me, then you're the biggest jackass I've ever met."

"Guess I'm a jackass."

The drive to the house was excruciatingly quiet. My desire for intimacy and Jake's lack of providing wasn't the problem, no matter what he believed. I had a hard time swallowing his unsavory opinion of me. As far as he was concerned, I wanted to be with someone, and that someone could've been anyone. He was wrong.

Jake had been loitering in my heart—and occasionally on my body—since the first night I laid eyes on him. Whenever he was near, I had a hard time regulating my emotions. My heart was ripe for picking, but Jake refused to harvest my crop…in more ways than one.

Sure, the hot and cold thing bothered me. It's simple. Don't start something you don't intend to finish. It wasn't about sex, though. I would've been angry if we'd been playing Monopoly and he'd quit in the middle of the game.

As we pulled up to the house, Jake said, "Let's go inside."

"I need a minute," I said, my voice wavering slightly.

He started to argue, but stopped himself. "Okay, I'll give you a few minutes alone." He knew I wasn't going anywhere since he pocketed the truck keys.

Once he went inside the cottage, I sighed in frustration. Maybe we were too different. I liked being reckless and carefree, foregoing all the rules. But I was in love with a frustratingly precise man of the law, one who adhered to responsibility and respected rules.

We weren't an ideal couple, and chances are, it'd never work. Probably the equivalent of trying to breed a duck to a chicken. I, of course, would consider myself the duck, since they're cuter. And everyone knows chickens have peckers. I knew I was drunk when the vision of a chicken's pecker made me giggle.

The more I thought about Jake, the more muddled my feelings became. The last week had taken a heavy toll on my heart. After Jake saved my life several times, most people would consider it White Knight Syndrome, but that wasn't it. I was in love with him. I'd never felt this sure of anything in my life.

Eventually, this whole ordeal would be over, and Jake wouldn't feel obligated to protect me anymore. But would he still care? After all, it's not like he said he loved me. Even I knew to care and to love are two very different things. I cared enough about the birds to not want Hank to pull off their heads, but I wasn't in love with them. And if Hank wanted to pull the head off something, why didn't he take care of the dreadful rooster?

I reached down to the floorboard and searched in the dark for my shoes. The first one I found immediately, but the other was still missing. My hand moved back and forth until I hit something that lit up. Closer inspection revealed a cell phone. It must belong to Floss. She drove the truck to the grocery store last. Laying it on the seat, I continued searching for my other shoe.

Jake's voice rang out, a touch of panic making it warble. "Emily…? Where are you?"

I popped my head up and saw him standing at the cottage door without a shirt. His bruised, swollen face looked worse under the porch light. "I'm looking for my shoes," I told him. "I'll be there in a minute."

"I'm getting ready for bed."

"You should put some ice on your face."

He nodded and shut the door as I stared at the pair of shoes in my hands. I'd found the second shoe as he called my name, but I let him believe I was still searching. I couldn't ask myself why because I already knew the answer. I placed my shoes on the seat and picked up the cell phone before I lost my nerve. One phone call. It's all I needed.

She answered after the third ring, sounding half-asleep. "Hello?"

"Gina?"

A slight pause lingered as voice recognition sunk in. "Oh, my God!" Gina shouted into the phone. "Where have you been? We didn't know what happened to you."

I sobbed quietly to myself. "They put me in witness protection."

She paused again. "Have you been drinking?" I giggled, but Gina must've heard the strain in my voice. "Are you okay?"

"I'm fine."

"Girl, people are looking for you. A couple of men stopped by here and pushed their way into our apartment. They tore the rooms up searching for you. I told them you weren't here, but they wouldn't listen."

"They're dangerous, Gina. If they come back, don't open the door. Just call the police. I saw them do something… terrible. It's why they're after me." I had to shake the image of Sergio's body from my mind.

"Is the other man with them?"

"What other man?"

"Two days after you disappeared, he showed up asking a lot of questions. He wants us to call him if we heard from you."

"Did he have a crooked nose and a gross-looking mole on his left cheek?"

"No, but he looked like he needed some sleep. His eyes were more bloodshot than Dale's that time we dared him to drink—"

"Okay, okay. Gina, this is important. Don't tell anyone you spoke to me. I mean it."

"You could've called us sooner, you know. We've been worried out of our minds. The police wouldn't — "

"You went to the police?"

"Yeah, but no one would tell us anything," she said, still irritated about it. "Then one cop said you were safe and that you were with Jake."

"Are you sure he was a cop?"

"I guess so. He was in the police station and wearing a uniform. Oh, and he had his arm in a sling."

"Officer Stevens?"

"Hey, yeah…I think that was his name. How'd you know?"

"He got shot when those men came after me," I told her. I was glad to hear Stevens was okay, but realized I was putting her in danger as well. "Gina, I can't talk any longer. I have to hang up now."

"You sure you're okay?"

Sighing, I closed my eyes and my jaw tensed. "I miss you guys. Tell Dale I asked about him, or the drama queen will never let me live it down."

Gina laughed. "Okay, I will."

I gripped the phone tighter. "Gina, I…I love you and Dale. You know you two are my family. Take care of yourselves." Then I hung up.

It hurt to hear Gina's voice. I thought I'd feel better, not worse. Depressed, I erased the call from the phone's memory and tried to do the same to my own.

I swung open the door and got out, leaving the cell phone on the seat of the truck where Floss would find it. I wobbled as I paced, belittling myself and wearing a not-quite-oval track in the dirt beneath my unsteady feet. Did I put my friends in danger by calling them? No, I couldn't let myself think that way. Man, how selfish could I be? I'm probably the only person in witness protection to ever come down with a case of the drunken dial-ies. *God, I'm dumb.*

As I walked up the stairs, I tripped and face-planted on the porch, almost landing on Dog. I didn't have the energy to get up. I stayed there, sprawled out on my stomach, anesthetized with alcohol. I crossed my ankles in the air behind me and ran my hand over Dog's spotted ears.

I grinned to myself. "Heavenly Father, we gather here today to remember the life of this loved one…"

"Dog doesn't need a funeral," Jake said, though I hadn't heard him open the door.

"Maybe not, but I'm starting to think my vagina does."

"Oh, come on. Don't start again. My face hurts, and I want to go to bed." He reached down and picked me up under my arms, setting me on my feet.

"Fine then, *coward*." I stumbled past him into the cottage, shakily making my way to the bedroom.

Jake followed me, watching from the door as I went into the bathroom. He was already lying down when I crawled onto the bed and plopped onto the pillow, giving him the silent treatment.

"Okay, I'll bite…how am I a coward?"

I turned over to face him. "The moment we start to get closer, you shut down. You keep our physical interaction in check and all of your emotions on the back burner."

"I'm an FBI agent, damn it. I'm trying to do what's right."

"And you think frisking me and leaving it unfinished is

right? Why do you have to pull out a magnifying glass every time your pants come off?" I realized how it sounded when both of us shifted our eyes down to his crotch. "Oh, you know what I mean. It's like you're looking for a way out."

"You actually think I wanted to stop? Emily, I wanted to take you right then. I could have. Hell, I would have. But don't you think you deserve more than fornicating in an old pickup?" He laced his fingers through mine and smiled. "I want to make love with you in a bed. Not screw you in the front seat of a truck because I'm angry with you and need to relieve some tension. And I prefer you to be mentally present, although, after tonight, I'm thinking that part could be optional."

I jabbed him lightly in the ribs with my elbow.

He pulled my hand up and kissed it lightly. "Ever been bedridden?"

"Is this a trick question?"

Something cold and hard slipped around my wrist. "This will keep you from running off again."

Chapter Sixteen

"You're handcuffing me to you?"

Jake grinned proudly. "Yep."

"This better be something kinky."

He rolled away, and the bracelet pulled at my arm. "If you think sleeping is kinky, then you're on the right track."

Between the drunken bar brawl and the guilt over the phone call to Gina, I didn't have it in me to argue. "You're enjoying this."

"Damn straight." He glanced over his shoulder at me. "But maybe tomorrow night, I'll throw you a bone."

"Big of you."

He laughed. "Yeah, I thought you'd like that."

I shot him a look of disbelief. "I can't believe you're scheduling sex with me. What are we, fifty years old?"

"I'm not scheduling. It's more like I'm telling you what's going to happen. God knows it hasn't worked out in our favor the way we've been doing it. Tomorrow, we're going to

try it my way."

"No thanks," I grumbled, declaring a Mexican standoff. "You've lost your chance."

"We'll see." The corners of his mouth crinkled slightly. "You can consider it a late birthday present."

"Wow. You're really full of yourself. Don't light a candle you don't intend to blow out."

"It'll be win-win, I promise. Now quit acting like it's going to be as bad as getting a tooth pulled and go to bed."

"I hope I piss on you in my sleep."

"Now that's kinky," he noted with a chuckle.

· · ·

It was the worst night of sleep I'd ever had. The handcuff dug into my wrist, making it sore, and at some point during the night, the sound of a rainstorm began slamming into the roof. Lightning crackled through the sky, brightening the room, and thunder roared in my ears. It was like sleeping in a drum while someone beat on the outside. It didn't stop until close to dawn, which is when I finally drifted off.

When I woke up, the handcuff still dangled from my wrist, but Jake wasn't attached. Thank God he hadn't hooked it to the bed frame. Otherwise, I would've peed myself waiting for him to come back. I wanted to go back to bed, but the stale scent of alcohol on my breath made me sick. I brushed my teeth and my hair, dressed in khaki shorts and a pink, stretchy tank top, and hurried over to the main house. I hoped I wasn't too late for breakfast, but wasn't sure how it would fare on my stomach.

Floss stood over a skillet, flipping pancakes and frying

pork sausage patties. Hank and Jake sipped coffee at the kitchen table with newspapers in front of their faces. Only Hank and Floss looked up as I entered.

"Good morning," she said. "Hungry? I've got a new batch of pancakes nearly ready and homemade blackberry syrup on the table."

"Sure, that'd be great," I replied. "Can I help you do anything?"

She eyeballed the handcuffs still attached to my wrist and smiled. "You can sit your hind end in a chair and eat some breakfast, that's what you can do."

I did as I was told, pulling up a chair next to Jake. He folded the newspaper up and set it on the table. His eye had completely swelled shut and the side of his face looked like someone had taken a tire iron to it.

He pointed to the cuffs. "Want me to take those off?"

"Definitely," I said, holding up my wrist as he pulled the key from his pocket and unlocked them. "Does your eye hurt?"

"My whole face hurts."

Hank glanced over at me from behind his newspaper. "Must've been some fight last night."

I leaned over, lightly touching the ugly purplish bruise on Jake's cheek, making him wince. "I'm sorry. I know it's my fault, but I didn't mean for any of it to happen."

Jake's good eye widened slightly. At first, I figured it was because he never thought he'd get an apology out of me, but then Hank spoke. "How was it your fault?"

"Didn't he tell you I caused the fight?"

"Jake told us he protected you from that little bastard, Jeremy."

"That's partially true," I said, looking back at Jake. "But there's more to it."

Jake touched my arm. "Emily, you don't have to — "

"No, it's okay." It was time I took responsibility for my own actions. I turned back toward Hank and let out a small sigh. "I flirted with Jeremy to make Jake jealous. It's why the fight broke out to begin with. It shouldn't have happened, and I feel terrible it went so far."

"Of course you do, dear," Floss said, bringing me a plate of food. "Now eat up. Don't let those pancakes get cold."

Hank returned to reading his paper.

"That's it? That's all you're going to say?"

"Well, for heaven's sake, what more is there?" Floss asked.

Hank peered around his newspaper at me. "Everyone makes mistakes, honey. But if it will make you feel better, I could take you out back, throw you over the fence, and let the buzzards eat you. I don't know what good it'll do, though." Hank laughed at himself. "Now finish your breakfast."

Floss broke in again. "By the way, Hank, I found my cell phone. I guess I'd left it in the truck yesterday when I went into town."

"Good," he murmured, his nose buried in his newspaper. "I didn't want to have to buy another one."

Instantly, I remembered the phone call I'd placed to Gina. It was dreamlike. I couldn't believe I did something so dumb. Then again, we were talking about me. My biggest fear was that I'd put Gina and Dale in danger with my phone call, all because I wanted to hear her voice. I couldn't berate myself enough.

"You look hung over," Jake said. "You need caffeine."

Still thinking about the phone call I'd made, I snapped at him. "Why? So I can do stupid things faster?" I caught myself, realizing Jake didn't know what I'd done. He couldn't read my mind. "I'm sorry. I…I had a rough night."

Jesus. I'm going to have to tell him the truth. Damn, he's going to think what I already know. I'm a freaking moron.

"Jake, I need to talk to you about—"

"Anybody home?" Cowboy yelled from the front room.

"In the kitchen," Floss yelled back.

When he walked in, I gaped in horror and covered my mouth. Swollen to twice its normal size, Cowboy's slightly crooked nose had a gash over it. The bruising around it looked painful.

"Oh God. I'm sorry about your nose."

He shrugged it off and winked. "Ah, I was too pretty, anyway."

"Is it broken?"

"Usually what happens when you get hit in the face with a beer bottle. It still works, though. That's all that matters." He leaned over Floss's shoulder. "That smells great."

"Sit on down, and I'll fix you up a plate," Floss said, slapping his hand as he reached for a piece of sausage. "And keep your filthy hands out of the food. Ain't no telling where those things have been. I've heard all the rumors."

"All lies," Cowboy said with a smug grin. Jake and I scooted around the table to make room for him. As he sat in the chair next to me, Cowboy snickered. "You guys should see Ox and Judd."

"How'd they fare?" Jake asked.

"Judd has two black eyes and a busted lip, but, as usual, Ox doesn't have a mark on him. He's a scrappy little thing, too quick for anyone to get ahold of. I told him the next time we all get into a fight, I'm going to hold him down and let someone beat the hell out of him. That way he'll match the rest of us."

"Well, at least one person escaped unharmed," I told them. They both looked at me like I was stupid. "Okay, I meant someone besides me."

· · ·

After breakfast, the boys tended to something in the barn for Hank. I helped Floss feed the animals. The horses were fed first, since they impatiently trotted up and down the fence line, snorting and stamping their feet on the soggy ground. It was the equivalent of beating utensils on a table and chanting, "We want food."

The rabbits were almost as demanding. Jack climbed the wire with his front paws while Twitcher ran in circles, growling, as I neared their cage with pellets. At least the birds would wait until I placed the newly replenished feeder down and walked away before they attacked it.

When Floss added a scoop of kibble to Dog's bowl, then poured greasy leftovers and raw fat on top, I cringed with disgust. Since he was not around, I imagined the only things that'd be eating out of that bowl were ants. At least I finally figured out how Dog died. A diet like that would kill anybody.

Once we were done, I watched Floss fill a small wire cage with a dozen baby guineas a man ordered earlier in the morning. It was almost noon before he arrived to pick them up. While Floss handled the transaction, I strolled over to the pigeon pen. I watched them strut back and forth, flapping their delicate wings as they cooed to me. It's where Floss found me.

"You like homing pigeons?" she asked.

"I like listening to them. It's soothing. Makes me want to fall asleep."

"Jake reminds me of a pigeon sometimes," she said.

I looked at her strangely, but didn't say anything. Jake definitely didn't make me want to fall asleep. I wouldn't have minded hearing him coo soft words in my ear, though.

The birds pecked at the ground, bobbing their heads as they walked. Floss was mesmerized by them. "Jake always finds his way home," she said. "Even if it does take him awhile."

Her eyes were watery. She sniffled, pulled a tissue from the pocket of her sundress, and wiped her nose. Not only did she love Jake, but she admired and respected him. He was the son she'd never had. Not wanting to embarrass her, I didn't linger on the emotion welling up in her voice.

"I'd never spent time on a farm before now, but there's no better way to relax than being outdoors," I told her.

"Want to take a little field trip with me?" Floss asked. "I'm going to pick some wild blackberries. I could use an extra hand."

"Sure…well, if Jake will let me. But he'll probably handcuff me to you."

She grinned. "He's a rotten scoundrel sometimes, isn't he?"

We found Hank and Jake in the pole barn repairing the gate to the colt's stall. Hank wiped his sweaty forehead with a handkerchief as Jake kneeled to put the last screw into the hinge.

"What happened to Cowboy?" I asked.

Jake finished drilling. "He left when his pager went off. A barn fire on the other side of Rickety Bridge, I believe." Jake grabbed a bottle of water off the top of the post and downed half of it.

"Have any objections to me picking berries with Floss?"

"Depends," he said, grinning mischievously. "How many pies is she making me?"

Floss grabbed a couple of white buckets from the small stack against the wall. "One. I'm using the rest for jam."

He turned his attention to her. "Two, and we got a deal."

"Jacob Ward! You can't bargain this girl's freedom with pies."

Bemused, Jake poked her some more. "I could ask for three. After all, I am injured."

"Two, and that's all," Floss said. "And if I use sugar instead of salt, you should consider yourself lucky."

Hank got a kick out of their exchange. "Floss, if you two are going to pick those berries, then you better get a move on. It's supposed to storm again this afternoon. We're going to finish up, board the horses, then we'll be done for the day."

"Then we'll be back before the rain starts," she promised.

• • •

Automatically, I assumed we'd be picking berries somewhere on the property. I was delighted when Floss told me to get in the truck. She drove us a few miles down a dirt road and pulled into a private drive resembling an overgrown trail.

Two long muddy ruts marked the way, divided by a

median of tall grass and small shrubs that scraped the belly of the truck. She slowed, veering around large water-filled potholes in the tracks as we bounced around the cab.

Floss parked at the fence line, grabbed the white buckets, and ducked under the barbed fence. We furthered our quest into the forest with me right behind her. By the time we got to the blackberry bushes, I could no longer see the truck and had worked up a sweat.

"Whew!" I said, wiping at my forehead with the back of my hand. "It's a bit of a hike."

Floss grinned, not looking the least bit winded. "Wait until we head back carrying buckets of fruit. Good exercise." She examined the bushes for a moment in silence. "Not all the berries are ripe. Don't pick anything pink or red, just the black ones."

There weren't many black ones, but plenty of red and pink. "Not many ripe ones, Floss. Maybe we came out too early."

"We did, but it had a purpose. I was checking to see if the bushes were overgrown. I'll have to get my loppers after these ornery things soon and prune them back, plus it's better to harvest the berries by hand after it rains. You don't run into as many bees."

"Is there a right way to do this?" I asked, brushing my hand along the deep-veined leaves before lifting a large juicy blackberry with my palm.

"Watch for thorns," Floss said, plucking a couple of berries and tossing them into her bucket.

We picked next to each other, then worked in opposite directions. If it wasn't for my ankles getting scratched by the scrubby brush, I probably would've enjoyed myself. I guess it was my own stupid fault for wearing sandals.

Bright sunlight beat down on us, burning my limbs and scalp with its consistently hot rays. I ignored the heat and focused on the pleasant, woodsy scent emitted from the green space around me. It reminded me of Jake, except his scent had an underlying citrusy tone. It was almost strange that I could recall the undertones of his scent so easily, when I couldn't even remember the sound of my mother's voice. Being in this place, surrounded by Jake's loved ones, had only left me aching for the family I had lost. Yet, I'd never felt closer to them.

Juice from the berries already stained the bucket's interior, as well as my fingers, when Floss suggested we take a break. We left our buckets and sat in the shade of some fountain-like trees a few yards away.

I plucked a dandelion out of the ground and threaded it into the hair above my ear as Jake had done before. How he had smiled at me afterward made me feel prettier, more feminine than I'd ever felt before. Like the flower had anything to do with it.

"Do you like flowers?" Floss asked.

"Oh, I love them!" I said. Then my face contorted.

Floss noticed. "You sure you like flowers? Your lip is curling up like you sniffed a skunk."

I laughed. "I just realized something, that's all. I've never actually been given flowers by anyone before, not even a man. I guess none of them ever thought I was special enough."

"Well, I get flowers every year."

"Aww. It's sweet Hank would go through the trouble—"

"He doesn't," she admitted. "The flowers I get are the

ones God sends my way every spring. All the flowers I'll ever need. He cares enough to send them, so I care enough to enjoy them."

"Honestly, I hardly ever noticed them before coming here," I said with a shrug. "Maybe that's why God's punishing me by putting me in this situation."

Floss shook her head. "Who said God is punishing you, dear? Maybe he wanted to surprise you. I see how he looks at you."

I gave her a smile. "God?"

"No, dear, I'm talking about Jake. Keep up with me." Floss rose to her feet. "I'm going to show you something." She walked over to the buckets on the ground, pulled out a berry and returned to where I sat. Gently breaking the berry open with her fingernail, she rubbed the stain over her lips, instantly brightening them. "See," she said, smacking her lips together. "God gives you everything you need. You just have to figure out how to use it to your advantage."

"Jake is a little more complicated. He has rules. I'm surprised he let me come out here with you. I'm not even sure why he did. Probably his way of buttering me up after handcuffing me last night."

"Complaining doesn't create solutions," Floss said, pulling the dandelion from my hair. She held it lightly under my chin. "Besides, you like butter." She winked with wise, knowing eyes. Then she went back to picking berries.

I joined her and we finished filling our buckets as dark gray clouds thickened in the distance, blocking out the sun's rays.

"Hey, Floss," I yelled. "These blackberry bushes over here have been trampled. Nothing left to pick."

"The deer have probably been through here a time or two," she said, looking off at the dark black clouds forming in the distance. "Can't stay much longer, but there are some more brambles near the creek. They produce better because they get more moisture, but we don't usually pick from them. Walking the hill hurts Hank's knee. Why don't you take this empty bucket down there and start picking while I take these to the truck?"

"Which way is the creek?"

"Over there, north of the large red oak. The creek's small, but feeds into the Trinity River. Walk straight that way and you'll find it," Floss said. "Be back in a minute."

Floss shrank into the trees as I walked down the hill looking for the blackberry bushes.

The air cooled as the wind picked up, gusting through the trees and warning creatures of the approaching storm.

Who knows how far I walked, but I hadn't come across the blackberry bushes. Had I strayed off course? All the trees looked the same, and it's not like my brain had a built-in compass. When I heard the sound of running water, I changed course slightly and strolled in that direction. The sound grew louder. I was getting closer, but still saw nothing.

I positioned myself on a tall dirt mound, trying to catch a glimpse of the creek. Ten seconds later, I realized the mistake I'd made. A biting, stinging pain overwhelmed me. Hundreds of angry, rust-colored fire ants swarmed my feet and ankles, attacking in great numbers. I disturbed their nest, and in return, they had proficiently declared war.

Jumping around in circles, I knocked them away. Every time I thought I got them all, more crawled out from between my toes or the backs of my heels. My feet were on fire, and the burning needed to be doused out. I made a run for the creek.

As I ran, I caught a glimpse of the water. But in a flash, I realized I hadn't found the small creek, but rather the larger Trinity River. I tried to stop abruptly, but the steep bank was slippery and the forward momentum wouldn't allow it.

My knees buckled, forcing me to slide down the bank ten feet before dropping into the river.

The runoff from last night's rainstorm had swelled the dirty river, creating a fast-moving monster, littered with debris. The swift current jostled me around underwater, lashing at me and depriving me of oxygen. It released its grip and I forced my way to the surface, but was only able to take a short breath before the monster dragged me under for the second time.

Again, I fought my way to the surface, smacking my skull on a large branch. Though dazed, I clung to the floating driftwood, using it as a life preserver. I'm not sure how many miles the river shoved me downstream, but somehow, I slowly maneuvered myself closer to the bank and climbed out.

Collapsing with fatigue on the sandy shore, my stomach rolled with nausea. I coughed and sputtered muddy river water from my burning lungs. My mouth felt gritty. I wanted to puke, but couldn't. Though the next wave of nausea cramped my stomach tightly, I pushed my tangled wet strands out of my face and peered around, trying to get my bearings.

"Hellooo?" I yelled out, though the fire in my feet had transferred to my throat. My voice echoed in the solitude. Swept away by the rushing water, my sandals were no longer on my feet. Catastrophic, since hiking barefoot through the woods would be a slow, tedious process. But it wasn't the first time I'd been alone in a bad situation and had to rely on myself.

Determined to make my way back to Floss, I crawled up the bank and stepped farther into the woods. Following the river upstream, I carefully made my way over rocks, rotting branches, and dead leaves. The brutal terrain bruised and scraped my feet.

By now, Floss had surely realized I was missing. She would've alerted Jake, who would be out searching. They'd find me and he'd yell at me for being an overbearing pain in his ass and tell me how stupid I was. And he'd be right, of course. Because who the hell in their right mind almost kills themselves picking stupid berries? Well, besides me. Just proves that I don't belong here. Damn it, Jake. Why'd you bring me here and make me fall for you? This is all *your* fault.

I snapped back to reality when something moved in the brush. A tiny reddish-brown piglet with broken stripes running down its sides stared back at me. The piglet squealed and ran skittishly back into the briars. It would've been funny that I startled the piglet, if several grunting adults hadn't stepped out.

Before coming to Texas, the only knowledge I'd had of pigs was what I learned from watching *Charlotte's Web*. Pigs were cute, pink, and friendly. But these weren't pigs; they were wild hogs. Hank had warned me how dangerous they could be. I suspected the two smaller ones were females.

Physically, the third hog was different. He was big, black, and so obviously male with thick, wiry hair raised on the back of his neck in an aggressive position.

His massive head was too large for his body, and his legs

and snout were longer than the females'. He made a scissor motion with his jaw to show me his exceptionally sharp tusks, ones he planned to put to good use. I could hear him grunting with agitation, my presence exciting him. Unlike Wilbur, he wasn't cute, pink, or friendly.

Then he charged me.

Chapter Seventeen

I barely had time to contemplate what to do, but managed to scramble up the tree next to me. Thank God the branches hung low enough for me to pull myself up.

The grunting, pissed-off hog tromped back and forth through the briars, taking out his frustration on the base of the tree, slashing deep gouges with its tusks. I tightened my grip on the branches, digging my fingers into the ridges of the bark.

From the safety of the tree, I saw more hogs on the other side of the briar patch. The herd consisted of eleven feral hogs, counting the five small piglets running jerkily behind their mother. I wasn't sure which piglet had noted my arrival, but now that I was helplessly stuck up a tree, I wanted to drop-kick the little fucker.

I pelted the hogs with small branches in hopes of scaring them off, but every time one of them squealed, the boar became even more agitated, lashing out at the tree trunk again.

I'd paid so much attention to the danger below me, I hadn't realized the danger from above. A sudden crack of lightning scared me almost as much as it scared the hogs. They startled and ran in circles, grunting and squealing as they regrouped. Once it started raining, they shot off into the woods, as if they didn't dare get wet. Who knew pigs were made of sugar?

My muscles hurt, and as badly as I wanted out of the tree, I forced myself to stay put, in case the hogs hadn't left the area. At least a half hour later, I swung out of the tree, picked up the largest stick I could find as a weapon, and resumed my hike, walking as fast as possible. Running would've been quicker, but not smart on bare feet.

Determined to keep moving, I waded through slick mud and trudged over sharp sticks and rocks that bruised and poked into my heels. Brush scratched against my legs. Thorny vines littered the ground, pricking into my feet as I stepped on them. My wet hair plastered to my scalp and rainwater dripped into my eyes, making me blink constantly to clear my vision.

I tried to think of it as a nature walk, but who in their right mind would be out in this weather? My clothes stuck to me, chafing my waterlogged, sunburned skin, but I had to keep moving. Every moment I stopped to rest or pull thorns from my dirty feet put me dangerously closer to nightfall.

The longer I walked, the more my stress level rose. What if Jake assumed I had run off again? Would he bother looking for me? No, I couldn't let myself think that. Though Jake couldn't go to the authorities and organize a search party without drawing attention, he'd definitely be looking for me.

I hoped.

Hefting myself over a large dead tree, I spotted a dilapidated hunting blind ahead. It was unoccupied, unless you counted the mud daubers building a home in the entryway. I didn't want to stop moving, but walking through the woods at night in the rain wasn't an option.

I climbed up the broken ladder into the moldy blind and found a dry spot in the far corner. The hunting blind probably hadn't been used in years and was falling apart at the seams. The leaky roof, rotted through in several places, left the wooden floor damp and swollen. One dry corner was all I needed and, apparently, all I was going to get.

I leaned my back against a wall of questionable sturdiness and shook from the inside out. It wasn't cold, but the cool rain had soaked my sunburned limbs, and the contrast in temperatures made me shiver with the chills. The idea of spending the night in the woods alone probably played a part in it as well.

My feet felt like raw, splinter-infested nubs, but were too caked with mud to see any real damage. I didn't bother wiping it away, though. The mud soothed the ant bites, keeping them from itching or burning. Dizzy and nauseated, I curled into a ball with severe muscle cramps.

The hunting blind darkened more and more until I could hardly see anything. I propped open a rotting, hinged window, but it was a moonless night and just as dark outside as it was inside. I closed my eyes and breathed deeply, listening to the sound of the rain slapping the roof and feeling the walls shake every time the thunder rolled. The storm kept up its strength, but after a while, I lost what was left of mine.

I slumped back, trying to doze off, but couldn't. When I opened my eyes again, panic hit me. It was pitch black, darker than dark, and I saw nothing, as if someone had stolen my vision. Many people are born not being able to see, but for a person with sight to go instantly blind, the terror is tremendous. It went against every grain in my body.

Fear weaved through my mind, conjuring up scenarios and tainted thoughts as to what happens to a girl alone in the woods at night. An image of Bigfoot popped into my head. Then one of vultures picking flesh from my bones. I guess I needed a legitimate cause for my insomnia, something besides staying alert in case Jake came looking for me.

Though I had blamed him earlier, I knew it wasn't Jake's fault that I was in this mess. If I were being honest with myself, I'd admit I had lost my way years before, after learning of my parents' deaths. In some ways, I still felt like that lost little girl who had no one to turn to. No one who cared. No one to trust.

But that wasn't true. Not anymore. I had people who were looking out for me. And Jake *would* find me. That I was sure of. He'd probably kill me once he did, but he would definitely not stop searching until he got the chance.

It was a comforting thought, but it still scared the hell out of me at the same time. Because what if I trusted him to come for me and he didn't? Like my parents...or my policeman...

After it finally stopped raining, sleep deprivation and fatigue kicked in.

I fell asleep, dreaming I was in some sort of terrarium. I hiked through a forest, crawling over sticks and rocks in my path, sluggishly trying to find my way through the never-ending greenery. As I piloted my way through the dream, I realized someone watched me, waited for me, called to me. The two men who stepped out of the woods with the rope and shovel entered my thoughts. Voodoo people? The one missing an eyeball reached for me and said, "I want to feel your nice, warm innards."

I cringed as his face morphed into Sergio's, his blank, dead stare sending chills through my bones. He touched his cold fingers to my neck, and I shoved his hand away. He grasped my shoulders, shaking me and, although I screamed, he wouldn't let go.

Then I heard a familiar whuffling sound. A horse? Yes, that's it. The same sound I heard when I went into the barn to talk to…Jake!

Disconnecting from my dream, I felt someone's hands on my shoulder and opened my eyes. The light of a lantern glowed behind a large, dark figure. It shadowed his face, but I knew the man wasn't Jake. I shot backward and put my hands up instinctually for protection.

"Emily…it's me."

"Junior?" I leaned closer, caught a whiff of wintergreen, and relief swept over me.

He gathered me in a tight bear hug I hadn't known I needed until he'd given it. "You're okay," he crooned softly, rubbing my shoulder. "Your feet…how bad are they?"

I pulled back from him and wiped at my face with the back of my hand. "They're sore. How'd you find me?"

"I used to be a tracker, remember?" He pulled a canteen from around his shoulder, unscrewed the cap, and handed it to me. "It's something I've always done well."

He watched as I guzzled a large amount of water. Then

he used the canteen to wash some of the mud off my feet, trying to get a better look at their condition. "You've got some thorns embedded."

"Can you get them out?"

Stone-faced, Junior pulled the large buck knife from the sheath on his belt. My mouth dropped open. Last thing I wanted was someone poking my feet with a pint-sized sword, making them hurt more.

"Wait! Isn't there a less painful solution?"

Amusement flickered in his eyes as he put his knife away. "Floss can take care of them for you when we get you back to the house. Can you stand?"

I tried to, but pain shot through my feet, pulling me back down.

"Scoot toward the door. I'll help you from there."

Junior slung the canteen strap over his shoulder and picked up the lantern. He pushed open the blind door and clicked his tongue. A large black stallion moved into view, wearing a saddle with the butt of a rifle sticking up next to it. The horse bobbed his head and gave a snort as he came closer, responding to his master's gentle command.

Effortlessly, Junior lifted me onto the horse. He grabbed the lantern and the reins, then led us away from the blind on foot.

"Junior, you're going the wrong way."

He shot me a challenging look. "You want to trade places? I'll ride and you can walk us out."

I winced. "Sorry, I don't mean to be a backseat driver. Sometimes I have control issues."

"Sometimes?" Junior laughed, as if he regarded me as entertainment. "I thought Lucy was demanding and free-spirited, but she never had anything on you."

"Lucy?"

"My daughter."

"Oh, yeah. The one with the great taste in clothes. I bet she wreaked havoc on your wallet," I said, gripping the saddle horn tighter as the horse followed Junior down a slight hill.

"It was always her taste in men I worried more about."

"She's dating someone you don't like?"

"Not anymore," he said abruptly, his tone becoming more serious.

I got the feeling he didn't want to talk about it, so I changed the subject. "Some hogs cornered me when I came through the woods."

He nodded. "I know."

"They trapped me up in a tree."

"I know that, too."

"The big one looked weird, and he was mean."

"Most wild hogs can become aggressive if cornered, but if you stay away from them, they'll usually leave you alone."

I shook my head, though he couldn't see because his back was to me. "I wasn't messing with him. It was the other way around. He charged me, and I don't mean by asking for my credit card."

He grinned back at me. "Why do you think he looked weird?" I gave him a quick description of the females and babies. "The sows sound like wild domesticates," Junior said. "Some of the locals call them Piney Wood Rooters. They're leaner because they don't pick up weight easily. What about the boar?"

"Gigantic, probably like four-hundred pounds," I told

him. "And he had a big nose."

"You mean a long nose?"

"Whatever. But smaller ears. His back sloped like this," I said, using my hand to demonstrate an uphill motion. "He had this short, straight tail with hair or something on the end that looked funny, like…oh, I know! Pumba's tail on *The Lion King*. Oh, never mind. You probably don't even know what movie I'm talking about… Anyway, he was different than the others. Much scarier and way more aggressive."

Junior stopped, walked up beside the horse, and glared at me, his face serious. "You're trying to tell me you went up against a pure Russian boar weighing four-hundred pounds?"

"Is that what he was?"

He shrugged, then started leading the horse again. "It's not like I'd call your description a reliable method for identification."

"Hey, I got a good look at him while stuck in the damn tree. Wasn't much else to do."

Junior flicked another grin over his shoulder.

After that, we drifted in and out of silence. The dark night air and the rocking motion of the horse made me groggy. Junior tried to keep me awake by talking. It must've been some chore, since I never saw him as someone who did much of it.

"Open your eyes, Emily, or you're not going to stay upright on that horse much longer," he ordered, stopping for a moment. "It's close to daylight." The blue tinge of morning happened upon us, so Junior extinguished the lantern and stowed it on the side of the saddle.

Up to this point, I hadn't had the courage to inquire

about Jake, but I needed to know before we got back to the house. "Okay, how pissed off is Jake at—"

"Shhhh!" Junior stood motionless for a second more, then reached for his rifle.

He stepped in front of the horse and motioned with his hand for me to stay put. He walked toward a sound I couldn't hear, guarding me from an unknown evil. Both his hands cradled the weapon in a defensive position, ready to react at a moment's notice.

Like a cannonball, the boar shot out of the brush straight toward him. Junior raised the rifle and aimed, but he didn't shoot. I wanted to yell, but wouldn't dare risk distracting him, which would inevitably endanger his life—and mine. The hog was closing in fast.

Now! Damn it, shoot him now!

I opened my mouth to scream, but he fired. The sound ricocheted off the surrounding trees. With a bullet hole between the eyes, the boar collapsed, hitting the ground and sliding to a dead stop next to Junior's booted feet.

The horse lurched skittishly under me. I grasped a handful of its mane and held on in case it bolted. A click of Junior's tongue settled the stallion instantly.

The sight was ridiculous. Junior stood over the massive boar as if it were a harmless puppy. The man had steel cable nerves and a pair of brass balls.

My eyes widened to the size of saucers. "Holy shit!"

Junior shrugged. "Hakuna matata."

• • •

Junior had parked his truck and horse trailer two miles

downstream from where he found my tracks on the bank. Once he trailered his horse, we drove toward the house.

"I can't believe you found me," I told him, the hero worship written all over my face. "Especially at night after it rained. You must be good at tracking." He smiled at me, but didn't say anything. "I don't really know how to thank you."

"You just did."

I lowered my eyes. "I thought Jake would be looking for me…but I guess…well, he must be mad…"

"Nobody's mad, Emily. Worried, but not mad. Jake and the other boys found the spot where you fell into the river and called me. I picked up my horse and parked my truck farther downstream while they all split up searching the banks from there on foot. Over the years, I've taught each of them boys how to track, and they're good"—he gave me a wink—"but I'm better."

I offered him a smile. "Should we call and tell them I'm with you?"

"Cell phones don't work back here. Too many trees, no clearings. When we hit the highway, we'll call Floss and let her spread the word. They're carrying two-way radios to stay in touch with Hank."

"It was kind of you and the others to help. You guys hardly know me."

"I know you, Emily. Better than you think. You are so much like my daughter, Lucy, in personality. The two of you could've passed for sisters."

"I'd like to meet her."

"You can't. She died four years ago."

The shock made my head whip around to him. "Oh, I…I'm sorry. No one told me. I thought the clothes…"

"I couldn't get rid of them before, but you came along and…well, I wanted to help. It made it easier to part with them."

I patted his hand with understanding. "May I ask how she died?"

"Lucy was in her first year of college when she met a man named Brian Wellington. They went out only a few times, but he was obsessed with her. He got jealous easily, so she broke it off. When he caught her at a party talking to another boy, he went crazy. After she left the party, he followed her back to her dorm and stabbed her to death. The bastard went into hiding before the police could arrest him."

"Did they find him?"

"No." Junior's eyes turned black, making him look more savage than I'd ever seen him. "And they never will."

I swallowed. He didn't have to spell it out for me. "Is that why you stopped working as a tracker?"

"Yes."

"What about Lucy's mother?"

"Suzanne died a year after Lucy from a brain aneurysm."

"I'm sorry. I know what it's like to lose everyone you care about. My parents…"

"I know."

I gave him a strange look. "Is there anything you *don't* know?"

He grinned, but didn't answer.

"Who told you?"

"The first time I met you, I knew something was going on. When Jake introduced you as his girlfriend, you were caught off guard." He chuckled softly, as if remembering the look on my face. "Few people can lie to me and get away with it. Jake's not one of them."

"I understand helping Jake find me when you thought I was his girlfriend, but now that you know I'm nothing to him, why bother?"

"I could find you faster than the boys could. I wasn't able to save my daughter...or my wife...but I could help you. It won't bring them back, but maybe it'll save my soul. " He gave me a knowing look. "And you're something to Jake, whether you two admit it or not."

• • •

Floss hugged me tightly, bringing a smile to my face, before Junior could lift me out of the truck. I didn't doubt she'd been standing in the driveway since we hung up with her.

"Hank and Jake are on their way back now," Floss said. "Let's get you inside and clean you up."

Junior carried me into the cottage with ease and sat me gently on the bed. He turned to leave, but I grabbed his hand, pulling him back. I touched the side of his face and kissed his cheek. "You're a good man, Junior."

With his Native American skin color it was hard to tell, but I was sure he blushed. "Take care," he said before leaving.

Floss played doctor, checking the bump on my head and looking at the scratches on my legs before pulling two thorns and a couple of large splinters out of my feet. Several small cuts had dirt packed in them, but I told her I'd scrub it out in the shower. She helped me stand—amazingly easy to do when you don't have spikes crippling your feet—and shuffled me into the bathroom.

I sat on the bed with fresh clothes and clean, damp hair

while Floss checked my feet again. With the dirt and mud gone, thorns and splinters would be easier to spot. She removed another sizable splinter, applied antibiotic cream to both feet, then wrapped them in gauze. I was glad I wouldn't have to look at the small white pustules that had formed where the fire ants stung me. It was like my feet had broken out with a bad case of acne.

As she finished, Jake exploded through the cottage door wearing his gun in his shoulder holster. I jumped, not having heard them pull up. He didn't say a word, just positioned himself in the doorway. I tried not to look directly at him. Flustered, I waited for him to move, to do something, to yell at me, but he didn't say anything.

"I'm going to let you two chat," Floss said before making herself scarce.

The room closed in on me and I couldn't breathe. If Floss was running, I had to expect the worst. I wished she'd taken Jake's gun with her.

He was bound to be upset that I caused more trouble, costing them all a sleepless night. I probably could guess his thoughts. *Hurricane Emily strikes again.* He openly and loudly disapproved of my stunts any other time. Why wasn't he shouting colorful words at me already?

After the bar fight, he struggled to control his temper in the parking lot. Before that, I hadn't thought he was capable of losing control. Not completely, anyway. Sure, he yelled at me a lot when I made him angry. Holy freaking cow! I must've done a bang-up job pushing his buttons if I left him speechless. He was never this quiet, this motionless, for any length of time.

I should say something, apologize or at least explain

what happened. I wasn't sure it was the smart thing to do. His silence and restricted movements were "Don't Feed The Bear" signs, if I'd ever seen them. If I opened my mouth now, I'd be inviting the danger. Maybe it's what he wanted. His way of surrounding me with fuel, striking a match, and letting the flames force me to react. With unwavering patience, Jake could easily wait me out.

Someone had to go first. "Before you say anything, I'd like to—"

"Don't." The only word he spoke.

Shit. "If you're going to yell at me, get it over—"

"Don't speak."

Fuck me. What's he going to say next, three words? The anticipation was killing me, but I sat quietly, wondering what he was thinking. Come on, Jake. Yell at me. Punch a wall. Do something. Anything.

When he moved toward me, I changed my mind.

He sat on the side of the bed, facing me. I instinctually drew away from him, but he wouldn't allow it. His arm slid around my waist, pulling me back and making me flinch. I still wasn't sure of his mindset. My eyes refused to meet his, avoiding the storm I imagined raging inside, but he caught my chin and lifted it.

I was surprised at what I saw. Jake looked terrible. No, he looked like shit. And it wasn't from the bruises left over from the bar brawl.

A painful scowl puckered his face and his dark, unruly hair was disheveled. His gray eyes appeared weathered, as if he had aged ten years overnight. Every bit of the strain showed on his face, but he didn't look mad. He looked... pitiful.

"Jake…?"

"Shhh," he said, pulling me into his chest. "Don't talk." His hand twisted into my hair as his fingers made feather-light strokes against my scalp. "Jesus, Emily. You were gone, dead for all I knew. I wasn't sure we'd find you in time and I couldn't stop thinking if I'd only—"

"Jake, I'm fine."

He studied my face as his eyes clouded over. "But I'm not." Then his mouth covered mine.

I tried not to lose my smarts, struggling to control the mind clutter and scattered feelings. But I had to contemplate whether Jake had a passive-aggressive disorder. When his tongue swept into my mouth, caressing mine, I no longer cared. After all, I'm no doctor. Hell, I was in the midst of spiking a fever myself.

When Jake resurfaced, his gray eyes had changed. Cold, murky ashes now smoldered with heat. He traced a velvety finger along my collarbone, as if finger painting across my skin, until he reached the strap of my halter top. Pushing it aside, he gently pressed his lips to my shoulder, then his tongue, making me shiver at his slight touch.

Confused, I pushed him back. "W-what are you doing?"

"If you don't know," Jake said, snaking his hand around my neck, "then you're way behind." He nipped at my bottom lip and trailed his mouth up my jaw.

"Wait…" I murmured unconvincingly, as his lips brushed across my ear, his tongue flicking at my lobe. But he wasn't stopping. "Jake, hold on." I put my hands on his chest and moved him back again. "Why are you acting like nothing happened?"

"I'm not," he said softly, settling his hands on my hips

and pulling me closer. "Something happened. Fine. We'll talk about it later."

"Later?" Did we switch roles somehow and I wasn't aware of it? "Why later? Why not right now?"

"Because, right now, we're busy." Jake nudged me onto my back and crawled over me, lifting my shirt to reveal my midriff. He tickled it with his soft lips, moving upward with the shirt until he neared my breasts.

Adrenaline coursed through my veins, disrupting the delicate balance of oxygen and carbon dioxide in my brain. It made it harder to think. Was he planning to yell at me later? If so, I wasn't sure I wanted to have sex with him before getting berated.

With my hands, I blocked his progression to my breasts. "Talk first, sex later."

He groaned with frustration and flopped onto his back. "Never thought I'd hear you say that," he grumbled.

"Neither did I," I admitted, trying to get control of my senses. "What is this? Aren't you mad at me?"

"For stopping me, yes. For falling into the river and getting lost in the woods, no."

I tossed him a suspicious glance. "You're not mad?"

"God, Emily, it was an accident. We knew what happened the moment we found where you fell into the water. What we didn't know was what happened to you afterward. I wasn't even sure you made it out of the river alive. Not until Floss reached us on the radio and told us Junior had found you." He ran his fingers through his hair, the stress of the memory showing plainly on his face. "I knew Junior would get to you first. The boys and I are good at tracking, but—"

"He's better," I said, finishing his sentence.

Jake's eyes narrowed. "Junior said that, didn't he?"

I smirked in confirmation.

"That stupid Indian has no modesty when it comes to his abilities," he said. "He's good at everything and damn well knows it. But I guess you know that already."

"Because he found me first?"

"We passed Junior on the road. He told us about the hogs. You don't know how lucky you are the Russian boar didn't get ahold of you."

"Well, I'm not stupid. I wasn't going to stand there and let a four-hundred pound pig—"

"Five."

"Huh?"

Jake sat upright. "Junior said the hog was closer to five hundred pounds."

"Oh." I wasn't sure if I was supposed to feel stupid for guessing low or smart for coming as close as I did.

"It was a good guess," Jake said, which made me feel better. He swiped a strand of hair from my cheek and pushed it behind my ear. His hand rested on my neck, his thumb rolling lightly over my cheek. His eyes glazed over with emotion. "I…I don't know what I would've done if something had happened to you, Emily."

I touched his face in an effort to comfort him, but didn't miss the shift in his posture or the stretched seam in his jeans. "Jake, I—"

"I need you, Emily. I need to touch you, to feel you under me. No more waiting. No more wanting. Right now."

"What about the rules? You said—"

"Screw the rules." He pushed me back onto my back, rolled on top of me, and nuzzled into my neck. "Now, where were we?"

Something dug into my rib cage. "Wait a second. You forgot something."

"I have condoms," he whispered, touching his lips to my skin.

"That's not what I meant," I said, though he ignored me, still licking and kissing my neck. "Jake…? Jake, stop."

Reluctantly, he paused, but I could feel his hard-on through his jeans. "Please tell me you're kidding."

"No. It's hurting me. Where are you putting your gun?"

Jake grinned widely. "Depends on which one you're referring to."

Chapter Eighteen

Once Jake's 9mm handgun rested safely on the nightstand, he returned to the bed. He slithered up my body, kissing and touching lightly. An orientation of sorts. As if he was accustoming me to his touch, preparing my body for the inevitable.

The stubble on his chin rasped across my sensitive skin like steel wool, making the pangs of longing start low in my belly. I craved the tenderness he offered. The need to fulfill ourselves threatened to amp up the passion quicker than expected. Our clothes were merely speed bumps in the road to stimulation.

With our clothing lying in a heap on the floor, Jake pressed his lips to my ear, whispering obscene rumblings of expectation and promise. "You have no idea what I want to do to you, Emily. What I'm *about* to do to you," he corrected. "God, I want to taste you."

I could've OD'd on his words alone. I licked my wet,

swollen lips. "So what are you waiting for?"

He propped himself up on his knees and flitted glances up and down my body, staring ravenously with a sex-starved expression. Jake resembled a man in a hunger crisis eyeing a buffet. It was a raunchy glare, his darkened eyes sponging up every detail of my naked flesh.

When his tender mouth closed on my inner thigh, I pressed my fist to my lips and let out a muffled cry. With feathery strokes of his tongue, Jake massaged my thighs, tempering me, adjusting me to his heat slowly before he tasted.

His ambitious mouth targeted me in all the right places. I arched under him, my hips undulating rhythmically in time with his pace. His creative fingers pulsed over my sensitive skin, causing the pressure to build. My hands fisted his hair as he pushed two large fingers inside me, rapidly building pressure that would result in an explosion.

The elusive orgasm I'd been chasing since I met Jake fiercely consumed my body like flames from a fire. I twitched and convulsed recklessly until my breath bottomed out and I finally let out a deep, satisfying moan.

I wanted to feel him plunging into me with the forcefulness he possessed. But he had other plans. Jake held on to my hips, pulled me back to him, and continued his exploration of my body with his mouth. I begged him to take me, but he ignored me. Instead, he carried me over the threshold of pleasure once more.

Waves of sensations vibrated inside me, making me purr with ecstasy. I appreciated the attentiveness, the generosity, but even then, for a brief second, I wasn't sure Jake would stop long enough to give himself to me fully.

I squirmed in his grip, begging for more. "God, Jake, I

want you. Please…"

The grin he wore as he rose to his knees wasn't lost on me. He wanted to hear me pleading, begging him to penetrate my body to alleviate the deep, throbbing ache only one part of his could. He quickly snapped on a condom and kneed my thighs apart, positioning himself with his hand. I could feel his erection prodding at my soft folds, but he didn't shove into me as expected.

"Open your eyes," he demanded, unwinding my fingers that were still coiled around the sheets and interlacing them with his.

The heavy-lidded, lust-filled gaze I offered lit up his face, and a primal urge took over. He pulled my hips up roughly and grunted as he buried his thick, hot shaft inside, grinding against me fully. He kept scorching eye contact that burned into me, searing me with his flesh as well as his mind. It wasn't fair for a person to have this much power over my emotions, my body, but I had accepted it the moment our clothes hit the floor.

No air was left in the room. I couldn't catch my breath. I was plummeting in a merciless freefall that sucked all of the oxygen from my lungs and, although I grasped for it, my ripcord of completion was still out of reach.

I swept my hands along his back, feeling the hard-packed muscles tightening, rippling under my fingers. He was getting closer. But Jake was going for the big O…mine, not his own. Purposefully, he was holding himself back until he got what he came for. Literally.

He didn't seem obsessed with trying to make me scream like a porn star, but I couldn't say the urge hadn't been there to do so. If I didn't come again soon, I'd surely end up with brain damage.

"Come for me," he demanded, shoving himself deeper into me. "Now, Emily. I want to feel it."

He intended to get what he wanted, even if it meant coercing it out of me like a modern day pirate. Jake had charted the route to my satisfaction, but on his map, X didn't mark the spot. G did. And he was obviously a "leave no stone unturned" kind of guy.

Shattering what strength I had left, my inner muscles contracted around him, milking him to orgasm. His body became rigid and he threw his head back, groaning loudly, enduring the sweet torture of his own gratification until finally collapsing next to me on the bed.

A half hour later, our heart rates returned to normal, but neither of us spoke. It wasn't a rewarding experience, but more of a head-to-toe euphoric buzz.

Jake tucked me possessively into his chest and held me with gentle hands, like a fragile baby bird that'd fallen from its nest. I drifted in and out of consciousness, but became aware of him as his finger doodled across my collarbone.

"Should I consider your closed eyes as a 'do not disturb' sign?" he asked.

I cracked one eye open and smiled with contentment. "I'm already disturbed…in more ways than one. What the hell was *that*?"

"What's wrong?" he said, grinning devilishly. "You didn't like?"

"Oh, no. I liked it a lot," I said. "But why do I suddenly have the urge to bless you with holy water?"

"Never had a woman complain before."

"Not a complaint, more of an observation." I hesitated to ask, but felt the need to. "Do you have any, uh…complaints?"

"Emily, I'm a man. We're not hard to please. I was just thrilled you were naked." He ran his hand lazily between my breasts. "Still am, in fact. Mother Nature's wardrobe," he said, leaning in for a quick kiss.

When he got out of bed, I watched the muscles tighten in his bare ass as he stalked across the room and opened the closet. A minute later, a blanket dropped over me. "You look cold," Jake said.

"Thanks." *Damn nipples.*

Jake continued leaning over me. "I can do you one better if you want to take a shower with me. I promise it'll be hot," he said with a wink.

"I would, but I think you crippled me for life. I lost all my basic motor functions. I'll probably never walk again."

Jake flashed a proud grin and stroked his finger across my eyelid. "Poor baby. Sleep then. I wouldn't want you to have any permanent damage."

Thinking of only my heart, two words came to mind. *Too late.*

• • •

Serenely, I drifted in and out of consciousness, but stirred when Jake crawled back into bed, his hair damp and his warm body smelling of soap. When I picked up my head, he glanced over at me.

"Hungry?" he asked.

"Is that an offer?"

"If we're talking about food, then yes. Earlier, I went over to get you something to eat. Floss had already made us some chicken salad sandwiches. She left them upstairs in the fridge with a note. I brought them back with me and put them in ours."

"A note? What'd it say?"

He did his best Floss impression. "Jake, I'm riding into town with Hank. I didn't want to disturb you while you were boning Emily."

I gigged him in the ribs with my elbow and laughed. "She did *not* say that!"

Jake laughed. "Well, close enough. I deciphered the hidden meaning behind what she wrote."

"Which was…?"

"*Enjoy*. Though I think she was referring to the sandwiches. Stay here. I'll get them."

Jake got out of bed naked and walked into the kitchen. As I glanced toward the bedroom window, I realized the room had darkened a little. The late afternoon sun had already descended behind the trees.

"I hope you wore clothes when you went over there," I yelled from the bedroom.

"I threw on a pair of shorts," Jake called out, rustling around the kitchen. When he came into the bedroom, he carried a plate in one hand and a glass of tea in the other. "I've got something for you."

I raised my eyebrows. "It better taste like chicken."

"Doesn't everything?"

I sat up, keeping the blanket tucked under my armpits to keep it from falling, exposing my nakedness. "You don't want me to answer that."

"Now you're just being crude," he said, scowling as he placed the plate in my lap. Two sandwiches cut into small triangles adorned the plate, along with a dill pickle.

I smiled at him. "I was talking about your pickled opossum and rattlesnake cheese. You know, all the wacky stuff you country people eat."

Jake laughed heartily. "All you're doing is giving me ideas. Rattlesnake cheese sounds pretty good."

I bit into a sandwich. "I'm too hungry right now to be grossed out."

"I should probably apologize for not letting you eat before attacking you."

"But you won't, right?"

He laughed. "Not a chance in hell. Be more careful about what you ask for."

I swallowed another bite. "You know we're going to have to talk about it."

"Eat first," Jake said, squeezing into the bed next to me. "We'll talk about it later. We have time."

I would've argued, but after going twenty-four hours without eating, food received precedence over curiosity. I inhaled the sandwich, then started on the pickle. When I finished, I set the plate aside and caught him staring at me.

"You did that on purpose. Absolutely no one eats a pickle like that, especially when they're in bed naked."

"What's wrong?" I asked, grinning slyly. "Thought you liked torture."

"Only when I'm doing the torturing," he grumbled. He watched me as I slid out of bed, walking carefully on my sensitive feet toward the bathroom. "Where you going?"

"I need to get ready for dinner."

"Dinner? You just ate," he noted. "You can't possibly eat again so soon."

I shrugged. "Didn't stop you earlier."

• • •

By the time I got out of the bathroom, Jake had disappeared. I wondered where he went until I heard a truck door shut. Hank and Floss were back. Wrapped in a towel, I sat on the edge of the bed and applied antibiotic cream to my swollen feet. Seconds later, Jake came back inside.

"Floss is going to start dinner, but it'll probably be a while before it's ready," he said, sitting beside me on the bed. "Want any help? While we're waiting for dinner, I could give you a little petting."

"You mean pampering?"

"Petting sounds like more fun, but yeah, that, too." He lifted my feet into his lap, reminding me of how he did the same thing to me the first night we arrived. I watched him doctor my battered feet and wrap them with gauze, just as Floss had.

Then he grabbed me around the waist, nuzzling his face into my damp hair. Jake's hands rubbed over my shoulders, kneading them hard, as if trying to work out the knots. It wasn't long before his gently massaging fingers moved from my arms to my chest, then from my chest to my hips.

"Special Agent Ward, I do believe we've tapped into one of your hidden talents," I said rolling my neck as he continued kneading his fingers into my shoulder blades.

"Mental medicine," Jake said, lowering his voice to a whisper, brushing my shoulder with his lips.

"Mmm-hmm," I murmured in agreement, concentrating more on the motion of his fingers as they etched into my skin.

Just when I thought our mental state would turn physical, someone knocked on the door. "Dinner's ready!"

Jake sighed and hollered back, "Thanks, Floss."

"Dinner? Already?" I said, looking at him. "That was fast. What'd she make...a bowl of cereal?"

He shrugged. "She must've decided it was leftover night or something. Better hurry and get dressed or we won't be making it to dinner," Jake said, eyeing the towel that had crept halfway down my breasts.

• • •

After a dinner of grilled cheese sandwiches and tomato soup, Jake offered to put some boxes into the attic for Floss. I came straight to the room, undressed completely, and slid into bed. A few minutes later, he joined me, stripping off his clothes before settling under the covers in the moonlit room.

He ran his hand the length of my body, as if to assure himself I was as naked as he was, then snuggled into me, resting his arm across my stomach.

"Seeing if I had another man under there?" I teased.

"With you, you never know."

Offended, I sat upright. "What's that supposed to mean?"

"Calm down," he said, pulling me back down. "I didn't mean it the way it came out. I meant you always do things to purposely upset me."

I let some of the tension out of my body, still trying to figure out if I wanted to be mad about his remark. Since I probably deserved it, I let it go. "Defense mechanism," I explained.

"What's the point?"

I sighed heavily. "To push people away, I guess. That way I don't build an attachment to someone who doesn't plan on sticking around."

"So if you abandon ship first, and the other person follows suit, you don't feel like you got left behind?"

"Something like that," I admitted.

"Has anybody ever tried to jump overboard to rescue you instead?"

I hesitated, not liking the direction the conversation had taken. "Let's just say I'm a strong swimmer."

"So you've dated cowards? That's strange. I wouldn't have pictured that type of guy for you."

"Truthfully, I haven't dated much at all. Two long-term relationships, but neither lasted for a year or was that serious," I said. "You know how some women say they stopped compromising in the boyfriend department? Well, I actually stopped shopping there altogether. It saves me from the disappointment."

"Sounds lonely."

I shrugged. "I've been alone since I was fourteen. Guess I'm used to it."

Jake rubbed his hand over my arm, comforting me. "You're not alone here, Emily. You know that, right? We all care about what happens to you. Hell, Bobbie Jo—"

"You've kidding me, right? Unbelievable! We're lying naked in bed together, and you want to talk about your ex-girlfriend?" Disgusted, I pushed him away and rolled out of the bed. "Bobbie Jo can't stay away from you, though she thinks you're dating me and you want to—"

"She knows we weren't dating, Emily. I told her in the

barn."

"God, Jake! First Cowboy, now Bobbie Jo? For an FBI agent, you suck at keeping secrets." I picked my shirt off the floor and tried to figure out if it was inside out.

Jake sighed. "Where are you going?"

"Outside." I waved my shirt around in frustration. "I don't want to be in the same room with you right now."

"You're not going out there by yourself. Get back in bed." I ignored him and started to pull my shirt over my head, but he leaned up and snatched it from my hands. "Emily, come on."

"Screw you."

Jake leaped from the bed and pulled me against him roughly. "Ever hear the saying, "Make love, not war?" Why don't we try it? I guarantee you'll like it."

"Not a chance." As tempting as it was, the mention of Bobbie Jo's name had completely obliterated my sex drive, making me cranky and unreasonable.

He struggled with his temper, trying to keep his anger in check, but the fumes between us were inflammable. One tiny spark could easily cause an explosion. So what better to do than to strike the match and throw it in his face.

"If Bobbie Jo has such an impact on you, then why don't you pass your offer along to her? I'm sure she'll be more than willing to accept."

The shouting match turned into a scuffle ending with my body jolted onto the bed. Jake's heavy body insulated mine, pressing me into the mattress, holding me firmly in place.

Fuming mad, I fought like a wildcat to get up, but he was stronger and pinned my arms above my head. When I tried to kick him, he shoved his way between my thighs. When I tried to bite him, he laughed.

"So we're back to that now, are we?" he asked, grinning. "Maybe I should nibble on you, see how you like it." Jake lifted his eyebrow as if he considered the idea, then something hard throbbed against my thigh.

"Don't even think about it," I warned, narrowing my eyes.

He chuckled again. "Not my fault I can't fight fair with a naked woman. You dangled the carrot. I just reached for it," he said with a lustful gaze. "I know this sounds strange, but I'm really turned on right now."

Jake's erection grew stronger between my legs, making my stomach flutter with excitement. "Then that makes two of us," I admitted breathlessly.

We both snickered at the idiocy of the situation.

"Look, I'm sorry. I don't want to argue. I know she's not your favorite person, and I can even understand why you'd be jealous. I wouldn't like it if you were friendly with an ex-boyfriend, either. But I'm telling you…there's nothing between her and me. Not anymore."

I sighed in surrender. "I don't want to talk about her. Can we just forget about her for now? We were on the right track before you took the detour and derailed us."

Jake smirked. "Then I guess it's up to me to get us back on track," he said with determination.

Methodically, he shifted a little to the left and buried himself inside me, making me gasp at the full brunt of him. My mind softened at the infusion of our bodies and the ingenuity of his effective pinning technique.

The weight of his body on mine was unbearable. Yet, I couldn't get him close enough. The sexual tension was magnetic, but we faced off in a mind-blowing, breath-defying battle to see who'd move first. Too bad for him I don't fight fair.

As my inner muscles clasped him, he let out a soft groan, but didn't move. I squeezed and relaxed again, applying more pressure and allowing my contractions to tempt him into knee-buckling bliss.

Jake swallowed hard in my ear. "I'm sorry…I shouldn't have…" I clenched my pelvic floor again, and his head shot up. "My God, I won't last much longer if you keep doing that."

"Then let go of my wrists and we'll try it a different way." He released me, and I pushed him over, rolling with him, as he landed on his back with me straddling his hips.

His eyes glossed over as he blew out a breath. "*That's* not going to be any better for me. The angle is…oh, sweet Jesus." His eyes rolled up into the back of his head.

"Did you think I was going to lie there and let you have your way with me again? How about I take the reins this time? You just sit back and…"

"Oh God," he murmured. "Keep doing that."

Slowly, I ricocheted my hips off his in a rhythmic, circular pattern. But it wasn't long before he was grunting and digging his fingers into the flesh of my hips. I changed tempo and wiggled wildly on top of him, whispering dirty suggestions that forced him to hold himself painfully back. The agony must've been too much. He gripped my ass and rocked both of us to an orgasm, his chasing mine with seconds to spare.

He was still hard inside me when I collapsed onto him, feeling his dark chest hair rasp across my sensitive nipples. Jake pulled my neck toward him, latching his mouth to mine and sucking on the tip of my tongue. We lay together, our bodies slickened with sweat, as our breathing slowed. Within minutes, he had me on my back, thrusting hard into me as he went for a bonus orgasm.

If our previous encounter had been red-hot, then this one was white-hot. Unable to get enough, his hands became rougher, gripping me with bruising force as he drove himself inward.

I moaned loudly, practically screaming out in pleasure, as Jake came closer. "Emily," he whispered. "I want to hear you say it."

It? What the hell did he want me to say?

When I didn't respond, he continued. "Say those three little words."

Oh God! "Jake, I can't…"

He stroked my nipples with his mouth as he plunged himself into my depths, wanting to take more than I was willing to give. His jaw tightened, and his eyes pierced into me with a strength that frightened me. "Tell me, damn it," he demanded, lifting my hips higher and pounding into me harder than before. "You feel it. I know you do."

Jake was right. I did love him, very much so. I just didn't want to be the first to say it. We both knew I'd never say it on my own, but he would force it out of me, if necessary. I could barely speak, much less think. His hands claimed my body, his mind branded my heart.

"I…I love you," I choked out.

Tears swam in my eyes over the mental release, as much as the physical one. My body clamped onto his, refusing to let go, and Jake shoved into me for the last time, groaning at his own completion. Once he regained his composure, he smiled at me and brushed his lips across mine.

As I lay quietly under him, I realized something. Awareness can be a funny thing. Jake was now completely aware of my feelings for him, and I was fully aware he hadn't returned the sentiment. But I was still one up on him in awareness and waited for his reaction.

"Shit," he muttered.

There.

Now, we were both aware we hadn't used a condom.

Chapter Nineteen

The morning sun was high in the sky when Jake's warmth slid out from under the covers. I propped my head on my elbow as he picked up his jeans from the floor.

"Can we talk, Jake?"

He pulled his jeans up over his hips. "I'm sorry about last night. It shouldn't have happened."

I told him I loved him, and he...*oh God! Of course, he regrets it. I'm such an idiot.*

He must've noticed a flash of hurt in my eyes because he sat beside me on the bed and took my hands in his. "I'm talking about the condom mishap, not the other stuff."

Then he kissed me lightly, lingering at my mouth for a moment before deciding against whatever else had passed through his mind. He pulled back and smiled, knowing I had guessed what he was thinking.

"I want to ask you something," I said.

"No, I've never done that before," he offered, brushing

my bangs out of my eyes. "Normally, I'm careful, but it was just the situation, I guess."

"It's not about that. I want to talk to you about…well, something else," I said, hesitating because I wasn't sure how he'd react.

"Okay, shoot."

"I wanted to ask you…um…well, I…" Was I brave enough to ask him how he felt about me if there was a chance he didn't feel the same way? "Where did you get the scar, the one on your leg?"

The flat, faded scar on his thigh was only noticeable from certain angles. Since I was roughly face level with his waist, I noticed. He hadn't wanted to talk about it before, but maybe he would now. It was a safer bet than asking him if he loved me. I'd have to work up to that one.

He didn't answer at first, which worried me. But then he sighed and shrugged. "It's probably about time I told you the truth, anyway." That worried me more. "My parents' names were Joseph and Marion Keller."

Recognition dawned on me, but I blinked with confusion. "That's strange," I said, trying to force my brain to recall something out of its grasp. "Their names sound familiar, but I don't know why."

"My dad was director of the FBI's Chicago division until last year. They were murdered," he said, pausing to let me take in his words. "Every local and national news network plastered their names and photos on their top story list for months. I would've found it strange if you hadn't heard their names."

The small jolt he gave me helped my memory kick in. "Gunned down in their home, right?" I asked, forgetting

I was callously referring to his parents. I should've edited myself better.

Jake nodded his answer, as if confirming it verbally hurt too much.

"A home invasion or something?" I asked, still trying to recall the news report I'd seen the year before.

"It was no home invasion," Jake said, gritting his teeth. "That was a mob hit, disguised as a burglary gone wrong." He closed his eyes and let out a slow breath, trying to calm himself down.

"But the news report said—"

"I was there, Emily." He ran his shaky fingers through his hair, as if startled by his own memories. "They invited me to dinner, and we watched a ball game on TV afterward. Dad and I drank a few too many beers, so Mom made me sleep it off in my old room.

"At four o'clock in the morning, I heard a noise that sounded like something fell on the floor. I wasn't alarmed enough to grab my gun off the dresser and walked into the hallway unarmed. One of the worst mistakes I've ever made. A man stepped out of my parents' bedroom carrying a silenced handgun. I didn't know who he was at the time, but later found out it was Curtis Manning."

At the mention of his name, I recognized it immediately and gasped. I remembered the large man with the cold, deadly eyes. He was one of the men who'd chased me from the lounge that night, wanting to kill me.

Jake acknowledged the horror in my eyes, but continued. "I hadn't turned on any lights. Manning couldn't see me standing in the shadows. But I must've shifted my weight or something because the wooden floor creaked under my foot. A wild shot hit me in the thigh as he ran out."

"You were lucky he was caught off guard. He probably would've killed you."

"No doubt in my mind," Jake agreed. "He didn't leave me alive out of the kindness of his heart. People who are caught unaware make mistakes. Like me, leaving my gun in the bedroom and walking out unarmed. It was stupid."

"What happened after Manning left?"

"I crawled back into my bedroom and armed myself, but by the time I got my gun, he was gone. I called the police. The dispatcher wanted me to stay on the line, but I hung up and dragged myself down the hall to my parents' bedroom. My mother was on the bed and my dad was on the floor, both with kill shots to the head."

Though I already knew the story didn't have a happy ending, it still disturbed me to hear his version of it. The look on his face as he told it reminded me of how I felt when I learned of my own parents' deaths.

I choked up. "I'm sorry. It was hard when I lost my parents, but I wasn't there when it happened. I can't imagine how horrible it would've been for you to find them like that." I paused long enough to wipe my eyes, but couldn't stop sniffling. "Why did he do it? Did Manning kill them because your dad was an FBI director?"

"No. My father had been investigating Frankie Felts for years. Manning's a flunky, an assassin, if you will. He doesn't do anything unless Frankie Felts orders it done, which means Felts has as much of my family's blood on his hands as Manning does." His eyes glistened with moisture as he added, "As much as I do."

"Jake, no." I reached for his hand as my voice cracked.

"How could it be your fault? You couldn't have known—"

"I should've known…I'm the reason it happened."

"Why do you think that?"

A tear escaped and rolled down the side of his nose. Judging by his lack of eye contact, his emotions made him uncomfortable. "Felts found out that someone received inside information from one of his employees. When he figured out who gave it, he pistol-whipped my dad's name out of him and killed the man. That's when Felts put out the kill order on my dad."

"I still don't see how…"

"The informant would only talk to someone higher up in the agency. The exchange was over the phone. I let the informant believe he was talking to FBI Director Joseph Keller."

A light bulb flashed on in my brain. I understood Jake's reasons for thinking it was his fault. Then the light bulb exploded, making my head hurt, since I knew nothing I said would convince him otherwise. But I had to try.

"When I was fourteen, my parents were hit by a drunk driver."

"I know," he said. "It was in your case file."

"I've always blamed myself."

Confusion took over Jake's face. "Why? How was it your fault?"

"I stayed over at a friend's house that night, but my friend, Cassie, wanted to go out without her parents knowing. I'd never done anything like that before. Believe it or not, I was a good girl back then."

"*You* followed rules?" Jake asked, shaking his head in disbelief.

"First night I'd ever disobeyed one. My parents were sticklers for rules and tried to instill them in me constantly. They slathered on sunscreen religiously, adamantly buckled their seatbelts, and—sometime after conceiving me—must've started practicing safe sex, since I'm an only child."

"They would've loved me, then," Jake said with a grin.

"I let Cassie talk me into sneaking out, and we went to the park to meet up with some friends. As soon as her parents found out we were missing, they called the police. A cop car picked us up and held us at the station until our parents could come for us. Cassie left with her dad, but I sat alone in a room for hours. Until an officer came to talk to me."

"The one you mentioned before?" Jake asked. "The officer who comforted you until they snatched you away?"

I gave a quick nod, trying to keep my composure. "My parents were on their way to get me when the drunk driver swerved into their car and pushed it off a bridge into the Mississippi River. Their injuries weren't severe, but my mom's seatbelt wouldn't release. According to eyewitnesses, my dad refused to get out of the car without her."

Jake scowled and shook his head. "All because of a damn seatbelt?"

"Y-yes. And me. All because of me," I said in a broken whisper before regaining control of my voice. He started to gather me in his arms, but I stopped him. "Don't you see, Jake? It wasn't your fault. No more than it was mine. Our parents wouldn't want us sitting here blaming ourselves."

"No, they wouldn't." He paused thoughtfully. "Actually," he said, smiling at his thoughts, "my mom would grab me up by the ear and my dad would threaten to take me out behind the barn and whoop my ass."

Jake's heart carried a load too heavy for any dump truck. He had tossed out some sharp, fragmented bits of regret from his dubious past, but he still couldn't hide the deep scars that had formed on the inside.

My eyes were no longer wet when the smile slid across my face. "I would've liked them," I told him. "Just like Hank and Floss. You're lucky to have them. I can see how much they love you."

"They would do anything for me," Jake said, nodding in agreement. "And have, in the past. Remember when I told you I'd been in witness protection?"

"Yeah."

"Well, it wasn't exactly witness protection. Not officially, anyway. When I was fifteen, my dad tried to prosecute Felts on a murder charge. Dad received death threats and wanted to keep us safe. He made my mom and I assume new identities and go into hiding. We came to live here with Hank and Floss."

For a moment, I had a touch of déjà vu, remembering when I had to change my identity. "Jake isn't your real name?"

"Actually it is…Jake Keller. Now, everyone knows me as Ward. Even after I told everyone the truth, they continued to call me by that name. I was used to it, so I kept it."

"I couldn't imagine you as Jake Keller. It would be weird, like when you first called me Emily Foster," I said with a laugh, remembering how I hadn't answered him much the first day. "Did you like living here?"

"I didn't want to at first," Jake said. "But I started hanging out with the boys and dating Bobbie Jo. Soon I didn't want to leave." I hadn't realized I'd made a face until he said, "Hey, don't look at me like that! You asked. I'm just trying to be honest."

"You can leave out the parts about *her*," I said, my face souring at the thought of Jake dating Bobbie Jo.

"If you gave her half a chance—"

"I don't want to talk about her," I said, clenching my teeth. "It'll only start an argument. Move on."

Jake sighed heavily with disapproval, but went back to his story. "Mom and I had been here six months when Felts bought off a judge. My dad's case against him was thrown out of court. When the death threats stopped, Dad thought it was safe for us to return home. Mom went, but I stayed to finish high school with the boys."

And to be with Bobbie Jugs, I imagined. "When did you end up moving back to Chicago?" I asked, hoping to hear about their breakup and a confession that her tits were fake.

"By the time I became a full-fledged agent, my dad had already taken over as director in Chicago. I transferred there and joined his mission in bringing Felts down. No one knew I was his son. Dad and I kept the information under our hats. I always took more after my mom, anyway, with her dark hair and gray eyes, so I kept Ward as my last name. We didn't want anyone to holler nepotism when he appointed me as the senior investigator on Felts's case file."

"I remember you said it was your case."

"It was. For nearly three years, but I didn't go undercover in Felts's organization until about six months ago. I spent years playing by the rules, but never could get Felts on anything solid. Manning had an airtight alibi for the night my parents were killed. Although he'd been there, I couldn't prove it. They killed my parents in cold blood and got away with it for a year. I couldn't take it anymore. The night he killed Sergio, I wanted to take Frankie Felts down one way or another. Since I hadn't been able to do it legally, I…well, let's say I was willing to try another method."

My heart thumped an extra beat at the hidden meaning. I had to ask, but wasn't sure I wanted to hear the answer. "What were you planning to do?" I swallowed hard, bracing for whatever he would tell me.

"You have to understand I'd been having a hard time dealing with my parents' deaths. If the FBI found out I was the director's son, they would've pulled me off the case immediately. No one could know. So I headed a memorial service for them in Chicago as Director Keller's coworker, but I buried Mom and Dad here in Texas as their son. I wasn't in the right frame of mind to be on the investigation, and I know I should've—"

"Jake! What were you going to do?"

His eyes narrowed and his jaw twitched. "Nothing Felts wouldn't have deserved," he said coldly. "That night in the club, I watched Felts, waiting for a chance to face off with him. I wanted to see the look in his eyes when I told him I was Joseph Keller's son. He would've known why I was there and would've been forced to draw his weapon."

"Are you suicidal? My God, why would you want him to do that?"

He stared off into space for a moment. "So I had a reason to kill him. A legal one, at least."

"But he wasn't alone. You could've got yourself killed."

"Curtis Manning wouldn't have lived long. He would've been the second one to hit the floor. Two kill shots, one to each of their heads."

His callousness shocked me. "You're not a killer!"

"You don't know what I am," he said, his tone darkened by his hatred. "I could've killed him. I would've killed him… if only…"

"Something kept you from doing it," I guessed. "What stopped you?"

"You did." His eyes softened as he glanced over at me. "You stopped me."

"What? How?"

"You were in the hallway and looked upset. The few minutes I talked to you gave me some perspective. I went to the bathroom to pull myself together. By the time I came out, the only thing I could think of was how you—how anyone— might look at me if you had known what I planned to do."

"But you followed them. I saw you go in the back room."

"I wasn't looking for Felts. Sergio went through there. I followed him to tell him to leave you alone, that you were with me. I wasn't sure which way he had gone. When I couldn't find him, I came out and searched for you. But you were gone. Then you flew out those doors a minute later. It was obvious you'd seen something. And, judging by how scared you were, I figured it had to be bad."

My body shuddered at the memory of Sergio's blank stare. "I thought you knew…that you worked for…"

"The only thing I knew was that they were searching for you. You were ducking through the crowd, trying to make your way to your friends. I had to get to you before you made it to them, or they would've been in danger as well."

"You should've told me…"

"Told you what? That you were the lucky break I'd been hoping for?"

"Lucky? You think it was luck I witnessed a murder?"

"Emily, you saw Felts commit a crime, and I hadn't been able to pin anything else on him. I hated that you had to see that, but truthfully, it was bittersweet."

The comment alone polluted and distorted my view of Jake. I had to bite back the words I actually wanted to say. "You should've at least told me about your parents and how involved with the case you were."

"I couldn't tell you how my parents died. Not in the beginning. I saw the reaction you had when I told you about the other three witnesses. It wasn't good." Jake shook his head insistently. "No, I couldn't take a chance you'd run. I needed your help to bring the murdering bastard to justice. It was my only alternative to killing him."

My heart felt like he'd taken a shotgun to it and had blown it to smithereens. "So this was a personal crusade?"

"Of course it was," Jake admitted, guilt-free.

Disbelief clouded my eyes and sent my stomach into a downward spiral. "It...it didn't have anything to do with protecting me. You weren't keeping *me* safe, Jake. You were keeping your precious fucking court date."

"I'm not going to lie and say I didn't have ulterior motives, Emily. But it had nothing to do with you or this thing between us."

This *thing* between us? What the hell was that supposed to mean? That it was just sex? He said he didn't do meaningless sex. Then again, it isn't like he said he loved me, either.

I became more enraged. "It has everything to do with me! I thought you weren't telling me about your parents because you didn't want to hurt me knowing I'd lost mine.

It's why I didn't push. But that wasn't it at all, was it, Jake? You kept it from me because you didn't want to lose your star witness. That's all you give a damn about."

"Emily, you're wrong. This thing. Us. It's—"

"It's what?" I asked, needing affirmation that he felt the same way about me.

"I don't know," he said in frustration. Jake moved away, infuriating me more.

I was livid he couldn't elaborate, couldn't verbalize it. I felt alienated and more alone than I'd ever felt since my parents died. After all, the man I'd fallen in love with wasn't in love with me. He might have pulled me closer physically, but emotionally he pushed me away.

I couldn't understand why, after what we had shared. Something was between us, but now, I was no longer sure what. It was like our relationship resembled the cell service out there. A connection was there, but kept getting lost in the trees.

"You fucking coward! That's fine, then. Chalk it up to one more notch on your belt for all I care. I should give you a standing ovation for the stunning performance you put on yesterday."

"Don't give me that bullshit." He swallowed hard, trying to keep his temper from flaring further. "You know it wasn't an act," he said more calmly.

I wanted to believe him, but I couldn't. Not after he admitted to having ulterior motives and not knowing what to call this thing between us. Dull pain in my fragile heart pulled at me, making me want to spew moisture from my eyes by the bucketful. But I couldn't let my guard down with him anymore.

Once I was alone, I'd worry about piecing the broken shards back together. For now, I was angry. Mad at him for making me admit I loved him while weakened by the throws of passion. Disgusted with myself for falling in love with him. In fact, I would've been happy to stuff all of my unwanted feelings into a trash bag, throw it into the burn pit, and light it with the raging flames blazing inside me.

"What was this, then? You and your friends getting your jollies off on the city slicker who can't do anything right? Jesus. You brought me out here so I could be the brunt of all of your jokes?" None of what I said was true, but he had hurt me and I wanted to hurt him back in self-defense.

"Emily, stop—"

"Well, I have news for you, Agent Ward, or whatever the hell your name is." My finger pushed into his chest, my tone all snark. "I'm not the joke here. All of you are. With your neglected lawns that look more like junkyards and your stupid southern accents."

Jake pushed my finger from his chest. "Emily, you're starting to try my patience."

"Well, it's about damn time! You're as slow as the rest of them. God knows no one out here has any sense."

He wasn't shocked by my outburst, but he was mad. "You can think we're all small-minded, if you want, but there aren't any ghettos out here, sweetheart."

"Only because everyone here already lives in the ghetto."

Once again, I had lashed out by attacking not only him, but his family and friends. I regretted the words the moment they flew from my lips, but I refused to take them back.

Jake flew into a fit, waving his hands in the air before

grabbing his boots and talking with a mock hillbilly accent. "Well, hell, darlin', I better get goin' then. My uneducated ass has to drive some cattle to market in the mornin'. Reckon I better get a move on."

He walked out and slammed the door as I yelled, "By the way, this fake relationship is off!"

Then I crumpled to the floor and burst into tears.

Chapter Twenty

I didn't have to face Jake again until I went over to the main house during lunchtime. I hoped I'd missed him, but leave it to me to judge something wrong. Like I didn't do enough of that already?

He had nothing to say. After verbally vomiting on each other earlier in the morning, we couldn't even stand to look at each other. Still upset over our argument, I would've skipped lunch to avoid him if I hadn't already skipped breakfast.

Hank and Jake had eaten, but were soaking up some air conditioning before venturing back out into the heat. The room was thick with tension, but Hank and Floss ignored it, talking casually about the Trinity River water levels.

It wasn't what I'd consider riveting conversation, but it held enough interest to keep me entertained without having to speak myself. I grabbed an apple from the bowl on the table and quietly listened to them talk.

We all heard the truck pull up, and Floss peered out the

window. "It's Bobbie Jo and her mother, Connie," she said, tossing a look my way. "I'll go meet them downstairs in the driveway."

Jake didn't look at me, but wore a smirk. "I'll go with you."

I stifled the eye roll and the groan.

"Emily, there's some chicken salad in the fridge from yesterday," Floss offered. "Help yourself."

"That's okay, Floss. I'm not in the mood for *leftovers*."

It was my turn to smirk at Jake, though I should've known better than to provoke him. It was like tapping the glass on a poisonous snake's aquarium. No matter how many times he struck at me, he couldn't get to me as long as the glass barriers were in place. Hank and Floss were obviously the barriers. But I wouldn't dare taunt a snake on the loose.

"Oh, Lordy, I don't want to know what that's all about," Floss said, heading outside.

Jake gritted his teeth with irritation while Hank grinned.

"Maybe I'll ask Bobbie Jo if she wants some *leftovers*," Jake said, to no one in particular. He lifted the brows on his smug face.

Uh-oh. The snake must have freed himself.

"She always liked what I had to offer," he added. Jake turned to leave, but stopped when an apple pegged him in his back. "Oh, real mature, Emily."

He picked the apple up off the floor, turned to face me, and saw I was still eating mine. I held my hands up, showing my innocence. He glared at Hank, who shrugged, grinning happily at his good aim.

Jake stared open-mouthed. "Traitor," he said, spinning on his heels and storming out the door.

Hank and I burst into hysterics. After a moment, I became overly emotional, and my laughing turned more to sobbing. Immediately, Hank pulled his chair over. He didn't say anything at first, just rubbed my shoulder, allowing me to get a handle on myself.

"I'm sorry," I said, wiping my eyes with a napkin Hank handed me. "I didn't mean to get upset."

"It's okay, honey. Everyone needs to have a good cry now and then. If I'd known Jake hurt your feelings this much, I'd have thrown the apple harder and aimed for his noggin."

"It's not that," I said, offering a trembling grin. "Jake and I had an argument this morning."

"So that's why he's in such a foul mood today," Hank said with a chuckle. "Jake's already hit his thumb with a hammer three times, thrown a shovel across the barn, and said more curse words than I thought he knew. And that was all in the last two hours. You must've really gotten under his skin this time," he said, still hooting.

"Yeah, that's the problem," I grumbled. "We keep getting under each other's skin. I don't know how the others believed Jake and I are supposed to be a couple."

"Honey, they all knew you two weren't a couple."

"You mean *aren't* a couple."

"Now, don't go telling me what I mean," Hank said. "I know what I'm saying. I meant *weren't*. Past tense. You two are practically married now."

I almost fell out of my chair with laughter. "Hank, I'm going to keep my opinions to myself. I'd hate to insult you by calling you crazy."

"You can't see it?" he asked, giving my arm a friendly pat. "That boy is stuck to you like a Band-Aid. He follows you everywhere, even if it's only with his eyes. That's devotion…the kind that comes from love. I watch Floss the same way. Especially when that rascal, Slick, comes around. I've threatened to blow his head off a time or two the way I caught him looking at my girl."

I couldn't help but smile, wondering if Jake really looked at me like that. It had to be wishful thinking on my part. If he watched me at all, it's because he was anticipating the next stunt I'd pull. It was purely physical attraction for him. No emotional attachment. Like it or not, I had to accept it.

But I appreciated what Hank tried to do. Kind words from an old man trying to make a young girl feel better. Hank was sweet.

"Okay, missy, I've got some work to do. I didn't get much of anything done yesterday."

"Being lazy, huh?"

"No, ma'am. I came downstairs yesterday to do some work, but ended up running back inside. The cottage was shaking something awful. Damn near thought it was a tornado," Hank said with a knowing wink.

I was left speechless and blushing. Hank wasn't sweet. He was perverse.

· · ·

I sat on the back porch with a glass of iced tea, leafing through a magazine I'd found on the coffee table. The magazine was more of a prop, really. My eyes stayed glued on the men the entire time. It was like watching my own personal comedy hour.

The storm that had passed through caused some problems

to the roof of the pole barn and it needed repairing. Hank climbed the ladder to assess the damage. Jake yelled for him to get down, saying he was too old to be up there. Hank told him to shut up, which made me laugh. I laughed harder when Jake smashed his finger with a hammer and cursed in tongues I couldn't translate.

I grinned when Hank jacked up the side of the barn using a car jack and ribbed Jake relentlessly about not doing his share of the workload. Then Hank set me off again when I caught sight of him holding a stud finder to his body and making beeping noises with his mouth.

"The two of them should take their act on the road."

I turned to see Bobbie Jo coming toward me, which wiped the smile off my face. Floss had invited Bobbie Jo and Connie inside for some tea, which was why I went outside. Bobbie Jo apparently didn't grasp the meaning of avoidance.

"I came out here to be alone," I told her, not bothering to watch my tone.

She sat in the chair beside me wearing white drawstring shorts and a peach knit top.

"You *will* be alone if you keep up that attitude," she said, her tone just as sour as mine, though she smiled as if offering me sugar.

"Where do you get off? You don't know anything about me."

"Because you won't give me a chance," she said, propping her feet up on the railing like mine. "You weren't happy about Jake and I going to the barn. I understand why. But I'd like to explain it to you, instead of having you hate me for no reason. If you still want to hate me afterward, then fine."

Noise from a circular saw caught my attention. Hank

worked on the ground cutting boards while Jake straddled the frame of the pole barn's roof wearing thick leather gloves. Realizing Bobbie Jo and I were on the back porch alone together, he looked worried. As if any minute our claws would come out and a catfight would begin. Too busy watching us to focus, he slipped through the framing, but caught himself. Bobbie Jo and I jumped out of our chairs at the same time. Neither of us relaxed again until he pulled himself back up and we saw he was all right.

"Wave and smile with me," I said. "That way he'll know everything is okay. I don't want him preoccupied while he's up there. It's dangerous."

Bobbie and I both waved with big grins on our faces. The worried look he wore disappeared, replaced by a puzzled one. It made both of us laugh. At least he seemed to pay more attention to what he was doing afterward and less attention to us.

"I helped look for you in the woods," Bobbie Jo said, surprising me. "It's one of the reasons I came by. I heard you went through a lot. I wanted to see if you were okay."

"I'm fine," I told her, giving her a slight nod. We settled back into our chairs. "By the way, I don't hate you."

She lifted her eyebrows slightly. "That's news to me."

"It's about Jake. Nothing personal."

"I never doubted that for a second," she said, nodding. "Have you forgotten I dated him? I know how other girls looked at him and how easy it is to get jealous over something trivial."

"I wouldn't call sneaking off to the barn with another woman's man trivial," I said matter-of-factly. "I took it seriously."

"That's the other reason I wanted to talk to you." Bobbie Jo clasped and unclasped her hands nervously. "I'd found out some unsettling news earlier that day and didn't want Jake to hear it from anyone else. He's still one of my best friends. We went to the barn only to keep others from listening in. In this neck of the woods, we have a few busybodies who'd love nothing more than to gossip."

I bit my lip, not knowing if I should ask or not. "You're pregnant, aren't you?"

Bobbie Jo reeled with astonishment. "H-how did you know?"

"Everyone around here drinks like a fish, but I haven't seen you touch the stuff. There's something else, but I don't know if it's normal for you. Maybe it's the pregnancy."

"What's that?"

"You glow," I said, making her smile widen. "No, I'm serious. Your skin, your hair, your eyes. It's like you're radioactive or something."

"I'll take that as a compliment," she said happily.

"You should." A moment of silence passed while I summoned the courage to ask her another question. "It's Cowboy's?"

She sat upright, no longer slouching in her chair. "Are you nuts? Where would you get a stupid idea like that?"

"I thought—"

"Oh, yuck! That would be like doing it with my brother," Bobbie Jo said, still making a face. "It's Jeremy's—you know, your *friend* from the bar. I left before the fight broke out, but I heard all about it the next day."

Now I made a disgusted face. "Oh God. No wonder why Ox didn't want me to go over there. He knew Jake would be looking for any reason to get into a fight with Jeremy." I hated to admit it, but was sure she already knew. "Jake's very protective of you. I'm surprised he didn't kill Jeremy. At least now I know it wasn't because of me."

"Oh, honey, the bar fight was definitely over you. Jake had already promised me he wouldn't lay a finger on Jeremy. Don't get me wrong, I'm sure he was glad to have a reason to clock him, but it was more about you than me."

"Great," I said sarcastically. "That makes me feel better."

"That's nothing," she said. "The others wanted to send a lynch mob over to Jeremy's house. I had to talk them out of it." Bobbie Jo leaned back into her chair casually and giggled. "My boys are something else, aren't they?"

"I know they don't like him, but did they think you'd stand by and let them kick the crap out of your boyfriend?"

Bobbie Jo laughed again. "Jeremy's not my boyfriend!"

"Oh God. Please don't tell me he's your husband," I said, remembering how I danced sexily on him in front of the entire bar.

"Nope. Jeremy wants nothing to do with me or the baby."

I tried to keep my expression casual, but sympathy tugged at my heart for her. It must've showed somewhere on my face. Bobbie Jo's eyes fixated on me as she shifted uncomfortably in her chair.

"Emily, don't you dare feel sorry for me," she warned. "This was my fault. Everyone told me to stay away from him, but I didn't listen. It may not be the ideal circumstances, but I've always wanted children. This baby's a blessing, not a burden." She waved her hand nonchalantly. "Besides, how many children do you know that get to have four godfathers?"

I hunched my shoulders. "Not many, I guess."

"None of my boys are happy about it, but I am. That's all that matters."

"Do you always refer to the four of them as your boys?"

"Well, yeah," Bobbie Jo said with a grin. "You're the first girl who ever wanted me to share, at least on a more permanent basis. Strange thing is, until now, I never wanted to."

I threw my head back against my chair and sighed. "It's probably not nearly as permanent as you think."

"Are you blind, Emily, or just stupid?"

Startled, I pulled my head upright and fastened my eyes to hers. "So much for trying to get along."

"Jake's crazy about you. He told me himself. How can you not know that that boy is in love with you?"

I bit into my bottom lip. "He should try telling *me*."

"Maybe he's waiting for the right time."

"He had his chance. I told him I loved him, but he didn't say anything back."

We both sagged farther down into our chairs, looking out toward the barn roof at Jake. "Honey, a man who views you as a fling won't put forth the extra effort to win you over outside the bedroom. I'm speaking from personal experience."

"Then I guess there's only one explanation," I said, looking over to Bobbie Jo. "Men are dumbasses."

Her eyes lit up as she smiled. "I couldn't have said it better myself."

We chatted for a while longer, while Bobbie Jo told me all about her family and stories about the boys when they were in high school together. She was more likeable than

I'd given her credit for. We got along great for the next hour before her mother got ready to leave and called her inside.

As she walked toward the back door, I stopped her. "Hey, Bobbie Jo... I'm sorry about calling you a slut at the bar. And I do want to clear up one last thing about that night. I was wearing underwear."

"That's funny...seeing how I *wasn't*," she said, giving me a friendly wink before heading through the door.

I smiled to myself.

Yep. Bobbie Jo and I would get along fine.

• • •

I helped Floss make a pot of beef stew, peeling and cutting carrots and potatoes for her, while she prepared the stew meat. With the ingredients thrown together in her large black boiler, the stew simmered, and Floss whipped up some sweet cornbread. She sent me downstairs to the cottage to tell Jake dinner was almost ready.

It was nearly dark outside. Dog had already taken up his post in his usual spot on the cottage porch. I toed him to see if he'd move, but as usual, he lay there like road kill. Bending at the waist, I gave him a quick pat on the head and stepped over him to go into the cottage.

Jake had just gotten out of the shower. Water droplets dotted his back, and his wavy brown hair looked almost black when wet. A towel, wrapped low around his waist, revealed a small treasure trail of hair under his belly button. Jeez. What I wouldn't give to be a leprechaun and follow it to his pot of gold. Though I doubted Jake's interest in short mischievous Irishmen with red beards.

I blinked the lust-filled glaze from my eyes and sighed inwardly. "Dinner will be ready soon."

"Okay," Jake said. "So, you want to talk about what happened now or later?"

"Nothing to talk about."

"I want to know why you're upset with me," he said from the bathroom.

"It was nothing." Only that he had conned me into foolishly admitting my feelings and hadn't bothered returning them. No biggie.

Defensively, I moved to the window and lifted the curtain. The last of the fading light made its escape behind the horizon. Through the pane of glass, I watched bugs swarm the security lights and listened to the crickets chirp.

A prickling sensation ran up my spine as Jake came up behind me. He pressed his muscled torso into my back, one hand at my waist. He gently pushed my hair off my neck and touched his lips to my skin. Hot waves of lust slid into my belly.

"It was something," Jake insisted. "So, like I said…now or later?"

I closed my eyes and inhaled a deep, slow breath, but didn't answer him. Preoccupied by his lips on my neck, I wasn't sure what to say. "I can't think…"

"If you say now, I'll stop," he breathed into my ear. "If you say later… Well, things are going to get much worse before they get better." I could hear the suggestive smirk in his voice.

Whether Jake loved me or not became a moot point. He wanted me, even if it was only for pleasure. We were two hamsters stuck in a cage together, running on a wheel nowhere fast. Although the outcome of the evening would only cause me pain, I didn't care. I wanted him, even if he didn't want me the same way.

He nibbled lightly on the side of my neck, waiting for an answer, but I couldn't speak. All I could do was bend my neck back, giving him further access to my throat—the only answer he needed.

"Later it is," he said, allowing his towel to fall at our feet.

I turned to face him, devouring him with my eyes. My fingers splayed across his chest, feeling the firm pectoral muscles stacked on top of the bulging six-pack he proudly displayed. He was excited and eager—obvious from the moment he dropped the towel—but his touch was surprisingly tender.

He framed my face with his large, callused hands, and his mouth moved over mine. I gripped his wrists, while his tongue slowly probed deep inside, seeking my response. A low moan escaped our tightly locked lips. I wasn't sure if it was his or mine. He pulled back slightly, running his tongue over my bottom lip and sucking gently before releasing it.

This was unlike the other times when he'd let passion consume him, practically ripping the clothes from my body. Most women want a man to take his time, gentling her, preparing her body for his lovemaking. But, to me, it felt like Jake held back.

As he maneuvered me to the bed, we heard a truck speeding down the driveway. Jake turned back to the window and peeked out the curtain.

"It's Cowboy," he said, looking concerned. "Something's wrong. He never hauls ass up the drive." Jake reached for the towel, wrapping it around his waist.

"You're going to have to do better than that," I said, stifling a surge of laughter. "You look like you're ready for a fencing match, and I doubt he's armed."

Jake looked down and gave me an impatient sigh. "Knowing Cowboy, I'd say he's always armed. Thankfully, he's not interested in a sword fight." Jake threw the towel on the floor and pulled on a pair of jeans that rested low on his hips. "I'll be back in a minute," he said, stepping out.

When I licked my lips, I could taste Jake. It was the taste of a confident, sensual lover, who would've delivered the performance of his life in bed. Had Cowboy showed up ten minutes later, I would've been writhing under Jake's hard frame, smothering in his masculinity. Sitting on the edge of the bed, I blew out a breath, calming my desire for intimacy to a more manageable level.

A few more minutes went by, but Jake hadn't returned. I peeked out the window to see him and Cowboy in deep conversation with Hank and Floss under the security lights in the driveway. Jake was upset, staring at the ground with his hands tightly clenched into fists. I went outside to join them. Everyone quieted as I walked up, and no one would look me in the eyes.

"What's going on?" I asked. Nobody answered. "Jake… tell me."

"A man in town is asking questions about you," he said, as the vein on his temple bulged outward.

My stomach felt squeamish. "Who is he?"

Cowboy spoke up. "No one knows. He's not from around here. That's why I came to warn Jake."

"But how could anyone know where to look for me?"

"I don't know," Jake said, looking puzzled. "No one

should've known where to find us. I haven't even spoken to Director Brockway, in case they tried to put out a trace."

"Why would anybody trace the…call?" Dim recollections of the drunken memories I suppressed came rushing back.

I stumbled back, my belly tightening with spasms. Jake and Cowboy both reached for me. Hank pulled down the tailgate on his truck and the boys lifted me, setting me on it. Jake pushed my hair back to look at my face while Cowboy gripped my arms, keeping me upright.

"You look like you're about to pass out," Jake said with a strained voice. "Take slow, deep breaths."

"I'll grab a cold washcloth for her," Floss said, already on her way inside.

"It's probably stress," Hank noted calmly.

In my daze, I could hear their voices, but did my best to tune them out of my head. More pressing issues had arisen, like figuring out how to tell Jake what I'd done and willing myself not to puke. I could almost hear him screaming at me already. Damn.

Then again, he didn't yell at me for getting lost in the woods. Surely, that was worse than making one lousy phone call. I snapped back to reality, trying to gather my composure. Everyone stared at me with blank looks.

"What's that about?" Jake asked me.

"Huh?"

"You said karma is biting you in the ass. What'd you mean?"

"Jake, I…I meant to tell you—"

"What did you do?" he asked suspiciously. He was like a powder keg filled with explosives, and I was the idiot who'd lit the fuse.

I gulped a deep breath, heated guilt burning inside me. "I called Gina from Floss's cell phone the night we came back from the bar."

A moment of silence passed while Jake tried to contain himself and the other men said a small prayer for me.

"Jesus Christ, Emily! What the hell were you thinking?" Jake yelled, pacing angrily back and forth. "I'm trying to keep your ass alive and you're…chatting on the phone with your girlfriend?"

"Calm down, Jake," Hank said, walking off toward the house. "Let me grab my pistol. We'll go into town and check it out. It may be nothing."

"I'll grab my gun out of the truck," Cowboy said, walking away from us to give us some privacy.

God, I felt stupid. "I'm sorry. It was a mistake."

"Yeah, you make a lot of those," Jake said with his teeth clenched, his eyes flashing with heat. He kicked the truck's fender a couple of times to let off some steam. It didn't help. "For God's sake, were you trying to get us all killed?"

Lowering my head, I whispered, "No, of course not. I wasn't thinking—"

"That's your damn problem! You don't think! I can't compensate for your stupidity."

"Jake!" Cowboy said, walking back over. "That's enough."

"She hasn't begun to have enough," Jake said, frustrated with Cowboy's interference. "She needs to learn there are consequences for her actions."

I hated listening to them talk about me as if I weren't there, but I knew if I opened my mouth, the sobs would erupt from my throat. I swallowed them, pushing them down as far as I could, but couldn't stop the moisture leaking from my eyes.

Cowboy watched me wipe my eyes and he patted my hand. "She knows, Jake. You can get off her ass now."

Jake let out a disgusted laugh. "We were sitting ducks for the past few days. She didn't even bother to warn us." He walked closer, glaring, as angry words of accusation poured from his mouth. "Emily, you better hope this turns out to be nothing because if anybody gets hurt, it's going to be all on *you*."

"I said that's enough," Cowboy yelled, shoving Jake away. "You're my boy and all, but if you say another word to her…"

"Damn it, you two, knock it off!" Hank came up behind Jake and put his hand on his shoulder, giving it a hard squeeze. "Son, you have no business talking to a woman like that. Now, go put on some clothes, get your gun, and get your ass in the truck. You're wasting time with this nonsense."

Jake stormed off without another word. I couldn't hold back the sobbing any longer. Cowboy put his arm around me and held me against his chest.

"It's okay, honey," Hank said softly. "Jake's just scared, and he's taking it out on you."

"Well, he crossed the line," Cowboy said angrily.

Hank nodded in agreement. "Someone has to stay here to protect the women. You want to volunteer?"

Cowboy smoothed his hand over my hair, brushing it from my wet cheeks. "Reckon I already have."

Hank opened the door to his truck and stepped in. "Take her into the main house and stay inside. We'll be back soon."

Cowboy walked me upstairs and opened the door to the house as Jake came out of the cottage. I watched him adjust his shoulder holster before getting into Hank's truck, but he didn't look at me. Then they drove away.

After ten minutes, my guilt and shame were replaced with an intense feeling of dread. Floss made us sit at the table and served us dinner. I pushed the stew around in my bowl and barely picked at the cornbread. Cowboy had no problem eating his, though.

An hour passed. Fret lines on my forehead deepened. Where were they? Surely, they had found out something by now. In the bathroom, I'd just recovered from another bout of mental anguish and was washing my face.

That's when the lights went off.

Chapter Twenty-one

I couldn't see my face in the mirror, but I imagined it looked twisted with fright. My heart banged against the walls of my chest as if it would burst any moment.

"Emily," Cowboy whispered, "open the door."

I groped for the doorknob in the darkness and unlocked it, shoving it open. Cowboy grabbed my arm and yanked me into the hall. My eyes adjusted to the moonlit room as he shoved a handgun into my palm.

"It's loaded. I hope you remember how to use it," he said, shoving his own handgun into his waistband.

"What the hell's going on?" I said, keeping my voice low like he did, though I didn't know why. "What happened to the lights?"

"Someone killed the power and phone lines from outside."

"And I left my darn cell phone in Hank's truck again," Floss added, standing next to Cowboy with a shotgun in her hands that was as big as her.

The blood drained from my face, and my body trembled. Another surge of fear ran through me. If anything happened to either of them, Jake would never forgive me. Hell, I'd never forgive myself.

"W-who's out there?" I asked.

"I'm not sure," Cowboy said. "I saw at least two men, but there might be more. We need to get out of here."

"Aren't we safer staying here?"

"Not if they set the house on fire, we aren't," Cowboy said, glancing at me to judge my reaction. "If they're trying to kill you, it'd be the easiest way. We'd be safer in the woods. But I'm sure they're watching the doors, and we're too high off the ground to go out any other way."

"Not necessarily," Floss said, making her way to her bedroom.

We followed her into the dark walk-in closet, where she clicked on one of those stick-it-anywhere dome lights, powered by batteries. We watched as she moved a large tote and threw some shoes out of the way. I wasn't sure what she was doing until she pulled back the carpet underneath, revealing a trap door in the floor.

"Hank put this in here when we moved in. He didn't like the idea of being caught unprepared in an emergency," she said, grinning.

With his gun readied, Cowboy pulled the door open with a good hard tug. A narrow wooden ladder led into a dark area somewhere under the house. He leaned down, gun in hand, and peered inside the hole. Everything must've checked out because he shoved his gun in his waistband and began climbing down.

"Once I'm on the ground, toss me the shotgun," he

muttered to Floss. "Then you two come down one at a time as fast as you can."

He ducked into the hole, practically sliding the rest of the way down the ladder and landing in a crouch on the ground. Cowboy peered around again to make sure he was alone. I doubted he saw much more than I could, which was nothing. He motioned, and I carefully dropped the shotgun to him. Then he waved for us to follow.

I made Floss go first and helped her into the hole. She climbed down slowly, taking one small step at a time until she stood safely on the ground beside Cowboy. Not wasting any time, I stuck the handgun Cowboy gave me in my waistband. The cold metal irritated my skin as I descended the creaky ladder.

It was uncomfortably dark, with a small amount of moonlight seeping through the slats of a gate leading to the outside. With guns drawn, we maneuvered toward it silently.

Cowboy checked to make sure we were clear. "Okay, we need to stay on the edge of the woods. Work our way to the back of the property as quietly as possible. Once we get on the trail, the footing will be easier," he promised. "Stay low, but keep moving."

At his signal, we made a run for the woods with Cowboy ushering us through the darkness. We weren't sure where the two men Cowboy had seen were, and we weren't waiting to find out.

We stumbled along the edge of the property toward the back fence, staying low to conceal our movements, guided by what little moonlight passed through the thick canopy of trees. The terrain was rough and uneven, which made running more difficult, but we went as fast as we could.

About halfway there, Floss stepped into a hole and fell to the ground, one leg sprawled behind her and the other bent under her in an agonizing shape. She cried out, but then stifled it immediately. It was the first time I'd ever heard a filthy word pass her lips. Her eyes watered as her hands shakily gripped her hurt ankle.

Cowboy tried to lift her, but any small manipulation of her ankle had Floss wailing in pain. It was the equivalent of us wearing flashing, neon signs that had "Yoo-hoo, over here!" written on them.

A man's voice yelled out, "They're not in the house! Search the property!"

"Darn thing's snapped like a twig," Floss said, her voice trembling with pain. "I'll just slow you down. You two go on without me."

"We're not leaving you here. Tell her, Cowboy." When he didn't say anything, I realized he didn't agree. We traded a quick glance. "You aren't serious," I said, the shock apparent in my voice. "She can't stay out here alone."

"She won't be alone," he said, propping Floss against the nearest tree and handing her the shotgun. "Shoot anybody who comes within a hundred yards," he said, making my eyes widen.

Floss grinned through the pained expression on her face. "You didn't think the shotgun was for looks, did you?"

Cowboy's gaze caught mine again, and my eyes pleaded with him. "Oh, come on. Stop looking at me like that. It's not like I want to leave her. Floss has a bad break. I won't be able to carry her without hurting her. I'm going to get you to safety, then come back for her."

"You two quit fussing over me and get a move on," Floss

ordered, grimacing. "I'll be fine."

Cowboy grabbed my gun and placed it in Floss's lap. She started to protest. "We still have my gun," he told her. "Reloading the shotgun takes too much time, and this will give you more ammunition until I come back. I'll sound a bird call before approaching."

"You better, or I'm liable to blow a hole clear through you," Floss said, her voice wavering. She gritted her teeth together. "Now, you two get out of here before I decide to tan your hides for not minding your elder."

I hugged her quickly before Cowboy grasped my arm and sprinted off in near darkness, towing me behind him. If walking through the woods barefoot during the day was dangerous, then running through them at night—even with shoes—was damn near suicidal. I couldn't see the ground. And the risk of falling only worsened by the numerous branches and vines grabbing at me.

Once I caught a bitter whiff of thick black mud and the pungent scent of algae, I knew we were close to the pond. We traveled along the tall weeds at the water's edge, then ducked behind a cypress tree. Cowboy scoped out the moonlit clearing where I had fallen into the water once before. We had to cross it if we wanted to get to the fence line, but he had reservations.

"Stay here," Cowboy said.

He sprinted across the opening, but didn't get ten feet when the sound of a gunshot rang out. His body crumpled lifelessly to the ground.

"NO!" Not thinking, I ran toward him, but stopped dead in my tracks as a man came out from behind a tree.

As he got closer, the moon lit up his face more clearly,

and I recognized him from the club and the photos Jake had shown me at the police station. It was Frankie Felts's cousin, Arnold. He held a dark, sinister-looking gun on me that matched the grin on his face.

"My cousin has been looking for you." Arnold grabbed me roughly by the back of my hair. "It's time for you to—"

We heard the growl at the same time.

A flash of white leaped through the air and latched onto his arm, snarling and biting. Thrown to the ground at the bank, I scrambled to my feet as Arnold got a shot off. The bullet hit Dog in his side and knocked him to the ground. He tried unsuccessfully to get up again. Arnold was poised over him with his shooting arm torn up, dripping blood, as he readied himself to shoot Dog again.

I screamed incoherently and barreled into Arnold from behind, knocking him into the pond with a large splash. He surfaced, his gun no longer in his hand. Pissed, he swore at me, threatening me with all the different ways he'd kill me when he found a way out of the water.

I ran straight to Cowboy, who wasn't moving, and kneeled beside him. He was lying on his side, something dark and wet dripping from his hair onto the dried, cracked mud. He had taken a bullet in the head. I buried my face in my hands and sobbed uncontrollably.

Then something touched my arm. Stunned, I instinctively flailed to protect myself and hit something solid.

"Ow," Cowboy said softly, followed by a groan.

I covered my mouth. "Y-you're alive?"

"You prefer something different?" He touched the side of his head and winced. "Jake would kill me if I died while babysitting you." He groaned and tried to get up.

I pushed him back gently, which didn't take much effort in his weakened state. "Don't get up, idiot. You've been shot in the head."

"You don't have to worry," he said, moaning and closing his eyes. "It hurts too much to do it again." His eyes cut toward the curse words echoing from the pond. "What's that?"

"Dog attacked the man who shot you, and when he shot Dog, I knocked him into the pond."

Cowboy grinned crookedly.

"What?" I asked.

"You risked your life for Dog, but you let me get shot?"

"Let you? I didn't know you were—"

We heard a rush of water and Arnold's choking scream as something pulled him under. The surface of the pond boiled and bubbled in chaos, then slowly went still as small ripples lapped at the sides of the bank.

"Jesus."

"No. Charlie," Cowboy said, closing his eyes again.

"I need to get you help. Tell me what to do."

He quietly thought to himself while I listened to his labored breathing. "You won't be able to find your way through the woods in the dark. Not by yourself, anyway. CB radio in my truck. If you can get to it, you can put out a call for help. Ox and Judd both monitor the channel it's on."

Cowboy's gun had landed on the ground near his body. I laid it on his chest and put his hand on top of it. "I'll be back."

"Take the gun with you," he said adamantly.

"But Charlie—"

"Charlie is preoccupied with digesting his snack," he

said, making me cringe. "I'll be fine. You take it. Chances are, you'll need it more than I will."

"I'll try to hurry." I gave his hand a comforting squeeze and picked up the gun.

I let my perpetual fear drive me, running faster than I ever have. The closer I came to the house, the lower I got to the ground until I was practically crawling on all fours. Then someone moved in the shadows near the bird pens, forcing me to duck inside the barn.

The barn was dark, riddled with shadows and moonbeams, but my eyes adjusted to the limited lighting. I searched for a quick hiding place, but the stall closest to the barn door belonged to the ornery colt. I didn't have time to slip into another one. I barely had time to unlock his gate when someone grabbed me from behind, threw me against the railing, and knocked the gun from my hand.

I slid to the ground, but turned enough to see Curtis Manning standing over me with a sneer of sheer pleasure and a large high-caliber handgun. Horses lurched skittishly in their stalls, snorting and clopping their feet. I scrambled backward in a crab crawl as Manning pointed his gun at me.

"Die, bitch."

I closed my eyes, flinching, as the shot rang out.

I'd always heard pain doesn't register when you're in shock. Because I hadn't felt the impact, I wasn't sure where I'd been hit. My eyes flew open as Manning fell to his knees, his dead eyes fixed on me. He dropped to the ground at my feet with a single, gaping hole in his forehead. A kill shot.

It meant only one thing. Jake!

He stood behind me to my left, his arm still posed in firing position. My legs wobbled as I ran to him. I threw my arms around his neck as relief washed over me. Overwhelmed, I broke down, clutching him to me and whimpering softly. Jake lowered his weapon, holding it at his side, while wrapping his other arm around me, pulling me tighter against him. When Jake spun me around, I thought he did so out of joy.

But I heard what sounded like an overblown balloon popping. The impact knocked Jake's body into mine, throwing us both off our feet. Uninjured and stunned, I sat up quickly to see Frankie Felts walking toward us with his weapon drawn. My breath caught in my throat as the last ten seconds dawned on me.

Dutifully, Jake had shielded me from a bullet that had torn into his right shoulder. He was lying next to me, holding his arm as blood seeped through his fingers. His gun had flown several feet away from us.

I scrambled for it and got to it at the same time Felts did. We both struggled for control of Jake's weapon while he kept his gun trained on Jake, who tried to get up. By sheer accident, Jake's gun went off and a bullet grazed Felts's leg. He cursed and backhanded me, knocking me farther away as he snatched the gun from my fingertips. I could taste the blood in my mouth from my busted lip. I scurried closer to Jake.

The shot had spooked the horses, each circling and kicking around in their stalls with sheer panic. As Felts came closer and shoved his weapon in my face, a stall door flung open behind him. The frightened colt bolted from his container. Felts limped out of the way to avoid being trampled as the colt ran out the barn door. Felts again pointed his weapon at me.

"Joseph Keller," Jake called out, his teeth gritted in pain.

The distraction worked, making Felts pause reluctantly. "What about him?"

Jake smiled proudly. "He was my father."

The mobster turned his eyes, and his gun, on Jake. Obviously, it was Jake's intention to keep the heat off me, though it would only be a temporary solution. After Felts killed Jake, I'd be next.

"You damn river bottom country hicks," Felts said, readying his finger on the trigger. "I have a rule about people who put their noses where they don't belong. Like father, like son."

"Nooo!" I screamed. It sounded more like an animalistic growl ripping from my throat, but my voice wasn't heard over the loud blast.

Jake's body jerked instinctively to shield me and push me out of harm's way. But, instead, Felts flew through the air. His body slammed against the stall door and sank to the ground, smearing blood on the wood all the way down.

Hank stood at the entrance of the barn holding a double barrel shotgun. "I have a rule too, you sonofabitch. Nobody messes with my family."

"Jake!" I scurried back to him, getting there seconds before Hank. I sat him up and quickly unbuttoned his shirt to get a better look in the moonlight. The finger-sized bullet hole oozed with dark blood. Hank handed me a work rag off a nearby table I was sure wasn't entirely sanitary. But I wadded it over the wound and applied firm pressure.

"Are you all right?" Jake asked, touching my face.

"I can't believe you're asking me that when you're the one who's been shot."

Hank placed a hand on my shoulder. "Emily, where's my

girl?" he asked, his voice wavering. "Where's Floss?"

"She's in the woods, somewhere past the compost pile. She's okay, but her ankle is hurt, probably broken."

"And Cowboy? Is he with her?"

Before I could answer, a noise came from behind Hank. He swiveled, pointing his shotgun in its direction.

Ox and Judd froze in the doorway, holding weapons of their own pointed in our direction. "Whoa! Don't shoot!" they yelled out in unison.

"About time you two got here," Jake said as Hank lowered his weapon. "I told you to hurry. What'd y'all do… stop for a sandwich?"

"Jesus," Ox said, looking at the two dead bodies on the ground. "Are those the mob guys?"

Jake confirmed with a nod. "Used to be."

"We saw Hank's truck parked on the road next to a black sedan we didn't recognize. Must've been their car, huh?" Judd said. "Guess you all walked in on foot."

"Yeah," Jake said. "But I don't know if there's anyone else with them. You two go check the property. Shoot anyone who doesn't belong here."

"Where's Cowboy?" Ox asked.

Everyone looked back, realizing I still hadn't answered yet. My lips trembled. "H-he's out by the pond, but—"

"You boys go get him," Hank said, rising to leave. "I'll check the property and find Floss."

"Hank, she's armed. Let her know it's you or she'll shoot you at a hundred yards."

Hank got up and set out for the door. Judd and Ox turned to go out as well. "Hold on…I need to tell you…guys, wait." They ignored me and kept walking. "Cowboy's been shot in the head!" I yelled to get their attention.

All three stopped in their tracks simultaneously, and Jake's head snapped toward me.

"I don't know if he's…alive," I said, my voice strained.

• • •

The driveway overflowed with vehicles and flashing red and blue lights beamed into the nearby pasture. It only spooked the horses more and had the birds on the property squawking. All of Hank's neighbors and friends came out to offer assistance as soon as word got out about the intruders.

The sheriff and his three deputies had been on the scene, but because the coroner had already arrived and the immediate danger was over, they'd left on another call. It didn't matter since they'd already taken our statements.

Two ambulances from the tri-county area remained. Floss was in one of them, given a drooling and sleep-inducing dose of painkiller. We sat in the other with Jake's arm in a sling while listening to Ox and Judd tease Cowboy mercilessly.

"Is it Halloween?" Judd asked, looking at Cowboy's mummified condition. "Or did someone toilet paper your noggin?"

"Well, let's not split any hairs," Ox said, grinning from ear to ear.

Cowboy shook his head, then winced because of it. "You guys suck, you know that?"

Looking at his bandaged head, I cringed. "I'm sorry you got hurt."

"Aw, shit, darlin', you've got to quit apologizing," Cowboy

said. "It wasn't your fault. Besides, now we get to compare the size of our bullet holes."

Hank walked up. "You don't *have* a bullet hole, you numbskull. All you have is a scuffmark on the side of your head. Floss has a worse injury than you."

It was the first smirk I'd seen on Jake's face all night. "If you're that bad off, Cowboy, we could take you out back and throw you over the fence."

"For what?" Cowboy asked.

Jake shrugged. "Buzzards got to eat, too."

I winced as a memory flashed through my mind of me sitting beside Dog, stroking his bloody fur as we waited for help to arrive. Jake must've felt my body tense and read my mind.

"Don't worry," he whispered into my ear. "Junior's taking care of Dog like he promised. The paramedics checked him out and said the bullet missed his vital organs. It was a clean exit wound and Junior's loading him into his truck right now to take him to the animal hospital. Dog's going to be fine. "

Before I could respond, Hank stepped away from the ambulance, his interest drawn to the driveway. "Who's this?" he asked.

We all piled from the back of the vehicle, watching as a convoy of three government vehicles parked nearby. Jake and I exchanged worried looks. Six men stepped out, all dressed in dark blue suits, but I only recognized one of them.

Director Harvey Brockway observed Jake's friends suspiciously, as did the other five agents. I figured it was probably because they all still held an arsenal of weapons. He scoped out the situation and approached, obviously uncomfortable with the grossly over-armed civilians.

"Agent Ward," Brockway said, nodding to Jake.

Jake didn't look happy to see him. "Director."

Brockway looked directly at me. "Miss Foster, I've come to take you into protective custody."

Jake didn't give me a chance to say anything. "No," he said to the director. "She's already being protected."

"Yes, apparently by a cavalry of armed citizens," Brockway said with disgust. "Ward, don't make this any harder than it has to be. You're already under investigation as it is. Last thing you need is to cause more problems for yourself."

"But she's—"

"Jake, it's okay," I said, not wanting him to get in any more trouble than he was already. "We'll get this straightened out after we all get checked out at the hospital. Right, Director Brockway?"

I hoped it would buy us more time together and give me a chance to figure out how to get Jake out of trouble.

"Oh...well, yes. I suppose so," Brockway stammered as the coroner wheeled a gurney, weighed down with a black body bag, past us. The director wore a disheveled, stressed out expression that matched his hair and his clothes. "So Felts is really dead?" he asked shakily.

Jake nodded in confirmation, and Brockway's face washed over with something familiar. Relief. I knew because I felt the same way.

Since nothing had to be resolved right away, Jake relaxed, but something whispered strangely to me. I pushed it away, not letting my anxieties take over and wig me out. But I couldn't shake it completely.

It was like whittling a piece of wood inside my mind. The more you scraped away, the smaller the object would get, but it'd start to take shape, even if you didn't know what it would become.

"You look like hell," Jake told the director.

"What do you expect when one of my agents goes rogue and kidnaps a federal witness? I haven't been sleeping well."

"You don't look like you've gotten any sleep since I last saw you," I said.

I wondered if his eyes were more bloodshot than Dale's the time Gina and I had dared him to drink— Something snapped. Gina had said the exact same thing about the man who paid them a visit, a man looking for me. But why would…

"Miss Foster, is something wrong?" Brockway asked.

The clarity overwhelmed me. "I…I know."

Jake and the others were confused, but Director Brockway looked more nervous now than when he first walked up surrounded by armed civilians.

"Miss Foster, I'll drive you to the hospital and get you checked out. From there we'll formalize the arrangements with the U.S. Marshals, and I'll transfer you to a safe house myself," Brockway said, a bead of sweat forming on his brow. It only confirmed what I knew.

At first, I thought I should be smart, keep my mouth shut, and not put myself in a precarious position. But my emotional state of mind wouldn't allow it. After all, it was me we were talking about.

Had Jake's arm not been in a sling, he would've been quicker and could've stopped me. I reached out, snatched Jake's gun from his shoulder holster, and pointed it at Director Brockway. All five of the agents in suits standing behind Brockway drew their weapons and returned the favor.

"Don't shoot!" Jake yelled to them. When he was sure they were holding fire, he turned to me. "Emily, what the hell are you doing?"

"It's him! He's the—"

"Miss Foster," Brockway interrupted, "I want to express my regrets for the events leading up to your situation. I know you're under a lot of stress, but if you don't drop the weapon, my men will shoot you."

"Wait!" Jake yelled, eyeing the men for itchy trigger fingers. "Emily, threatening an FBI director is a federal crime. Give me the damn gun."

I kept the gun locked on Brockway with trembling hands, knowing I only ever hit one out of three targets at close range. Chances were good that I'd die. Chances were better that Brockway wouldn't. For peace of mind in the event of the unthinkable, I wanted Jake to know the truth about this man. A man he trusted.

"Jake, he's in on it," I said, my voice straining to get him to understand. "Gina said he went by her apartment looking for me."

Brockway let out a nervous chuckle. "Of course I did," he said. "The FBI was looking for their agent and their lead witness. It's only natural we'd question your friends."

"Then why didn't you identify yourself as a fed?"

"I did," he said, though I knew it was a lie.

"No, you didn't. Gina had no clue who you were. She's the only person I talked to. How would Felts know where to look for me unless you bugged her phone somehow?" I glanced over to Jake. "It's how they found us. He passed the information to Felts."

"That's ridiculous. Agent Ward, you have ten seconds to get the gun out of her hand before I order my men to fire."

Jake tried to be objective, but wasn't sure what to believe. "Emily, please…" Jake pleaded. "Give me the gun."

"Jake, you once said people caught unaware made mistakes. Brockway made a mistake because he couldn't have foreseen you taking off with his only witness. Felts must've been pressuring him to find me. He was relieved to learn Felts was dead. The same relief I felt."

"Okay, enough," Brockway said. "Ten, nine, eight…"

"Emily, give me the gun. Please…" Jake held out his hand.

Adding insult to injury, I realized Jake didn't believe me. My heart shattered. I was in love with him—probably had been since I first laid eyes on him. And he didn't trust me. Hell, I wasn't even sure he liked me half the time. This person in front of me wasn't Jake, though. It was Agent Ward. It was the first time I understood the difference.

"Four, three, two…"

I heard the quick shuffling sounds and cocking of guns as Cowboy, Judd, Ox, Hank, and the other neighbors reached for their weapons and aimed them at the FBI agents. The cavalry chose to be on my side.

"Drop 'em, boys!" Hank yelled out.

"You better do as he says," Brockway called out to our entire group.

"I was talking to *your* boys," Hank said, nodding toward the five government men. "Not mine."

The blood drained from Brockway's face, and I knew he was a man backed into a corner. He didn't like being challenged and was starting to unravel.

Unlike Jake, the rest of them believed me. I saw it in their faces. But it only made me question my lingering self-doubt. What if I was wrong? It's not like it would be the first time. I couldn't forgive myself if any of them got hurt again because of me. Especially if Brockway wasn't the culprit.

Jake kept me safe all this time, and it was time for me to return the favor. It was like walking a plank above a man-eating shark, but I handed Jake the gun. I refused to leave him unarmed for what I was about to do.

Chapter Twenty-two

I stepped toward Brockway. "I have proof you helped Felts," I said, deliberately misleading him, knowing the fear would push him over the edge. He'd be forced to react.

Director Brockway grabbed me forcefully around the neck, throwing my body off balance. He turned me around and pressed the cool metal of his gun against my temple. He blew on my back like a bull, the pressure of my words having thrown him off-kilter.

"Nobody move or I'll kill her."

Jake and the others turned their guns on Director Brockway, who shielded his body with mine. The other five agents decided the civilians were no longer the bigger threat and did the same.

"Let her go, Brockway!" Jake called out.

Brockway walked backward, taking us out of the bright lights and into the shadows toward the government vehicles. I didn't think he'd kill me…at least not yet. He needed me alive to get away. But as soon as he got away, I'd become disposable. Physically and emotionally drained, the knowledge brought unexpected tears to my eyes. It was a terrifying, recurring nightmare.

Then something happened.

I closed my eyes and gasped a deep breath, feeling his presence before I smelled the warm, familiar minty scent. A strong sense of safety washed over me, wrapping me in a veil of comfort and peace. I opened my eyes as Junior came at Brockway, moving with lightning speed and brute force.

Junior slashed with the large buck knife, slicing away flesh from both of Brockway's arms. It was the efficiency of a hunter. Brockway dropped the gun and released me at the same time. The enraged look on Junior's face had shown how unstable he was in that moment. The fear that he'd kill Brockway to protect me held everyone else at bay. As if an invisible, impenetrable ring of fire circled us.

Brockway was on the ground, howling in pain and bleeding profusely from both arms. Junior held the large knife to his neck, daring him to move, looking for a reason to kill him. He wanted to. I could feel it. As if Junior's thoughts and emotions flowed through me. I laid a comforting hand on his shoulder and his body relaxed. He released a calming breath.

Junior rose slowly, wiped the bloody knife on his jeans, and slid it into the leather sheath on his side. We traded glances. There were no words for what had just happened. Just heartache. No one had been there to stop him when he killed the man who'd murdered his daughter. Though I don't think he regretted it, Junior wasn't a man who'd snuff out another man's life without it penetrating his soul.

He kissed my temple, squeezed my hand, and walked

out into the pasture, blending into the shadows. I knew his keen hawk-eyes kept watch over me, though. He was a good man who fiercely protected the ones he loved. And I was fortunate to be loved by him.

The whole group swarmed me. Hank and the other boys hovered, making sure I was all right, while Jake picked up Brockway's gun and shoved it into his waistband for safekeeping. After squeezing his way through and groping for me in the crowd, Jake pulled me out of Hank's big bear arms and into his own.

The feds allowed the paramedics to load Director Brockway into the ambulance. They stood guard as the deep lacerations on his arms were treated and bandaged.

Jake didn't say anything, but he stayed close. He kept one hand on his gun and both eyes fixed on me. I wasn't sure what it meant, but I thought it was a sign. He and I were nowhere near out of the woods.

. . .

At the hospital, I stayed with Hank as we waited for news on Floss and Jake. Floss had to have surgery to reset her anklebone with pins and screws. Jake had to have the bullet removed from his shoulder, though it hadn't done any major damage. Director Brockway was having surgery as well.

I overheard one of the doctors question the nurse about the man who had cut Director Brockway. "Was he a surgeon?"

The nurse shook her head. "No, I was told he's a hunter."

"Of animals or people?" the doctor asked seriously. "The man who did this would've had extensive knowledge of where to slice through a human arm to incapacitate him and cause the most damage by severing the correct tendons. Even if we can repair the damage, the director may never be able to use his hands again."

A shiver ran down my spine as Hank came over with a cup of coffee. "Hank, do you think Junior is dangerous?"

Hank chuckled at me. "Honey, I *know* Junior is dangerous. He did government contract work back when I was still in the FBI—"

"You were in the FBI?"

"I was Director of the Chicago Division, like Brockway," Hank replied. "Jake's father worked under me. It's how we met. I passed the position on to him when I retired. He was a good man, like his son. I guess no one told you Jake's not my nephew…not biologically, anyway."

Lightly touching my hand to his, I smiled. "Jake's your family, blood or not. Like you said to Felts, nobody messes with your family. And Jake's the son you and Floss never had."

"Emily, when I said that, I wasn't talking about Jake. That boy can take care of himself. I was talking about *you*. You're as much our family now as he is."

Sweet of him to say, even if it wasn't true. This wasn't my family. It was Jake's. I didn't doubt their concern for my well-being, but I didn't want their sympathy any more than I wanted their pity. I wanted to be loved and have a family to call my own, but it wasn't something Jake had offered me.

Riddled with guilt, I couldn't stop thinking about what Jake had said. *If anybody gets hurt, it's going to be all on you.* He was right. This was my fault, and they should all hate me. Probably would after they thought about it long enough.

I'd been unfairly thrust into all of their lives because of the situation.

I was a temporary fixture and had already overstayed my welcome. I didn't want to say good-bye to any of them, especially Jake, but I didn't see any other option. Maybe there is such a thing as becoming too enmeshed in someone else's life.

I blinked, keeping my emotions in check and forcing the sadness back down as three U.S. Marshals entered the lobby.

"Emily Foster?" one of them asked.

I nodded in response.

"Can you come with us? We need to speak with you privately." One of the nurses buzzed us in and led us to one of the conference rooms at the end of the hallway. "Please sit," he said as he shut the door, leaving the other two marshals outside to guard the door. "I'm Carter Sullivan with the US Federal Marshals Service," he said, offering his hand.

"Is that necessary?" I asked, motioning to the men on the other side of the glass door. "Frankie Felts is dead."

"Until his organization is broken up, you'll need to be protected. There's still a contract on your head…at least until the news of his death is made public. Money talks, you know. That's why we think Director Brockway gave information to Felts, to pay off some gambling debts he had accumulated."

I cut right to the chase. "Is Agent Ward in trouble?"

"Yes, ma'am," he answered. "An investigation is already under way as to his conduct. Kidnapping a federal witness is a serious crime."

"Kidnapping? He saved me…and more than once, I might add."

"Yes, but Agent Ward's methods are questionable. He's

going to have to have some higher connections to get out of this one with his career still intact."

I think he was referring to God, but my mind instantly went to Hank. Maybe he still had some connections in the department who could help Jake, especially now that the informant had been caught. That would certainly help Jake's case.

But what about me? I hadn't even considered where that would leave me after this was all over. Jake would no longer feel responsible for my well-being and probably end up resenting me for weighing him down. Then I'd be abandoned. Again. And that was something I couldn't bear to think about. I'd have to get used to the idea of returning to my old life…a life without Jake.

"We need to take you to a safe house," Sullivan said. "I can understand if you're reluctant to cooperate with the U.S. Marshals Service, but — "

"Okay."

He looked confused and almost put out. "Excuse my surprise, ma'am, but from everything I've been told about you, I thought you would put up more of a fight."

"What'd you think…you'd have to drag me out of here kicking and screaming?"

"It seemed to be the general consensus."

"Well, I do have a few stipulations."

The agent grinned, but shook his head. "This isn't a negotiation."

"It is now," I said. "Unless you'd rather I talk to the press."

His smiled faded. "Ma'am, I could arrest you and keep you in a cell for the duration, if I have to. The government doesn't take kindly to threats."

"Neither do I." I cocked an eyebrow at him. "If you want my full cooperation, then I want two things. One being an update on Agent Ward's medical condition after we leave here. So I know he's okay. And two, I want you to keep my whereabouts a secret."

The Marshal laughed heartily. "Miss Foster, isn't that the point of witness protection?"

"You don't understand," I told him. "I don't want Agent Ward or anybody in connection with him, including the FBI, to know where I am."

"It won't be a problem." The agent grinned at the thought of hiding me from the FBI. "Would you like to say good-bye to Agent Ward? I understand you and he became…close," he said, politely trying to find an appropriate word.

Thinking of saying good-bye to Jake made me feel vulnerable. My throat tightened, and my bottom lip quivered. I wouldn't be able to do it. And I didn't want Jake or the others to see me like this.

I had foolishly fallen in love with a man who didn't love me back. Jake was like a really good book, where you want to savor the whole thing, but then you're disappointed when it ends. That was my problem. I wasn't going to get my happily ever after. It was the end.

Jake had been my compass for the last few weeks, guiding me and pointing me in the right direction. Now it was time to take matters into my own hands. Even if it meant changing course. Jake had protected my body, but only I could protect my heart.

I smiled tearfully at the marshal. "I don't do good-byes."

· · ·

TWO MONTHS LATER...

"Someone get the door," I yelled from the kitchen.

Gina and Dale continued sitting on the couch, watching a movie, as if they never heard me.

Irritated, I walked past them. "Seriously? First, you two refuse to help me unpack. Now I have to make popcorn *and* answer your door?"

Gina flashed me a grin. "It's your door now, too."

"Yeah," Dale agreed, "The rules state the newest household member has to answer the door."

"Whose rules?"

"Ours."

"You can't make up rules as you go along," I said, swinging the door open. I froze as my eyes raked over Jake standing in the doorway.

He glared at me with stormy eyes of fury and a throbbing vein bulged out of his neck. "Okay," he grumbled, "Who the hell are you, and what did you do with Emily? Because the Emily I knew never followed anyone's rules."

At first I stood there, robotic, unable to react. Jake's commanding presence had a bewildering power over me. My buried emotions clawed their way to the surface and came out in the form of a two-month-old grudge.

"My name's not Emily. It's—"

"You're still Emily to *me*."

"What can I do for you, Agent Ward?" I asked, my tone sizzling with attitude.

"Don't give me that crap. We need to talk," Jake said as

he started to enter the apartment.

I blocked his entry with my arm. "No, we don't. There's nothing left to say."

"I just spent two very long months looking for you." He gave me a look that sent a chill through my bones. "I disagree."

I sighed with impatience. "Jake, what do you want?"

"What I want is to fit your ass with a transmitter or a homing device," he said, still eyeing my arm on the doorjamb. "Are you going to let me in or what?"

"Do I have a choice?"

He lifted an eyebrow and grinned.

"Fine," I told him as I stepped to the side. "You get two minutes."

Gina and Dale had turned completely, watching us with their arms hooked around the back of the couch. Apparently, this scene was better than the one on TV.

"Do you guys mind giving us the room?" I thought asking them to leave was safer than being alone with Jake in a bedroom.

"Man, you always spoil our fun," Dale said.

Gina grinned. "It's okay. We'll go to my room and listen through the door." They disappeared into her bedroom.

I turned to Jake. "I've been out of federal custody and back in Chicago for less than twenty-four hours. How did you find me?"

"I didn't," Jake said with a smirk. "I had your friends call me the moment you got back."

"Tattletale!" Gina called out from the bedroom.

Jake reached for me, but I pulled away, making him grunt in disapproval. "Emily, I went crazy when I realized you left. No one would tell me where you were. They said it was at your request. Why would you block me from finding you?"

"Because I obviously didn't *want* you to find me. Not that I thought it would matter," I said, shrugging. "After all, you have your own personal Indian tracker."

He ran his fingers through his hair in frustration, and his jaw tightened with a grimace. "Chief Dumbshit wouldn't help me. He said you needed to come back on your own. That it should be your choice, not mine."

"Good man," I said with a smirk.

"He said to tell you hello, and Floss wanted me to thank you for the flowers."

I smiled with delight. "She knew I sent them?"

"I don't know how, since the card was signed from God. But, yeah, she knew." Jake shuffled his feet uncomfortably. "Everyone misses you."

I didn't want to cry, but knew I was on the verge of it. "I think I've tainted all of their lives enough," I said in a callous tone as I moved farther away.

Jake snagged me up by my elbow before I could get out of reach. "You're a real piece of work, you know that? You don't just burn bridges. Oh, no, not you, Emily... You have to blow the sonofabitches up."

I shook my arm loose from his grip. "Well, then I guess it makes me no better than you. I don't appreciate you using them to get to me. If you have something to say, then say it."

"Fine." He stuffed his hands in his pockets and shuffled his feet on the floor. "Why'd you leave me?"

"*Leave you*?" I asked, confused. "Jake, you're making it sound like we broke up. It was a fake relationship. We weren't dating, remember?"

"Well, what the hell would you call what we were doing because we damn sure weren't playing Scrabble in that bed."

Dale snickered from the other room. Great. I'd never live that one down.

"You ran while I was in surgery, knowing I wouldn't be able to chase you," Jake accused. "Pretty chickenshit, if you ask me."

"I didn't run."

"Oh, you ran all right," Jake said, "Like a scared rabbit, running from the…what did you call me again, Gina?"

"The big, bad wolf," she said, giggling on the other side of the door.

"Stay out of it!" I hollered. Then I shook my head. "This is stupid, Jake. Tell me what you want."

"You," he said, grabbing a handful of my shirt and pushing me against the wall. "I want you."

My brain had to work extra hard with his body pressed into mine. The mixture of our emotions threatened to explode, and the result would be damaging to my heart. "Jake…please, don't."

He didn't listen. Jake and I were from the same country, but we were speaking different languages, and his was definitely not verbal. He pulled me in for a kiss, clamping his mouth over mine, and my legs buckled under me. Jake held me limply in his arms, like a rag doll for him to play with. He slid his muscled thigh between mine and moved his mouth down to my neck. His hands caressed my hair, twirling it with his fingers.

"I want you to come home with me," he breathed.

I gave him a quick, dismissive glance as I fought back the urge to pull off his clothes. "Why?"

"Because I want to protect you…"

He wasn't glad he found me because he loved me. It was about the stupid case again. I pushed him away. "Damn it, Jake! I don't need a bodyguard."

"Good," Jake said. "There are things I want to do to your body, but guarding it isn't one of them."

"But you said—"

"I do want to protect you. The way any husband wants to protect his wife."

"Jake, I—" His words made my head spin. "Wait, what'd you say?"

"I want to marry you."

"W-why?"

Jake chuckled. "That wasn't quite the reaction I hoped for."

I was annoyed he thought it was funny. "I'm serious. Why would you want to marry someone you don't love?"

"I don't," Jake said. "I want to marry *you*."

"But you don't love me."

"What the hell are you talking about?" His eyebrows squished together, giving him a disgusted look. "Of course I do."

"Jake, you don't have to pretend it was anything more than sex. I know that's all—"

With the speed of a striking snake, Jake latched onto my arm and pulled me closer. "I told you before, I don't do meaningless sex. I meant it then, and I mean it now. If you think I spent two months looking for you because I wanted to have sex with you, then you're crazier than I thought. Why the hell would you think I'm not in love with you?"

"Because you never told me."

"Yeah, I did. I remember telling you I care about you."

"Exactly. You *care* about me. It isn't the same thing. I care about Cowboy, but I wouldn't want to sleep with him every night."

Jake was irritated. "If you're going to marry me, then you'd better not want to sleep with him *any* night."

"I didn't say I'd marry you," I reminded.

"Damn it, Emily! Why not?"

"You still haven't said it."

Jake smiled, brushed the hair out of my eyes, and tilted my chin up toward his face. "Emily, I love you. I've been in love with you for months. I want to spend the rest of my life loving you, if you'll let me. Now tell me you'll marry me and you'll sleep in my bed for the rest of yours, and I'll be a happy man."

"Probably won't get much sleep," I warned him.

He smirked. "I'm counting on it."

I smiled at him. "Then, yes, I'll marry you." Then I narrowed my eyes. "But if you think for one second—"

Jake placed his finger over my lips. "Emily, when a man proposes to you, you're supposed to kiss him, not bitch at him."

"Says who?"

"It's a rule."

"You and your rules," I said, shaking my head. "Still making them up as you go along, I see."

"Mmm-hmm," he murmured, leaning down to brush his lips against mine. "Keeps things interesting."

"Hold on. One more thing, Jake." He breathed out heavily, but paused, waiting for me to continue. "So when do we go home?"

His lips curved into a smile. "The moving van's outside. Cowboy, Judd, and Ox are out there as well. They're waiting for my signal to come in and start loading your stuff. Gina and Dale knew your stay here was temporary, and they said they'd keep you from unpacking."

My mouth hinged open. "What if I'd said I didn't want to marry you?"

"I wasn't taking no for an answer. Besides, you didn't."

"But I could have. In fact, it's still a possibility, you know. A girl has a right to change her mind."

"I wouldn't do that if I were you," he warned, narrowing his eyes.

It was a challenge if I'd ever seen one, and I never backed down from a challenge. "Good thing you aren't me," I said.

I tried to outrun him, but Jake lunged for me. He caught me around the waist and pinned my wrists behind my back with one hand. His mouth covered mine as his tongue dipped into my mouth, teasing and taunting. My boneless body melded to his like a pliable piece of warm putty.

Then the cold click of handcuffs bound my wrists. Jake threw me over his shoulder and carried me toward the door.

"What the hell are you doing?"

"Hey, I warned you," Jake said, laughing. "You never learn."

"This is kidnapping! You're already in trouble because of this—"

"Oh, you haven't heard? I've been cleared of all charges, and I'm no longer suspended. I put in my transfer to Texas weeks ago. Guess you should've stayed in touch."

"Okay, Jake, I'm sorry. Take the handcuffs off. Jake, come on...please?"

"Rule number one: no begging. At least not until I get you naked and into a bed, then you can beg all you want. Rule number two: no sneaking out on me, especially right before the wedding. Rule number three…"

"Jake, you know I'm not any good at following rules."

"No shit," he said, patting me on the rear. "That's why I'm changing them. Rule number three: the only name you're changing is your last one…"

Epilogue

It was a sunny afternoon, and almost all of the guests had arrived at Miller's Bird Farm. They sat lazily under the shade trees, sipping iced tea as they waited for our wedding to begin.

Floss and Bobbie Jo helped me plan an intimate, non-traditional wedding, thrown together almost as fast as Jake and I'd been. It was the largest "small wedding" I'd ever seen, with over a hundred guests. But it was perfect.

Jake and I watched Cowboy, who was dressed in a new pair of Wranglers and a pressed western-style shirt, saunter over to us.

Cowboy eyeballed my body through the short, formfitting white eyelet lace dress. "Hey, beautiful! You look amazing!"

I blushed at his flattery. "Thanks. You do, too."

He then glanced to Jake and scanned over his pressed slacks and white button-down shirt. "Nice outfit. Are you taking her to the prom?"

Jake glared at him. "Shut up."

Grinning, Cowboy leaned over to me. "Wow, someone's in a mood today. Cold feet?"

"Like he's been walking barefoot through snow," I said, giggling. I'd never seen Jake nervous before, but I couldn't help enjoying it.

"How's the swear jar coming along?" Cowboy asked with a smirk.

"It's about half full already. I should probably have a five-gallon swear bucket instead."

Cowboy chuckled. "Well, I wanted to be the first to kiss the new bride," Cowboy said, hesitating and looking over to Jake, as if he were asking permission.

Jake became more annoyed. "You do know you're supposed to do that after we're married, right?"

"Well, yeah," Cowboy said, "That only applies to traditional weddings. But it's okay, Jake. If you're afraid she might back out of marrying you after locking lips with me, then I can't blame you." Cowboy winked at me to let me know he was goading Jake.

I smiled, but it faded, along with the color in my cheeks, when Jake said, "Go ahead."

Cowboy looked as shocked as I was. "What?"

"You heard me," Jake said. "One kiss. That's all you get, so you better make it good. Because after that, if you even think of putting another one of your body parts near her, I'm going to see if I can't straighten out the bone in your nose by breaking it a second time."

He had to be kidding, right? "Jake, this isn't funn—"

Cowboy didn't waste any time. His fingers dug into my waist as he cradled me against him, securing his mouth over mine. My lips froze and I tried to push my hands against his chest, but he held me tighter. He was taking this one kiss, whether I liked it or not.

Satisfied he had done the best job he could on an unwilling partner, he released me from his death grip. I swayed to the left, and Jake had to keep me from falling.

"Oh, give me a break. It wasn't *that* good," Jake insisted angrily.

A proud smile smeared across Cowboy's face.

"Oh God! I think I'm going to be sick," I replied, placing my hand over my mouth.

Cowboy's grin faded and transformed into a smirk on Jake's mouth. "Do you want to sit for a minute?" Jake asked.

"No, I think I got overheated."

The frustration and confusion showed on both of their faces. "Okay, it isn't funny anymore," Cowboy said, irritated. "Did I make you sick or hot?"

"I'd like to know myself," Jake muttered.

I groaned, annoyed with both of them. "I'm pregnant, you morons!"

Cowboy's eyes widened. "Damn. I'm better than I thought."

Jake's face paled, and I realized I'd ruined my own surprise. I planned to tell him once we were alone and in bed on our wedding night, not after I had made out with his best friend.

"Hey, ho!" Gina called out. She and Dale walked over with huge smiles, obviously having seen the kiss. "How's the big, bad wolf treating you?"

"I'm pregnant."

"Man, that was fast," Dale said, giving Cowboy a fist bump. "Immaculate conception?"

I sighed with frustration. "It's Jake's, dork."

Momma Bell was within earshot and must've had her hearing aid turned up. "Did I hear you say you're with child, girl?" I nodded, though I should've known better. "Well, what a blessing. Congratulations!"

"Thanks."

"Now, I forgot what I came over to tell you. Oh, I know. My dog, Missy, well, she's a bit of a hussy…" Momma Bell paused, and I wondered if she was going to add the word "too." But she didn't. "Anyway, she got herself in a bind with Dog and had herself a litter of pups. Floss said you took a liking to the lazy hound and thought you might like one."

"Oh, how sweet. I'd love to have one of Dog's puppies."

"She's the spitting image of her daddy, but I think she's got some health issues, seizures or something. I left her over there in the shade."

I followed her finger with my eyes. A small white puppy with speckled ears slept peacefully on her side on the cottage porch where Dog normally lay. As usual, he was nowhere to be found, but the thought of him exchanging places with his narcoleptic daughter come nightfall made me smile.

"Thanks, Momma Bell. She's perfect."

"Well, I guess I need to find me a seat for the wedding. It won't be long now." She leaned over and whispered into my ear, "My Earl used to rub milk on my boobies for me every night. He said it kept 'em nice and perky. You be sure to have Jakey help you with that."

I glanced at her deflated breasts with nipples pointed to the ground and realized something. Earl was a con man.

"Uh…yeah, I'll do that," I told her.

Jake hadn't said a word since I blurted out I was pregnant and I started to get a little worried. "Hey, guys, I need to talk to Jake alone for a minute." Once they all cleared out, I locked eyes with him. "I'm sorry. I didn't mean to—"

"You're pregnant?" Jake asked, as if he hadn't heard anything since the first time I announced it. His reaction had been unpredictably scary.

"Jake, are you okay? I'm sorry. I thought you'd be happy about the pregnancy—"

"Sweetheart, of course, I'm happy about it." He framed my face with his hands and gave me a quick kiss. "Don't ever think otherwise."

"Then what's wrong?"

"I…well…" He paused, searching for the right words. "Our child won't have any grandparents," he said, lowering his head.

I understood his pain, but hoped he'd look at it the same way I did. "This kid isn't going to miss out on anything. Look around, Jake. Everyone will love this baby. Our child won't grow up feeling the way I did."

"I want my child to have everything."

"It will," I promised. "It has us…and all of them."

Something over my shoulder caught Jake's attention and he grinned. "Since you gave me an early wedding present, then I think it's only fair I give you one. I want you to meet someone." He turned me around.

I recognized the man immediately. "Officer Stevens! I didn't know you were coming. It's great to see you again. How's your shoulder?"

"As good as new," he said, kissing me on the cheek. "I sure am glad everything turned out all right for you, hon. I worried about you after you left the police station that night."

"That's sweet. Thank you." I looked back to Jake. "What,

you thought I wouldn't remember one of the men who took a bullet for me?"

He smiled slyly. "I wasn't talking about Stevens. I wanted to introduce you to someone he brought with him. Detective Eric Mercer."

"Who?"

"Turn around and see for yourself."

I caught a glimpse of him from a distance and gasped. Fifteen years later, I still recognized the policeman who held me in his arms as a child and heroically comforted me in my time of need. No passage of time would allow me to forget his face. My breath caught in my throat, choking me, as I ran to him. He spread his arms to catch me.

The memory of curling into his lap, as he stroked my hair and soothed my broken soul, overwhelmed me. I had carried it with me all these years locked deep within. Now, the trauma I had endured came pouring out, flooding my eyes with droplets of sadness and mourning. I wept inconsolably.

Eric stroked my hair as he had before and whispered into my ear. "I'm sorry. They wouldn't tell me what happened to you or what foster home you were in. I searched for you over the years, but you kept getting moved around. I never stopped thinking about the little girl who needed me."

His emotions flowed from him in soft words and gentle gestures. He was still the same mild-mannered, compassionate man who had captured my heart all those years before.

"I've wanted to say something to you all these years and never thought I'd get the chance," I told him. "You couldn't save my parents, but you've always been my hero."

After a few minutes, my reservoirs dried up, and Eric wiped the smudges of makeup from beneath my eyes with his handkerchief. "So I hear you're going by Emily these days."

I nodded. "The FBI suggested I keep the name as part of my new life. The mobsters are dead, but Jake didn't want to take any chances that someone else from Frankie Felts's organization would come after me. Besides, I wanted a fresh start. A new name for a new beginning...with Jake."

We spent a few more moments together, but knew there'd be plenty of time to talk after the wedding. He went to mingle with the other guests, promising to save me a dance. Feeling more at peace than I had in years, I stood alone, looking out at all the guests in attendance.

I couldn't wipe the smile off my face.

Dale and Ox sat together, grinning and laughing with their gaydar meters fully in sync. Judd showed Gina his size fifteens, and I had no doubt she'd be showing him her double Ds later. Cowboy stroked his own ego by hitting on every girl within a twenty-yard radius, offering them what he called "southern hospitality." Bobbie Jo kept the children entertained. Hank and Floss seated guests, welcoming them, as they had done with me.

"Emily!" Jake shouted. "Don't move!"

"What's wrong?" I asked, though I knew the moment I caught the scent. "Oh God. Where is it?"

"Right beside you," he said, getting ready to lunge at me.

"Jake, if you tackle me in this wedding dress, you're going to marry yourself today. Besides, you could hurt the baby."

"Shit. What do you want me to do, then?"

"It's a watermelon snake! Get your gun and shoot the damn thing like a normal person."

Jake grinned. "God, I love you," he said, as he reached down into his boot, pulled out a .22 caliber handgun, and shot the snake in the head. Its body thrashed and twitched. Because Jake wasn't about to let me chop it into pieces and set it on fire, I settled for moving away from it.

Junior walked over, grinning. "You two going to stand around shooting things, or do you want to get married?"

Jake winked at me. "Emily, you've got two minutes to get your ass down the aisle before I come looking for you."

"Three would be better."

"Two…or else," Jake threatened as he made his way to the preacher.

I reached for Junior's hand. "Thanks for doing this. I appreciate it."

"Emily, it's an honor," he replied, lacing my arm through his as his eyes glossed over. "I didn't get to walk my little girl down the aisle."

Glossy-eyed, I smiled up at him. "Neither did my dad."

Moments later, I stood with Jake, our hands linked under the open sky as the preacher united us as a couple. He spoke of love, and everyone smiled. He spoke of honor, and everyone swelled with pride. He spoke of forsaking all others, and everyone glared suspiciously at Cowboy.

When a gust of wind whipped across the pasture, it began snowing dandelion seeds, as if God had blown them just for us. Floss and I exchanged knowing glances, and I caught Jake watching me with adoring eyes.

He didn't wait for his prompt. Jake kissed me, his mouth sweetly caressing mine. The kiss made me dizzy, but Jake steadied me with his firm hands and placed a protective hand over my stomach. He lingered at my lips, making my heart skip a beat.

"Jake, you're supposed to wait until the preacher says *'you may now kiss the bride.'*"

"Why?" Jake whispered. "What does it matter?"

"I don't know. I guess it's against the rules."

"So what," he said shrugging and smiling lightly. "Rules are made to be broken."

I laughed and threw my arms around his neck. "Then you're in for a shitload of trouble!"

Acknowledgments

First and foremost, I'd like to thank my husband and kids for encouraging my passion for writing and supporting me while I pursued this dream. Thank you to my mom, dad, and my sisters, Annita and Amanda, for letting me walk through my stories out loud while dealing with my crazy. To my friends and family, who were also my very first fans: Terry, Bobbie, Shelley, Kristy, and Debbie, for believing in me and offering me moral support when I needed it most.

A big high five goes out to my fantastic critique partners: Heather, Carol, Joy, Sarah, Sam, Renee, Kelly, and the two crazy girls who make up Elizabeth Hayley. Thanks for the encouragement, the brutal editing, and challenging me to be the best writer I can be.

A special shout-out goes to Julie Abston for taking my beautiful author photo, the "chicks" at Chickswagger who welcomed me into their henhouse and took me under their wings, Samanthe Beck for being my first and most awesome

Entangled friend (don't tell the others), and my Pure Bliss Street Team for blindly supporting a debut author in every way imaginable. You guys are the best!

I'd also like to thank my rock star agent, Andrea Somberg, for taking a chance on a new author, guiding me through the crazy world of publishing, and for laughing at all my stupid jokes.

Big thanks to my editors, Theresa Cole and Gwen Hayes, who not only "got" my vision and gave me some truly amazing edits, but also offered moral support in the form of cocktail recipes. You ladies kept me sane…and grammatically correct. Thank you to Fiona Jayde and Kerri-Leigh Grady for my gorgeous cover.

As for Liz and everyone else within my Entangled Publishing family, thank you for all the unwavering support you offered a new writer. All of you were necessary components to making this book the very best it could be and making my dreams a reality. Thank you all from the bottom of my heart!

About the Author

As the youngest of five girls, Alison Bliss has never turned
down a challenge…or been called by the right name. Her
writing career *may* have started out as a dare by one of her
sisters, but Alison hasn't put her pen down since.

She grew up on a small island off the Texas Gulf Coast,
where most of her childhood vacations consisted of camping
or hunting trips to the deer lease. Although she'll always be
a Texan at heart, Alison currently resides in the Midwest
with her Iowa farm-boy husband and their two sons. With
so much testosterone in her home, it's no wonder she writes
"girl books."

Alison is an animal lover, a closet video game enthusiast,
and believes the best way to know if someone is your soul
mate is by canoeing with them because if you both make it
back alive, it's obviously meant to be. She's an avid romance
reader who enjoys penning the type of books she loves to
read most: fun, steamy love stories with heart, heat, laughter,

and usually a cowboy or two. As she calls it, "Romance… with a sense of humor."

To learn more about Alison Bliss, visit her website at http://authoralisonbliss.com, where you can sign up for her newsletter to keep up with her latest book news. You can also email her at authoralisonbliss@hotmail.com or connect with her on social media. She'd love to hear from you!

Manufactured by Amazon.ca
Bolton, ON